To Cézanne

1

Reece

THE FIRST THING I notice are her hands. They're fine boned and small with short nails that are painted bright red. They're not elegant hands. But they're beautiful. Hands whose character has been shaped by use. They look capable and strong.

And, apparently, they are. Those hands wrote the book that has taken the country by storm. *Throw Away the Key* has been sitting at the number one spot on *The New York Times* Best Seller list for almost thirty weeks. It's being hailed as *the* book of the year. And all of this from a first-time author, who self-published her book, initially. Those hands have my respect.

As does the rest of her.

She hasn't done a single television interview since the book gained national prominence. Her pen name L. Vega and her bio, which refers to her in the first person, don't indicate whether she's a woman or a man. Honestly, I hadn't cared either way.

Until I saw her.

Now, that I *know* she's a woman, it's *all* I can think about. She's beyond beautiful.

She's tiny. She can't be more than a couple of inches above five feet tall. And every single part of her in perfect proportion. Her dark hair tumbles in seemingly perpetual waves, spilling over her shoulders and hanging almost to her waist in the back. Her full lips are painted in the same vivid red as her nails. Otherwise, she is completely devoid of makeup.

In this town where people dress to impress, she appears to have made practically no effort at all. She's not even wearing a suit. Her jeans have more holes than fabric, her white shirt sits off one shoulder and falls short of reaching her belly button. All that caramel, smooth skin is a feast for my eyes, almost daring me *not* to look.

Her beauty, her appeal is all effortless. She has what we, in this business, call presence. She's captivating and I already know that she's going to sell this film for us. When we put her in front of a camera, the public will eat her up. Add that to her obvious talent and clear ambition, and I can tell this woman's a winner.

She's sitting across from me, her beautiful face placid. It's like she doesn't have a care in the world. She shouldn't. When it comes to her book and the movie studios vying for the options, it's definitely a seller's market. The film belongs at Artemis Film and I'm prepared to do what it takes to make that happen.

"Thank you for agreeing to talk to us, Ms. Vega. I know you've been approached by several other studios about your book," Zev says in his trademark, brisk, no nonsense tone. He's my President of Development and normally he'd be running this meeting without me present. But I don't trust him not to fuck this up.

He's not interested in turning Lucía Vega's book into a film. He thinks it's a waste of time and money. Normally his opinion is worth its weight in gold. But, not today.

I've got a good feeling about this book. The timing and the story are perfect. It's a topic that's on a lot of people's minds. If it's not, it should be. This film is going to win us awards and make a shitload of money. So, I'm here to make sure we get this done.

"We were surprised to get your call," her agent, Sol Kline, responds. Sol is one of the country's biggest literary agents. He knows everyone, understands the ins and outs of this business, and can smell bullshit a mile off. The fact that he is her agent tells me that they aren't surprised at all. He only seeks out and represents very successful writers.

"I was surprised to be making it," Zev says, with a chuckle that fails to mask his disdain. "But Mr. Carras insisted."

I cut an ire-filled glance at him before I interject. I lean forward and look at her directly for the first time.

"Yes, I did insist. I read your book. It's great. I believe it's a story that needs to be adapted into film so that we can reach an even wider audience. I'm going to be stepping into the role Zev would normally play on this project and will oversee it myself."

The room is silent at my declaration. I've surprised everyone. Including myself. I feel Zev's eyes bore into me, but ignore him. Sol tips his head to the side, studying me. I don't give him more than a passing glance as I train my gaze on Lucía.

"You know who I am, don't you?" I ask her, looking only at her. Speaking only to her. When our eyes meet, I can see things in her expression that I didn't before. Her wide, rich brown eyes give me a glimpse into her thoughts. She's excited, but wary. Hopeful, but unsure. Whatever she sees in my expression makes her eyes widen with surprise.

She blinks hard and when she opens her eyes, the surprise is gone, the calm enigmatic expression back in place.

"Yes, I do," she answers. Her voice is deep—almost smoky —and surprisingly soft. She tips her head to the side. Her hair falls with the motion, and it caresses her bare shoulder leaving a ripple of gooseflesh in its wake. I force my eyes back to her face and my mind back to the conversation. I clear my throat.

"So, then you know that I've spent years involved in activism on this issue. Trying to raise awareness, to get people talking and thinking and to get lawmakers to take action. Your book has done, in a matter of months, what I've spent a decade trying to achieve." She flushes and I can't tell if it's in pride or embarrassment. But it lends her an air of innocence that's unexpected and charming.

"It shouldn't surprise you that I am chasing the option rights for this book so stridently. I want to take this story and put it in front of an even wider audience than you've reached already."

Her book, *Throw Away the Key* is told from the point of view of a young girl, named Azalia. She belongs to a class of people who have entered this country illegally as minors, typically with parents and not of their own volition. They earned the moniker of DREAMERs from an acronym for a piece of legislation that's currently rotting in committee in the United States Congress. The Development, Relief, and Education for Alien Minors (DREAM) Act would give the millions of people who meet the criteria, a path to permanent and legal residency status in this country.

In reading the book, the reader gets to walk in Azalia's shoes as she navigates life with this cloud of being undocumented over her head. The book is a work of fiction; yet her characters' struggles are real. I've heard real stories like the ones she tells. I've seen them with my own two eyes. I've *lived* them.

She regards me, her darks eyes catch the light and are lit with so many dimensions of brown color, they glitter. I return her regard and raise my eyebrows, prompting her to respond. She shifts to look at Sol and then back to me. Her eyes are still calm, but I can see her throat working before she speaks.

"I appreciate your passion, Mr. Carras, but I'm just not sure . . ."

When her voice trails off, I take the opportunity to cut to the chase. "Ms. Vega, let's not waste each other's time. Tell me what it would take for you to say yes," I say to her, making sure that my intent shows on my face.

I find myself, for the first time in my professional life, completely uninterested in the idea of driving a hard bargain. I want this so badly, that I know I'm going to give her whatever she asks for. So, I cut to the chase.

She folds her arms across her chest, her chin juts forward slightly. "Tell me what you loved about the story. Which specific scene really struck you?"

It's my turn to blink. I'm taken aback that she's testing me. Clearly, she doesn't believe I've read it.

But my affront fades quickly and leaves behind respect tinged with guilt.

I don't want to tell her, at least not right now, that I didn't actually finish the book. So, I pick the scene that made me stop reading, pick up the phone, and call Zev.

"Well, I'll begin by saying that I found Azalia very relatable and easy to empathize with. Your writing was clear and vivid." She sighs with impatience and I rush on. "But the part of the story that struck me was the playground scene. Where an argument about a toy escalates and another child hits Azalia."

I see a flare of surprise in her eyes. Her shoulders hitch the tiniest bit.

"What . . . why that scene?" she asks, clearly flustered and trying not to show it.

"Her mother's muted response to seeing her child being bullied and hit infuriated me. I could feel Azalia's heart breaking as, instead of receiving comfort from her mother, she was told that she should have just given the child her toy. The reader and Azalia's resentment toward her mother are borne in exactly the same moment. For Azalia that resentment takes years to leave. Yet, you make sure the reader understands her mother's heartbreak and guilt. The powerlessness she experienced in that moment turns the reader's resentment into empathy and—" Lucía starts to cough. She grabs the glass of water in front of her and takes a sip. Sol pats her back and even though she's still coughing, she waves him away. He stops and we all wait for her to catch her breath.

"I'm sorry, dry throat," she says sheepishly once she's recovered. "Please, go on." She shifts uncomfortably in her chair and glances at Zev before she looks back at me, this time not quite meeting my eyes. I look at Sol but he just nods for me to continue.

"Well, that scene and the ones that follow are a turning point in the story. They crystalized, perfectly, how defenseless a child is when they live in a country that's unwilling to give them protections of residency. Even though more harrowing things happen to her later in the book, that's where her character's refusal to accept the meager scraps she was being offered came from. As much as I know about this issue and care about it, I spend most of my time talking to adults. Reading as a seven-year-old child learns that she's to spend her entire life being punished for a crime she didn't commit, was really powerful. I think audiences will respond well and will feel compelled to act."

I glance at Zev. He's looking at me wide-eyed. I've kept my politics separate from the studio. He's probably never heard me talk about this before and I know that my passion probably surprises him. He knows me as a pragmatist. Objective and unemotional. My motto is: *What we feel isn't as important as what we know.* But this, for me, is an issue where what *I* feel and what *I* know are perfectly aligned.

"We have an obligation to the DREAMERs. They've been raised here, educated here. They love this country and it's their home. *Throw Away the Key*, through its characters and its message, makes that argument in a visceral and honest way that will translate beautifully to the screen."

Her expression has softened, and it's as if she's seeing me in a different light. She gives me an almost imperceptible, but very real, smile before she looks at Sol and nods.

He opens his briefcase and pulls out a thick document. He sets it on the table in front of them. When he starts to slide it across the table toward me, Lucía lays a protective hand on top of it and stops Sol's from pushing it any farther.

He gives Lucía a small frown, and she pushes the document in my direction. "This is an agreement we drafted." I don't pick it up yet. Sol continues, "The highlights are this: She wants to write the screenplay, she wants to be involved in casting and have the right of refusal. We've detailed her requests for an advance and back-end royalties.

She doesn't want to do any press—the studio and the actors can have all the screen time. Everything else is pretty standard." He taps the stack with a finger and says, "Read it, let your lawyers look over it. Sign it, and we have a deal."

These terms are almost unheard of. Yet, I don't miss a beat responding.

"Fine," I return, even as I feel Zev's eyes burning a hole into the side of my face.

She looks at Sol and gives him a broad, joyous grin. The energy of it brightens the entire room.

I want her to smile at me like that.

Where that thought came from, I don't know, but I banish it. I'm on a mission.

Just like every beautiful woman in this town, I'm sure she knows exactly how she affects men. I'm not falling for that. Been there, done that.

I glance at Zev, and he's staring at me. His bafflement and anger are on unfettered display across his face. I'll have to deal with him in a minute. I look back at Sol and Lucía, "We'll have this reviewed and signed by early next week."

Sol raises a surprised eyebrow at me but only nods. Then, pats Lucía's hand in a very fatherly gesture. This surprises me, Sol is not known for his warmth, not even with his oldest clients. "Well, then we'll consider this meeting adjourned until then. We're looking forward to working with you." They start to stand, but I stop them.

"So, we sign your paperwork and the story is ours?" I ask, wanting to be sure that we're all on the same page.

Lucía straightens completely and I have to stop my eyes from looking at the scar, jagged and angry, that runs down the right side of her belly button. I want to ask her what happened.

I want to touch it, and see how it feels in contrast to the otherwise smooth skin of her stomach.

What the fuck is wrong with me?

"Yes. If you sign that document," she says pulling me back to the conversation. She nods at the papers on the table. "We'll have a deal." She puts her hand out for me to shake and I do. Her grip is firm and when our palms touch, I *feel* it and so does she. Her eyes fly to mine as she pulls her hand back. Her eyes are wide, and her lips slightly parted in surprise.

I can still feel the energy from her palm in my now empty hand, and I can hear the rasp in my voice when I say, "Thank you for coming in."

Her nod is a quick, jerky motion and she glances between my face and her hand.

"Sure. Thank you for inviting us." Without saying goodbye, or waiting for Sol, she turns and walks out of the room. I watch her go, my eyes on the patchwork of torn fabric interspersed with bronzed skin that runs the length of her shapely legs.

"Reece, you have until Monday with those papers and then we're talking to other studios," Sol says. He's also followed my gaze. When he looks back at me, he's frowning, his expression one of rebuke and warning, then he follows her out. I close my eyes, annoyed that he saw me ogling her.

As soon as the door closes behind him, Zev pounces.

"Reece. What. The. Fuck? You can't be serious." He leans toward me and says this in a loud whisper as he if he's afraid someone will overhear us.

"I'm dead serious. You haven't read the book," I respond in a tone that's calmer than how I feel.

"I don't need to read the book. We don't make movies like this. We chase box office dollars, not critical acclaim." He slams his fist on the table.

Zev's worked here longer than I have. I know he resented my promotion to Studio President last year. I've been sensitive to that and have treated him with the respect I believe he's earned. But no matter how he feels, I'm his boss and he clearly needs to be reminded.

I raise an eyebrow at him. "Since when did you decide the creative or financial strategies of this movie studio?" I ask him, my tone quiet, but my anger not disguised.

He pales a little, and when he speaks again, his tone is less combative.

"Fine. But you're going to have to explain this to the writing team. You're going to have to get legal to sign off on it and you'll also have to explain to the board when we dump money into it and don't make it back at the box office."

I sigh. I don't want to alienate Zev, I respect him. I know he's got the conventional wisdom right, but I *know* this movie will be a success. I won't let it be anything else.

"I want to tell this story. I'm willing to take a risk. If it does well, it'll be great for the studio. Yeah, we chase box office success over critical acclaim. This is our chance to have both. I think Ms. Vega's got real star power. She'll be great when we start doing promo for it."

All of a sudden his expression loses some of its hardness, and a conspiratorial grin spreads across his face.

"You want to fuck her, right? I get it, she's gorgeous. I mean, I'm married, but I wouldn't mind getting my hands on that hot little body." He slaps my shoulder as he stands up and starts toward the door. "But, Reece, there are cheaper ways to get some ass. I bet she'd be on her knees for you if you just asked."

I close my eyes and exhale. This is the movie business. The casting couch is real. People use sex as currency all the time, and this sort of banter is common. But not at Artemis Film. My father and I are two of only four male Chief Executives across the entire organization. We've worked hard to create a culture that rewards creativity and hard work. This is where the brightest people want to work because they know that nothing but their effort and attitude counts.

I pick up the contract and start to flip through it, letting Zev know that I'm done talking. Just as he reaches the door, I call his name. When he stops I look him straight in the eyes. "I'll only say this one time. Consider it your warning." He frowns in confusion. "If I hear you talking about anyone who works for or with us, like that again, I don't care how long you've known my father. You'll be gone."

I look back at the contract and flip to the next page. He doesn't say anything as he leaves, but the door closes with a tiny slam. I don't really care how he feels. I meant every word.

I pick up my pen and add a few provisions to the contract. Lucía Vega is asking for a lot. I'm going to give it to her.

2

Lucia

THE RIDE BACK TO LOS FELIZ FEELS INTERMINABLE. SOL IS bursting with excitement and I'm coming out of my skin.

"That went better than I could have expected," he says. It's mid-September and the weather is picture perfect. The windows are down and I'm grateful for the fresh air. I feel hot and unsettled. He's practically bouncing in his seat. "I hadn't expected Reece to be at the meeting."

"Yeah, that was a surprise," I mumble as I stare unseeingly out of the window. All of the other studios had a mid-level executive make their pitch. They'd all just wanted to buy my rights. Then they'll write the screenplay to tell the story they think will be most marketable. I couldn't stomach the thought of my story being exploited like that. Sol and I drafted that agreement thinking no one, especially not one of the largest and most successful film studios in the world, would say yes. We'd never presented it to anyone before. No one had made it past the pitch. I hadn't expected anyone to, but then, I hadn't anticipated Reece Carras or his passion.

My pulse jumps as I remember the real thrill I felt when I walked into the room and saw him there. I recognized him right away. He's as famous as most of the stars in the movies he produces. The only son of the Carras Media Dynasty, he's the heir to a fortune that is made up of assets that span the globe.

He's also a former Olympic athlete. He won gold five times for Team USA. When he came home from his final Olympic games, triumphant, but badly injured, he picked up the mantle of responsibility and worked his way up to head of the studio over the last ten years.

At the same time, he started making a name for himself in the immigrant rights movement. He's put his money where his mouth is. He has a legal defense fund that is set up to pay immigration attorneys who represent people when they are detained. He's used his celebrity to campaign for politicians who share his point of view. I've followed his activism and he's been a hero of mine for years. Meeting him today was surreal.

He's not what you'd call classically handsome. His features are too strong, his brow too brooding, his lips too full. But that five 'o'clock shadow at ten in the morning? I didn't realize how attractive that could be until I saw it on his strong jaw. My fingers itched to touch it. The intensity of his gaze was nearly hypnotic, I found myself losing track of my thoughts when he looked at me.

I can see why he was voted "Sexiest Man Alive" by a major

magazine last year. He's sinfully compelling. And tall, and still as broad and wide as he'd been when he was swimming competitively. I remember watching him at the Olympics and being awed by his agility in the water.

My reaction to him has surprised me, I've never thought much about men. But, I've also never met a man like him before.

It takes us ninety minutes to get back to Los Feliz and Sol talks almost the entire time. I'm lost in my thoughts. The scene from the book, the one he said struck him, was one of the hardest to write. I took it straight from my own experience as a child and the hurt from that day is something I've never forgotten. It was a turning point in my life and that he understood it so clearly, moved me.

For the first time since the idea of selling the film rights came up, I find myself hoping it will happen. I'm not sure that he'll actually sign the agreement once he reads it thoroughly. I'm asking for a lot of money—and a lot of control.

Big budget action films are his studio's bread and butter. So, this book adaptation is definitely not in their wheelhouse.

I know immigrant rights and immigration reform is his cause célèbre. But I can't believe he would concede so much, to make it into a film. He could just have his screenwriters write something else.

The other studio we met with said they'd let me advise on casting, but wouldn't let me be part of the screenplay development. I had Sol send them an email declining as soon as we got home from the meeting. I'm glad I did. If Artemis actually agrees to my terms, it will be more than I could have hoped for.

We pull up to the bungalow I share with my friend, Jessica. Sol unlocks the car door for me, but puts a hand on my shoulder when I start to reach for the handle. I look at him quizzically, his eyes are soft, and there's a small smile on his usually frowning mouth.

"He's going to sign it, Lucía. He wants to be the one to make the film. He's a smart man. He's young, but he's trying to shake things up over there. He'll have it back to us before Monday."

I lean over to peck him on the cheek. "Well, we'll see," I say, reluctant to count my chickens before they hatch.

"Oh, ye of little faith. Trust me. I know him. He's never sat in on one of these meetings. They've never pursued a book-to-film adaptation. He wouldn't be doing this if he didn't want this story." He pats my shoulder. "He'll give you whatever you want. His lawyers aren't going to find anything in that contract that'll be a deal breaker. Monday, you'll see."

I smile at him. He has yet to steer me wrong. But I grew up knowing that nothing is guaranteed. I won't believe it until it's in my hands.

"Talk to you Monday, Sol," I say noncommittally before I hop out of his car. I watch him pull away before I walk up the short flight of stairs that lead to our front porch.

I don't go inside right away. Instead, I sit on one of the black wrought iron, cushioned chairs we keep there and survey my surroundings.

A quiet street, potted plants on my stoop, neighbors waving as they walk by—these are all things I dreamt of when I was growing up.

I love Los Feliz. It's full of history and character. This is the neighborhood where the artists, the real ones, live. Our house was built in the 1920s. It's been renovated, but many of its original features, including the stained-glass door that creates a kaleidoscope of color on the foyer's parquet wood floors, remain.

I started practicing yoga when I got my first job. Every morning, I greet the sun on the back porch. I commune with the sounds around me. I focus on the positive things in my life and spend time making those the narratives I carry with me all day.

When I sat down to write *Throw Away the Key*, I hoped that I could shed some light on what it's like to grow up feeling like an American, loving America, but not being loved in return. I also wanted to pay tribute to my brother, Julian, by telling his story. That story is just one of many in a book that spans the first twenty-one years of my main character's life. But I borrowed heavily from my own experiences throughout. I let my bitterness and rage bleed into the pages of this book. It's covered in my fear and vulnerability; bound together with the hope that someone would read it and be moved. It was such a cathartic experience, pouring out onto paper what lives in my heart every day.

When I'd finished writing, Jessica edited and proofread it for me. We bought a cover from someone Jessica met on Facebook and uploaded it to online retailers, sold paperbacks of it in Jessica's store, Amour, on Hillhurst Avenue in the trendy Silver Lake neighborhood of Los Angeles.

The reception it's received and its success have exceeded my wildest dreams. It's also made me money. I couldn't believe it when I started getting my royalty checks from online retailers. I went from living one paycheck away from disaster to being able to write my mother a check for almost fifty thousand dollars overnight.

Amour is a wildly successful store and boasts a clientele that reads like the who's who of Hollywood. She sells all of her handmade jewelry, ceramics and furniture there. One of *O Magazine's* editors is a client and picked up the book. She read it, loved it, and next thing I knew, it was being featured in their magazine. Then, Sol found me and things really took off. I had already sold over two hundred thousand copies when he negotiated a six-figure advance and a nice royalty-share for a paperback deal with a huge traditional publisher. And everywhere I went, I saw copies of *Throw Away the Key*. It was incredible.

Then, I started getting calls to do television interviews and magazine features. The attention frightened me and I turned them all down. My life has been focused on survival. I've never had the luxury to dream beyond that. And survival has meant living off the radar.

Attention means questions and there are many that I can't afford to answer. I also worry about my mother and how this might impact her.

Lucía Vega is not my real name. It's the name I chose when I decided to publish my book. And now it feels like I'm living vicariously through her. Lucía's not undocumented. Lucía's a published author, with a nice house in Los Feliz and a tattoo of the word *Libertad*—Spanish for freedom—next to her left breast, right over her heart. Lucía's confident, smart and brave. When I step into her shoes, I feel like I can do anything. Be anything. In writing this book, I also wrote the ticket to my own emancipation. I'm free, at least while the world thinks I'm Lucía Vega. I'll protect Lucía and her existence fiercely. Ana Maria De La Vega Rios—the undocumented, scared, tired girl —doesn't exist in the reality I've created.

Reece Carras symbolizes everything girls like Ana aren't supposed to dream about: Power, money, autonomy . . . sex.

But girls like Lucía Vega? They can dream about those things and they can go after them. It's a pipe dream, but today it was close enough to touch.

My stomach grumbles and I glance at my watch. It's getting

late. Just as I'm getting ready to go inside and scrounge for dinner, Jessica pulls up in her little bright blue Mini Cooper. She's my roommate, my friend and my inspiration. She lives her life exactly as she likes. She's thirty-five and has been widowed for more than ten years. She's French, came here as a student, but got married before she even graduated. Her husband died less than a year later. He left everything to her. The house, all his money—and he had a lot of it. She's lived here ever since.

She's never been back to France. It holds bad memories for her and she won't talk about her life there at all. When her mother died last year, she refused her sibling's pleas to attend the funeral. She was stone-faced as she talked about it, but I heard her sobbing in her room later on. It's a subject that she never talks about. I have some of those too, so I don't push.

She doesn't need to work for the income, but she's an artist and loves it too much not to. Amour is where she sells all of her creations, and now she has a small section for books, too.

I watch as she hops out of her car. She looks like the quintessential California girl. Blond, tall, skinny, except for her surgically enhanced breasts. Her face is Botoxed, filled and peeled to make sure that not one line creases her skin. I think she looks amazing. So does every man who lays eyes on her.

She's a modern-day Lothario—loves them then leaves them and never looks back. She's not cruel, but she doesn't do attachments anymore. She always tells me that she likes her independence too much to settle down again. I think it's because she still misses her husband.

"Bonjour, my little soufflé. Why are you sitting here looking around like you just moved here?" she asks cheerfully as she plops down into the chair next to mine. We've become so close. We are family to each other. She loves effusively and is generous with her affection. I love her.

"Just thinking, enjoying the nice evening before I go inside."

"You were pretty pessimistic this morning, did the meeting at Artemis not go well?" She slings a sympathetic arm over my shoulder.

"No, actually, it went very well. And . . . Reece Carras himself was there," I sing at her and prepare for her reaction.

She shrieks, her grip on my shoulders tightening to a near choke hold. "*Mon Dieu!* Reece "Sexiest Man in The World" Carras was there? You were in the same room with him?" She jumps to her feet and looks down at me, eyes narrowed. "What in the world are you doing here and not in his bed? I can't imagine he looked at you and didn't come on to you."

"He definitely didn't come on to me. He was there to try to get a deal done." I try to sound nonchalant. I know all that intensity and focus I felt from him today was about the book and not me. I look down at my right hand and remember the current of energy that traveled up my arm when we shook hands.

I grimace at my calloused palms. I got my first manicure this morning, but no amount of pampering can disguise the fact that I've worked with my hands most of my life. The women in his world are beautiful, dressed in couture and perfectly made up. My clothes come from secondhand stores, though these days, they're upscale consignment ones. And the only makeup I wear is my red lipstick, and that's only because it reminds me of my mother. At least, what she was like when we were young.

She rolls her eyes at my lack of enthusiasm and pouts. "You don't even care. Such an experience is wasted on a person like you. You met the sexiest man in the world and you're acting like it's nothing. Did you at least take a picture?" She sits back down and puts her elbows on her knees and cups her chin with her hands. She looks at me with a mixture of pity and disgust.

I laugh. She's obsessed with celebrity gossip. She watches E! religiously and knows more about celebrities than she knows about me. She told me that she's waiting for Tom Cruise to discover her store. Her more famous clients never come to the store themselves. They send in personal assistants and drivers instead. She's dying for a celebrity encounter.

Reece is one of her favorites. Last year, he went through a very public, very ugly divorce. He and his ex-wife Fabienne had been together for ten years when they split. They married young, right after he won his Olympic Gold. She's a world famous supermodel from Brazil and he was the dashing young athlete who was going to inherit a huge movie empire. They were tabloid darlings and their split was major news.

Jessica read me daily updates on his divorce proceedings. His ex-wife accused him of cheating on her. He never responded publicly. They had a prenup and apparently, she made a mint off him. Once the divorce was finalized, he disappeared from the public eye, only making appearances in relation to his immigration activism.

"Did you at least tell him you have a roommate who adores him?" Jessica asks, still pouting.

I roll my eyes back at her. "I was there for a meeting, Jess. Which by the way, went very well. I think it's going to happen; he really wants the option rights."

"Of course it's going to happen, my little brioche bun," she says with a small, sad smile. "When it does, I hope it will take some of that sadness out of your eyes. I know you think you hide it well, but my heart aches at the emotions you wear plainly on your face. Especially when you think no one's watching." She pats me on the knee, stands up and heads for the door.

"I'm grilling portobellos for dinner tonight!" she calls over her shoulder as she opens the door.

I groan and call after her, "I'll never become a vegetarian and I'm not on a diet! Stop trying to convert and starve me." She laughs that tinkling laugh and disappears inside.

I laugh, too, but her parting words stay with me and sober me. She's right, I don't remember a day in more than fifteen years that I haven't felt sad. Because at the end of the day, my brother is still dead. My heart has a permanent hole in it.

I've lost a lot. I've given up even more. But, in writing this book, in telling my brother's story, I feel like I've started to get some of it back.

Today, I sat across from one of the most powerful men in this town and made demands. And he took me seriously. But even if he hadn't, I would have been fine. It feels good to have what I need; to not feel desperate, for once.

I stand up to walk inside and take a deep breath, letting myself absorb the sound of Los Feliz at dusk. It's quiet, but there is a hum of contentment in the air. The sounds of people going about their lives in total peace.

I grew up in a neighborhood where everyone looked over their shoulders. They didn't loiter outside talking to their neighbors. They didn't cook on their back decks and play music that they sang along to. They didn't speed down the freeway with their tops down, not caring if it meant you might get a ticket. Living in the shadows meant you didn't do things to draw attention to yourself.

I want to live free. Just like my neighbors in Los Feliz; enjoying the small pleasures of life without worrying that doing so would mean my undocumented status could be discovered.

I've been considering how to make that a reality. One option is to voluntarily depart. It would mean waiting three years before I could apply to return. But, if I'm deported before I can leave on my own, part of the penalty would be a ten-year wait before I could apply.

I'm not sure if I'm ready to leave the country I call home.

But, for the chance to become a real member of the orchestra that gives Los Feliz the sound of freedom, I'm willing to try.

3

Reece

It's Sunday night and my father is on a tear. He just finished reading Lucía's contract and he's livid.

"Reece, this makes no fucking sense. Why are you giving her so much control? She's written one book. One!"

His palm slaps the table and I stifle a sigh. I expected this. Prepared for it, even. But that doesn't make it any less aggravating. He wouldn't talk to Zev like this. But he's my boss and my father, and I've just learned that conversations like these come with the territory.

"It's one of the most important books I've ever read," I say simply.

"Important?" he sputters like the word tastes terrible on his tongue. "It doesn't have any action. It doesn't have any sex. It's fucking Young Adult fiction, Reece," he says.

My father is the most powerful man in this business. He's the head of the world's largest entertainment conglomerate. He hasn't gotten there because he has bad instincts. But, even he doesn't understand the motion picture industry the way I do.

He knows it; it's why he made me President of Artemis Film.

I know the adaptation will be a stretch for us. I admit that some of my motives are personal. But I wouldn't be risking the studio's reputation, or money, based solely on my need for absolution.

I know that this could bring our studio our first acting, directing and screenwriting awards. We're going to win Oscars with this film. The marketing I've planned is going to make it a box office success.

"Dad, she wrote the story. She wants to write the screenplay. She wants to make sure the actors we cast are close to her vision. I don't see what's wrong with that."

"She's asking for a lot of money. What's her justification?" he demands.

"Because she can. She's an international bestseller, holding nominations for the Orange Prize for Fiction, The Man Booker Prize, and the National Book Award," I respond, trying to keep my voice level, but I know my temper is showing.

My mother, Diana, breezes into my father's study.

"I can hear you from the front foyer," she says to both of us, her tone disapproving.

She pats my father on the shoulder and perches on the edge of his desk.

"Darling, you're wasting your breath. He's already signed the contract. Isn't that right?"

Her eyes cut to me and she doesn't disguise her annoyance. I bristle.

"Yes, I have. Legal reviewed it. They didn't find anything unenforceable. They gave me their formal opinion. I signed it and sent it over this morning. I added a few stipulations, but I don't think they'll be deal breakers for her," I respond and try not to swallow hard. My mother isn't someone I like tangling with when it comes to business.

Diana Carras runs the entire organization's operations with an iron fist. She and my father met while they were both MBA students at Wharton. She's worked for Artemis for thirty-five years and they are always on the same page. Except when it comes to me.

My father is supportive of my passion about immigration. He's the son of a Greek immigrant. He's the first generation of Carras' born in America. So, he understands, somewhat, how important this is. My mother on the other hand, doesn't think she has any skin in the game. Her sole concern is how it affects the studio.

"Reece, we promoted you to the head of the studio because we trust you. You've proven yourself to be an excellent leader. I just wish you'd talked to us about it a little before you committed yourself to this project." She comes to stand next to me and puts a hand on my shoulder. I look down at her, her light blue eyes, shrewd as ever as she talks to me. "I've heard the buzz about this book, so I understand why so many studios want it. Given the issues it raises, I understand why *you* do. I know you believe this film will do well. So, go ahead. But after the script is written, you've got to bring it before the committee, just like everyone else does, and let them decide whether or not it's got the green light."

"We'll support you, son. However we can," my father interjects.

My father saying this helps ease the knots that I had inside of me during this entire conversation.

"Of course he has our support," my mother snaps at him. "We're all allowed one fuck up, and this film will have one of the smallest budgets we've ever worked with, so if it doesn't do well, the board won't be calling for your head," my mother says as she pulls out her to phone and starts reading email.

"Thanks, Mom. Glad you believe in this," I mumble not hiding my sarcasm. I can't wait to prove her wrong.

"Look, Reece—" my dad starts but my phone buzzes and I grab it from the table where it's resting. One glance at the screen, has me out of my seat and pacing my dad's study. I've been waiting for this call all day.

"Sol, talk to me," I say as soon as I accept his call.

"She said no." He cuts straight to the point. I stop in my tracks.

"How? We gave her everything she wanted." My voice is raised and my parents look up from their respective devices at the same time. I turn my back to them and walk to the large bay window that overlooks their rear garden.

"You added somethings she didn't like, Reece," Sol returns calmly.

"For fuck's sake. No one writes an entire screenplay alone. She needs a team," I hiss into the phone, trying to deprive my audience of a performance.

"That's not it. Listen, take out the language about Malibu and I think she'll be on board," he says.

I balk.

"*That's* her problem? Sol, you need to advise your client.

You know that no one else is going to give her so much and ask so little in return."

I hear his exasperated exhale. "I'll talk to her, Reece. But, let me just warn you right now. You better not be doing this because you're hoping something extra comes along with her book. That girl has been through enough. If it even starts to feel like you're doing this because you think you're going to add her to your harem, I'll make sure that she walks."

I see red. Yes, the author is beautiful, but I also read the fucking book—most of it anyway. That story needs to be told and I need to be the one to make it happen.

"I've known you a long time, Sol. So, I'm going to ignore that insult. Talk to your client. Get her to say yes. Then, call me back."

I disconnect the call and sit down.

I look up to see my parents watching me, concern on both of their faces. My mother comes to where I'm standing and touches my arm.

"You should be grateful. Yes, it's a good story, but it doesn't make sense for the studio's brand. I know you care about this topic, but it's risky."

Her gentle voice only annoys me because I know she's happy this happened.

"Mother, every time we begin this process, we take a risk. The upside of those risks are usually just that we're going to make a tremendous return on our investment. This project? We could do that *and* we could actually tell a story that matters." I look between them. "I read the book. You should, too. You'll see why it's so special."

"If you can't get her to agree, none of that even matters," my father says softly.

He's absolutely right. "You're right, Dad. Thanks for the advice," I say as I stand up and stalk out of the room.

"What advice?" he calls after me, but I don't respond.

I'm not going to sit here and hope that Sol Kline can convince her. I grab my keys, jump into my car and head to Los Feliz. If she's going to turn us down because of one clause that I actually thought she'd jump at, I need her to look me in the face and tell me why.

Not that it matters. I'm not taking no for an answer.

4

Lucia

SUNDAY NIGHT MEANS *THE WALKING DEAD*, SHRIMP TACOS and margaritas. Tonight, I've doubled the tequila in my drink. I need it. Sol is pissed at me and I'm avoiding him. I know he thinks I'm crazy. Hell, I think I'm crazy, but I can't accept the clause Artemis added. It would throw my life into total disarray. I'd have to rent a place in Malibu and I can't afford that in addition to the rent at Jessica's for three months, or however long I'd be there. Even if I could, getting someone to rent me a space once they learn I'm undocumented is next to impossible. So, I can't.

I'm disappointed. Getting this close to the film actually

happening made me realize how much I wanted it. And then there's Reece. I haven't stopped thinking about Reece since we met. I keep replaying his impassioned speech he made during our meeting. His eyes were so intense as he told me why this matters to him. I would have enjoyed working with him.

I assumed the reason he became head of the film studio was only due to the fact that his parents own it. But yesterday, I could see that he's flexible and decisive at the same time. It's rare to see those qualities in people who've had everything handed to them and haven't had to compromise or sacrifice much.

I take a sip of my drink and wish Jessica were here instead of out on a date. I could use a little company and comfort tonight. I'm just piling the pico and guac on my taco when I see the headlights of a vehicle as it parks in front of our house. I barely register it because we live on a busy street. When our doorbell rings less than thirty seconds later, I almost jump out of my skin.

I already know it's not for me. Sol and Jessica are the only friends I have who know where I live and Sol wouldn't show up without calling. It must be one of Jessica's guys who got their date night wrong. I contemplate not answering—I'm not in the mood to console one of her love-sick boyfriends—but the doorbell rings again and I know that the lights and the television make it obvious someone is home.

I look down at myself. I'm wearing one of my gauzy beach cover ups, but it's decent enough. Reluctantly, I pause my show with a sigh, push off the couch and rush to the door. As I approach, I see a tall, obviously male silhouette through the door's glass.

I swing the door open. "Jess isn't—" I can't control the squawk of surprise that escapes when I open it and see Reece

Carras standing on the other side. He's the last person I'd expected to see and for a minute I just stand and gape at him. He's dressed so differently from when I last saw him. In his office, he wore a suit, his hair styled off his face. Then, he'd looked every inch the young movie mogul-and that he is.

But tonight, he's dressed in jeans, Chucks, a V-neck white T-shirt that clings to his muscular chest and reveals a tattoo that covers his entire right bicep. His tanned, muscled bicep. His five o'clock shadow is more like a light beard now and a dark lock of hair rests on his forehead.

His eyes are hooded and he's looking me up and down in a way that makes me feel as if I'm standing in front of him naked. His gaze feels like the touch of a hand. I feel my nipples harden as his eyes sweep past them.

I cough and he brings his unfathomably dark eyes to my face. He doesn't look the slightest bit chagrined when I scowl at him.

"Are you done?" I ask him, placing my hands on my hips.

"Well, I was just giving you a chance to finish," he drawls and I blush.

I brush my hair with my fingers and straighten my dress before I step outside and pull the door closed behind me. "What are you doing here? How do you even know where I live?" I cross my arms over my chest and plant my feet. I hate how defensive I sound, but I've been thrown completely off balance by his unexpected visit.

His eyes flare with annoyance. "Your address was in the paperwork you filled out to enter our office building. All of our visitors' information gets scanned into my address book," he returns evenly, folding his arms across his chest and leaning against one of the porch columns. "You know exactly why I'm here," he snaps, all traces of humor disappearing from his dark eyes. I have to stop myself from gulping down the ball of nerves lodged in my throat. Suddenly I see the executive who runs his movie studio like a well-oiled machine. Someone who isn't used to hearing no. He's not here to flirt with me or make small talk.

"Don't play coy, Lucía." He pronounces my name the way a lot of Europeans do—with the c pronounced ch.

I correct him. "It's Loo-seeah. I'm Mexican, not Italian. And I'm not playing coy." I draw out the last syllable.

His left eyebrow quirks up and he smiles as if surprised. A dimple I didn't noticed before appears in his right cheek. "Forgive the mispronunciation, Lucía." He says my name correctly this time. He runs his fingers through his closely cropped dark hair and sighs. My eyes are drawn to his gorgeous mouth; fascinated at the way it purses on his exhale.

"Tell me why you said no," he asks, his voice still demanding, but gentler this time.

My heart thuds against my chest so hard that I'm sure he can hear it. I glance down at my hands and try to gather my thoughts.

This man, who until yesterday, I'd only seen on television or in magazines is standing on my doorstep because he wants to make my book into a movie. It's surreal and intimidating. My reason for saying no now feels very flimsy. I force myself to look at him and answer his question.

His handsome face is impassive, but his eyes are anything but. The urgency in them only heightens my anxiety. I clear my throat. "I thought Sol told you. I can't move to Malibu for an undetermined amount of time. I pay rent here."

He raises his eyebrows as if to say and? I sigh.

"I can't leave my roommate high and dry. It doesn't matter how much you pay me, I can't afford to pay rent here and at some place in Malibu. I need to work a commutable distance from where I live." I cross my arms, stick out my chin as I admit, "I don't drive."

He doesn't hesitate when he responds. "'That clause was not a random whim. Our Malibu office is where our screenwriting team always collaborates. Most of them live in Malibu or close by and it's just always been an easy central place. The studio can provide your accommodation while you're there."

"You'd house me?" I say hesitantly. I didn't expect that.

"Yes, if that's what it takes."

Shit. I don't want to move to Malibu. It's so far away from what I've come to think of as my home. I've never lived anywhere but this city. I feel safe here. Although, at times, my inability to leave makes me feel like a captive. A change of scenery might not be a bad thing. "I won't work weekends; I'll want to come home every Friday night."

His eyes roll and he sighs. But he doesn't miss a beat before responding. "You won't be a prisoner. You can leave whenever you want. But you'll need to build a writing schedule with your team and stick to it." I don't have any other excuses at this point and as if he knows it, he laughs. The rich, deep, triumphant sound washes over me, mingling with my anxiety, creating a feeling of trepidation that I can't tamp down.

I feel cornered. I don't know why, because what I want the most is finally within reach. I'm letting my fear keep me from grabbing a hold of it. Nothing in my life has ever been this easy. It's all too good to be true. And that makes me very nervous.

I have one more thing to add. I take a deep breath and let it out.

"Sol's warned me about how some of these things work. I'm not interested in sleeping with you, so if all of this is a ploy to make that happen, you're wasting your time."

He mumbles something under his breath and stands up

straight and he narrows his eyes at me in anger. "You're the third person who's suggested that I'm doing this to sleep with you." His eyes flick over me again. "Yes, Ms. Vega, you're very beautiful." I'm grateful for the setting sun as I feel my entire body flush. "But I don't need to spend millions of dollars to get a beautiful woman to sleep with me." His dark, lushly lashed eyes rake over me. He grins sardonically and says, "Honestly, you're not my type." His frank eyes don't leave mine and I can feel my chin jut out as I try to pretend that his words didn't feel like a slap to my face. "No offense," he adds, as an afterthought.

"Glad it's mutual," I scoff.

He runs a hand over his face. "Look, I've given you everything you've asked for. Stop making excuses. Come to Malibu. Write the screenplay. Let's see if we can get past that." He puts his sunglasses on. "You've made a lot of demands. I've met them all. It's time for you to deliver." He turns to walk down the steps. I watch his long, denim clad legs eating up my pavement. Just as he reaches his car—which looks like something from the future, all black and smoky gray—he looks over his shoulder at me. I haven't moved. I'm not sure that I can. His sunglasses are shielding his eyes, but I can still feel them on me and I wish he would just leave.

"Let me know by tomorrow at noon," he calls. Then he gives me a two-finger salute and pulls away.

I stand there for a few minutes feeling like such a fool. Of course I'm not his type. I don't know what possessed me to say that. I step back inside and sit down. My taco is soggy and cold, and my margarita is no longer frozen.

I can't waste food, so I force myself to eat everything and that just sours my mood even further. I decide *The Walking Dead* can wait and get ready for bed.

As I start to drift into what will prove to be a fitful sleep, I tell myself that I'm going to sleep on it. But my heart knows that I've already made a decision. I can't turn this down because I don't want to spend a couple of months in Malibu. This is a once in a lifetime chance, and I know it. I'll call him in the morning and get the ball rolling. I pray I don't regret it.

5

Lucia

CHANGE HAS BEEN MY ONLY CONSTANT. I'VE MOVED MORE times than I can count. Before I came to live with Jessica, I moved at least once a year So, I don't know why, as Sol and I sit in the back of a chauffeured SUV, cruising down the Pacific Coast Highway, I feel like I'm on a rollercoaster straight to hell.

I want to tell our driver to turn around and take me back to the safety of my house. But, it's too late. We've all signed the contract, they've already paid me my twenty-five percent advance. I made my choice and there's no turning back. Sol's got his headphones on and his eyes are closed. I try to breathe and relax as we speed down the 101 towards Malibu.

Every day this week, I've dreamed of Julian and the last time I saw him. I was eight. He was sixteen. He was leaving for school and told me that he had to do something for a friend after school and that he'd be home late.

My dream would then jump to later that evening; me coming in from playing to find my parents in a panic.

My father's cousin was on the police force and he called to let us know that Julian had been arrested. They were throwing things in bags and screaming at each other in Spanish. When I asked them what was going on, my mother shouted that Immigration was going to deport us. She dissolved into tears. When I turned to my father to ask him where Julian was, he slapped me across the face and told me to go to my room and pack. He'd never hit me before, and a combination of fear and shock propelled me to my room where I obeyed his order. We hid in a neighbor's garage that night, my mother's wails keeping us up all night.

The next day, my dad went in search of my brother's court-appointed attorney. He brought me along to translate for him. It took us almost two hours to locate the lawyer. All he told us was that Julian had been identified as a suspect in a crime by an eyewitness. He'd already been arraigned and then handed to Immigration Enforcement. They were preparing to take him to a detention center near San Diego where he'd await his deportation hearing.

He read from the file and closed it, then told us he was expecting a client. He didn't even have the decency to look my father in the eye as he delivered the news. I could feel my father's heart cracking as we stood there; the fear on his face turning to anguish with every word the lawyer spoke.

Julian was going to be deported and we couldn't do anything about it. We couldn't go to San Diego. We relied on my parents' income. If they didn't work, they didn't get paid, and not getting paid meant risking homelessness.

Then, the crime he'd been initially arrested for was solved less than two weeks later. The real perpetrator struck again and was caught at the scene. His DNA matched DNA found on the first victim.

Not that it mattered for Julian. It didn't matter whether he committed that particular crime or not, he was still here illegally and they were going to deport him. No one cared that he was a straight A student or that he had a little sister who worshiped him. When we got the news a few weeks later that Julian died in the detention center, my life spiraled so wildly off center that I've never recovered.

That was the first time I'd ever seen my father cry. He pulled his hair as he howled; it was an anguished, desperate sound that made my blood run cold with fear. He prowled the living room of our apartment sobbing and ranting. His son was gone, and there was nothing he could do. He had failed to protect him. His cousin offered to go and claim Julian's body for us. But my father insisted on going himself. He didn't care if it meant he would be detained, too. My mother begged him not to go. Her pleas fell on deaf ears. He was consumed by grief and guilt.

Scared, confused and feeling utterly alone, I stood and watched them have this battle, while I tried to absorb the fact that my big brother wasn't coming home. Ever.

I miss my brother. He was the only person in the entire world who understood me and he'd been my only real friend. And when he died, my life as I knew it ended.

My father went to the morgue to claim the body. He got into an altercation with one of the medical examiner's staff, was arrested and then detained. When his deportation order was issued a year later, he didn't fight it.

He was sent back to Mexico and has never tried to return. He settled in the small resort town of Playa Del Rosarito and to this day works at one of the large resorts that dot the beach of that town. We saw him once when we drove to the border. We talked to him through a chain link fence that none of us dared cross. I only speak to him once a year, when I call him on his birthday. He and my mother never talk.

I wasn't sure that I blamed him for not wanting to stay in touch. My parents came to this country to see us well-educated. My father broke his back cutting lawns, keeping flowerbeds mulched, pruning trees, cleaning gutters—whatever he needed to do to make sure that my brother and I went to school. My brother got a soccer scholarship to one of the best private Catholic schools in the city. My parents were so proud. I was only six and still enrolled in our public elementary school, but they had hopes that I'd get a scholarship for my art or music to the conservatory when it was my turn. But in the span of one day, everything he'd given his life to was destroyed. Once he was gone, and his income was gone, we couldn't afford the rent on our little house any more.

My mother took a live-in cleaning position and they let me stay with her. We shared her room, but it was spacious enough. She got to walk me to school every morning and pick me up in the afternoon. I stayed out of their way, and made sure they never saw me. Being invisible became part of who I was.

When I was twelve, the youngest son of the family cornered me in my room, tried to kiss me and touch me. My mother walked in and stopped him. He told us if we told on him, he'd "turn our illegal asses in." That was enough to silence my mother.

A week later, she sent me to live with my father's cousin and his wife. I still went to school, but when I got home I was their nanny, maid and cook. At fourteen they put me to work in the family restaurant he and his wife ran, and said I owed them the work for my room and board.

I didn't complain. I kept my head down, worked hard and did as I was told. Every day my goal was just to survive.

I only saw my mother once a month after she sent me away. On the first Sunday of every month, she would come and take me to mass and then to get something to eat. Her bitterness was always palpable and it created a distance between us that felt impossible to bridge. But, she was my mother. And I clung to those visits, even when it was obvious she would rather be anywhere else than with me.

I graduated from high school the same year that the President of the United States created a way for people like me, who came to this country with their parents when they were minors, to work legally. And he deferred any action on deportation for two years. You just had to have a clean record and proof that you were a minor when you entered the US. My mother didn't want me to apply, she said I'd be exposing myself, but I did it anyway. It was a chance to work legally, to earn a living that would allow me to support myself.

I looked for a job as soon as my work permit came through. I moved out of my uncle's house and into a tiny studio I shared with another girl I met at a job I had cleaning offices in Beverly Hills overnight. During the day, I worked in a grocery store and on my days off, I wrote.

My apartment building was full of undocumented people from all over the world. The landlord overlooked our status as long as rent was paid a month in advance. It was small, crowded, loud and unbearably hot, but it got me away from my relatives. I even had enough money to start taking yoga classes instead of following along with a YouTube video I stumbled upon one day.

And that's when my life started to change for the better. During my first class, I made friends with Jessica. She looked like a Barbie and sounded like a French bar maid. We bonded over our inability to pronounce the names of some of the moves. When she dropped out of yoga and moved on to spinning, we stayed friends.

I ran into her one evening when I was leaving yoga and she invited herself over for dinner. When we got to my apartment that night, I found my roommate, and my meager valuables, gone. I sat down in the middle of my empty apartment and cried when I realized she'd taken my small suitcase that had Julian's class ring, a book of his drawings and most of the pictures I had of him inside. My neighbors told me that there'd been a raid by the immigration authorities at her day job and she got scared and decided to move. I was paralyzed by sadness; Jessica took charge, and took me home with her.

We've been roommates ever since. She charged me the same rent I was paying in my shitty shared studio. Living in Los Feliz was a game changer. Suddenly, I had the space and quiet I needed to write. And I finished *Throw Away the Key*.

The rest is history. Here I am, on my way to start writing the screenplay for the film adaptation of my book.

And I know that in many ways my life choices are still limited, but I was going to try to squeeze every last drop of life out of my existence. I'm only twenty-three, but life has shown me that moving past your fear is the only way forward.

So, as we sit in the back of the car that Artemis Film sent to bring me to Malibu, I grab Sol's hand and give it a grateful squeeze. I didn't even have to ask him to make this drive with me. He insisted on coming. He's been so good to me.

His eyes pop open and he looks over at me. "This is it, kid. You ready?" He's asking rhetorically. I smile in response, because I'm not so sure that I am.

He knows I don't have an answer to that question. Since I signed the contract with Artemis, things have been moving at warp speed. The studio wanted me to get started writing as soon as possible. When the money hit my account, I got a call from Reece's assistant, Liza, who told me she would be handling all my arrangements personally. She asked me what I ate (*everything*), what kind of mattress and pillows I needed (*the regular kind*), if I had any environmental allergies (*who doesn't?*) and told me that I'd have a car and driver at my disposal in Malibu. I can't believe all of this happening.

I'll be living in my own guesthouse on the estate that the Carras family owns in Malibu. The writing team will be there first thing in the morning for us to get acquainted. The family's private residence is part of the estate, but Sol said they only use it in the summer and are in Los Angeles this time of year. That's a relief. I couldn't handle seeing Reece every day. It's mortifying that he's gotten under my skin when my presence barely registers with him.

That's probably for the best. I'm finally financially secure, but I still feel like my life is too unsettled to bring anyone into it. I don't date because that would mean I'd have to share my status and I'm afraid to do that. Jessica had an employee, Kelvin, who worked for her at Amour. He was from Germany and came to LA to study, but overstayed his visa. His "best friend" from college agreed to marry him so that he could stay. But as soon as they were married, she began blackmailing him. She demanded money, made him buy her a new car. She even had him pay rent on an apartment where her boyfriend lived. After a year of scrambling to meet her demands, he eventually filed for divorce and went back to Germany. Those are the kinds of things that happen when you tell people about your status.

I can't take the risk, so I keep it to myself.

By the time we arrive at the wrought iron gate, the sun has set. All I can see are the two giant *Cs* that adorn each side, which our headlights are illuminating.

Our driver, Constantine, rolls the window down, punches a code into the little keypad to open the gate. We drive down what must be the longest and best-lit driveway in the world. It's lined with dozens of torches on either side. At the top of the driveway, we stop in front of a beautiful house. It's a modern structure made of glass and white stone. Constantine kills the engine and hops out of the car.

Sol's dozed off and I nudge him awake. His eyes shoot open and before he can speak, I demand, "I thought they were putting me up in a guest house?" He shrugs sleepily and stretches.

"This *is* your guesthouse, Ms. Vega," Constantine says as he opens my door.

"This is a guesthouse? All of this is for me?" I say as I step out of the car and look around. This guesthouse is three times the size of our house in Los Feliz.

He nods. "Yes, this is part of the Carras Estate, and the offices are also on the property."

"Where's the main house?" I ask him, unable to tear my eyes away from the beautiful structure that is going to be my home for the next few months.

"It's farther down the beach, about a quarter of a mile away. It's a quick jog but you can also take the golf cart that's in the garage." He holds up a pair of keys and jingles them. "These are for you. House, golf cart and access fob for the office building.

It's another half a mile beyond the main house so you should definitely use the cart to get to and from the office."

I can hear the unmistakable crash of the ocean. The first thought I have is that I'll be doing my yoga to that sound every morning.

"Sol, I think things are going to be okay," I say with a smile before I start to walk up the steps that lead to the house. I peer inside through the floor-to-ceiling glass windows that sit on either side of two huge white wood doors. They are battered and look like they were salvaged from the original structure that this modern structure replaced.

It's a single-story, open-plan home. All the lights are on inside and I can see furniture in a style I've heard called shabby chic dotting the huge open-plan space. I can see straight through to another wall of glass that leads to what looks like a back deck. It's dark, but there are two fire pits burning, and beyond them I see a pool with a ledge that looks like it's meeting the horizon. "It's nice, right?" Constantine says as he comes to stand behind me.

I turn around to face him. He doesn't look a day older than twenty-five, but he told us he's Reece's older cousin. I can see a resemblance. They have the same coloring and similar facial structures. He has a huge friendly grin on his face. I've not yet seen one like that on Reece's face. And . . . I'm thinking about Reece again. I frown and Constantine misreads it and says, "There is a porch that wraps around the entire house so you can access the back deck without going inside. Even though you can't see it from here, beach access is just down those stairs at the end of the deck."

I walk over to look, and indeed, there are steps built into the side of the hill leading down to the beach.

He comes to stand next to me and smiles down at me. "You'll like it here, Ms. Vega."

I return his smile, "I hope so, Constantine. And please, call me Lucía."

"Okay, Lucía. But only if you call me Coco."

Sol comes to stand beside us. "Coco," he says mockingly, "I want to get back to LA tonight. Can we get Ms. Vega settled and be on our way?" His voice is gruff and unfriendly.

Coco's smile disappears and he mumbles a quick, "Yes, sir," before he jogs back to the car to get my bags out.

I bump Sol with my hip and whisper, "That wasn't nice, Sol. He was just being friendly."

"You've got a lot to learn, kiddo. But *friends* like him are usually the ones named as 'a source close to the star' when you hear juicy tidbits in the news. I don't have to remind you that you've got a lot to lose here, Lucía. Focus on what you're here for. Be careful who you talk to." After giving me that bitter pill to swallow, he tests the door, finds it unlocked and walks inside.

Coco returns with my luggage in both hands. As he passes me, he gives me a friendly wink and I try to smile easily back at him.

6

Reece

LUCÍA'S NOT MY TYPE. I WASN'T BEING DISHONEST WHEN I said that. I can smell the innocence on her from a mile away. She has no guile; no poker face. Yet despite that and all the other reasons I should stay away, I can't stop thinking about her. It's not just that she's beautiful. It's that on her, innocence doesn't equal naïveté. Her lack of guile doesn't manifest as a lack of self-awareness. She's clever and direct. The way she demanded what she wanted, and was prepared to walk away if she didn't get it, won my respect.

It's been a long time since I've seen that kind of conviction from anyone who's trying to make a career in this industry. I'm fucking glad that she sold us those rights. This film is important.

I think back to the night that changed my whole life and spurred this journey. It's been fifteen years and I still feel cold when I think about it. I've dedicated myself to trying to make sure that what happened then doesn't happen to anyone else. Recently, I realized that no matter how much money I raised, how many people's legal defenses I funded, how many times I testified before Congress, I wasn't tipping the scales enough to have an impact. Immigration has become a political football that no one wants to run with. *Throw Away the Key* has given us the chance to change the narrative by putting relatable, likable faces to the issue. This film could be a game changer.

So, it's a real inconvenience that I'm insanely attracted to the author. I can tell she feels it too because I saw her looking at me the same way I was looking at her. The attraction and tension between us is so thick, I can almost touch it. Her entire body flinched when I said she wasn't my type. But, if I hadn't put that barrier up, we'd be in bed faster than either of us can think better of it. I can't let that happen. But, fuck me. I want it to.

Since I'm in Malibu this week, I'm going to keep an eye on Lucía as she gets her team together. I'll try to offer advice and help her make informed decisions. Then I'm hightailing it back to LA. I need to put physical distance between us because when I'm near her, it's easy to forget why I need to stay away.

Going to her house got her to agree, but it left me with a hard cock that couldn't seem to control itself. In the shower, I've stroked myself and come to visions of her that night. She was wearing this thin, white dress. Her nipples pebbled beneath it, begging me to pinch them. Her beautiful face was completely bare, even that red lipstick was gone. Those plump lips were the same color as her face, except for the soft pink inner part, that peeked out when she pursed her lips. I've imagined that mouth around my cock more times than I can count.

I want to meet with her this morning before she heads to the office, so I stop by her house. We'll be working closely on the project; I need to be able to spend time with her without getting a chubby. I figured this meeting would be good practice.

Now that I'm here, I realize it was a terrible idea. She's on the deck, moving through what I think are yoga poses. She is focused on what she's doing and oblivious to my presence. She looks invincible and completely at peace. I'm captivated as I watch her body's graceful movements.

She comes out of her last pose and then walks over to the pool. She dips her toe in and then sits down so that her legs are submerged. Her head tips back to let the morning's weak sun bathe her face. In profile, her perfect bone structure is revealed. The movement arches her back and forces her chest out. Her nipples are hard underneath her sports bra, and from where I'm standing, they're like beacons begging me to move in their direction.

I feel my body responding to her. "You're here for a reason, Reece, stop acting like a Peeping Tom and get your shit together," I mumble under my breath. I turn the corner. Before I can say a word, the sun casts my shadow over her and she lets out a yelp and jumps up. She whips around and her eyes widen in surprise when she sees me, then she wavers just enough to lose her balance and fall backward into the pool.

It takes me a couple of seconds to realize she's struggling. I drop my phone along with the bag I'm holding and jump into the pool wrapping my arms around her. That only makes her even more frantic. She starts to fight me and I throw her over my shoulder. She's screaming like a banshee, arms flailing and pummeling me as she continues to panic. Thank God she's so small, otherwise it would have been impossible to get us both out of the water safely.

"Stop moving, dammit," I shout, trying to be heard over the ruckus she's making. I put her down in front of me. Her eyes are closed, and she's screaming bloody murder. She's trembling and I start to rub my hands up and down her biceps to try to calm her down. "Luc, you're fine," I say, not shouting but still loudly enough for her to hear me. She stops screaming almost immediately, but doesn't open her eyes.

"Lucía, open your eyes. You're safe. You're out the water," I say, this time in a softer voice. I can see the terror on her face and I don't want to do anything to agitate her and set her screaming again.

She doesn't say anything but her eyes remain squeezed shut. Her trembling turns to a shiver. It's early on a September morning, so there's a slight chill in the air. I feel a shiver run through my body, too. I'm soaked; I didn't even stop to kick my shoes off before I dove into the pool.

"Lucía, can you hear me? Let's go inside so we can dry off. You'll get sick if you stand out here like this."

I've just decided that I need to pick her up and carry her inside when she speaks. Softly, in that low husky voice.

"I can't swim." Her eyes are open now, but glued to my chest.

"No shit," I quip and that seems to snap her out of whatever trance she's in.

Her eyes come up to my face and she takes a step back, putting not just physical distance, but a palpable emotional barrier between us. She frowns at me as she lifts her arms to wring the water out of her hair.

"You scared me. What are you doing here, anyway?" She

doesn't sound combative, but the glint in her eyes and the tight set of her jaw tell me she's pissed and that it's taking a Herculean effort to hide it.

"Well, for starters, I live here," I say.

Her eyes go as wide as saucers. "I thought this was the guesthouse." Her eyes dart around like she is looking for the nearest exit. "I thought you lived in LA. And I thought you were only here in the summer. Sol said I'd be alone." The alarm is completely undisguised. And a part of me is tempted to tease her, but I have a feeling it wouldn't go over well. So, I put her out of her misery.

"This is the guesthouse, I'm up at the main house. And while I do live in LA, for the next couple of weeks, I'll be here full time. I've staked a lot on this film and I want to make sure things go smoothly."

"Don't you have clients in LA? Meetings?"

God she's transparent. I didn't realize that me being here would make her so uncomfortable. Does she *dislike* me?

"It's LA, not Las Vegas. It's a forty-five-minute drive. I'll be back and forth." I see her shoulders sag in relief. It shouldn't bother me that she doesn't want me here, but it does.

"Oh, okay." She smiles the most insincere smile I've ever seen.

"It's a good thing you're not pursuing a career as an actress," I say entering the house. I kick my shoes off before I open the door and step inside. She trots in after me, leaving a trail of water in her wake.

"I'm sorry. I don't mean to seem like I don't want you here. It's just not what I expected."

I dismiss her statement with a wave of my hand.

"Listen, we're dripping wet, why don't you go and get

changed and then come back. I came over to talk to you before you meet with your team this morning."

"What about you?" she asks, raising her eyebrows at my equally sodden clothes.

"I've got some clothes in my truck, I'll go out and get them and I'll change, too."

She smiles another uncomfortable, closed mouth smile and then dashes off to her room.

I watch her go. Her yoga pants are a light blue and wet. I can see straight through them. God, she has a luscious ass.

I groan to myself. I can't afford to fuck up this film. But the more I look at her, the more I want to fuck her. I know I didn't just imagine the way she was looking at me that night at her house. I want to follow her to her room, and play with her body until she begs me to fuck her. Make her admit she wants me.

I step back outside to the deck and walk to where I'd left the breakfast and coffee I brought with me and bring them inside. Thankfully my phone and keys weren't a casualty of my impromptu swim. I look down at myself and grimace, my jeans are already stiffening uncomfortably. I run out to get my things, and when I come in, I can hear the water in the master bath running. I imagine her wet and naked in the shower. Her soapy hand sliding over her stomach and slipping between her legs. I wonder if she's touching herself. I want to walk in there and find out. "Not even an option, Reece," I mumble as I duck into the hallway bathroom to change.

Once I'm dressed, I step back into the living room to wait for her. I'm reading emails when one from my father pops up, wishing me good luck today. It's just what I need to remind me that I can't indulge in this kind of self-sabotage. This film, and its success is too important. I'm not going to let myself get distracted by Lucía Vega's ass. It has disaster written all over it.

I'll have this meeting and then I won't come back to the guest-house. "Lucía Vega is your much younger employee," I say to myself. If I could just get my dick to listen, I might survive this morning.

Like a genie popping out of a bottle I rubbed, she walks into the living room. She's wearing tiny denim shorts, a light pink sleeveless top that barely covers her belly but flows to her knees in the back and flip-flops. Her hair is still wet, and her lips are bright red again. She looks good enough to eat.

She's also holding a pile of towels in her hand. She drops them onto the floor and gets on her hands and knees and starts wiping. I'm distracted by the swaying of her ass and the toned muscles of her legs and so it takes me a minute to process what she's doing.

"We have staff that cleans up, Lucía," I say dryly. She stills, her back stiffening for a moment before she starts wiping again.

"I'm sure you do," she says without looking up.

"Then, why are you on the floor?" I ask as I stand over her.

"Because I made a mess. I'm cleaning it up. I don't want whoever you've hired to come in here and slip and fall because I was too lazy . . . or *entitled* to mop up a little water," she says. When she says the word entitled, she's implying that's exactly what I am.

"Fine." I walk back to the island. "When you're done being righteous, I'd like to talk with you about the job I've actually *hired* you to do. I brought breakfast, but I'll start without you."

"That's fine, Mr. Carras. I'll be done in a minute," she says stiffly.

Fuck, this woman is difficult.

"Call me Reece," I say as I unpack the bag of pastries. I take the two coffees out of the drink carrier and wait for her to join me.

When she's finally finished, my coffee is cold and my patience has worn thin.

"This all looks delicious, thank you," she says, her eyes studiously on the food and purposely avoiding me.

I nearly laugh.

"You're welcome," I say to her with an equal lack of sincerity while I watch her pick up a croissant and sit down.

"I haven't worked this closely on a project in a long time. I've also got my other studio responsibilities to think about, so I won't waste time by beating around the bush."

Her eyes finally come to mine.

She looks wary, but she's paying attention.

"I came here to help you get ready for the first day with your writers, but it seems we need to clear the air first." She looks confused, but I know she's not.

"You clearly have a problem with me. I'm not sure why. I want you to get over it. Fast. Ball's in your court. If you decide you want things to be unpleasant, that's fine, too, but it will make the next few months feel endless." I pick up my pastry. "So, eat, and think about it. When you're done. We'll talk."

Her eyes narrow before they drop to the counter. I see her hands balled into tiny fists. Her control is slipping. Good, maybe now we can have a real conversation.

I sit back, take a huge bite of out the *pain au chocolate* and wait for her to respond.

7

Lucia

OH, HOW I *WISH* I COULD UNLEASH ON HIM. FOR showing up here unannounced, scaring me, making me fall in that damn pool and making me feel like a fool.

But I swallow all of that. He's my boss. I don't want to do anything to mess this up. I also know my dislike of him is irrational. His *"you're not my type"* declaration stung more than I wanted to admit initially. Seeing him this morning, looking more handsome than he should, makes that sting feel fresh. I've got to put that aside and behave like a professional.

I struggle to calm myself before I lift my eyes from the snow-white marble countertop and look at him. Of course, he's not even looking at me. He's scrolling through his phone while he munches on that chocolate croissant. The one I'd planned on eating, but didn't pick up because I was afraid to look greedy for taking two.

I clear my throat to make sure I don't sound angry before I speak. "I'm sorry if I came across that way. Falling into the pool rattled me. I have no reason to dislike you. I'm looking forward to working together."

"Good. Glad you made that decision quickly."

I pick up the coffee he brought. It's strong and black, just the way I hate it. But, I drink it like it's the most delicious beverage I've ever had.

When I was little and my dad would scold me, Julian would always say, "*If you don't want people to talk down to you, then behave yourself.*" It's a piece of advice I live by. God, I miss Julian.

Thinking of him makes my eyes sting. I look back at Reece to see him watching me. His expression is pensive. I remind myself where I am and who I'm with and the sting in my eyes goes away.

"Okay, let's get down to business."

I glance at my watch and see it's already seven thirty. I'd asked the two screenwriters to meet me at the office at eight thirty.

As if reading my mind, Reece says, "We have time." He strolls over to the other side of the kitchen island and presses a button. A drawer pops open and I watch in horror as he drops his half-eaten pastry inside. Wasting food is a sin. My mother never threw anything away and neither did I. When he looks up and catches my eye he must misunderstand the cause for the horror on my face.

"Oh, that's the trash can. Did you think I was putting garbage into your kitchen drawer?"

"I *know* that's the trash. Why did you throw that away?" I ask him.

"Because . . . I'm full," he says slowly, as if I'm the dense one.

"There was almost an entire half left. Why didn't you just save it for later?"

He quirks his head like he's just seen a three-legged kangaroo.

"Save it for later? What? Like put it in my pocket?" He's amused.

I roll my eyes unable to hide my exasperation. "Of course not. Just wrap it in a paper towel and put it the bag. That was so wasteful." I huff.

His eyes widen with genuine surprise. Then, he walks back to the drawer, presses the button to open it again and peers inside. He starts mumbling to himself.

"Nothing else in here . . . Should be safe enough."

He reaches inside and pulls out the pastry. With a wink, he takes a huge bite.

I know my mouth is open. I know I've got bug eyes, too. I don't care.

He finishes chewing and sits down on one of the barstools. "What? I've never really thought about it before, but you're totally right," he says matter-of-factly before taking a huge gulp of coffee. He looks at me and smirks.

"I'm not a monster, Lucía. I can admit when I'm wrong." He does a ceremonial drum roll on the counter and my eyes follow the motion of his hands. They are huge with a dusting of hair on the backs of them. I was in a panic when he lifted me out of the pool, but I remember the way they felt as he rubbed my arms to warm me up. They're strong. There was a sureness in his touch that helped me to calm down.

"Are you imagining my hands around your throat? You're staring at them like you've just seen me use them for something nefarious."

"I wasn't thinking anything. I'm just waiting for you to tell me whatever it is you came here to say."

He laughs, but it's more of a scoff and I know I'm blushing again. I'm annoyed with myself for being so transparent.

"Okay, Lucía. I know this is all new to you and I want you to understand some of the dynamics. A novice leading a screenwriting team is nearly unheard of. So, prepare yourself for pushback from your team. They are going to test you, push you, they might even try to undermine you." He takes a sip of his coffee, his eyes never leaving mine. He must see the mild panic as it skitters across my face. "I'm not trying to scare you. It's just the nature of the beast," he says, his tone reassuring.

"You have two jobs. The first one, obviously, is to get the screenplay written. The second is to *lead* the team. To be the person who makes difficult calls and then deals with the fallout. You've got to manage the group dynamic. They'll feed off your energy. So, you need to do whatever it is you do to keep yourself even and focused. You guys will write almost every day except for whatever you decide are your off days. You'll have read-backs where you go over what you've written. Ultimately, *you* decide what works, what doesn't and where you're going next with the story."

He hops off the stool and starts pacing.

"And when the team is done, you need to go over the pieces everyone wrote and make sure that you're getting the best from people. The strength of the writing is going to be important.

This story is character driven, and dialogue is what's going to tell it well or fuck it up."

He stops his pacing and looks at me. "You have any questions?"

I have a million questions; I feel like I've bitten off more than I can chew. Talk about being careful what you ask for. I haven't had much time to prepare or get ready. I'm grateful he's telling me all of this. I know he wants the film to do well. But I can tell he wants me to do well, too.

I know Reece is watching me. My brain spins as I try to make sense of everything that is happening and I don't want him to see all of that. So, I just say, "Not right now. Thank you. It's a lot to absorb, but I'll do my best to not let you down."

He walks to stand in front of me, so that we're just a few inches shy of toe-to-toe. Besides this morning in the pool, it's probably the closest I've been to him. I can feel the energy radiating from him. It's magnetic—and it takes real effort to resist the pull of it. I just want to lean forward a little . . .

Oh God. This isn't good. I can't be into the man I work for and who's made it clear that he's not into me.

"Lucía, don't worry about letting me down." He puts his hands on my shoulders. I stifle my gasp at the nearly electric charge that his touch sends through me. It's too much. I step out of his grasp as casually as I can and grab my coffee from the counter. He picks his up, too. But he only holds it as he continues to speak. His eyes never leaving mine.

"Focus on yourself. This is *your* dream. *You* wrote that book. You want to bring this story to life. Don't let anything get in the way of that. It's not going to be easy. But, I'll help you, if you let me. I'm not saying we need to be best friends. But us getting along would make all of this easier."

I take all of this in and I try to reconcile it with what I

thought he'd be like, and I can't. This display of graciousness has thrown me for a loop. He's . . . nice.

"Reece. Thank you. I know I'm not the easiest person in the world. But I promise, I'll work hard—"

"And that's all I ask, Luc." His voice is gentle as he cuts me off and I'm actually relieved. I feel like I was about to reveal more of myself than I'm really ready to.

Suddenly he snaps his fingers and points at me. "*You* need to learn how to swim," he says excitedly.

"What?" I ask.

"I can teach you how to swim. Kill two birds with one stone. You can learn how to swim and it's a great trust building exercise," he says with a shrug.

I can't suppress the shocked bark of laughter. "Oh, no. I don't want to learn how to swim. I've gone twenty-three years without knowing how and I don't want to learn now."

Reece laughs, too. "Are you serious? I saw you looking at the water. You wanted to get in. Don't let your fear stop you."

"I'm not afraid."

"You absolutely are. Why else would you say no?"

"Aren't we going to be busy? When will we even have time?"

"We'll do it in the mornings. You only need thirty minutes a session. Come on. When will you ever get the chance to take lessons from an Olympic swimming champion?"

I regard him. He looks sincere, despite the teasing note in his voice. He's right. I do want to get into the water. I hate that I don't know how to swim. I've always wanted to learn and haven't ever had the chance. Spending time with him might be awkward at first, but I'm sure I'll get over this silly crush. And it *would* be a good way to get to know each other. "Okay. That's fine, but let me return the favor and give you some yoga lessons."

He leans back and groans.

"I'm too big for yoga. Can't you teach me to crochet or bake banana muffins? Something useful?" he says with a pained look on his face.

"I can't bake or crochet. And yoga *is* useful. It centers me and helps me get ready for each day." I grin up at him as I pat my stomach. "It's the reason I have such incredible core strength."

He stills and I worry that I've said something wrong. "What's wrong? I mean, if you really don't want to learn yoga, we can skip it."

He shakes his head, a slow smile spreading on his face, revealing that dimple again. "No, it's not that. You smiled at me. Sincerely and with all your teeth. That's a first. So, if yoga makes you feel like that, then hell, you can teach me yoga. We can even start with the yoga. Four weeks of yoga, four weeks of swimming."

"Okay . . ." I'm so surprised by his words that I can't think of anything to say in return.

He stands up, gathering his phone and keys and starts toward the front door. "Take the golf cart behind the house. The keys are in the ignition. Ride up the red brick path until you get to the third building with the huge parking lot on the side. You can't miss it. Your team's meeting room is on the second floor. They'll be there in thirty minutes."

"Where are you going?" I ask, sad that he's leaving just as the conversation was getting good.

"To work. Where you should be going, too. I've got to change before I head in." He gestures to his casual clothes with his hands. "I'll see you later, Luc. Remember: you're the leader." And with that he turns around and walks out the door.

I watch him go and try to collect my chaotic thoughts. It's

only eight in the morning and it already feels like I've had a full day. Reece surprised, confused and excited me this morning. And if it's any indication of what the next few months will be like, I'm going to need to keep my wits about me. I look down at myself and head back to my bedroom to change. This is the first day of the rest of my life, and I want my team to know I'm serious and ready to work. I'll save my cut offs for tomorrow.

8

Reece

I FEEL LIKE I'M LOSING MY MIND. I'VE ONLY HAD THREE face-to-face conversations with Lucía and the lines are already blurring. I'm seeing her less as my screenwriter and more as Lucía Vega, the sexiest, smartest, most driven, and most sincere woman I've ever met.

I don't know why I offered to teach her how to swim. It means I'll have my hands on her . . . while she's wearing a bathing suit. I'll need to beat one out every morning before I go meet her just to get through the lessons.

I can't believe she doesn't know how to swim. You can't live in California and not. Our lifestyle requires you be comfortable being in the water: days at the beach, out on the boat, pool parties. So, I really am doing her a favor.

I meant it when I said I wanted us to break the ice. We can talk about the screenplay and discuss policy. I can make sure the screenplay is on track. I didn't plan on being so attracted to Lucía. But it's just a physical attraction. I'm not an animal. I can handle this. So swimming, yoga and talking. It should all go well.

I just wrapped up a status meeting on one of our productions. We're still under budget, but our lead has been getting some bad press for a DUI he just picked up. I don't understand these actors. It makes me not want to take risks on unknowns, but this kid was perfect for the role. I had our executive producer talk to him. I've given him advice, introduced him to financial planners and hired him an excellent personal assistant. But apparently, that was all in vain.

They get a lucky break. A once in a lifetime chance that millions would sell their soul for. Instead of keeping their heads down and working hard, they take their first check, the first real money they've ever had, and buy a house and car they can't really afford, start drinking excessively, some even fall into drug use. It's all such a headache.

I'm just hanging up when Liza comes rushing into my office. Her blond corkscrew curls are more disheveled than normal and I can see she's flushed under the layers of makeup she wears every day.

"Reece, you need to get to the second floor. The writers are screaming at each other." She sounds panicked, and beckons me to follow her.

I step into the hallway and am greeted by silence. "Hurry and get down there, Reece. They sound pissed," she says as she rushes after me.

I stop and turn to face her. I look at her and realize that what I thought was panic, is actually excitement. I narrow my eyes at her. "*I* can't hear anything, Liza."

She lifts her chin and shrugs her shoulders. "Well, I could… when I rode the elevator down there." She has the grace to blush when I shake my head at her. "What? Annelle called and told me she was afraid they were going to start brawling. Come on, we're missing it," she says, grabbing my arm, practically pulling me toward the stairs.

"Wait here."

She frowns at me but says, "Fine. I'll just get the highlights from Annelle." And walks off in a huff.

I suck in a deep breath as I head to the stairs. As soon as I reach the door for the second floor, I hear it.

They aren't screaming, what I hear is more like a bellow. I glance at my watch. It's ten in the morning. They haven't even been working for two hours. What the fuck could have happened?

I walk into the suite and gape at the scene in front of me.

The two staff screenwriters, the so-called professionals, are standing on either side of her desk from one another yelling in each other's faces. The only person not screaming is Lucía. She's sitting at her desk typing away like nothing's happening.

I walk over to the desk and when the two see me, they stop speaking mid-word.

"Mr. Carras. He's being ridiculous."

"Reece, tell this shithead that I've actually read the book and understand it."

They speak simultaneously.

"Both of you just stop talking," I say in a scathing tone. Their shoulders slump at the same time and they comply.

I pull up a chair and sit next to Lucía. She doesn't look at me or even stop typing, but I can see that jaw working. "Lucía, can you tell me what's going on?"

I put a hand on her arm and she finally stops and looks up at me. The expression in her eyes is pained and she seems to be trying to tell me something. But I don't know her well enough to understand what it is she wants to convey. Even if I did, I wouldn't let her avoid this confrontation. If she can't be direct with her team, then she'll never get this screenplay written. I know Todd and Dan have different approaches to this story; I heard their pitches when I hired them. But, they're also the talent I need for this project.

"You're going to have to tell me, Lucía." I use the same tone I used with the men. I won't coddle her. I won't make this easy for her. She'll have to toughen up. Quickly.

She purses her lips in frustration and shuts her eyes for a few seconds. She opens, them, runs a hand through her hair, glances back at her screen and takes what appears to be a fortifying inhale.

"Well, Todd thinks we should start the story on the night of Julio's death. Dan thinks we should start the story with the family's arrival to the United States. Show a dramatic river crossing and have the father drown and die in that scene." Reciting words she's clearly heard repeatedly.

I glance up at them and nod to the chairs that are across from me.

I turn back to Lucía. "Okay, what do you think?"

She doesn't hesitate. "I disagree with them both. I want to tell the story chronologically. I'm not interested in shock value or rewriting the family's history so that it sensationalizes what is already dramatic enough." She speaks slowly and her voice is steady.

"Well then," I look back at the two writers, "what's the problem?"

They exchange a look that tells me they have at least one point on which they agree, they think she's wrong.

Todd looks at me, apparently the designated spokesperson for them now. "Well, this is her first screenplay, so we understand her desire to write chronologically. She doesn't understand the methodology of screenwriting. You can't tell a story like this chronologically. The audience doesn't have the patience a reader does. I think we need to decide whether this story is about policy or about people. Opening with the boy's death will make the story more compelling."

Dan groans. "I agree we can't do this chronologically, but starting with his death gives so much away, too soon. Given the political climate in the country, we're better off starting with the river crossing."

Todd slams his fist on the table. "There was no fucking river crossing, Todd."

"Just because she didn't write it doesn't mean it doesn't happen all the time. It's dramatic and more compelling than the father's deportation story."

"If you add that to the beginning, it will ruin the rest of it. That's not who the family in this story is," Todd yells, as he pushes his chair back from the table and stands up.

I look at Lucía. She's staring at her computer screen helplessly. I suppress a groan.

"Guys, she's your boss. And she wrote the fucking book." They both start talking again, at the same time. I cut them off.

"The screenplay will have to be green lighted by the studio once it's completed. If the opening doesn't work, you can fix it in re-writes."

The gratitude in Lucía's eyes makes it hard for me to hold

eye contact. But I do. "I'm going back up to my office. I don't want to be dragged down here to resolve disagreements. You need to manage your team." I say firmly.

You can hear a pin drop as I leave. I want to look over my shoulder, but I don't. I'm confident she's capable of getting people to do what she wants. She'll have to figure this out on her own. I witnessed her controlled, peaceful and powerful expression as she went through her yoga poses this morning. I know she's got the strength in her to get them to follow her lead.

When I look back, the scene is less than inspiring. They're all staring at the computer screens, not looking at each other. At least they're not yelling. I hope I'm doing the right thing.

BEFORE LEAVING the office later that evening, I stop by the second floor. Lucía is sitting there by herself. Her back is to me, and she's pulled her hair up into a huge mess of a knot on top of her head. She has her headphones on and she's singing "The Greatest" by Sia at the top of her lungs. Her singing voice is terrible. But she's got the emotion right. I can hear her conviction and determination in her voice.

If I was a wagering man, this film's success is a bet I'd gladly take. Everyone at the studio is treating me like it's an early mid-life crisis or vanity project. I don't give a fuck. I know what I'm doing and I think Lucía Vega is going to be my lucky charm. She's beautiful, has a sexy voice, and, most importantly, has a real passion for this project. She's going to be fantastic when we start doing the press for this.

I'm tempted to interrupt her. I want to hear about her day and what happened after I left.

And because I want to, I won't. I let myself look at her one more time, watch the motion of her head as she sways with the music. The curve of her neck, the glints of light in her hair mesmerize me for a minute . . . and then I force myself to walk away.

9

"You ready?" Reece asks as he drops down onto the yoga mat I laid out for him.

No, I'm not fucking ready. I don't want to do any of this. I'm both tired and anxious. Yesterday with Dan and Todd was a disaster. I need today to be better. And I don't feel like giving yoga lessons when what I need is a real session to make today bearable. But I don't say any of that. Instead, I smile pleasantly at him and say, "Sure thing."

He rolls his eyes and laughs. "Liar." He's in a good mood. Even though I'm irritated, his enthusiasm is contagious.

I let myself take a long look at him. From the tips of his

toes, to his long, thick, muscled legs and thighs. He's wearing swimming trunks, and a white T-shirt that exposes his tattoo.

"How long have you had that?" I ask him, breaking the quiet.

"Only a year." He looks down at it and then smiles rakishly at me. "You like it?".

I scoff. "It's fine. Just wondering how I didn't notice it before."

"And when would you have seen it?" he asks and I try to look casual.

"I've seen pictures of you. From when you used to swim. That's all. You didn't have it then."

I'm not going to confess that two nights ago I stayed up all night trying to find a picture of him where the tattoo was visible.

Most of them were taken at premiers, award shows and fundraisers. A few were candid shots of him in street clothes taken while he was married, so his ex-wife was in the pictures, too.

As I scrolled through them on my laptop, I felt the bitterness of jealousy in the back of my throat. They looked so good together. Both tall, beautiful, tanned and dressed in designer clothes.

"I got it after my divorce. It's a collection of symbols from all over the world. They all mean the same thing —freedom," he says the last word with real relish.

I'm mesmerized by the way *freedom* spills so easily from his mouth. I instinctually bring my hand up to cover my heart, where my own ode to freedom is also tattooed.

"Well, then congratulations. Nothing feels better than emancipation," I quip and I sit back down next to him.

"Indeed . . . and what do you know about being shackled?

From where I'm sitting you appear to very much be the master of your own destiny."

"If only you knew," I mutter inaudibly.

"What?" he asks.

"Let's get started," I say with a forced frown. I couldn't begin to explain, even if I tried. He's found his freedom; I was only getting a taste of someone else's. No matter how much I pretend, I won't ever forget that Lucía's life isn't *really* mine.

He closes his eyes as the rising sun kisses his face, looking like he doesn't have a care in the world. I wonder what that would be like.

When our eyes meet, his are so open, so calm that I feel myself relax a little. He smiles at me gratefully as if he can feel the change. I try to focus on why we're here.

"I thought I'd start by demonstrating the twelve basic poses called *Asanas*. You don't have to master them and you can modify them for now. After that, I'll show you the Sun Salutations. Those are less challenging and you should be able to do them with me."

Instead of waiting for his reply, I start with the headstand and move through the twelve poses, quickly, naming them as I go.

When I finish, I find his gaze is riveted on me. "You're strong. I'm impressed." I know he's paying me a compliment, but his scrutiny makes me uncomfortable. It reminds me of why I stopped taking group classes.

Yoga is where I open my mind, it's where I leave all my stress. It's where I can let my guard down in a way I can't when I'm with other people. My time on my mat is where I find my sanity. It's how I make it through each day. It grounds me, reminds me of who I really am. It's a safe place for me to feel all my hurt, all my desires. The part of me that is desperate to be free and honest. The part that cries. The side I don't let anyone see.

I need yoga. I know that sharing my practice with him means he'll catch glimpses of me that I don't show to anyone. The thought leaves me slightly breathless.

"Did you get all of that? I'll write down the names of the poses for you so you can practice them later. But for now, let's move to the Sun Salutations. You've got to sync your breathing to your movements. So you only inhale or exhale when you move."

He nods, his dark eyes are serious again. "Okay, I'll follow your lead."

That comment feels loaded, but I only nod and say, "Fine."

So, we begin. We move through this exercise that I've done every day without fail for almost five years. He's quiet and attentive and as we move together and breathe together. When we finish, my senses are heightened. I can feel fine hairs on my arms rustle in the light ocean breeze. I smell the salt in the air with each inhale. I can taste it in the back of my throat with each exhale. Reece's scent is like sweat mixed with sun. Every single nerve ending in my body is aware of him.

I feel . . . great. He's staring out at the horizon, his posture relaxed. I study his profile. My eyes trace the gentle slope of his forehead where it meets his dark, thick brows. The bridge of his nose is perfectly straight, his lips full and so . . . appealing. If I were an artist, I would want to draw him and then never let anyone see my work. His morning beard covers his jaw and chin and I wonder, again, how it would feel beneath my hands.

"That was great," he says, as if it was the last thing he expected.

I've never been so tongue tied in my life. I just give him a quick smile before I busy myself with my mat. "Tomorrow, we'll start with the Sun Salutations and then we'll work on the first position, the *Sirisena*, or headstand. You've already got good core strength from swimming, so we'll focus on your balance."

"Okay . . . do you think I should get a manual or something to study?" he asks and I finally force myself to look back at him. He's so sexy. I want to stomp my foot at the unfairness of it all.

"No, you don't need a manual. I'll write the basics down for you. Just practice when you can. If you want to continue learning after we're done, I can recommend some great teachers in Calabasas or even here."

"When we're done? Who says we'll ever be done? I might want you to teach me forever," he quips. I laugh. He's charming when he's relaxed and it's so easy to forget myself.

I'm worried about not being able to relax during the session, but surprisingly, I feel even more relaxed than I normally do. But this was . . . a revelation. Our synchronous movements and breathing felt intimate and comfortable.

"I can't be your teacher forever, Reece. Unless you're a fast learner, working with you will mean I'm not making progress in my own practice. You'll be holding me back," I say with a laugh.

"We'll see. I'm a natural born athlete, kid. Maybe by the time this is all said and done, I'll be teaching you."

"When pigs fly," I shoot back.

"Oh, man, Luc. Don't dare me. I can't say no to a challenge."

He's been calling me "Luc" since the day he fished me out of the pool. Everyone shortens my name. But somehow, on Reece's lips it sounds special.

"I don't have time to argue, I have a writing team to wrangle and I don't want to be late. Same time tomorrow?" I say as I start toward the house.

He calls over his shoulder, "Yeah, handle your team." It's the only reference he's made to yesterday's debacle. "See you tomorrow, same time. Bring your A-game. I'm going to make that headstand my bitch."

I sing in the shower, and as I make breakfast, and then on the way to the office. It's a good day.

10

Reece

It's our second week of yoga practice and I'm so fucking sore, I can barely walk. Lucía's constantly fighting her laughter when we see each other around the office. I'm practically limping. Yoga uses different muscles than swimming and my thighs feel like they've taken a beating.

I'm still trying to master the fucking headstand. At this rate, it will take me another week to get comfortable enough to move on to the next Asana. She makes it look easy.

It crushed my ego when I told her that maybe I was just too big for the poses she was trying to teach me, because then she showed me YouTube videos of these huge football players resting like bosses in the headstand. So now, I'm determined.

I get to her house a little early so that I can be on the deck when she gets there. I want to spare myself the laugh she'll have at my expense when I hobble up the stairs.

I hear "Crush on You" by the Jets blaring over the outdoor speakers.

Ah, she has good taste in music. Another check in the "characteristics of a perfect woman" column. I see her through the glass doors, standing in front of her blender. She's dressed for yoga in these tiny, sexy-ass hot pink yoga pants and her sports bra. Her hair is still loose, and flying as she moves to the music. She hasn't put on the T-shirt she always wears when we practice together. I can see her stomach and sides. Her skin looks like satin. I rub my palms together at the thought of touching it.

These mornings are starting to be my favorite part of the day. We laugh a lot. And she's a good teacher. She acts like every single inch of progress is amazing. I leave feeling relaxed and ready for whatever bullshit the day brings. We're becoming friends. Real friends. I look forward to seeing her. And although the attraction is there, I've managed to keep it in check and focus on what she's teaching me.

She whirls in surprise when I knock. A wide smile spreading across her face as she sees me. Shit, that feels amazing.

"You're early," she says good naturedly as I join her in the kitchen. She grabs two glasses from the cabinet, and holds them up to me. "Want to share my breakfast?" she asks as she pours the dark green liquid into two glasses.

"Ugh. It looks disgusting. Like what I used to drink when I was training, but worse," I say as I take a sniff of whatever vile concoction she's just handed me. "And it smells awful. No thanks."

"It'll help your muscles. You can barely walk." She laughs as she grabs her glass and gulps it down.

"You talk a lot of shit, you show off. I bet you couldn't walk when you first started, either."

"Yeah, but I wasn't an Olympic athlete."

"I'm not an Olympic athlete anymore. That was more than ten years ago."

"Excuses, excuses," she tsks. "But given your advanced age, some soreness should be expected." She cackles.

"Keep laughing. I'm going to come early tomorrow and have my video recorder ready to catch you in the act. You've got those Paula Abdul moves down pat. It'll make excellent blackmail material."

She laughs at me, throwing her head back in delight. "As if anyone would care about a video of me dancing."

"You haven't seen yourself. Believe me, they would care."

She stops laughing and gives a playful swat on my arm. Her laughter softens to a smile and her eyes turn nostalgic.

"That was my brother's favorite song. We used to dance to it all the time. In fact, we wanted to grow up and join the Jets." Her face falls slightly, but then she forces a smile.

"Come on, you don't want to hear my childhood stories." She starts toward the door.

"I want to know you; whatever you want to share."

"Really?" Her eyes search my face.

I answer honestly. "Of course, why wouldn't I?"

Her eyes grow sad and she walks over to one of the blue leather and chrome barstools. Her shoulders look like she's carrying a heavy load on them.

"I was only eight when he died." Her voice is tinged with

nostalgia, her voice just above a whisper. I can see her throat working and her eyes glistening. I'm intrigued. At the same time, I'm not sure I want her to continue. Weeping, sad women have always been my weakness. It's how Fabienne managed to keep us going for so long. She knew if she cried or admitted some fear or heartbreak to me, I wouldn't be able to walk away from her.

I know it's cynical. But, I need to be careful here. Especially because I'm also more attracted to her than I've ever been to anyone. One minute, I'll be patting her shoulder to make her feel better, and then the next, I'll be begging her to let me kiss her.

She sniffles and accepts the tissue I hand her with a sheepish smile. When our hands brush each other, I feel it. Not quite a spark or a tingle . . . but a strong awareness. The connection makes us both stop and pay attention. It would be so easy, to just do what I've been wanting to do for the last few weeks. Her skin is calling to me; I only want one more touch. When I put my hands on her shoulders that first day, I felt the smooth texture of her skin against my palm. I want to touch her. So badly. I want to know what she feels like everywhere.

She's beautiful and far too tempting. I need to get the fuck out of here.

I look down at my watch and step back. "Listen, we'll be late if we do the lesson today. Let's pick this up tomorrow."

There's a pause before she responds, but I don't look at her. I can't.

"Tomorrow's my day off, and I want to sleep in." She sounds completely relaxed so I take my eyes off my watch. She's turned her back to me and is rinsing her glass in the sink.

"The day after, then?" I ask. She gathers her hair and piles it on top of her head with a black rubber band that has a permanent home on her wrist.

And when she does that, the soft skin on the gentle slope of her shoulders is exposed. My resolve to keep my distance disappears and I involuntarily take a step toward her. I want to put my mouth there. Just as I start to move, she turns around to face me and I freeze. When she sees my hand outstretched, and me in mid-stride, she looks concerned. "Are you sure you're okay?"

I re-route my hand's destination and in a lame save, I rub my neck like it's sore and her expression goes from concerned to confused.

"I'm fine," I say. "Just a little stiffness in my neck. I need a good hard swim." God I sound like an idiot. "But, really. I'm glad you felt like you could tell me."

She smiles brightly and my cock jumps. That decides it. I'm leaving right now and tonight, I'm going to LA. Maybe I just need to get laid.

"I'll be in LA day after tomorrow, so three days from now?"

"Okay. It'll give you time to recuperate." She shoots me a grin and I'm glad the conversation is light again. As if she can feel my relief, she says, "I know it was heavy, but I have to admit it feels good to have gotten that off my chest. I haven't said those words aloud in a long time. Thank you." She walks over and steps up onto her tiptoes and presses the softest kiss to my undeserving cheek. I catch a whiff of her vanilla scent and I have to stop myself from wrapping my arm around her waist and holding her to me.

11

Lucia

A LITTLE AFTER NOON, I HEAD TO THE OFFICE CAFETERIA for lunch with Dan and Todd. We reached a detente last week. And then on Monday, I brought in some homemade banana muffins for us to share. While we broke bread, we found that we were all dying for the next season of *Game of Thrones* to start. They decided I couldn't be a *total* idiot if I could see how everything that went wrong for the Starks started with Kaitlyn Stark's myopia when it came to Jon Snow. We've gotten along well ever since. We still have disagreements about the screenplay, but they listen to me and I'm learning a lot from them, too.

We're about to sit down when I see Coco by himself at one of the tables that overlooks the water. I meant to speak to him earlier, so I excuse myself and walk over to him.

Despite what Sol said, he's been nice every time I've seen him.

"Hey, is this seat taken?" When he sees it's me, he smiles warmly. "It's all yours, Lu." His use of a nickname surprises me, but we've become pretty friendly in the last few weeks, so I ignore the slight discomfort I feel at hearing it.

"Thanks, Coco. You've got the best view in the room. I could look out at that all day."

"Yeah, me too. It's one of the reasons I never mind me being on assignment out here. That, and the fact that I get to drive *you* around."

"I'm sure the view beats driving me any time." I laugh, but when he doesn't join me, I look at him. He's watching me closely and my laughter dies.

"I'm starving!" I tell him as I try to hide my discomfort.

"You settling in okay? Hope they're not working you too hard." he says as I dig into my huge salad.

I finish chewing my mouthful of chicken and tabbouleh before I respond. "No, it's fine. Just lots to do. It's just the normal stuff that comes with finding a rhythm and getting the story direction together, but I think we're off to a good start."

"Well, let me know if you need anything. I know how intimidating Reece can be." He smiles knowingly at me.

I want to say that Reece isn't intimidating at all. That he's been nice and has my back. But I don't say any of that. I don't want to give anyone the wrong impression.

"Thank you." I smile warmly at him. "Uh, I actually stopped by to tell you that I need to go into town to do some grocery shopping and get a few things. I have tomorrow off. Do you think you could take me in the morning?"

His smile dims, but his voice is friendly when he says, "Sure thing. I'm around and you're my priority when it comes to driving. So just tell me when you need me and I'll be there." He winks and stands up.

"Thanks, Coco. I'll just text you when I'm ready."

"It's a date, Lu." And with a short wave, he walks away. *Was he flirting with me?* He's been so nice to me that I decide to give him the benefit of the doubt. But recalling Sol's warning, I resolve to be a little more professional in our future interactions.

I catch a glimpse of Reece. He's in one of the conference rooms. He's on the phone, his face a mask of concentration. He's cleanly shaven, wearing shirtsleeves and no tie, but much more formal than this morning. As if he senses me looking at him, he looks up as I walk by. His eyes light up and he flashes me a quick smile, and waves for me to come into the room.

"Sure, Zev. I agree," He's saying when I walk in.

"I still think it would be good to have those numbers ready before we're done." He holds up a finger, as if saying he'll only be another minute.

"If she's being difficult, cut her loose. I'm sure we can find someone to replace her who'd be happy for screen time." He leans back in his chair, tension creating brackets on either side of his mouth as he purses his lips.

He rolls his eyes and holds the phone away from his ear. I can hear Zev talking and Reece mouths a silent "sorry" before he puts the phone back to his ear with a resigned shake of his head. I smile sympathetically and then wave before I duck out of the room. And just like that, my unease about Coco is forgotten. I walk back to my desk with a huge smile on my face.

It's Friday morning and I've put off my shopping trip as long as I can. I hate shopping. So, I try to be really efficient about it. I already know which two stores I want to pop into. I need a bathing suit and groceries. I send Coco a text to tell him I'm ready and then sit down to wait.

It's weird being driven by someone other than an Uber driver, a bus driver or Jess. It's strange having doors held open and a car waiting for me when I exit a store. I'm not sure that it's something I want to get comfortable with.

For anyone who's ever been in a position of service, it's hard to forget what it feels like to smile at someone who barely acknowledges your existence. The experience is exhausting, but it builds character at the same time.

The first time I went out to eat with Sol and his family, he told me to stop thanking the waiter every time he refilled my water glass. I can't imagine not thanking him. He's someone's child, father, brother or uncle. How can I act like he's invisible just because he's serving me?

That's how the family my mother works for treats her. She lives in the same house they do, yet, they only seem to remember she's there when something is broken or goes missing.

She's like a ghost who cleans up after them. She keeps their house running so they don't have to think about it. When she started working there, they made it very clear I was to be not seen or heard. I stayed in my room and only left it when I was going to school. I ate there, played there and never made any noise. And despite all of that, their children found ways to make me miserable. They sought me out to pick on me.

That's how it was until the day she sent me to live with my aunt and uncle.

That was the night our relationship changed for good. She distanced herself from me. Sometimes, I can tell she's thinking about what happened because she can't bring herself to look me in the eye. She still works for that family, but I don't blame her. I know she was scared. And she knew I'd be okay. But her losing her job would have meant both of us were out on the street.

I start to pick up my phone to invite her here for dinner when my doorbell rings. I grab my purse and keys and rush out to the door. Coco is standing on the porch and when he sees me, he smiles his friendly smile. "Your chariot awaits, my lady," he says with a dramatic bow.

"Hey, Coco. Thanks." I smile at him and get in the car. My phone buzzes and when I look down, I see it's a notification from the Google Alert I created.

I've been anxious for news about what the new President is going to do with the DACA program that allows me the right to work. My application is pending, but I've never had trouble getting it renewed before. I'm deep in thought and don't realize we've arrived at our destination until my door opens and Coco's standing there smiling at me.

"Sorry, I spaced out. I won't be long," I say to him as I start toward the boutique where I plan to buy a swimsuit. It's the first one I've ever owned.

"Take your time, princess," he calls after me. I know he's just being friendly, but that nickname . . . it isn't right coming out of his mouth.

I manage an awkward wave as I set off for Nati's boutique. This shopping center is typical of Malibu; rustic, eco-friendly and expensive as hell. I grab the first white one-piece I find, check the size and then head to try it on. This is the part of shopping I hate, trying clothes on. But, they have a huge No Returns sign over the bathing suit section, so I can't take any chances with it.

As I approach the dressing rooms I see a tall, gorgeous blonde smiling widely at me. "Hi, I'm Lila. Let's get you into a room," she says as I approach. She touches my arm and steers me to one of the dressing rooms. It's bigger than my closet in Los Feliz and very brightly lit. The mirrored walls create a three hundred and sixty-degree reflection, that lets you see your whole body at once. I keep my panties on, but otherwise strip.

I pull the bathing suit on and immediately see why it won't work. It's white, without a lining in the top and I can see my cinnamon colored nipples clearly. I can only imagine how much more transparent it would be if it was wet. But I like the cut, the fit and decide to ask for it in black.

"Hello, Lila?" I call out.

When no response comes, I call out one more time. "Of course. Get me in here and abandon me," I grumble to myself as I step out to see if I can see her.

I shriek when I see Coco sitting on one of the benches outside of the dressing room. He's staring at my door and smiles in a way that sends chills up my spine. My hands come up to cover my breasts when his eyes fixate on them and he doesn't look away.

"Coco, what are you doing here?" I sputter.

"You were taking longer than I expected so I came in to look for you. I asked the girl at the front and she said you were in the dressing room. So, I just came here to wait."

"Why didn't you say anything when I called out for her?" I ask as I hop back inside the dressing room and close the door behind me.

"My name isn't Lila," he says with a chuckle.

Even with the door closed, I feel uncomfortable stripping with him there.

"That bathing suit looked just right, in my opinion. Step back out, and I'll take another look," he drawls when I don't say anything.

My heart begins to race and I try to hide the panic I'm feeling when I say, "Can you go see if you can find Lila for me, please?"

"If you need something, Lu, you can just ask me and I'll get it for you," he says in a tone that is full of so much innuendo and suggestion that I feel like he can see through the wood of the door that separates us.

"That's okay. Can you just get her, please?"

He doesn't respond right away and I'm afraid he's going to refuse when he says silkily, "No problem. Be right back"

As soon as I hear his footsteps receding. I rip the swim suit off my body and throw my shorts and T-shirt back on. I leave the dressing room and go back to the rack where I got the swimsuit, grab a black one and then beat a path to the register.

When I get there, the girl at the register gives me a friendly smile and says, "Did anyone help you with your purchase?"

"Lila abandoned her station, but I got what I wanted," I say as I hand her the bathing suit and my debit card. I know I'm being rude, but I just want to get out of there.

Her smile falls as she takes my card. "But if it doesn't work, you can't return it." All of her earlier friendliness is gone. I'm glad. It makes the transaction go a lot faster when she isn't making small talk. I'm heading for the door when Coco steps into my path. I stop short of running straight into him.

"Where'd you go?" he asks, his friendly, affable demeanor back in place.

I'm not fooled. The way his eyes raked over my body earlier

made his real intentions clear. I don't return his smile. I don't want him to think that his attention is welcomed.

"I got what I needed. I just need to run to the grocery store really quickly. I'll meet you in front in fifteen?" I say as I dash past him.

"I can take your purchase to the car for you," he says with his hand held out for my shopping bag. A vision of him sniffing my bathing suit's crotch flashes into my mind and I clutch the bag closely to my chest.

"No, thanks! I got it. See you out front." I turn and practically run out of the store before he can respond.

When I step into the cool interior of the grocery store, I realize how overheated I am.

The way Coco looks at me has me freaked out. I'm not what anyone would call beautiful, at least not in this town. I've got a little too much meat on my bones to be considered ideal. I'll never wear a size zero, nor do I want to. I know there is something about my body that men like. I've heard the catcalls. I've fended off the gropes at stores and in restaurants where I've worked. The thought of having to deal with this from Coco every time I need to go somewhere creates a ball of dread in the pit of my stomach.

Shit. I need to find another driver.

I speed through the aisles. Grabbing the items on my list without checking to see what's on sale. And in less than ten minutes I'm out of the store. I think about calling an Uber but decide that would be too dramatic. I'll just pretend to be on the phone the entire time I'm in the car.

He's waiting for me at the curb when I step outside. I pull my phone out and pretend to answer it. He opens the door while I fake a conversation with Jessica and avoid eye contact. Our ten-minute ride home is a special kind of hell. I pretend to talk to Jessica about a trailer I just saw for the new Marvel movie. Every time I glance up, I see Coco watching me through the rear view mirror.

When we pull up outside my house, I'm ready and have the door open before Coco can come to a complete stop.

"I have to use the bathroom. See you later!" I call over my shoulder. I sprint up the stairs, open the sliding door and step inside before he can even respond.

I rush to my bedroom and only then do I let myself indulge in the panic that's been running riot inside of me. *What the fuck was that?* Thank goodness I don't need to leave the estate again for at least a few more days. I'll send Liza an email in the morning about getting a new driver assigned. I rush into the shower and wash off the feeling left behind from the way Coco looked at me.

12

Reece

I'VE BEEN IN LA FOR THE LAST COUPLE OF DAYS. MY attempts to keep Lucía out of my mind have turned out to be a total failure. She's all I've been able to think about. I went out for drinks with my three best friends from high school, Oman, Graham and Dave. Not a single woman I saw sparked any interest. I just kept comparing them to her.

Plus, the email she sent this morning makes me feel guilty for not keeping a closer eye on her.

"Liza, get operations on the phone and get Lucía Vega a new driver," I say into my speakerphone. "Already on it, Reece," she responds. Of course she is. Lucía's email was addressed to Liza, but she put me on copy. It was only a couple of lines, asking how she could go about getting a new driver assigned. She didn't say why, but I know my cousin. He's an asshole, and always has been. I wish my dad would let us fire him. But when my father's younger brother died, my father promised to take care of his son. And he has.

He's only a couple years older than me. When we were kids, we were close. But as we've gotten older he's changed. He's accused my dad of treating me differently than he treats him. The truth is, when it comes to Artemis, my dad doesn't mix his personal feelings with the interest of the company. He's passed me over for promotions before because someone else was better. His actions just made me want to work harder.

But Coco? It made him angry and he's acted out in ways that have left my parents up at night worrying and making excuses for him. He's a shit of a person. I shouldn't have let him be assigned to her in the first place. I open my email and write to Lucía.

To: Lucía@Throwawaythekey.com
From:RCarras@ArtemisFilms.com
Subject: Your request
Luc,
Got your email. I've requested a new driver be assigned. He'll be there this afternoon. Care to tell me why you need a new driver?
R.

LESS THAN TWO MINUTES LATER, her response pops into my mailbox.
To: RCarras
From: Lucía
Subject: RE: Your request.

Reece,

Thanks for the heads up. I'm not trying to get Coco fired, just felt a little uncomfortable. I can tell you more tomorrow during our yoga lesson.

See ya,

LV

I RESPOND RIGHT AWAY.

To: Lucía

From: RCarras

Subject: Re: re: Your request

All right 55, I'll let you off the hook. But tomorrow, we're swimming. We've had four days of yoga. I need to spend some time in the water. I do have other things to do, but if you need something, I'll take care of it for you. Coco's not getting fired, unless what you tell me tomorrow warrants it.

See you in the morning.

R

I START to close my browser when another message come through.

To: RCarras

From: Lucía

Subject: Re:re:re Your request.

What's 55? I'm not ready to swim. And your yoga isn't progressing, you need more practice.

See you tomorrow.

LV

I CHUCKLE. She's right that I'm not progressing. I still can't do that fucking headstand.

From: RCarras
To: Lucía
Subject: Roman numerals.
LV = 55. You're more than ready to swim.
R.

AN HOUR LATER, she hasn't responded. But our email exchange has made me want to talk to her some more. I decide I'm going back to Malibu tonight. I pick up the phone and call her.

She answers on the first ring.

"Hello?" Her voice is so sultry. Her hello sounds like a "come here."

I clear my throat. "Fifty-five, it's me. Dinner tonight. I'll pick you up at seven."

"Please don't call me that. It's weird. And seven o'clock should be fine."

"It's not weird. It's actually perfect. If that's how you always sign your name, I'm sure there are a bunch of people who call you that for short."

She huffs, but I can tell she's smiling. "Fine."

As I hang up, I feel myself perking up at the thought of seeing her. She's got me tied in knots. And I'm not sure that I mind anymore.

AT SEVEN ON THE DOT, I knock on Lucía's front door. I see her come out of her bedroom. I'm holding flowers and when she looks at me and sees them, she smiles widely. She looks gorgeous. Her white dress is sleeveless and shows off her beautiful shoulders. Her silky, golden skin glistens where her breasts swell at the top of the dress and my mouth waters. The dress's bodice is caught at the waist with a wide white belt that shows off her amazing body. Her hair is shining and her lips are coated in that red lipstick that I think of as her trademark. She's wearing black open toe heels tonight and her legs look amazing. They'd look even better draped over my shoulders. . .

When she opens the door, the ocean breeze catches the short lacy skirt of her dress. It billows around her thighs, showing me more of that incredible skin of hers. Her scent is different tonight. All flowery and sultry.

I can't seem to remember why I needed to keep my distance from her. Every time I see her, I learn something about her that makes me feel like I'm crazy for not pursuing her.

"Hey," I say hoping I don't sound as hungry for her as I feel. I bend to press a kiss to her cheek. Her hair is floating around her face and I push it back a little to expose her ear and let another kiss land there.

"Hi," she breathes back as she sways toward me.

I step back and hand her the flowers. It's a bouquet I picked up from the florist on my way here, a cluster of white petals shot through with a verdant leaf. As she brings them to her nose and takes a sniff, I wish I'd gotten her something more vibrant. They pale in comparison to her.

"These are gorgeous. Thank you." She smiles up at me, and it's *that* smile. The one she gave Sol that day in my office. But, it's got a little secret behind it tonight, and I can't help but think of this as my very own.

She steps aside. "Please, come in." I look around the house. I notice she's put little touches of herself into the space. I see a small painting of a girl *en pointe* in her pink ballet shoes. There are a couple of framed pictures on the dining room table that she's turned into her workstation. I see her bright red shawl, one that she wears almost every day at the office, hanging on the back of the chair. And there is a row of multi-colored vases on the kitchen counter. She grabs one of them and fills it with water for the flowers.

"I'm glad you're making yourself at home," I say as I walk into the living room.

She turns to me and looks up at me, her smile a little less bright, but her eyes full of light. "No one has ever bought me flowers before."

"That's a crime."

She scoffs quietly, "Hardly. Let me put these in some water before we go. They'll be so pretty on my dining table." She grabs one of the multi-colored vases from her counter and fills it with water. She handles the flowers with a gentleness that borders on reverence. "Thank you so much for these." When she looks at me, her large eyes are luminous and questioning.

"Lucía…" I'm not sure what I want to say, but drawn by a force that I can't resist, I take a step closer to her.

A loud ding sounds from my pocket, and the moment is broken. I pull it out and see that it's a calendar alert Liza created for our reservation tonight. "We better get going, if we're going to make it in time for dinner."

She sighs and looks like she is about to say something. But she doesn't. She just grabs her purse and heads out the door.

ONCE WE'RE SEATED, Lucía twists and turns, taking in the restaurant and ambiance. I've been here before. I know the view is amazing, but seeing the excitement in her eyes as she takes it all in makes me feel like I'm seeing it again for the first time.

The tide is moving to a rhythm that the moon demands. I watch as the waves rise and break in front of us. Then, I look at Lucía who is even more beautiful than the magnificent display of nature that serves as the restaurant's backdrop. The waitress takes our orders, fills both of our glasses with a delicious California sauvignon blanc and then leaves us alone.

"So, tell me what happened with Coco," I ask right away.

She looks startled, but smiles gamely.

"He came on to me. And I think it's best to nip this is in the bud now before something really uncomfortable happens," she says simply.

"What do you mean? Did he say something?" My good humor is completely gone.

She winces a little.

"No. I mean…I just know when a man is looking at me in a way he shouldn't. I don't want things to get any more awkward than they are already." She squares her shoulders. "I know he's your cousin. I'm not trying to disparage him." She sounds defensive. And I don't like it. I want to nip *that* in the bud immediately.

"Hey, you don't need to explain yourself. Yeah, he's my cousin but that has nothing to do with knowing the difference between right and wrong."

Her shoulders lose some of their tension and realization dawns. "Did you think I was going to ask you for evidence. Or try to defend him?"

"I don't know." She pauses and looks down. Then she looks back up at me and her eyes are full of uncertainty.

"I want to ask you something, but I'm not sure if it's a good idea," she says and she worries her lower lip with her teeth.

"You can ask me anything." And I mean it. I'll answer whatever she asks me, honestly.

She looks skeptical, but says, "You didn't say why you wanted to have dinner. It wasn't exactly an invitation. More like . . . my boss ordering me to have dinner with him."

The straightforward question, the unexpectedness of it, catches me by surprise.

She's really this innocent. She really doesn't have an agenda. She has no clue I'm one of the men who is looking at her *the way he shouldn't*. "I know I'm not your *type*." She says *type* with air quotes.

If she knew how untrue that was, she might be afraid. She's not my type, she's something much better. I wouldn't have been able to dream her up if I'd tried. She's fucking charming. And I'm completely bewitched by her.

"I can't read you. I don't know what you want from me. But I know it's not just to make this movie. So, if it's not sex, I don't know what else it could be."

Oh God, I want so much more than sex from her. I can't say that to her, at least not yet. So, I answer as honestly as I can.

"It was an invitation. I'm so used to giving orders that sometimes, I forget to switch it off. But, I want you to know that even if it had been a work invitation, you can say no to me. You're an employee, not a servant. If something doesn't sit well with you, tell me." She nods shyly, but I can see the relief in her eyes.

"Now, you answer a question for me." Her look turns wary. "What happened in the past to make you think sex could be the only other thing I want from you?"

She tents her fingers under her chin, elbows resting on the table. Her eyes are solemn and frank. She swallows hard and then says, "There haven't been many people who have given me a chance without wanting something in return."

"Well, that just proves that the world is full of fools." She rolls her eyes.

"No really, Reece. You've done much more than give me a chance. You've taken a huge risk and given me the opportunity of a lifetime. I've admired you from afar for a long time. I know you could be anywhere else in the world tonight. With people who are much more interesting than I am—"

I interrupt her with a chuckle. "I find you endlessly fascinating. You work hard and you don't bullshit anyone. You're teaching me yoga. What's not to like?" I don't add that it doesn't hurt that her eyes captivate me. Or that when she smiles, I feel motivated to make it happen again.

My humor disappears as I look at her and see that she's not smiling back.

Her tone is resigned when she speaks. "I started working when I was twelve. I've cleaned other people's toilets. I've parked cars, I've bussed tables. I've worked for every single thing I have. I'm not sophisticated or well-educated." Her laugh is short and humorless. "The first people who didn't ask for anything other than friendship were Jessica, and then Sol. And even they are really just my landlord and my agent." Her shoulders slump a little.

"I don't want to start thinking we're friends if we're not. I know you want this film made. And I'm afraid that's the only reason you're spending time with me. I've learned the hard way that life is too short for assumptions and innuendo. So, if it's just to get the movie made, cool. I promise I want that, too. You don't have to hang out with me, teach me how to swim, take me out to dinner, tell me I look nice, and act like you care that Coco hit on me just to keep me around. This," she spreads her arms out as if she could hold the whole universe in them, yet she never takes her eyes off me, "is already more than I ever thought my life would amount to."

She brings her hands down, and rests them on the table. "So, if you're doing this for any reason beside enjoying my company, you can stop. Tell me now, and there won't be any hard feelings."

Her eyes are naked, and her vulnerability bared. So, I return her gaze, and hope she can see the sincerity in my eyes.

"I want to make this film to honor the story you told in your book. It touched me. I have the ability to bring it to a huge audience. So, I'm doing it." I sit back and look away as I speak less candid thoughts. "I also really enjoy your company. I think your honesty is refreshing and I admire that you're not willing to compromise on anything that's really important to you. So, yes, I want to be your friend, Lucía. And I want you to be my friend too."

She rewards me with one of those smiles that makes me feel like a fucking superhero. "That's awesome. Thank you."

"Thank *you,* Lucía. Now, that's settled." I lift my hand and signal our waitress. "Let's eat, I'm starved."

We're half way through dinner, and the company, food and view are the best I remember experiencing in a long time. The conversation has moved from less emotional things to progress on the screenplay. She asks me a lot of questions about my swimming career. I love talking about that. It was the most important part of my life for so many years. Throughout my entire childhood and until I was twenty-four and swam in my final Olympic trials. The injury I suffered in a car accident on the way to the airport, fractured my leg and tore a muscle in my rotator cuff. The injury cut my swimming career short. It meant downtime that I hadn't had in years.

"So, what sparked your interest in the issue of immigration. One minute you were a famous swimmer, the next you were setting up a foundation, attending rallies." I wish I could tell her, but I'm not ready to yet. I want to know her better and have her know me better too. It makes what I did easier to explain.

So, I give her my canned response. "While I was recuperating from my injuries, I started seeing stories in the news that bothered me. And when I did some reading to learn more, I discovered what a crisis it was, especially for the DREAMERs. I mean, you already know that. You wrote a whole book about it." I shrug. "And I found that I had the right platform to elevate the conversation."

"You said the new driver would be here tomorrow? Haven't you wondered why I don't drive myself?"

I'm perplexed, and I frown at her. "No, I haven't wondered. A lot of people don't drive here, even though I don't understand how. I can teach you, it's not hard. And then you can drive yourself."

And the smile that's been dancing on her face for most of the night disappears, as quickly as an extinguished flame on a candle. "What did I say?" I ask her, the urgency in my tone not disguised.

"I know *how* to drive, Reece," she says softly, exasperation giving her voice an edge.

"Okay, I'm not following, then, why don't you?"

Her hands, which had been moving fluidly between her wine glass and her cutlery are now balled into fists on the table.

"Can't you guess?"

"No. I can't guess. Tell me what I'm missing?"

She looks at me like I should understand, but I don't.

I'm truly lost. "I don't understand. What are you trying to say?"

"Reece, I can't get a driver's license. California doesn't allow undocumented immigrants to have one."

I scoff. I know this to be untrue. "Of course they do. The lady who worked for us had one."

She looks at me like I'm a moron and then what she said finally registers.

"You're undocumented?" I ask dropping my voice to a whisper. I glance around us, even though I know our table's isolated and private.

She looks nervous and says, "Yes. Should I have told you? I have a work permit. Through DACA, I swear it's legal for me to work for—"

I cut her off. "Lucía, you don't have to explain yourself. Legal wouldn't have approved this deal if there were any issues in that regard. That's the last thing I'm concerned with."

She visibly relaxes and seems to regain her composure. But I'm still trying to process what that means as she continues to talk. "There was a time, yes. Now, you have to have documents, unexpired ones, from your country of origin to get one. My parents left Mexico when I was two years old. I haven't been back since. My Mexican documents, my passport, my identification cards, the things I would need to get a driver's license are gone. All I have is my DACA work permit. I'd have to go back to Mexico to get the documents I need and if I do that, I wouldn't be allowed to return."

I'm stunned, not just by what she's telling me, but by her poise. She lives a life I can't imagine. Driving, traveling and working are all things I don't think about as privileges. I take so much for granted that she has to negotiate every single day. Yet here she sits, wanting to contribute. To serve a country that renders her invisible and believes she should stay that way.

I grab her hand across the table. It's completely impromptu, but as soon as her hand is in mine, I feel that spark. The connection we make whenever we touch that tells me her hand was meant to be held by mine. She links our fingers and I stroke the back of her hand with my thumb.

"Lucía Vega is just a pen name." She pre-empts my next question by adding "L. Vega is an LLC I created so I could do business and not have to sign legal documents with my real name." She guessed my next question. "It's Ana Maria. But, I'm living as Lucía now, and that's how I want you to think of me." Her tone is testy and it makes me smile.

"Okay, Lucía Vega, Let's make this movie," I say and I bring her hand, that delicate, beautiful, powerful hand to my mouth and press a kiss to the back of it. "And let's be friends." I want so much more from her, but right now, it's all I know I can honestly take.

"Fuck, yeah."

I laugh out loud and say, "Fuck, yeah, Fifty-five."

"Don't call me that," she says with a frown and I just laugh again.

13

Lucía

THIS IS OUR FOURTH WEEK OF WRITING. IT'S BEEN SUCH an incredible experience. And since I told Reece that I was undocumented, the sky hasn't fallen in. Ana Maria's fearful existence hasn't come back to claim Lucía's. He's still spending time with me. Coming to yoga practice and making a real effort and giving me a lot of guidance as we reach the half-way point in our writing. Sometimes it even feels like he's flirting with me.

"Ready to switch places?" I say as we wrap up our yoga lesson. I've put off the swimming lessons every time he's brought them up. But, I promised that we could start today, after a quick session of yoga.

I glance at him, and his tanned, muscled forearms flex as he reaches down to grab the hem of his shirt. "Hell yeah, it's about time." And then he proceeds to pull his T-shirt off. My eyes are glued his perfect torso, all that smooth, tanned skin making the blood rush through my ears so loudly, it drowns out the crash of the waves behind us. His eyes are glued to the pool, he looks eager to get in and only spares me a glance when he asks, rather brusquely, "Do you have a suit? You should probably go and get changed."

"We're getting into the water? Today?" I croak as my fear quickly overtakes the reaction I was having to watching him strip.

"It's a swimming lesson, Lucía. Typically, you need to be in a body of water to swim. Air doesn't have quite the same viscosity," he responds sarcastically.

I want to run and hide. "I didn't realize we'd be getting in the water today." I'm stalling, but I'm not ready for this.

"So, go. I'll wait." He has stooped to roll up his mat and looks relaxed, but his tone is tense. I'm afraid I've annoyed him.

"I could just do it in my clothes," I say quickly, and start rolling up my mat, too.

"You'd have to at least take off your T-shirt." My head whips in his direction and even though he's not looking at me, it's like he can feel the protest forming on my lips. "Clothing adds weight and makes moving cumbersome. It's not ideal. But since you're wearing shorts you should be fine if you just take off your top. I assume you're wearing one of those sports bra things, right?" He stuffs his mat into the bag that was lying on the deck chair next to us and stands up fully. He pulls his shorts off and reveals one of those itsy-bitsy speedos that I'd seen him wear in competition.

Unlike then, he's got a healthy sprinkling of dark, wispy

hairs all over his chest that thins into a silky and tantalizing trail before disappearing into the top of his very high-cut bottoms. Beside the tattoo, nothing else has changed—his body looks like he swims every day. His swim shorts leave very little to the imagination.

"Unfair, Lucía," he mumbles, his voice low and silky.

My eyes shoot to his. He's watching me watch him and he looks . . . hungry.

"What?" I ask a little dazed, mesmerized by the way his eyes are roaming my face.

"I'm practically naked and I'm still waiting for you to take your top off," he says as he starts to walk toward the pool, not giving me a chance to respond. Which is fine; Witty comebacks aren't my forte. And even if they were, he didn't sound like he was being funny.

I take a deep breath and whip my T-shirt off. I try to act casual, but it's the very first time in my life that I've taken off an article of clothing in front of a man. I can't believe I'm having this experience with a man who won't ever know or appreciate what a milestone this is for me. I walk toward the edge of the pool and stand beside him. He's staring into the water and I don't speak because he looks lost in thought. I wish I knew what he was thinking.

"We're going to start with breathing today," he says, cutting into my thoughts. And then he dives head first into the water. His entry, graceful and fast, barely makes a ripple. He swims to the other end of the pool before he resurfaces and then he flips around and swims at a leisurely pace back to the edge where I'm standing.

If yoga is where I find my center, my peace, the water is very clearly where he finds his. He looks almost amphibian in the way he moves. His muscles move in perfect concert with each other, barely disturbing the water around him. He only comes up for air right before he reaches me.

He pushes the wet hair that's fallen into his eyes back and grins up at me. "Well, are you getting in?"

I want to say, "No, I'm not." I've never voluntarily gotten into a pool except to dangle my legs or feet in the water. But I swallow my fear and say instead, "Yeah, I'm going to use the stairs." I nod in their direction. "Can you meet me over there?" Without waiting for him to respond, I walk over and start my descent into the shallowest part of the pool. The depth marker says 3.5 feet. The water is warm, but refreshing after our light yoga workout. I try to relax as I walk until the water is just up to my ribs and stop.

He swims to the center of the pool and then walks the rest of the way, each step bringing more of his body in focus. He stops a few feet away from me and crooks his finger at me, beckoning me to take a few more steps, to come into the water deeper than I feel ready for. I shake my head no, eyes closed. Partially because I want to try to forget that I'm in water, and partially because I don't want to see the disappointment in his eyes.

"Lucía, you have to choose. Are you going to be afraid or are you going to do this?" My eyes pop open and the air rushes from my lungs. My brother, Julian used to say a variation of those words all the time. He would say, "Faith or fear, Luc. Choose one."

My heart aches at the thought of him, but it also renews my determination. I want to learn how to swim. I want one less thing to be afraid of. And I have the man who is possibly the best swimmer in the state of California willing to teach me.

So, I take a step toward him. And I can see the flash of relief that crosses his face.

He takes a step towards me, too and we do this, one after the other, until we are finally standing less than an arm's length away from each other.

"You ready?" he asks and I sense that he's asking about more than just these lessons. I nod. He stretches out his hand toward me, palm up. I mimic the gesture.

His laughter is unexpected. It's melodious and genuine and comes from deep in his belly. With his head thrown back, his arms hanging loosely at his sides, he looks like a man ten years his junior as he laughs. I'm not even able to muster the annoyance I should. It doesn't stop me from splashing water in his face and asking, "Share the joke?"

His laughter dies to a chuckle. "Nothing. I was putting my hand out for you to take it. But you mimicked me instead. It was funny."

"Okay. Do it again." The three words, said as one before I lose my nerve.

"Do what again? Laugh?" he asks, his expression confused.

"Hold out your hand," I repeat. Quietly, shyly.

His expression changes, softens a little and he does as I've asked. This time, as his hand extends toward me, he holds my eyes and says, "Give me your hand, Lucía."

The air changes. I feel it. As I reach for his hand, it feels like a step toward something more than just the hand of someone who's teaching me to swim.

As soon as our hands touch, I start to fear the moment we'll have to pull them apart. I know that when he lets go, I'll miss his touch.

And it's wrong being this close to a man who is essentially my boss. A man I'm intrigued by and attracted to and who is so far out of my league that it's laughable. His fingers close around mine and he yanks me forward while spinning me around so that my back is to him.

I let out a yelp of surprise as his other hand comes to rest on my stomach. He covers it with our joined hands. "What are you doing?" My voice has a breathless quality that I attribute to surprise, but it's also partially due to the pleasure of having his hands on me like this. *Why does this feel so good?*

"I'm going to teach you to breathe, and I want you to feel what I'm talking about as I explain." He bends his head down so his mouth is beside my ear. It's not touching, but it's close enough that I can feel the heat of his breath on my skin. The goose bumps take me by surprise. I feel my nipples harden and I have to close my eyes and concentrate so I don't groan and lean into him.

"The most important thing to remember is that you're not holding your breath when you're under water. You're releasing the air you capture in your lungs with each exhale. When you put your head underwater, you should be at one hundred percent of your lung capacity and you shouldn't come up for air again until you're at zero." He presses our layered hands into my torso and says, "Take a deep breath. As deep as you can."

I do as he instructs.

"Your breath should fill your chest, not your abdomen." The hand that was on top of mine moves up to sit on my chest, just above the rise of my breasts.

"Do it again and this time, this hand," he wiggles the fingers of the one on my chest, "should be the one that rises. The one on your stomach shouldn't move at all."

I try and immediately feel the difference.

He mumbles in my ear, which is closer now, "That's it, Luc. Fill your lungs so that you have the air you need to let you make the most of your time underwater."

I nod and his lips brush my ear with every ascent and descent of my head. He pulls his head away. And then I realize that I'm standing as close to him as I can without us touching. And without even thinking I take a step backward and bring us skin to skin.

I feel the unfamiliar but unmistakable hardness of his erection in my ass for the briefest moment before he jumps away from me like he's been burned by my touch. Humiliation from his rejection burns hot and fast through me. I don't just think I've made a mistake. I know I have.

14

Reece

THIS WAS A MISTAKE. I KNEW IT AS SOON AS I TOUCHED her. I'm fucked. This is the woman whose legend I've been spinning since I laid eyes on her. She's ambitious. She's not a slave to her fears and she is sexy as fuck. In the month that I've known her, I've come to see that she's special. And I'm so wildly attracted to her that it hurts. I shouldn't be doing this. She's my employee. She is so fucking young.

But fuck if I can help how hard I am, being this close to her. I'm a selfish asshole. Because I can't *not* do this.

I was purposely keeping her body away from mine so she wouldn't feel how little control I have. I didn't anticipate her taking a step backward. And as soon as I felt that soft ass of hers cradle my cock, I jumped. And now she thinks I was rejecting her and she's leaving.

Fuck.

"Lucía," I begin, but she just turns around and starts walking toward the stairs.

"Don't worry about it, no big deal. I'm sorry. I didn't mean to," she says without turning around.

I swim after her and in a few strokes, I'm able to grab her by the waist, under water, just as she is putting her foot on the first step.

"It is a big deal and I'm sorry," I say as I come to standing and turn her around to face me. And when I see her eyes, those big brown, beautiful eyes, I know I should probably let her leave. I see the pain in them before she erases it and sets her entire expression to neutral; the last thing I want to do is hurt her. I should let her walk away because I can't be thinking about fucking her when we both have so much riding on this whole experiment. But I know I won't.

She sighs, "Reece, forget it. You don't have to sit here and try of think of something to say. I don't know why I stepped back when it was obvious you were holding me away."

"No, Lucía." I put my arm on her elbow to stop her from leaving again. "I'm trying to think of what to say. Yes, I was holding you away." She slips her arm out of my grasp and this time I grab her hand. It's so small, and yet there's nothing fragile about it, or her. I can feel the callouses in her palm and I remember that this woman has worked hard and fought for every single inch of paved road she's traveled. I shouldn't do anything to jeopardize that. But her hand, it feels so *right* in mine.

"No. Shit. I'm fucking this up. Lucía . . ."

"Reece, it's okay. Really."

"Stop interrupting me, dammit," I growl at her.

She clamps her mouth shut and her eyes grow wide. She looks as shocked as I feel, she actually did what I said without arguing. That's a first.

"I was holding you away because I didn't want to make you uncomfortable. I shouldn't be getting hard while I'm teaching you how to swim. I shouldn't be getting boners with you at all. You're—"

"I know, I'm not your type." She tries to tug her hand out of my grasp and in frustration, I pull her flush against me. She melts into me, connecting us from hip to thigh.

"Does that feel like you're not my type, Luc?" I mumble when I feel her hips rotate and against my erection.

"But you said . . ." she whispers and looks up at me. The look of wonder on her face makes me want to take her mouth in a wild kiss.

I let go of her hand and move both of my hands up her body. One stops at her waist, the other goes to brush away the loose hair that is sticking to her neck. As soon as my hand touches her, her eyes close and I feel a shudder pass through her.

I lean in and down and put my nose on the side of her neck and inhale, she smells like sweat and vanilla and chlorine. I press a kiss to the base of her throat and move my hand to cup her neck.

"I lied," I say against the spot I just kissed.

Her head falls onto my chest and she says my name, and in her tone I hear so much of what I'm feeling: confusion, frustration, need. I tilt her head up to look at me. Her eyes remain closed.

"Luc, look at me."

She shakes her head no.

"Luc—"

And then, the air and the moment is cleaved in half by a loud, all too familiar voice shouting my name

"Reeeeece!"

Lucía and I both jump, breaking contact. Without another word she turns and starts up the stairs just as fucking Fabienne comes around the corner.

She comes to a halt as she sees Lucía. Her eyes dart back and forth between us and I see them narrow in a way that I dislike.

"Fabienne, what are you doing here?" I ask her as I start to follow Lucía out of the pool. She's already at her mat and hurriedly pulling her T-shirt on by the time I'm out of the pool.

"I could ask you the same thing Reece's Pieces," she taunts, using the nickname she knows I hate. She holds out a towel to me.

I roll my eyes as I snatch the towel from her. Fabienne is my ex-wife. Our marriage was years of tantrums, breaking up, making up, accusations and drama. Our divorce was even worse. Unfortunately, she's been cast in a film the studio is producing, but she has no reason to be here, in Malibu, looking for me.

"Can you just answer a question without being cryptic. Why are you here? How did you know I was at the guesthouse?"

She glances at Lucía who is drying her hair with a towel and not facing us. God, could this be anymore awkward?

"I went to your house and Alma said you were here. So, I took the golf cart. Sorry to interrupt." Her gleeful tone says the exact opposite.

"Cut the shit. Why were you at my house?" I ask her, ignoring her evasion.

"I just thought we could have breakfast, you know . . . I want to talk." She looks at Lucía again and this time Lucía looks up at her, too.

Her expression is shuttered, but I can see the tension in her jaw and I know she is anything but calm. And then she turns to face me.

"I'm going to get ready for work. I'll see you at the office. Thanks for the lesson." And then she walks towards the sliding door without acknowledging Fabienne.

"Lucía, can you wait?" I start after her.

She stops and turns to face me, her expression no longer shuttered. Her eyes are cold but her chin is quivering, and I can see that she is struggling to hold on her to her composure.

"No." She gives her head a gentle shake. "I can't." And then she turns to go, closing the sliding glass door behind her.

"So, that's the famous authoress?" Fabienne drawls as she drops into one of the lounge chairs on the deck. "I read her book, you know," she quips.

"Good for you. And I don't have time for breakfast," I say as I start to walk past her into the house. I can't imagine what Lucía's thinking.

"What? You always have time for breakfast," she calls after me, and I can hear that she is not perturbed in the slightest. She knows she's done some damage and that makes her happy. She used to be one of the nicest people I'd ever met. Her fame changed her and I went from being her boyfriend to being a tool she used whenever she wanted to make headlines.

"Not anymore. At least not with you. If you need something, talk to your production team. You can show yourself out," I say, not bothering to look back at her.

"Reece, I read chapter fifteen of the book. I know why you're desperate to get it made," she singsongs, but her voice has the edge to it, the one it normally gets when she's about to say something she knows is going to sting. I stop and turn to face her.

"You don't know anything, Fabienne," I say slowly. I don't want her even thinking about Lucía. She looks at me, her expression puzzled at first and then delighted.

"Oh, you haven't read it." She claps excitedly as she stands up. "This is perfect," she says with a giggle. Her glee making me all kinds of nervous. She's never happier than when someone else's day is about to be ruined.

"Fabienne, please leave."

I hear her laugh as I shut the door behind me. I walk to the front of the house and watch as she hops into her convertible Jaguar coupe and drives off.

"Lucía," I call as I enter the house. The shower in her bathroom is running. I want to walk in there and make her listen. When she was pressed against me, I could feel every single curve of her body melt into mine. I could feel the pulse in her neck when I kissed it.

I owe her a conversation and I want to make sure Fabienne's really gone. So, I grab a piece of paper and pen from her counter and write her a note.

I'm just about to walk out of the kitchen when a picture catches my eye. It's a silver framed picture of her and a boy, I assume he's her brother . . . he looks vaguely familiar, but I don't know why. She looks like she's about five years old. She's sitting on his shoulders with a wand of bright pink cotton candy in one fist. He's smiling up at her and she's staring up at the sky, her mouth open in a laugh, her eyes full of wonder.

I'm going to put that smile back on her face. I let my fingers skim her face in the picture before I let myself out.

15

Lucia

I'M GETTING READY TO LEAVE THE HOUSE WHEN I SEE THE slip of paper with my name on it. It stops me in my tracks. I pick it up and run my fingers over it before I read it. Reece wrote this. With the hands that had been on my body. Holding me, while he told me that he wanted me.

His handwriting is unexpectedly neat and restrained. I scan the short note.

LV,

Sorry we were interruped. Please come by my office so we can finish talking.

Reece

COME TO HIS OFFICE? As if. So much happened this morning. My shower didn't help me process any of that. Reece wants me. The same way I want him. But . . . his ex-wife. She wasn't acting like an ex. Not that I have much experience with relationships, but she looked at me like some dirty side-piece.

I walk out back and hop in my golf cart to head toward the offices. I let my eyes scan the beach as I drive. I can't imagine ever taking this view or these sounds for granted. The waves are lapping at the beach gently this morning. The gulls call to each other as they frolic above the surf. It's cool here this morning, but the breeze feels amazing as I zip along the path.

I pass the main house where Reece lives and see that all the lights are on and his golf cart is still there. I wonder if she's there, too?

I can't really afford to let myself get distracted or involved in their drama. I feel a pull toward Reece. We've become friends and now I know that we're also both fighting an attraction. He's become one of my favorite people. He's smart, he's compassionate, he's funny and he's got a great laugh. You know how the say there are some people you just have chemistry with? I thought that was just a saying. But now, I know it's real. We feel good together. Not just romantically. But in every way.

I know I was holding back—I didn't think he was interested. But I'm not sure what his reason could be. It could be my status, but he hasn't seemed fazed by that. Maybe it's my age. Or, because I'm a nobody in Hollywood and he only dates A-Listers. Maybe it's because I work for him. Or maybe it's because he's still not over Fabienne. I want to know, but I don't want to push it. Maybe it's for the best that nothing happened between us. We're at a crucial point in the screenwriting process. Next week, we are headed to LA to share our script progress with some of the other studio executives. I'm nervous and excited. I think we've done good work and I hope I've proven myself a little. But this meeting is important, if it goes really well, we could get the green light right away. That would mean we'd be moving on to casting and then production. It's totally surreal to think that my book, my little book that was written as fiction, but is inspired by my life, is going to be a fucking movie.

I squeal as I drive. It's been hard work. But then again, I've worked hard my whole life and always will. But all of this is so much more than even my wildest dreams could have conjured.

I'm on cloud nine as I park my golf cart, thinking about the book and screenplay has totally lifted my spirits. I almost skip into the office and head straight for the elevator. Just as I hit the call button, I hear familiar voices coming from around the corner. It's Reece and Fabienne. My pulse spikes and like a bird struck by an arrow in mid-flight, my good mood comes crashing down. I brace myself for impact as they come around the corner, toward the elevator. They look so . . . right. I didn't let myself really look at her this morning. She's even more beautiful in person than in print or on screen. Her hair is incredible; her skin is flawless. *She* looks like she belongs next to Reece. I don't feel bad about the way I look, but I know I don't look like *that*. When he finally sees me, Reece stops short.

"Hey, did you get my note?" he asks. He's looking at me intently, and I can see the worry in his eyes. It verges on desperation.

"Yes. I did." I nod and start to move toward him. But Fabienne reaches him before I do. Her emerald green eyes livid as she watches me, daring me to step closer. Reece doesn't seem to notice her as he searches my face. But I do. And suddenly, I'm Ana Maria again. I'm back on that playground and the thing I want most is being taken from me.

I feel hot tears prick the back of my eyes. Shame wells in my chest and forces me to look away. "Luc," Reece starts to say. Two men join us in front of the elevator and he stops. They both greet him and Fabienne. I stand there, wishing the ground would open up and swallow me whole.

And then the elevator dings and the doors open. We all step on, I press the button for my floor and quickly move to stand across from them. I keep my eyes on the door as the elevator begins its short climb to my floor. You could cut the awkward tension in the air with a knife. I can feel Reece's eyes on me, but I can't look at him. Not with her there.

The elevator stops on my floor and the doors pop open right away. I step off without another glance in their direction. My heart is racing and my palms are sweating. Those thirty seconds in the elevator with them felt like torture. I take a big gulp of air as my constricted lungs ease open.

"Lucía, I'll be in my office," Reece calls after me. I don't turn around. I can't. I don't need to see them standing together again. That image is burned into my brain.

I head to my office and turn my computer on. Dan and Todd are late, as usual, so I pull out my notes from yesterday and start responding to emails from Sol, and various blogs and news outlets asking me for interviews.

I'm about to close my inbox, when I see a new email pop up. It's from Reece. My mouse hovers over the message as I decide whether or not to open it. I don't want to have this conversation now. I have a lot of work to get ready for our meeting in LA.

"Hey, early bird," Dan calls as he and Todd come bounding in, coffees in hand. That decides it for me. I'll read it later.

THREE HOURS later and we've gotten through the toughest scene in the book—the sequence of Julio's arrest, death and their father's deportation. I've been dreading today. Writing those scenes in the book had been cathartic. But today, it was like reliving a nightmare. Todd and Dan were also moved by it, but they have no clue that this is *my* life story. And after spending hours having to be clinical in my approach to how we constructed this part of the screenplay, I'm emotionally spent. I tell them that we should take an extra hour for lunch.

I grab my phone and walk outside. My fingers tremble as I finally let myself open the email I haven't been able to stop thinking about. Every time I let my mind relax while we were writing, Reece's name would pop into my head.

To:LVega@ThrowAwayTheKey.com
From RCarras@Artemisfilm.com
Subject: Today
Fifty-five,
I need to talk to you . . . but something's come up. I'm headed back to LA right now. I'll email or call when I have the chance.

R.

My heart sinks. He's gone back to LA. With Fabienne probably. My heart twists in my chest at the thought. I don't know what this means. Did I misunderstand what happened in the pool? Should I call him and just ask?

I walk back to my desk and sit down. Dan is nowhere to be seen and Todd is busy typing away at his computer. He gives me a very fleeting, but assessing glance before his eyes go back to his screen. "What's wrong, sweets? You look like you lost your puppy."

I'm in over my head here, and I'm tempted to ask them for advice but I don't want to gossip or talk about Reece. I bite my lip and look up at him. "Well, can I give you a scenario and see what you think?"

"Scenario for the screenplay or real life?" he asks as he types on his computer.

"Real life," I respond.

His fingers come to an immediate halt and his head snaps to me, his hazel eyes twinkling. "Oooh, yes. Real life! Hit me with it."

I pause and try to think of how to phrase my scenario without giving away who I'm talking about.

"I know this girl. And there's a man she likes. A lot."

"Like, in what way? The way I like you or the way I like Jason Momoa?" he asks.

I roll my eyes at him. "I'm being serious, Todd."

"Me too, girl. I never kid about Jason Momoa."

"The latter," I say impatiently. "As I was saying . . . she likes him, thinks he might like her back, but he's got an ex who's still hanging around and as soon as she shows up, he disappears.

Should she call or just take a hint and leave him well enough alone?"

Todd considers me like he's weighing his words very carefully. I look down, feeling foolish.

"You know what, forget it. It's silly."

"Oh, no, no . . . It's not silly, Lucía," he says reassuringly. "I'm just trying to think."

Just then, Dan walks around the corner. "You're thinking. God help us," he says dryly as he drapes his long, lanky frame onto his chair. He looks at us and says, "What are you guys talking about?"

"Oh, Lucía's just asking me for advice about her and Reece," comes Todd's nonchalant response.

"Ooh, what about her and Reece?" Dan says, with real excitement.

I sit up in my chair and gape at them, my heart beating triple time. "I never mentioned his name or said it was about me!" I shout at him.

"Calm your tits, kid. We're not blind. We see you two making heart eyes at each other. Smiling as you walk by. When you first got here, I thought you must have fucked him for the job. He's not really the casting couch type, but I figured that maybe you were too much of a temptation for him to resist." He looks at me and bursts out laughing. "You should see your face. Your mouth is hanging open," he says laughing.

I shut my mouth. "We don't make heart eyes, nothing has ever even happened between us," I protest.

"Hey, you've got real writing chops, kid, you don't need to feel bad about anything," says Todd, looking at me sympathetically.

"I don't have anything to feel bad about. *Nothing* has ever happened between Reece and me. We're friends," I repeat emphatically.

Dan rolls his eyes and goes back to his computer. "Okay. Sure. Listen, you don't need to tell us your business. But anyone with eyes can see how you get all calf-eyed when he's around, and every time he looks at you, you'd think he'd never seen you before. He always does a double take." They both laugh out loud as Dan does an impression of Reece. Whipping his head around and making his eyes bug out.

I groan and sink down in my chair.

"Hey, if you're really *not* fucking . . . then you've got some pretty good mental foreplay going on. So, when you finally *get* to fucking—"

I cut him off. "Stop saying fucking. No one is fucking. Reece and I . . . we're just friends." I'm reeling on the inside. My protests are to convince myself as much as they are to convince them.

Todd gives Dan a knowing glance. "Oh, babe, you should relax. If you could see what we do, I think you'd rest a lot easier. And as for that ex of his. She's history. Never say never, but I think she might really have to be the last woman on earth. She made his life a living hell."

My curiosity is piqued. I want to know more, but I won't gossip, especially not about Reece. When I don't respond, Todd sighs and says, "Listen, here's what I'd tell your friend: Don't play games. If you want to call him, call him. If you're wondering where you stand, ask him."

"Okay, enough of this shit. I've got work to do," says Dan as he slips his headphones on and faces his computer.

"Thanks, T." I smile gratefully at him.

He smiles at me. "Don't thank me yet. I'm sending you a

bill for that little therapy session." And then he turns back to his own computer.

I do the same. I open my email and write back to Reece.

To: RCarras

From: LVega

Subject: Re: Today

Reece, I'm sorry I missed seeing you before you left. Is everything okay? I want to talk to you, too. About what happened in the pool. Call me when you can.

LV.

I READ it ten times before I press send. And then I wait. And wait. When, by the end of the day, Reece hasn't responded, I feel so despondent that I decide I need another session of yoga tonight. The kinks and aches in my heart are telling me that they need to be worked out.

I'm in my golf cart on my way home when my phone's alert tells me that I have an email. I stop the golf cart, right there in the middle of the path, and pull it out. It's from him.

To: LVega

From: RCarras

Subject: Re: re: Today

LV,

I'm okay. My dad had a minor heart attack today. He's okay now, but we had quite a scare this morning. I'll be in LA for the next week or so, trying to get settled.

Things are pretty hectic, so it'll be difficult to do it this week, but we need to talk.

I meant what I said in the pool. I want to pick up where we left off. I'll check on you tomorrow.

Night,

R.

MY HEART GOES through a series of emotions as I read the letter. Fear, relief, disappointment, happiness, doubt and now worry. I can't imagine what his morning was like. I know how much he idolizes his father.

I email him back right away

To: RCarras

From: LVega

Reece,

I'm so sorry about your dad. I'm glad he's okay. Call me if you need anything.

I miss you,

LV

I WAFFLED on adding that last sentence, but Todd told me not to play games. So, I won't. I press send and start back down the path to the house.

I'm just walking into the house when my phone rings, I answer without looking at it.

"Hello?" I answer as I kick the door shut behind me and slip my shoes off.

"You miss me?" Reece's deep voice responds. It's gruff with fatigue, but I can hear the smile in it.

"I do. Reece, your dad, I'm so sorry. Are you all right?"

I walk into the house, turn all the lights on and walk to the fridge to pour myself a glass of water.

"It's okay. He's okay. And I'm just tired. It was mild and he got to the hospital really fast," he says, sounding like he's not quite convinced yet. "He's in otherwise really good health, so he's going to make a full recovery. But, Luc . . ." His voice trails off like he doesn't want to finish his sentence.

"What? What else happened?" I demand, when he doesn't say anything.

"I'm going to need to start working from the LA office again. I won't be back in Malibu for a few weeks."

I feel selfish for feeling so profoundly disappointed at this news. I try to disguise it. "Okay . . . well the screenplay's coming along really well. I'll make sure you get daily upda—"

"I'm not worried about the screenplay," he says softly, but I can hear the frustration in his voice. "This morning, in the pool, I want to continue that and the conversation." The gruffness is gone from his voice, and it resonates through me. And my heart smiles; full and wide.

"Me, too," I respond and am surprised when my voice comes out as a whisper.

"Good. Let me spend the week getting things straight. And I'll come up next weekend and take you to dinner again. And we'll talk it out, face-to-face."

"Sounds good, I can't wait. Let me know how your dad is doing, okay?"

"I will. And I miss you, too Luc. Sleep tight."

When I get into bed a few hours later, I've replayed our phone call so many times that I feel like it's imprinted on my brain. Reece misses me. He didn't leave because of Fabienne. I snuggle into my pillow floating on cloud nine.

This man, this amazing, gorgeous, funny and brilliant man

wants me. As much as I want him, if not more. Whatever he's thinks we've got to talk about—my age, the fact that I work for him, maybe even my status—whatever it is, we'll be able to get over it.

I hope Todd's right about Fabienne. I didn't plan on any of this, but now that it's happening, I want it so badly. I want *Reece* so badly.

I fall asleep with a smile on my face and a little tendril of hope starts to grow in my heart.

16

Reece

I've been in LA for a week. My dad's being released from the hospital today. As much as I want to get back to Lucía, I'm needed here. Our conversation the night I arrived gave me hope that helped me get to sleep.

But that feels like years go. I've been neck deep in work. When I'm not at the office, I'm at my parents' house. My mother doesn't trust anyone else to be alone with my father. So, on the weekend when she had to run some errands, she asked me to come and spend the afternoon in the house.

I called Lucía today to say that I wouldn't be able to come back this weekend like we'd planned. I'd expected her to sound as disappointed as I felt. Instead, she'd just assured me that she was really busy anyway. Her voice was chirpy when she told me that they were hitting it pretty hard on the screenplay and making good progress. But, the lightness in her tone was false. I could hear her biting her tongue.

I started to ask her to tell me what was on her mind, when my phone buzzed. I had a potential partner waiting outside my office. I apologized and disconnected the call.

The studio has done some major juggling. My dad won't be able to work for at least a month. Today's been so busy, I didn't even stop to eat lunch.

At the end of the day, I walk into my dad's office and take a seat. It's the first time all day I've had more than a couple of minutes to even think. And my thoughts go straight to Lucía.

I look at Lucía and I see endless possibilities. She could be more than just my partner in bed. I'm done fighting what I feel for her.

I'll find time to drive to Malibu tomorrow, even if it's just for a couple of hours. I'm going to tell her how I feel.

I settle down at my dad's desk and pull out my phone. I decide to tackle the other thing that's been gnawing at me at all week. I bring up my Kindle app and open Lucía's book. Fabienne's taunting voice rings in my ear as I jump from the last page I read to chapter fifteen.

I start to read. And half way through the chapter, I stop, convinced that I've misread it. I go back to the beginning of the chapter and read it again, but it's the same. The incident she describes . . . I know it. But, how does Lucía? My gut twists.

There are only six people besides me who know that story. Fabienne is one of them. My parents and my three best friends are the others. The only one in that group that would ever use it to hurt me is Fabienne. I close my eyes and I see those beautiful brown eyes, so full of honesty. Was that all a lie? I can't believe it, but there's no other explanation that makes sense.

I've just been sitting here thinking she's the woman of my dreams, and she's been in cahoots with my ex-wife all along.

Rage makes my hands tremble as I dial her number. She doesn't answer. I call again. It goes to voicemail again, but I don't leave a message. I need to talk to her face-to-face. I walk out of my father's office and head to my car. I'm going to Malibu tonight.

17

Lucia

MY FATHER ALWAYS TOLD ME THAT IF SOMETHING WERE meant to be, I wouldn't have to chase it. That fate and I would meet just where we should, at just the right time.

Seven days ago, in the pool, I thought that my destiny and I had finally collided. Now, I'm starting to wonder if I imagined it. I re-read his email every day to make sure I haven't. We hadn't talked all week until today when he called to say he wasn't going to be coming to Malibu for the weekend after all.

I'd let hope have a home in my heart after our conversation that night. And each day that's passed without hearing from him, it's faded a little. I know he's been busy and I decided to let him have the space to focus on his family and work. But when he called today and said he wasn't coming up this weekend, I'd wanted to beg him to come.

Instead, I pretended I was fine while we spoke and I've spent the day trying to ignore the ache in my chest. I had the day off so I spent most of it bingeing on my favorite show, *Master of None*. It's what I wish my immigrant story looked like. Legal, successful and with an intact family.

I ordered in Thai food and besides the delivery man, I haven't seen or spoken to another human being all day. It's the kind of day I'd normally relish. But instead I've been miserable.

Finally sick of sulking, I force myself to go outside. The fire pit is roaring and I'm sitting, watching the waves as they crash onto the shore, over and over. The majesty of it all is incredible. I wish Julian was here to share it with me. I miss him so much.

I know he'd be proud of me. He thought I could do anything. And even though my parents were building all their hopes on him, he used to tell me that I was going to change the world. That we would do something great together. Well, now we are.

I lift my glass to the sky and toast him. His death won't be in vain. I'm just taking a sip when I hear a noise from the side of the house. I jump off the chair and grab the bottle of wine I brought outside with me. It's not an ideal weapon, but it's all I've got.

"Who's there?" I call out to the dark, my heart sprinting as I wait . . . and then I see him.

Reece steps out of the dark of the house's shadow and onto the deck. The light from the fire illuminates him and my heart leaps with joy as I take him in. He's dressed in a suit, like he's just come from the office, but he's taken off his tie and opened the top button of his shirt. I can see the smooth, tan column of his neck. I want to run to him and place a kiss on that exposed skin. I want to tell him how much I've missed him.

But the look on his face stops me. He doesn't look happy to see me. My joy at seeing him is replaced with a foreboding feeling that something terrible is about to happen.

"Reece, are you okay?" I ask when he doesn't say anything. His face is in partial shadow, but I can sense that anger and hurt hold equal weight in his expression. Tears prick my eyes because I know what's coming is going to hurt.

"Why didn't you answer the phone?" His voice is hoarse, like he hasn't slept in days.

"What do you mean?" I ask honestly confused.

He takes a step toward me.

"The phone. I called it. Twice."

"My phone is inside. I didn't know you'd been calling."

He takes another step forward and I look up at him. The look in his eyes sends a shiver through me. They're flat, cold. I don't move. A thousand butterflies spread their wings and take flight inside my gut. Icy fear pricks my veins.

"Is your dad okay, Reece?" I ask him.

"He's fine," he snaps, but doesn't say anything else.

I come to step in front of him, to look him in the eye, his voice is so grave.

My heart skips a beat.

"Reece, tell me what's wrong. You're scaring me." My voice breaks on that last sentence and he flinches.

"I learned a lot of things from my marriage. But if I had to choose one life lesson that is non-negotiable for me, it's dishonesty."

I am suddenly on alert. Reece's eyes have a dangerous glitter to them and I can see that he's angry and I have no clue why.

"Tell me about chapter fifteen, Lucía."

I draw a blank. "What's chapter fifteen?"

He flexes his jaw, and my heart is sprinting now. What could have made him so angry? "Chapter fifteen in your *fucking* book. Where did you get that story from? I know you. It's not from your imagination."

Goose bumps erupt from my scalp to the soles of my feet. How does he know that?

"*Throw Away the Key* is fiction—" I start to say.

He growls and stops me by grabbing my arms and puts his face close to mine. He seethes. "No. It's. Not."

I wince and he loosens his grip on my arms. "Tell me the truth, Lucía. I'm warning you—if you lie to me, I'll fire you. And I'll make sure no one else will work with you either."

My heart catches in my throat and I feel a surge of fear. What is going on? I try to sound calm and try to answer his question.

I look at him, feel the pinch of his fingers on my arms and rage, hot and wild supplants my fear. How dare he threaten me? I wrench my arms out of his hold and meet his accusations head on. "I have never lied to you."

He steps toward me and I put my hands on his chest, holding him away. "Don't you dare touch me again," I say, my voice shaking with my anger. "Yes, parts of the story are taken from my real life. And you can't come in here, put your *fucking* hands on me and threaten me. I don't have to tell you shit."

"The hell you don't. Tell me about chapter fifteen," he roars and I can see real anguish in his eyes. I don't understand any of this.

"Reece, chapter fifteen is based on what happened to my brother, Julian. I wanted to pay to tribute to him, by including what happened to him in this story," I tell him as I look into his eyes. I'm tired and unable to fight any longer.

He steps back. His eyes going from angry to horrified. The dread almost overwhelms me and I take a stumbling step backward, too. I have a feeling that distance between us might be a very good thing right now.

"I thought you'd read the book months ago. Why are you only now asking about chapter fifteen?"

His shoulders sag a little and he turns to face me. When he speaks his voice is mournful.

"I hadn't finished it. I got to the half way point and knew I had to find you and make it into film, I didn't even care how it turned out. I've been meaning to finish it… but I've been busy."

Any other day, I'd be upset that he'd only pretended to read it all, but right now, that feels insignificant.

"Then, how do you know about chapter fifteen and how did you know it isn't fiction?" I ask, dread creeping into me, hope, seeping out.

Far from the angry way he started this conversation, Reece seems almost despondent.

"Lucía, I want to tell you a story. But before that, I want to tell you that I meant what I said in the pool. And I meant what I said in my email." He tugs me into his chest and holds me there. I let myself savor the contact. My anger has lost its fuel. It's been replaced by icy fear.

"Reece, whatever it is. I don't want to know. Please," I beg.

His lips caress the top of my head when he speaks. "I've got real feelings for you." My arms circle his waist. "I've been struggling this week. I've thought about us being in a relationship and worried that you were too young to be locked into one." I squeeze him. "I thought it might be too soon for you. And there was also the whole 'you work for me' thing that I thought would make things difficult. But I'm not a kid. I've got an ex-wife who's a pain in the ass. And you're not ready for the kind of media attention you'll get when we get together. And then there's your status. We've got to figure out a way to do something about it."

Even though he's in my arms, with each sentence, I feel like he's taking a step away from me.

His hands come up and skim my face, his eyes mournful, his fingers wiping the moisture from my cheeks. It's only then that I realize I'm crying. "But fuck me, I can't stay away from you. I have moments every day, where you're all I can think about. So, I decided I was going to drive out here tomorrow and just tell you how I feel and what I want."

Hope, a small and fragile fleck of it, flutters in my chest.

"And then I read chapter fifteen, And Luc, I've been so angry ever since. I drove here to rip you a new one. I thought you'd been lying to me . . . but this is so much worse."

I've clearly missed something, but just like that my hope is gone again. I take a deep breath, close my eyes and brace myself.

"I know that story, Lucía. It's my story."

18

Reece

Lucía's eyes pop open and she stares at me unblinking. I let go of her hands and stand back. And then, I tell her.

"The summer I turned nineteen, I was back in LA. I had just competed at my first Olympics and I'd medaled. My coach was kicking my ass getting me ready for my next meet. I was in the gym and swimming ten, sometimes twelve hours a day. I was exhausted at the end of those days." Her face is a study in patient curiosity. I look away, I blow out a breath and keep going.

"One night after practice, I was leaving the gym and I saw a woman being attacked in the parking lot. A man had her pinned to the ground, facedown and he had her dress up around her waist. I ran over and pulled him off her. He ran off as soon as I got him loose. I thought about chasing him, but she was a mess, petrified and I didn't want to leave her alone. So, I sat with her and called the police. They came, took my statement, I gave a general description and went home." I can remember that night like it was yesterday. I'd gotten a pretty good look at the guy. Or so I'd thought.

Lucía's perfectly still. Her curious expression completely blank as she takes in what I'm saying.

"The next day they called, said they'd picked someone up and wanted me to come down to the station to see if I could pick the guy out in a line up. The lady who'd been attacked had never seen his face. I went, picked the guy that looked like the one from the night before. They thanked me, told me I'd picked their guy and that they'd let me know if they needed anything else from me. I never heard from them again.

"Fast forward four years. I won a gold in the Olympics, but came home injured after that car accident. My shoulder was shredded and no amount of surgery would have made me whole. I retired but had months of physical therapy to deal with. Fabienne was out of the country for work and I was staying with my parents. One day over lunch, I asked my mom if she'd ever gotten an update.

"She told me they'd gotten a call, a couple of weeks after the initial incident. Another woman had been attacked near the pool. The woman that was attacked had a Taser and stunned him repeatedly until the police arrived. The DNA they took from him matched the DNA they took from the attack I helped to stop."

I take her hand and she doesn't even seem to notice. Her eyes are completely unfocused and swim with unshed tears.

"I'd picked the wrong guy out of the lineup. She and my father decided it was best not to tell me because the news came right before a major meet. She said she didn't know anything about what happened to the poor kid I'd originally identified."

I look at Lucía and can see that even before I finish my story, realization is dawning on her. She snatches her hand out mine.

"Luc . . ."

She shakes her head, quick and fast and I plow ahead to finish the story. I just need to lay it all out and see where we go from there.

"I called the police officer who'd been assigned to that case and I asked after the first suspect. The case had been closed. I had to bribe him with movie premier tickets to get him to look up the boy's information. But then he told me that even though the boy had been arrested for the attempted rape, they'd also charged him with unlawful entry into the U.S. and he'd been in ICE custody within forty-eight hours of being arrested."

She whimpers . . . it's feeble and broken and I feel a trickle of cold sweat run down my back. Yet, I push on.

"And then he told me his file showed that he was deceased. Died in the detention center awaiting deportation. At the age of sixteen."

She starts to sob, quietly, but her shoulders are shaking.

I move to her, to put my arms around her. As soon as I do, she pulls away. Her eyes ablaze and her jaw clenched, her mouth pinched. She rises on her toes to put her face in mine, and between gritted teeth, she spits, "Get out." And then she bursts into tears.

"Lucía . . . I'm sorry."

I stop talking because she is crying so loudly. Sobbing uncontrollably. I don't know what to do. Driving over here, I could only think one thing and that was I was going to have it out with her for lying to me. I'd assumed *that* was the worst thing. But *this* is the worst thing. I never suspected that she would tell me the story in her book was her story, too. That the boy whose life I'd ruined was her brother's.

"I know sorry isn't good enough, but it's why this issue, this movie is so important." I know I can hear the plea in my voice. But right now, I'm ready to beg if it would make her listen to me.

"Luc—"

"Shuuuuut up!" Lucía roars at me suddenly, in the middle of a crying jag. She fights her way out of my loose hold and jumps up. "I don't want to hear any of this!" she shouts at me. She is vibrating with rage and every word she bellows is punctuated with her jabbing a finger in my direction. Her face is tear streaked, her nose is red and her lips are puffy.

"He was my brother. My blood. And you're telling me it was you who put him behind bars? *You* who cut his life short? And why? Because you were tired from your swim practice and didn't get a good look at him? Or do all Mexicans look the same to you?" Her hands are waving around her head as she screams. She's still crying, her rage and sorrow creating a tempest before my eyes.

"What do you want me to say? That I forgive you?" She clutches her chest, tears streaming from her burning eyes. She doesn't bother to wipe at them as she faces me.

I can't answer her. I have no idea what I want to say. She rushes into the house and I follow her.

She grabs the front door and pulls it open.

"Get out," she says, not looking at me, her voice barely above a whisper. But I hear her loud and clear.

"Lucía, please. I know you're angry, but let's talk," I say, not budging. I need more from her, even if it's fury.

"Leave, Reece. Please," she says through gritted teeth.

"We need to talk."

All of a sudden the phone that was in her hand is flying in my direction, it lands at my feet, and the screen shatters.

"Whoa," I say just as she grabs a basket of potpourri that's sitting on the table in her foyer and hurls it in my direction. Her aim is way off and it lands three feet to my left. But I get her point and she's running around her foyer, looking around for other things to throw as I rush past her and out the front door that's now hanging open.

"Okay, Lucía, I'm out, but I'm not leaving. We need to talk."

She leans out towards me. Her eyes are wild; her hair is flying.

"Fuck talking. Fuck you. I don't care if you don't leave. Stand there all night for all I care." And then she slams the door so hard that the windows that frame it shudder.

Shit.

Just as I raise my fist to strike the door, the entire house falls into darkness. Every single light is extinguished. And for a beat, it is both dark and completely silent. A minute later, I hear sobs coming from the back of the house. I know if I follow the sound to its source I'll find Lucía on her back deck. Her crying is mournful and unrestrained. She is crying, talking, screaming all at once. My ears burn with the heat of it. And I know I need to leave her to this. I wish I knew someone I could call to come be with her. She shouldn't be alone. That I can't be the one to comfort her makes me feel helpless.

I stand there until the violence of her sobs subside. And then, I leave to give her some privacy. I owe her at least that. But I'll be back.

19

Lucia

I'M BACK IN LOS FELIZ. I'M HAVING DINNER WITH JESSICA and my mother. Jess is leaving for a date soon, so my mother and I will be alone for most of the evening. I called her when I got back home and finally told her about the screenplay. She was actually excited. So, I extended the proverbial olive branch and invited her to join us tonight. And I was shocked when she agreed. I haven't seen her in almost two months and it's her first time visiting me here. So, I'm nervous. I'm outside manning the grill and they're inside getting the wine we've had chilling most of the afternoon.

She and Jess have hit it off, color me surprised, but I'm glad.

It's been a week since Reece dropped his bomb on me. I spent the first two days crying, praying for relief from the pain. Then, I got back to work and lost myself in it by working almost around the clock. I haven't allowed myself the time to process what he told me. He's called, emailed, texted. He even came back to my house the next day. I couldn't find the courage to face him. I had no idea what to say. And this week, I've felt like I was trapped in a terrible purgatory.

Dan and Todd both hate me for being so demanding. But, I don't feel bad. This presentation is important. It will decide the fate of this project and I haven't left anything to chance. I also know that Reece will be there and I'll have no choice but to face him. It's just another layer of anxiety that has made this week more stressful.

When we finished ahead of schedule, we decided that we earned a break after the way we'd been working as of late. So, I came down to LA to try and relax. While I've been here, I've been trying to lose myself in the book I'm writing for my publisher. It's a young adult fiction novel about a Syrian girl's coming of age while living in a refugee camp in Greece. It's a story I'm connecting with, so it's been nice to have time to really work on it.

Yesterday, I spent the day at Artemis' headquarters. I met with some of the other screenwriters and spent some time in their legendary museum. I managed to avoid Reece, but being in the building conjured so many feelings. Knowing I was sharing space with him made me crave him. But in trying to avoid seeing him, I only left the writer's pit once the entire day.

At lunch, I'd gone to visit the on-site museum that takes up the entire tenth floor of the building. I wandered through the displays, looking at costumes, props and other collectibles from Artemis' nearly seventy-year history. I'd found myself in the section dedicated to the Carras family history. It's a fascinating story, told in pictures, of Reece's grandfather's immigration from Greece as a young man and how he headed West to start making movies. And from those humble beginnings, he started building what would become one of the largest media empires in the world. What the family accomplished in just one generation, is the epitome of the American Dream. And that's all I want for myself, a chance to fulfill my potential.

The last photos in the collection were of Reece and his parents. His mother is a striking woman. Her dark hair and icy blue eyes give her a regal bearing. Even in the picture I find her intimidating. And Reece looks just like his father. Strong, bold features. Heavy brows, full lips, tall, broad and so serious. He was a teenager in that picture. Not older than sixteen. The same age my brother was when he was arrested and sent to jail.

My heart ached. What a cruel twist of fate. But is Reece to blame? Does it matter if he's not? I know him. He is a good man. But is it a betrayal of my brother to feel this way?

These are the thoughts that have weighed me down all week and it's still not clear to me what I should do.

I'm pulled back to the present by the spitting fire of the grill as a drop of oil falls from the cooking shrimp. I look at my backyard and take a deep, fortifying breath. The air here is not as clear as it is in Malibu, but it's still so gorgeous. My neighbors to the right have this amazing lemon tree. The branches dangle over our fence when it's bearing fruit and lemons, ripe and juicy, fall into our yard every day. We go outside each morning to collect them. The cool October air carries with it the sweet citrusy smell of the Frangipani tree we planted from a cutting our neighbor gave us. It's a paradise back here.

I love being in Malibu, but Los Feliz, is my home. I feel

anchored here. Sure of myself and safe. Being home the last few days has made the fracas of this week tolerable.

Jessica and my mother come outside with two big bottles of wine and three huge wine glasses. They are talking animatedly and I smile to see them getting along so well.

My mother is only ten years older than Jessica, but she looks old enough to be her mother. I feel a flash of guilt that she's had to work so hard.

My mother wasn't thrilled when I told her I was going to publish a book. She couldn't believe I was "wasting" my income that way. She said, "We didn't come here so you could follow your passions, *mija*. We came here so that you could find a profession. So that you could build a secure life. What does writing do?" I remember that day like it was yesterday. Even when I got my book deal and was able to give her more money, she'd asked, "Now that you've had your fun, are you going to focus on your real job?"

"It's so nice to have you back. It hasn't been the same without you. I'd started eating inside more," Jessica says flashing me a quick smile as she lays everything out on the dining table we have outside.

"It feels so good to be home," I say over my shoulder pulling the shrimp and vegetables off the grill, and piling them on the plate I'd planned to serve them on.

"It is so beautiful. I'm sorry I haven't come sooner." My mother's English is flawless but heavily accented. When we were growing up my mother made Julian and I speak only English at home. She and my father wanted to make sure that we sounded "American." Her own accent always made her reluctant to speak if we weren't home. In our old neighborhood, when we were among family and friends, she had been a social butterfly. It's nice to see her enjoying being around people again.

I smile at her and say, "I'm glad you're here." It's been a while since we've sat down like this, not in a restaurant, but in a home and broken bread. It feels good.

Jessica pours us each a glass of wine and sits down. I walk over with the pan of our taco fillings and put the contents on our plates. We have tortillas, pico, guac and cheese all laid out for dinner tonight. Jessica piles her tortilla high with veggies and the other fixings then says, "I have to leave in a minute. But, I want to know, have you talked to Reece?"

I am in the middle of sipping my wine and choke on it. My mother and Jessica both stand up and come to bang on my back. I catch my breath and tell them, "I'm fine," while I fix Jess with my death glare.

My mother looks back and forth between us and then asks, "Who is Reece?"

I don't say a word and Jessica sits back with her eyebrows raised and looks at me. She is obviously not bothered by my glare.

My mother turns to me and says, "Is anyone going to tell me?" I look away from Jessica and at my mother and the expression on her face alarms me. She looks like she is going to cry. My mother stopped crying when my father left. She would get angry, curse him, but she never cried.

"Mama, it's nothing," I say and reach for her hand.

Jessica stands up with a flourish. "I've got to get ready. I'll be back. You can tell me then." She floats out of the yard and back into the house, seemingly unfazed that she's opened a can of worms that I had hoped to keep firmly shut.

I close my eyes, silently count to three and turn to face my mother. She's watching me expectantly.

"Really, it's nothing. I have some things to figure out with the man I'm working for," I say trying not to lie without revealing too much. I don't know how my mother will react to hearing that I'm in love with the man who's responsible for her son's death.

She sighs, a long sigh and looks down at our joined hands.

"Ana," Hearing myself called by that name makes me cringe. "I know that I made a mistake when I sent you to your Uncle Jorge. I knew it then. But I didn't think I had a choice. It was the only way I could afford to keep you in clothes and keep you safe. I needed that job." Her voice cracks on the word "needed."

"And that boy—he's grown up now to be as vindictive of a man as he was a child—would have turned us in."

My blood starts rushing through my ears. "That's what it's always come down to. Don't make noise. Don't draw attention to yourself. Don't get hurt. Don't fight back," I say quietly, but bitterly.

"Ana. I'm human, too. It hasn't been easy to suppress my anger. To let people abuse me and my children. I did it so that you could have a good life. I know it doesn't seem like it. But look, you've written a book. It's being made into a film. All of that . . . these are my dreams come true. And so are you."

The backyard is alive with the evening song of the creatures that live in our trees and bushes, but I don't hear any of that. I can only hear my mother and my heart pumping the blood straight to my head. I'm at a loss for words. My mind wants to hold onto my bitterness, but my heart wants to let go and fall into her arms. I've missed the family I used to have. I grab hold of her hand and she squeezes mine. Tears spill down my cheeks as she brings our joined hands up to her face and presses the back of my hand into her cheek. She closes her eyes, and takes a deep breath.

"I owe you so many apologies, *mija*, and I will give them to you. I think I'll need a lifetime to atone for everything. But, maybe I can start by being here for you. I know I haven't earned the right to ask you for anything." She looks around the garden, looks through the sliding glass doors into the house. "I'm grateful you have such a lovely home. You deserve it. And I'm glad Jessica is someone you've been able to confide in. I fear that I've left you to face the world alone. Yet, you've managed to make something of your life despite that."

For the second time this week, I feel like I'm having an out of body experience. I thought my mother resented me. I thought she had kept her distance because I reminded her of all the terrible things she wanted to forget. Our conversations have been brief and infrequent.

And we have never talked about what happened at her employer's house. But before I can bring that up, she sits up straight, and drops my hand. Her voice has lost its wistfulness as she continues speaking. "I know it will take time for you to trust me again. But, for now, I want to know who Reece is, and I want to know what he's done to upset you." And then she takes a bite of her taco and looks at me eagerly while she chews.

I just stare at her for a second. And then I decide to let her change the subject. I'll take the progress we've made tonight and know that we have a lot more to say before our relationship is healed. I also realize that the words she just spoke took a lot of courage and I'm not going to throw them back in her face. So, I tell her about Reece. "He is the head of the movie studio that I told you bought the rights to the film. We've been spending time together, getting to know each other."

My mother puts her taco down and smiles broadly. I haven't seen that smile in fifteen years. "He's a movie producer? Is he rich?" she asks excitedly.

"Yes, Mama. Very," I respond. "And famous," I add.

Her smile slips a little. This probably gives her the same pause that it gives me. Fame means exposure.

"When I met him, he told me that he'd read the whole book. But I found out last week that he'd only gotten half way through." I close my eyes as I remember him standing on my deck telling me his story.

My mother leans over. "Is this why you're having a problem? Because he didn't finish the book?" she asks looking a little confused. "That's not a life altering situation. You've gotta loosen up, Ana."

I stand up and I walk over to the railing that runs along our patio and with my back to her, I tell her.

"I wish that was all, Mama. He's the 'witness' who identified Julian in that line up. The one that sent him to jail, and then detention."

My mother's "*Dios Mio*" has me turning around to face her. Her horror is apparent.

"So, yes. I was falling for a man I can never be with." My mother's face goes from horrified to confused.

"Why? What else? Why can't you be with him?" she asks me, stuttering over her questions.

I look at her, surprise and annoyance dripping from my words. "Did you not hear what I said? How could I be with him after that?"

My mother walks over and puts an arm around me. I'm shorter than her and my head fits perfectly into the crook of her neck. I nestle it there and the ball that's been in the middle of my chest expands. I haven't had my mother's comfort for so long and I've forgotten how good it feels to be in her arms.

"Ana, you're so young. It's easy to be dismissive of people when you think you've got your whole life stretched out in front of you."

"I'm not so young, Mama. And I'm not being dismissive. I've thought about this all week."

Her dry, humorless laugh punctuates the air.

"A week? You're going to be grappling with this for the rest of your life. But that doesn't mean it's impossible to overcome." She runs a caressing hand up and down my arm. It's an absent-minded motion, but so comforting.

"Ana Maria." I lift my head at her use of my full name. She only said it when she really wanted me to pay attention as a child. "Maybe it's my fault, I didn't show you how to be forgiving when you were a child. I held so much anger inside of me that you never saw me be gracious."

I start to protest and she cuts me off by putting a finger to my lips. "This young man, Reece? He pulled Julian out of a lineup. He looked like someone he thought he'd seen committing a crime, right?" she asks.

"Yes," I whisper, my sadness clogging my throat. My mother grabs my chin and forces me to look her in the eye. Her expression is stern, determined.

"I've had years to weigh this, Ana. Right after it happened, I used to fantasize about confronting the man who sent Julian to prison. But I soon realized that my anger was directed at the wrong person. He's not the one who arrested Julian. He wasn't the one who charged him based on the words of one witness. He didn't hand him over to the authorities to be sent to detention. He didn't kill Julian. And if anyone is responsible for his death, it's your father and me," She says quietly, her voice thick with unshed tears and regret.

I pull out of her grasp, her words shocking me out of my melancholy.

"What are you saying? How are you to blame?" I ask vehemently.

She looks at me, her lips pursed, her eyes glassy and wide. "Your father and I decided to leave Mexico when you were born. We're not well-educated people, our parents didn't have any connections. Your father was working at a tire factory in Mazatlán. He worked fourteen-hour days and I worked at a resort there, as a housekeeper." She sits back down at the table and picks up a napkin that she begins to shred as she speaks. "We were scraping out a living, and your Uncle Jorge told us that one of his friends was looking for someone to work as a landscaper. The pay was almost ten times what we were earning and so we came to see. We applied for visas and they were granted. We knew that if we liked what we found, we probably wouldn't go back home. It was wrong, but we thought we were doing the right thing. Your brother was almost nine, we wanted him to get a good education. You were just a baby and we wanted the same for you. So, we made a decision. You and your brother have paid for it."

I blink in shock. I've spent many nights resenting them for taking away my chance to be a productive citizen of this country. But I've never blamed them for what happened to Julian. I know they loved him. I know that they did what they did because they wanted to give us a better life.

I shake my head. "No. You can't blame yourself. It's not your fault." I try to reassure her.

"How is it Reece's?" she shoots back. "You should be angry at me, at your father, at the court system, at the immigration laws. Reece only did his civic duty."

"Civic duty? Julian was my brother," I say, my voice clogged by a ball of emotion that makes getting words out painful.

"It is the greatest tragedy of my life that your brother was misidentified. But I also know that under normal circumstances, they might have charged him and let him sit and wait for trial. But because —" Her voice cracks as she starts to cry. "your father and I brought him here. He was turned over to the Immigration people. He was gone." She composes herself and wipes her tears and puts an arm around my shoulder. She speaks softly into my ear.

"Ana, there are plenty of reasons why you and Reece may not be able to work things out, but this should not be one of them. Not if you really care for each other. He told you the truth as soon as he knew it. He didn't do anything malicious or dishonest."

That only makes me feel more miserable, because she's right. Reece is such a wonderful man. "Aren't I betraying Julian? He's my blood," I say through a sob.

My mother puts a hand under my chin again. Her eyes are angry as she lifts my face to hers.

"Look at your life. Where has your blood been? Where are your aunt and uncle? Where was *I?* Don't be a fool. Your grandmother, God rest her soul, used to say love is thicker than water. Blood means nothing without *love.*"

Each word, so harsh and yet, so healing. It's true. Look at the family I've built. Jessica, Sol . . . Reece. Blood had nothing to do with it.

She sags into her seat and says, "I'm tired. I should go home. I have to be up at six tomorrow morning."

Jessica steps out on the patio just then. She's wearing a pretty pink dress. It's short, but otherwise demure. With her blond hair caught in clips on the sides and her flawless makeup, she looks like a walking advertisement for Ms. All American.

"Oh, you're leaving? I can give you a ride, if you'd like. I'm heading out in about ten minutes," she says as she breezes in. If she notices the heavy mood, she doesn't pay it any heed.

"Okay, that would be nice," my mother says quietly. I can

tell she wants to keep talking. But, I'm glad our conversation's been cut short. It was a lot. And as glad as I am that we're talking again, I'm not used to all of this openness with her.

We move to our seats around the table and sit down. I'm lost in my thoughts, mulling over what my mother said and knowing in my heart that she's right.

"So, have you talked to him?" Jessica repeats the question that got this conversation started. I twirl my wine glass in between my fingers.

"No. His dad's been sick, he's been working . . . and I've been avoiding him," I say, feeling miserable and ashamed of myself.

"Well, stop doing that. You know where he lives, right? Go there. Get it over with before you have to see him when you give your presentation. That would be all sorts of awkward. It's Monday night, I'm sure he's home."

Why didn't I think of that? I put my fork down and look at her. "Yes." I clap my hands together. That's a great idea.

Jessica whoops in delight. I laugh, too. I'd forgotten what a shit stirrer she is. She lives for drama. She's probably hoping Reece and I will get into a fight and it'll be on TMZ. But after two glasses of wine it sounds like a great idea to me, too.

So, I turn to my mother and say, "What do you think?"

"Go and get your answers. I'm going to finish my tacos and then let Jessica take me home." I kiss her cheek. I open my Uber app and order a ride to Reece's place in Calabasas. My fingers tremble as I press Request Ride. I hope I'm doing the right thing.

"Wish me luck ladies," I call as I stick my head outside the patio's sliding doors. We see the sweep of headlights as my car pulls into the driveway.

"Go get your man." She calls after me as I speed to the door.

I text Reece, afraid showing up unannounced might be a bad idea. All I write is: ***I'm coming to your house, be there in thirty***. I just hope he'll see me.

20

IT'S LATER THAN USUAL AS I PULL ONTO MY STREET. I'VE been in a meeting with my father all evening and I'm exhausted. This week has been one of the most difficult of my life. One of our projects is seriously over budget because our lead has missed days of work, which cost us hundreds of thousands of dollars each time. My father's recuperating, but he's still very weak and my mother's been a nightmare. And then, there's Lucía.

I need to figure out what I'm going to do make things right with her.

I pull into my driveway, tired but resolved. I'm heading back out as soon as I change. After our confrontation, I called, texted and emailed Lucía every day. I even went by her house once to see if I could get her to talk to me. She wouldn't speak to me or see me. Not that I blame her.

The conversation we had last time I saw her got out of control so fast.

I think back to that night and how angry I was on the drive to her house. I thought maybe Fabienne gave her the story. The scenario I imagined ended with her confessing to misleading me. These thoughts, played over and over again in my head and were fuel for my anger.

And in one sentence, she blew that all to bits. Her brother. I'd sent him to jail.

It took me years to get to a place where I could forgive myself after finding out what I'd done.

When the police asked me to come in, I didn't think twice about it. When I picked her brother out of the lineup, he was just the guy I'd seen the night before. I thought I'd done something heroic. But, I hadn't. Not only did my actions cause the police to halt an investigation that left a real rapist out on the streets, they ruined an entire family.

My guilt has always been overwhelming. The foundation, the legal defense fund, and the advocacy made me feel like I was making a difference. But, Lucía brought the real-life consequences into sharp relief in a way it hadn't been before. Seeing the living, breathing consequences of my actions has been nearly debilitating.

Now, I don't know how to look at her and ask her to forgive me for something so utterly unforgivable.

I told her I was developing feelings for her that night. I didn't even know the half of it. This week, after coming so close to losing her, I know that what I feel is real. The thought that I might have to let her go terrifies me. If she can't stomach the thought of being with me, I won't have a choice. But I'm going to fight with every ounce of strength I have. I've never been so sure about my feelings for someone as I am with Lucia.

I know she's in town. I heard she was at the office, but I couldn't risk approaching her there. I didn't know if she'd ignore me or throw things at me. They have a big day on Wednesday, I don't want to be the reason that she's distracted or upset. So, I've left her alone.

I was starting to feel like a stalker. So tonight, I confided in my father. He knew something was off. I hadn't planned on telling any of it, but when he asked, the story poured out me.

He listened, he even took a few notes. When I was done, he'd said, "Reece, it's not going to be easy."

I'd agreed with him, "Yeah . . . I don't know if she'll even give me a chance to explain."

He shook his head at me and said, "That's not what I mean. That, son, will be the easiest part of this. She'll talk to you. She'll understand that you made a mistake. But once you're together, that's when things will become hard. You're going to get a lot of press attention and for someone like her, that's very risky. What are you going to do about her status? You can't marry her. She can't travel. She can't drive. If you did get married, she could be deported at any time and then what would you do?"

I'd forgotten that my father was a pragmatist. He's more laid-back than my mother, but he's very rarely emotional about things. I should have known he'd say the equivalent of *"So what if you love her?"*

When he meets her, he'll understand. He'll love her. He won't have a choice. She's special. The bright, shiny goodness that lives inside her is obvious the instant you meet her. And courage is her super power. She feels fear, but never lets it stop her.

My father's declarations of doom felt damning. And I didn't have any answers for him. But I'm certain that if I can get her to forgive me, we can handle anything else life throws at us. I'm going to convince her of that. Tonight. I want a chance. I pray she'll give me one.

I hop out of my car, new purpose lengthening my stride. As I approach my front door, my steps falter.

She's there. Sitting on my doorstep illuminated by the security light. I can see the highlights in her dark, chocolate colored hair as it spills down her shoulders. Her lips are painted that red I've been seeing in my sleep. She's wearing a pair of tiny white shorts and a black tank top, and she's got a sweater bunched up in her lap. Her toes flex and arch in her red flip-flops as she watches me approach.

She tips her face up and looks at me. Her eyes are clear, and angry.

Shit.

"Do you want to come in?"

In what I take as a good sign, she accepts my proffered hand. I let her walk ahead of me into the house.

I hit the switch on the panel to the left of the door and the whole house comes to life. So does Lucía. She whirls on me, her hair still moving even after she's stopped. Her eyes dart around the house, taking it in.

"We need to talk, Reece. It's long overdue." Her eyes finally land on me and I can see the anxiety in them. "You look terrible. Did you stop shaving?"

I laugh in disbelief. That's the last thing I was expecting to hear. After a week of holding my breath, of thinking that we'd gone past the point of no return, her observation, so casual and familiar, makes me inexplicably angry.

I take a step toward her. My eyes narrowing as hers widen in surprise.

"We had an epic confrontation last week. I called you, texted you, emailed, stood outside your house for days." She looks down.

"You ignored me. I understood why. I decided to give you your space, because you clearly needed it. And no, I haven't been shaving. I've been a little preoccupied," I snap at her.

She takes a step back at my raised voice, but she looks concerned and says, "Is your dad okay? Is it working?"

"Lucía, am I in the *Twilight Zone*?" I ask her incredulously.

"What do you mean?" she asks sounding genuinely perplexed.

"I'm beginning to wonder if you're not slightly psychotic," I say, frustration now mingling with my confusion. I lean in close to her face, so she can see my eyes. "You threw me out of your house last week. You've basically gone into hiding to avoid me. And now, suddenly, you're here saying our talk is overdue and asking what's wrong. Luc, it's not my dad that has me stressed the fuck out. It's you."

She starts to respond and then seems to think better of it. I can hear her counting to ten under her breath.

Fuck, I've missed her. I want to stop talking and kiss that plump bottom lip of hers.

She sighs and looks down at her hands.

"I'm sorry. You're right, I was avoiding you. I didn't know what to say. We both dropped bombs on each other. Mine was a grenade, yours was nuclear. I had to think. I needed to process . . ." She looks up at me through her lashes, a tear dangling from the tip and I feel her pain deep in my gut. It has been a lot. Almost, too much.

A lot was said the other night. And even though I don't

understand where this change of heart has come from, I'm glad. I'd hoped she would get here eventually. I prayed that her reaction was driven by surprise and hurt, but that she'd see her way to at least talking to me. It happened faster than I expected and apparently without any help from me.

"I told you how I felt before everything went crazy. My feelings are unchanged." She's still looking at her hands. "I understood your reaction the other night. I even welcomed it, felt like I deserved it. Do you feel differently now?"

Her eyes come slowly to mine, she looks unbearably sad.

"Yes. I feel differently. I . . . won't apologize for my reaction the night you told me. It was like . . . a tsunami of pain and anger overtook me. I couldn't control it, Reece. Everything hurt so much. All at once." She wraps her arms around herself like she's cold. I want to pull her to me and be the one to comfort her.

"But, I've had time to think and I talked to my mother."

My stomach drops. Her mother. I'd forgotten she has other family members I'll have to face. She's not looking at me as she speaks, her eyes seem glued to her feet. But, I'm watching her. I can see that she's struggling to keep her composure. She amazes me.

"The other night was intense. But, Reece, what happened all of those years ago to Julian; I know it wasn't your fault." My chest tightens at the mention of his name.

She raises her head to look me. Her eyes burn with regret. I know they mirror my own.

"I needed someone to show me the way, because I was stuck in a bad place. I loved Julian so much. His death changed my life in so many ways." She shivers slightly, but doesn't look away.

"He committed suicide."

All of the air leaves my lungs. I didn't know.

"My mother tells everyone he died in a fight. We're Catholic," she says, knowing that I need no further explanation. "To me, the method wasn't a factor. He was gone. And suddenly my whole world was destroyed. My family . . ." She chokes on a sob and I pull her to me. Keeping her at a distance is no longer an option. I can't stand there and watch her in pain and not respond. She wraps her arms around my waist and holds on while she cries.

"My brother, Reece . . . my heart . . . it broke when he died," she says in a near moan. She seems to be reliving it all again, right now. Her shoulders shake and I can feel the pain radiating from her. Like a living thing, it seeps from her into me. Her sobs quiet, but she stays burrowed in my chest.

"I'll never get over him being gone, Reece. Never. I didn't even know what it meant to miss someone until he was gone. My parents, it broke them. Broke my family. My dad . . ." She sniffles. "And when he left, my mother was *so* angry. She cursed him. She cursed my brother. And she stopped being my mother," she mumbles quietly. I don't know what to say to comfort her.

I have so many questions. Where is her mother now? How did someone who had such a hard beginning, turn her life into something so beautiful? How did she learn to live so freely, live so fully?

"Oh my God, I'm so sorry . . ." she says as she pulls her arms from around my waist and steps back, putting several feet of distance between us.

My arms scream for her to come back, but I try to give her space.

"Please, Lucía. Don't apologize . . ." I say, my voice thick with emotion. This week has been hell, and for the first time since this nightmare unfolded, I can see a way forward for us.

"You had to have known I was in the office today, that I was in LA. I've missed you. Why didn't you come and find me?" Relief like I've never known propels my hands up and I cup her cheeks, brushing the tears away as I look down into her beautiful face.

"I was coming to find you, Fifty-five. Tonight. I came home to shower and then head to your place. Work has been crazy this week. I've needed to be with my dad. But I haven't stopped thinking about you. And I *was* coming to you. You beat me to it." Her arms snake around my waist and she lays her head on my chest. Feeling her soft, sexy body pressed against me, giving me hope . . . it all feels so fucking good.

"Reece, I've been so confused." She looks up at me, her eyes wary. "Maybe I still am."

"That's okay. I'm confused, too." I lean down to brush my lips along her hair line, I get whiffs of the notes unique to her; vanilla, flowers, wine and smoke.

Her hands stroke my back and she whispers, "We might feel that for a while, but . . ."

"I'm not confused about two very important things, Luc," I tell her, pushing her away from my body. I miss the heat right away. But, I need her at arm's length so I can look into her eyes when I say this.

"Have you missed me this week? Or did you just want to talk to me to clear the air?" I ask her.

"I've missed you,"

I cup her face. "Do you trust me?"

"Yes. Completely,"

"Then, babe, we can be confused, upset, whatever. But what we can't be, is apart."

She nods, and I see her throat moving. She bites her lower lip, and my teeth feel jealous. I lean in, nip it and pull.

I lick the bruised flesh and press a kiss to her top lip. I start to kiss her again, and she pulls away.

"No, Reece . . ." She steps completely out my hold. She's flushed and a few wisps of her hair are sticking to her neck. Her eyes wide and incredulous.

"I have questions. Don't you have questions for me?" she asks, breathless but serious.

"Yeah, I do," I respond shortly. "But they can wait until I've kissed you." I reach for her. She steps out of my reach. Her eyes wide and serious.

"No. If we start kissing, we won't stop. I really need to finish talking." She crosses her arms, sets her chin and I resign myself to listening.

21

Lucia

REECE SIGHS, PUTS AN ARM AROUND ME AND LEADS ME through to the kitchen. Silently, while I watch, he snags two bottles of wine from his wine fridge. He's obviously impatient. His jaw flexes, and even through the days' worth of growth on his face, I can see the clenching. He's dressed in his shirt and tie. My fingers feel the urge to walk over and loosen it for him. Instead, I go to him and pick up the wine bottles while he grabs two glasses and the opener. He nods for me to follow him. When we reach the doors that lead to his backyard, he lets me step out ahead of him.

I sit down on the collection of chaise lounges he has there.

In perfect, awkward silence, he opens a bottle, and pours us a glass. I take a sip and try to find the courage to speak.

"I want to tell you a story, Reece." I finish the rest of my wine in two gulps and pour myself a second glass. I feel the compounding effect of this glass of wine and the ones from earlier, right away.

I look out into the evening, my eyes trained on the waves without really seeing them.

"When I was five, I fell into a pool at the house of one of my parents' clients and the groundskeeper had to jump in to rescue me. I'd never been so frightened in my life. I ran to my father seeking comfort; wanting him to reassure me I'd be okay. Instead of being distraught that I almost drowned, he was furious that I had wandered off to the pool by myself when he'd explicitly warned me not to. He told me that I'd risked his job." That night, he sat Julian and I down, and gave us the "if you bring attention to us, we'll be deported" speech. I close my eyes and think back to that night.

I remember sitting there, next to Julian, both of us so scared while my father yelled.

"He kept saying that being deported was worse than a death sentence. It was the worst thing that could happen to our family. That he would die before he did anything to expose us to the life he'd left behind."

I've never forgotten the look in my father's eyes as he said those words. He was really afraid. Discovery and deportation were worse than death, was what he taught us. And Julian, who was not afraid of anything, was terrified. He didn't sleep that night. And he never forgot my father's message.

I open my eyes and look at Reece, I want him to know that I mean what I'm about to say. "We all knew that if we drew attention to ourselves, we'd be in danger of deportation or worse. We all knew once he'd been handed over to ICE, that we wouldn't see him again. Detention Center deaths are common. People either die or are deported. Very rarely are they released to live happily ever after with their families. His death wasn't your doing."

"So, all of this activism has been some sort of penance for Julian's death?" I ask, my voice quiet. I'm suddenly bone tired.

He leans forward, staring out at the water. His voice heavy with the conviction of his words. "It was at first. But I've learned so much since I started and now it's a real passion. One I care about fiercely. But yes, this started because I didn't want what happened to him to happen to anyone else. And I don't know what to do with the knowledge that my mistake sent him there. I don't know what to do with the knowledge that he was your brother and it's your story." He sighs. "I finished it, for real this time," he says with a dark smirk. "I'm afraid that you'll never be able to look at me without thinking that I'm the person who ruined your life."

I turn to look at him and our eyes meet. I try to look away, but he grabs my chin and makes me hold his gaze. His eyes are windows to his soul. I can see the turmoil there.

"I know that right now, things seem bad. And there's a lot we've got to figure out, Luc. But none of that comes close to how right the thought of there being an 'us' feels. But you've got to be one hundred percent sure about this because it won't be easy. And if you're feeling angry or resentful about the role I played in what happened to Julian, I need you to be honest with me about it."

"Reece, I first heard your name when I was twelve years old. You'd come home from your final Olympic Games and retired from swimming, gone to work in your family's business and overnight made yourself the public face for the immigration right's cause. I've always thought you were amazing. Having your studio produce a movie based on a book that I wrote, it's all felt like a dream come true. And then I got to know you, I found this instant friend. And that's turned into something as beautiful as it is unexpected. Maybe if you'd still been a stranger when I found out you'd misidentified Julian, I'd have called for your head. But, now . . . you're someone . . ." I cup his face, looking down at him. "Reece, I know you. I trust you."

By saying those words aloud for the first time, I endow myself with a new coat of armor. That knowledge will be the fuel I'll need to get through whatever comes our way. I feel a sense of calm wash over me.

Reece puts his hands lightly onto my shoulders and looks down at me. His rich brown eyes pull me in and my thoughts scatter. I want to finish what I have to say before we go any further, so I step out of his grasp.

"I can't say that I won't look at you and think about Julian, but I don't blame you."

I smile sadly at him. "Reece, you made a mistake. Years ago. Forgive *yourself.*" I feel a need to touch him; I grab his strong, warm hands and squeeze them as I speak. "None of us are perfect. I'm certainly not. I'm damaged in so many ways. But those cracks and breaks? Mistakes I've made? They've strength-ened me." He shakes his head as if to deny the truth of what I'm saying.

"You've managed to turn a tragedy into something good. I know you've changed a lot of people's lives with your legal defense fund. You're amazing."

He cups my face. I close my eyes and press my cheek into his hold.

"You're practically purring." I feel his breath on my mouth and I open my eyes. His lips are an inch away from mine. His hold is firm and when he tilts my head and leans forward, his intent is clear in his eyes. A stream of panic shoots through and I step back.

"I thought . . ." he says as he retreats, confusion in his eyes.

I nod my head vigorously, trying to convince myself as well as him.

"I have more questions. Major ones. And so should you." I place my open palm on his chest, to keep him at arm's length. He grabs my wrist and using his hand like a cuff, holds it in place.

His eyes search mine, and when I swallow, audibly, he lets go of my wrist. He makes a sound in the back of his throat and sits down. "Okay, ask away. Anything."

His sits with his legs spread, arms thrown over the back of the chair. It's an invitation. I want to accept, but I know that if I do, the conversation I want to have won't go any further. So, I pick up my wine glass and start pacing.

"Tell me about Fabienne. Are you really done or is there a possibility you'll reconcile?"

He looks at me like I'm speaking a foreign language

"Come again? Fabienne?" he asks.

"Yes, Reece. The last time I saw you, she interrupted us and she looked at me like I was playing with her favorite toy."

He chuckles, and sounds truly amused. He loosens his tie and unbuttons the top button of his shirt like he's making himself comfortable.

I start to pace again, back and forth between the chaises. My empty wine glass swinging between my fingers.

"It's not funny. I want you to tell me where things are with you. I can overcome a lot, but if you're unresolved when it comes to her, this is a non-starter."

When I'm done with this declaration, I expect him to look

concerned or thoughtful. Instead, he's watching me, smiling broadly, his eyes full of mirth.

It startles me so much that I collide into the chaise that's in front of me. And the next thing I know, the ground is rushing up to meet me. I hear the glass in my hand shatter as it hits the pebble-covered ground and I can't do anything to stop myself from falling straight onto it.

22

SHE FALLS IN SLOW MOTION, BUT I STILL CAN'T DO anything to stop it. The sound of the glass shattering precedes her sharp cry as she lands on top of it. By the time I reach her, she's cradling her hand and I can see blood pouring down her arm, and dripping onto the ground beside her.

I drop to my knees next to her, trying to appear calm, even though panic is surging inside of me. She's struggling to push herself up, using only one arm, but can't get enough of a hold on the chair to do it. I lift her up and place her on the chair so I can take a look at her hand.

My stomach turns and blood runs cold. There is a huge piece of glass sticking out of her palm. She looks down at it, her eyes wide with shock. I touch the arm she's cradling and she winces and looks up at me, her eyes are full of tears and her chin wobbles.

"Luc, does your arm hurt besides the cut?" I ask her gently.

She whimpers in response and I spring into action, running inside to grab a towel from the kitchen.

I sit on the side of her body where she appears least injured. I scoop her into my lap. I want to wrap her hand in the towel, but as I start to, she snatches her hand back and says, "You're pushing the glass deeper."

Shit, I need to get her to the ER. I wrap the towel around her forearm to catch some of the blood that's dripping down and she moans. Her head falls onto my chest and she starts to cry softly.

Hearing my girl, with the heart of a lion, crying makes me move faster.

When I reach my car, I put her down as gingerly as I can and reach over her to buckle her in. "You need to keep your arm elevated while we're driving," I tell her. As soon as I sit down, she reaches out to touch me with her good hand.

I look at her face, her eyes are closed tightly. Her lips are sucked in and I can tell she's trying to keep herself composed. I pull the hem of my T-shirt up and wipe the blood. She licks her lips but doesn't say anything.

"You're going to be fine, Luc," I say to her as I back up and then turn out on the road.

I hold her hand as I drive, keeping my eyes firmly on the road, aware that every bump must be agony for her. She hasn't made a peep since we got in the car. All I can think of is getting her to the ER.

When pulled into the hospital's driveway, I run inside and ask for a wheelchair and help. A man dressed in scrubs follows me back to the car. I lift her out and put her in the chair. "We've got her, sir. You can go and park. I'll take her to the Emergency Room. You can meet us there." I'm confused, and look up at the sign and see that I've brought us to the general entrance. I glance at Lucía; her eyes are still closed. I just nod at him and hop back into my car and go park.

Five minutes later, I find Lucía, in her wheelchair, sitting by herself in the waiting area. There are no other patients waiting and I look around, confused as to why she's been left there.

I walk up to her wheelchair. Her eyes are closed and she's clutching her arm, trying hard to stay sitting up. Her pale face is drawn I can see she's in a lot of pain.

"Luc, I'm here."

She's sweating, and gives a minute nod in response.

"I'll be right back." I brush a kiss on her forehead and stalk to the reception desk. The man sitting behind it doesn't notice me approach. His head is bent and he's doing something on his phone.

"Excuse me," I say trying to keep my tone down and my anger in check. "There's a critically injured woman waiting to be seen and you're busy texting."

He looks up at me. The bored expression on his face almost sends me over the edge.

"Sir, do you need help?" he asks like he clearly doesn't care whether or not I answer.

"Yes. I do. My girlfriend is sitting there in a wheelchair, bleeding. And no one is doing anything to help her," I grit out, so angry I see red.

He his eyes widen in surprise and then he looks around me to survey the waiting room. His eyes come back to me and he looks disinterested again. "Sir, the only person in the waiting room is that woman." He points at Lucía. "Perhaps they've already taken your girlfriend back."

I look at him incredulously.

"That is my girlfriend."

His widen again and then he jumps up. "Oh, I'm sorry, sir. They told me she didn't have any papers and was uninsured when she came in. They must have made a mistake. I'll just go and get her insurance and get her taken back." He stands up and starts to move toward her.

"I have no idea if she has insurance, but why should that matter? You're required to treat everyone equally when they come in regardless of their insured status."

He stops walking, and addresses me. His voice is clipped, his eyes are flashing.

"Sir, there are three other hospitals within a mile of here. When people come in without insurance, if they're not in critical condition, we wait a few minutes to make sure no insured emergencies come in behind them. We're a small ER, if we make insured patients wait, they'll just leave and go try their luck somewhere else."

I stop, stunned. "You cannot be serious."

He stops too, and crosses his arms across his chest. "This hospital's a business. We get *paid* for insured patients, so we prioritize them. If you don't like it, take it up with hospital's management. I'm just doing my job." He starts walking again and reaches Lucía before I do.

"Ma'am do you have insurance?" he's asking her as I reach them.

She doesn't open her eyes, but shakes her head in the negative. He looks back at me.

"Are you going to be financially responsible for her? If so, we'll take her back right now," he says as he starts to wheel her back to the desk.

"Of course I'll be," I say in exasperation. "Just get her a doctor." I can't believe any of this.

"Fine, we just need you to sign the form that assigns you financial responsibility."

He walks behind the desk, pulls out some papers attached to a clipboard and shoves them at me. I fill them and he clacks away on his computer while he talks on the phone. He asks someone to come and get Lucía and put her in a room. I look over to her, she's slumped in her chair. I write faster.

"Is the doctor free to see her now?" I ask him as I push the papers, along with my driver's license, back in his direction. I look down at Lucía again. Her eyes are still closed, but she has sagged a little in her chair.

I turn to find the attendant looking at me. Recognition lights his eyes. He picks up his phone and dials a number, while smiling at me like I'm the fucking Queen of England. He mumbles some code into the phone and then hangs up. "The doctor's actually coming for her himself. She'll be seen to right away. You should have told me who you were."

He bats his eyelashes at me.

I stare at him in disbelief. I want to knock his ass out. Being recognizable is a double-edged sword. Every time something like this happens, it feels like an invasion of privacy. The last thing I need is for him to call TMZ. So, I force a smile and say, "If I'd known it would have made a difference, I would have." He grins and starts to respond when the double doors swing open and out comes a man who looks more like he *plays* a doctor on television than he does like a real one.

"I'm Dr. Maxit, I'll take," he looks at the file in his hand and then looks up, "Lucía, back with me."

He pronounces her name correctly the first time. I don't like the way he's looking at her. Like she's a snack instead of a patient.

"Sure, let's go," I say, and grab the handles of her wheel chair.

"Sorry, sir. But I'll need to take her back with me alone. You're not family, we can't allow it. I'll make sure to send someone out to give you updates if the patient asks us to."

Then *he* grabs the handles of her wheelchair and rolls off. I don't have a chance to say more than "I'll be here," to her as he walks off with her.

I sit there for an hour feeling like I'm losing my mind. I've watched a stream of patients come in. Almost all of them sit and wait before anyone sees to them. None of them insist on being seen right away. Even the woman holding a screaming child with blood all over her clothes doesn't protest when the man at the desk tells her to wait. I don't understand why people aren't more forceful. I've had enough of waiting. Not knowing what's happening to her is torturous.

The reception desk attendant eyes me warily as I approach.

"Can you get me an update on Ms. Vega, please?"

"Of course, Mr. Carras." His response is coy and it grates on my already-frayed nerves. But I manage to smile stiffly. He speaks quietly into his phone and then hangs up. He smiles brightly up at me.

"Good news. She's ready to be discharged. They are getting ready to send her out."

I feel relief wash over me. She's fine. She can go home.

I thank him, my gratitude sincere this time. Ten minutes later, Lucía and Dr. Fuckface walk out. He's laughing. She's smiling up at him, too. As soon she feels my gaze, she looks at me and our eyes meet. Relief and joy war for prominence in her expression. When we reach each other she mumbles, a shy,

"Hi." I take her in. Her left arm is in a sling and her hand has a huge dressing on it. I drop to a crouch so we're face-to-face.

"You okay?" I ask her. She nods, but her eyes tell me everything I need to know. *I've missed you. I need you.*

I reach up and brush her hair back from her face. Her head sways so that her cheek rests in my palm.

"You scared me," I whisper. I feel a slight shudder wrack her body

"I know, I'm sorry. I was scared, too." Her smile is wistful, but her eyes shine as she whispers, "Come closer."

I lean in so we are an inch shy of being nose to nose.

"Closer," she says again. I bring my nose to brush the side of hers. We're so close that our lips are almost touching. My hand combs through her silky hair. I know what's coming; my need and anticipation reach a fever pitch.

She tilts her head and presses her lips to mine. I sigh in relief at the feel of her mouth, soft and pliant as she kisses me . . . quickly, softly. As soon as my lips start to search for more, she pulls back. Like warmth of the sun covered by an errant cloud, the loss of her lips leaves me cold.

"Thank you for taking care of me, Reece," she whispers, still close enough for me to feel her breath on my lips.

"That's not enough," I say gruffly. Almost reflexively, I start to reach out to bring her closer to me. Then, I hear a cough. I'd forgotten Dr. Fuckface was standing there. I stand up slowly to meet his eyes.

He looks amused and returns my gaze easily. "She has a sprain in her right arm, and a deep cut in her palm on the same side. Luckily, no major muscles or arteries were severed. But she needed several layers of stitches. I used dissolvable stitches, so she won't need to come back to have them removed. I've given her a pain reliever, a very strong one, so she might be a little 'high' for a few hours. I've written her a prescription for more, you should stop and get it filled on your way home. Otherwise, she's fine. And she can return to work tomorrow if she feels up to it. She'll have to rest her hand and arm. So, typing is probably out of the question." He glances down at Lucía fondly. "She'll be pretty sore, so try to make her take it easy. I have a feeling that might be difficult."

Why is he acting like he and Lucía are friends? I start to step around her wheelchair. I'm ready to get the hell out of here. "Thanks, I'll take it from here."

He steps aside and moves to stand in front of us.

"I'm sending a nurse to wheel her out and wait while you go and get your car. It's hospital policy."

His smile has a little bit of a challenge, but I'm not sure my mind isn't playing tricks on me. He puts a hand on her shoulder and smiles at her.

"Take care of yourself, Lucía."

"Thank you, Dr. Maxit," she returns

"It's Gael. It was a pleasure to meet you," he says and with a curt nod at me, he walks away as the nurse approaches.

"I'm Sue, Ms. Vega, I'm going to wheel you out." the tall, redheaded woman wearing nurse's scrubs says to Lucía. She grabs the handles of the wheelchair before she addresses me. "Can you go bring your car around, Mr. Carras? I'll wait with the patient in the pick-up lane outside."

I stoop to look at Lucía and give her a reassuring smile before looking at the nurse. "Yeah, sure." I push Lucía's hair out of her face and tell her, "I'll be right back."

When I pull up, I can see the nurse laughing at something Lucía's saying and I'm relieved she feels well enough to speak.

As soon as I stop the car, the nurse opens the door and then helps Lucía out of the chair. By the time I'm around to their side of the car, Lucía's already in the passenger's seat. "Drive safely. She has her discharge instructions." And she starts to turn away.

She stops and then looks back at me, an expression on her face that I recognize. She wants to ask for a picture or an autograph. I don't say anything, but hope her better judgment will win out. It does and she keeps walking.

I lean over her to buckle Lucía in and I want to press a kiss to her mouth as I stand back up, but I don't dare. Not with the way I'm feeling. If I start to kiss her, I might never stop.

We're on the road, heading to her house before I speak.

"So, you and that doctor were friendly," I say to her. Trying to keep my tone light, but I can hear the accusation in it.

"Excuse me?" she says, her affront clear. She jerks her head to the side to look at me.

"I'm just making an observation." But I already feel like fool. How could that be the first thing I say to her after this ordeal.

She sighs but her voice is tender when she speaks. "Reece, what's wrong? Why would you ask a question like that?"

"I'm sorry. I'm tired. A lot has happened in the last few days. It was a stupid thing to say," I grind out. I feel uncomfortable with the feeling of shame that's starting to creep into my conscience. She doesn't say anything and I can feel her watching me.

"You've got me wide open, Lucía. I feel . . . exposed." I almost choke on the word. I hate feeling that way. I hate admitting it even more. "So yeah. I'm jealous of anyone who looks at you. I want to be able to tell him to fuck off because you're my girl." Her eyes widen at that, and I amend my last sentence. "You feel like my girl."

Her eyes grow even wider, and just as she starts to speak, a yawn escapes her mouth and she winces slightly.

I'm such an asshole. She's tired and in a lot of pain. Lack of sleep and stress have made me crazy.

"Shit, Luc. I'm sorry. Let's get you home."

She only nods, but doesn't respond. The car is quiet except for "Hallelujah" by Pentatonix playing on the radio. She starts to sing at the lines

"Maybe there's a God above
All I've ever learned from love
Was how to shoot somebody who outdrew you..."

Her voice is soft and haunting. She hums the chorus and then trails off as the song ends. The next song starts and she reaches for the volume knob on the console and turns the volume down. My hand is on the gear shift and she covers it with her own.

"You shouldn't feel jealous, Reece. I know we've got things to sort out, but what I feel for you isn't something that could be threatened by a good looking ER doctor. I feel like your girl, too."

My heart lightens at her admission. That's a step in the right direction. It's so tempting to keep pushing. To get her to say what I need to hear; to try to just move past this. To pick up where that kiss left off.

I know we can't. I know we have some hurdles to surmount, but this is definitely progress.

Her rich, husky voice breaks the silence that fills the car. "You were great tonight, baby." She's sleepy and her words are a little slurred. She's never called me anything but Reece before and despite what a shitty night it's been, I smile. I join our hands, link our fingers. The thread of the pulse that beats at the base of her palm is in sync with my own. Our connection feels like a live wire; volatile, but strong.

After a few minutes, her voice cuts through the silence in the car. "Thank you for getting them to take me back so fast. I've never been seen to so quickly before. I've gone in with more severe injuries than what I had going on tonight. You know that scar on my side?"

I nod.

"It started as a small scratch from a fence I was climbing. My parents didn't take me to the ER until it got infected. And even then they made as little fuss as possible. By that point, the infection was so bad they had to cut away pieces of skin." She lets go of my hand and rubs the scar through her shirt.

I feel a surge of anger at this. I can't believe anyone is treated like that.

"So, you don't have insurance?" I ask

"Nope. Undocumented immigrants are prevented from participating in the health care exchanges. If I had an employer, I could get it through them, but I'm self-employed," she says tiredly. "Thanks to the book and now the screenplay, I have money to pay for things like this."

We ride in silence for about five minutes before she says, "And tomorrow, when I'm less groggy and hopefully not in so much pain, we're going to finish talking. I want this shit out of the way so I can start kissing you whenever I want to."

I see a smile tugging at the side of her face.

I'm not a praying man, but I say a silent "thank you" as I speed down Melrose Avenue toward Los Feliz.

23

I FEEL LIKE I'VE BEEN HIT BY A GOLF CART REPEATEDLY. I roll over in my bed as yesterday's dramatic ending speeds through my mind like a movie trailer. Scene after scene—me storming over to Reece's house; having it out with him; falling; the hospital; kissing him and coming home—replays through my awakening mind.

The sun is shining in through my window and I know I've overslept. I start to think about all the things I need to get done today. Jess should be gone to the shop already. I'll be saved having to explain my bandaged arm at least until tonight.

I groan as habit has me using both hands to brace myself as

I start to stand up. I can't believe I fell. The hospital bill is going to be expensive. A year ago, that would have felt like a mountain I'd never be able to climb. Today, I know I have enough money in my checking account to pay for what happened yesterday.

It's amazing how having that layer of stress removed makes everything feel a lot easier to handle.

I gingerly feel the ground with my toes, grateful for the luxury of heated floors throughout the house when my feet meet a comfortable, lukewarm floor. I walk over to open the blinds and gaze out at our beautiful backyard. Two squirrels race through the branches of a tree that's in one corner of our yard.

What a luxury it must be to know exactly where you belong. To be doing exactly what you're meant to without anyone trying to stop you.

It's been a few weeks coming, but I feel like it happened overnight. Reece and I are . . . an "us." I'm part of a "we."

All the lights were off when we got here last night. Reece asked to stay, but I said no. I told him I'd talk to Jessica in the morning and let her take care of me. I was exhausted, bruised and just wanted to go to bed. And, I was afraid of what would happen if we're alone together in my bedroom. That kiss, God, it was so good . . . and quick. It had to be, I could feel his lips start to demand more from me. I could feel his hunger. I could feel the potential of what's to come with us.

I am brushing my teeth as I remember what he said to me in the car. Wide open? I feel like his girl? Butterflies erupt in my stomach. How is it possible that Reece Carras feels like that about *me*?

I meant what I said yesterday, I want to get everything out into the open and I want to talk about Fabienne.

I hope we can do this part quickly because I want him so badly. I didn't even know it was possible to need someone's physical presence. Yesterday when they took me back into the exam room and didn't let him come with, I thought I was going to die from missing having him there. By the time they were ready to discharge me, my need to see him was acute.

Relief and happiness overwhelmed me when I saw him as we came out into the ER's lobby. The look on his face said he felt the same way. When he looked at me and asked me if I was okay, I had to kiss him.

I can still feel his lips on my mouth. So wanting, grasping, accepting.

I'm falling for him, fast and hard. There are so many practical things that will make this difficult to figure out. I'd planned on leaving the country as soon as the screenplay was done. My plan was to come back, but it wouldn't be an option for three years from the time I left.

My ability to stay in this country is currently dependent on tenuous and contentious Executive Order. I can't travel beyond its borders—I wouldn't be allowed re-entry. Reece can't whisk me off for a weekend to Cabo or Paris or wherever he's used to vacationing. I can't accept that I'll never have the right to vote in elections that have real consequences for my life. I've never felt more resentful of my status as I do now.

"Enough of this pity party," I say to my reflection before I turn to leave the bathroom.

Gingerly, I make my way to the bed, trying not to jostle my arm. I'm about to pull the comforter back and climb back in when there's a knock on my bedroom door. I figure it's Jess, though she rarely knocks. When I open it, confusion and excitement make me gasp. Reece and Jessica stand there, together and smiling.

"Oh, my little macaron," Jessica says as she pulls me into her arms. She hugs me and strokes my hair and calls me her little beignet over and over while assuring me that she is going to take care of me. I look over her shoulder at Reece, silently asking for an explanation.

He holds my phone up, waving it before he puts it down on the desk in my room, "You left this at my house last night."

Jessica doesn't loosen her hold on me as Reece enters the room. He's never been in here before and I can see him surveying it as he does a broad sweep of the place.

"Jess, I'm okay," I say trying to reassure her. I wrap my arm around her and hug her back. She relaxes her hold and scans me from head to toe. Her face is as expressive as her Botox will allow.

"I'm so glad you have me listed as your In Case of Emergency, my little bonbon. When Reece called this morning, I came up and peeked in on you and saw you were sleeping. And then I went off to the store."

"Thank you, Reece, for caring enough to call me. I can see you already know her well enough to know that she wouldn't ask for help on her own, even if she needed it." She beams at him and squeezes me.

I feel a ball of emotion forming in my throat. This woman is my family. My own may have fallen apart, but I've started to build a new one. One that's based on choice and love. It holds us together with a bond that's thicker than one formed merely by blood could ever be.

I squeeze her back and say a "thank you" that comes out strangled as it works around that ball in my throat.

"Come on, I know you're basically okay, but I'm going to cook some food, do your laundry and make sure you have everything you need while you're here. And you can take some back to Malibu with you." I watch as she grabs my overflowing clothes hamper from my closet.

"I'll take that," Reece says as he lifts it from her arms.

She gives him a grateful smile.

"Now, muffin, I know you're going to try and write and other naughty things you shouldn't be doing. But Reece thought that maybe if you didn't have to do the other stuff you'd actually get some rest when you're not trying to write . . . with one hand." She grins down at me. She gives my shoulder a squeeze and then heads back out the door.

"Reece, come on. Help me unload the groceries out of my car. I've bought the entire grocery store for our girl here," she calls over her shoulder as she leaves.

He smiles at me and follows her out, running his hand gently down my arm as he passes me.

I'm smiling, genuinely, from my very soul for the first time in a very long time. That smile stays in place until I fall asleep that night. I'm loved. I'm seen. I belong to someone who will fight for me.

I thought my heart was permanently broken. I never thought anything would feel good again. But today, between Jessica's love and Reece's protectiveness and desire to take care of me—I feel great. I can feel the jagged tear in my heart start to knit back together.

"You look so much better this morning," Jessica exclaims when I come down for breakfast the next morning. She's smiling broadly as she gives me a hug.

"I feel better," I say as I hug her back. "Thank you for yesterday."

"Of course, *ma chere*. I hope you're hungry," she says smiling as she extends her arm over all of the food she's made for breakfast. There is a mountain of turkey bacon—I can't believe she touched meat for me—and a bowl of fluffy scrambled eggs sitting there waiting to be devoured. A tray of cinnamon rolls covered in a white glaze, still steaming from the oven—its rich, spicy aroma dances under my nose, making my mouth water.

"Jessica, you're going to spoil me. Come. Sit with me." I beckon her with my hands.

I look her in the eye and grab her hands.

"Thank you so much for everything. It's been years since anyone has done anything like this for me. Not since I was a kid. I wanted to say this yesterday, but we were so busy being us . . . talking nonstop and then I fell asleep. So I want to say it right now. Thank you. All the food, clean clothes, all my appointments entered into my calendar." I giggle at the memory of her entering them last night and cursing the tiny buttons on my phone as I dictated things to her. She scowls. "You've got so much work to do and your own life. And you dropped everything to take care of me." I feel a tear escape and run down my cheek.

"Don't cry, my little éclair," she says as she wipes the tear away.

"I'm happy, that's all."

"Lucía." I startle at her use of my name. "I didn't ever think I'd have a family after Thomas died. And I don't want to diminish your biological family, but I love you like I would a sister." She brushes a stray hair off my forehead. "I know you want to do everything yourself. You need to feel like you're the master of your own destiny. I've never wanted to overstep or demand that you let me do more for you. But, I'm glad Reece decided to not ask you before he called me. I'm happy to be able to take care of you, Lucía. It's my honor." She squeezes my hand as she hops down from the stool and walks around to get plates from the cabinet. "You and I are each other's life vest in this crazy city and I know you'd be there for me if I needed it," she says, her back to me.

"Yes. Of course I would." And it's true.

She turns around, plates in hand, a conspiratorial grin on her face.

"And oh my God. Reece Carras is obviously totally fucking in love with you," she says on a delighted whoop.

"Do you think so?" I say fishing for her opinion. It feels too good to be true.

"Umm, Luc. Open your eyes," she crows. "It's absolutely obvious that he is and that you are totally in love with him, too," she says as she piles food onto my plate.

"Neither of you have to say a word, you both practically vibrate when you're in the same room. I mean, I felt like I was in some fucking force field of love," she says, a delighted smile on her face.

"No… we have so much to work out, Jess. I don't want to get my hopes up if things fall apart," I say to her in an agonized tone.

"Get yourself together. You don't *think* about being in love. You can't help being in love. You can't fight it. You're just there whether you want to be or not. And, babe, you couldn't have picked a better man to have that happen with. Because some of us fall in love with total cunts. They cheat on us, and treat us like dirt. And we put up with the crap because we are in love with them. And if the sex is good? Then fuck it, you are totally screwed. Leaving him is almost impossible. Even if he hurts you in between the moments where he makes you feel like you're on top of the world."

She puts my plate of food down in front of me and grabs us forks from the drawer and comes to sit with me again.

"Trust me. Don't waste a moment of time you have with a man like that. He's actually good enough for you, pudding. He's gorgeous, he's rich, he has a conscience and he's crazy about you. He wants to take care of you. Let him. You deserve that, Luc. You don't have to do everything yourself. If you find someone you can share your life with, you don't let stuff get between you."

"I know. We're going to try. But, Jess, I worry about living my entire life looking over my shoulder. . ."

She grabs my hands and gives me a searching look. And then her face softens into a sweet smile.

"I understand, donut. There will be some hard choices to make. But, you should keep your eyes on the prize. You've come so far in the years I've known you. You're this close," she holds up her thumb and index finger, leaving a tiny gap between them, "to having what you want."

She's right. I need to get it straight in my head. Hanging out with them together yesterday was great. I rested on the couch while Jessica cooked and put Reece to work chopping, stirring, straining and just being her general kitchen bitch.

Jessica told us about some weird customers she'd had this week while she filled a dozen Tupperware containers with meals, salads and snacks. Reece talked about getting his first gold medal. He told us that he'd thought about hiring someone to come and do this stuff for me this week. He dismissed that idea almost as soon as he'd had it because he knew I wouldn't be comfortable with a stranger in my house. It felt good to know that he understood me so well.

"Anyway, eat up. I've got to get going. I can leave the store for a day, but more than that, and the place starts to get disorganized. I'll try to come home early. Call your mother." Gosh, she's calling me on all my shit today.

"I will," I mumble. "I'm going to try and do some reading today. Rest my arm. We have our meeting tomorrow and I want to be rested up."

She frowns at me disapprovingly and says, "Tomorrow? So soon? You should take a couple of days. You fell pretty hard. You're lucky it's not worse."

"Jess. Really. The doctor said I could go back to work. I probably look worse than I feel," I protest.

"Okay. But when you're done, home and then rest."

"Sure," I mumble and roll my eyes.

"Don't sound so glum, my little bowl of cassoulet."

I laugh out loud at that one. "Cassoulet? Moved up from desserts to full blown meals, have I? That's what you should have made for me today." I pout playfully. Her cassoulet—a savory bean stew, a French staple—is one of my favorite things to eat in the world. I want to go to France just to eat the different varieties. Especially the ones with sausage in them; she always leaves it out. And it's still one of the most delicious things I've ever tasted.

"My cassoulet takes a full day, my sweet. One day, I'll take you to France and take you to have the best cassoulet in the world. There's a restaurant in Carcassonne . . . ah, how I miss it." She looks up when I don't respond.

I'm smiling, but it's stilted. We both know that that trip will never happen. Her eyes soften with understanding and she smiles brightly.

"Or even better, I'll make it. And I'll even add a little

sausage, just for you," she says and that draws a small smile out of me.

Out of nowhere and suddenly, a pang of longing courses through me.

"Deal." I hop off the stool. "I want to call Reece and say thank you for yesterday. Then I'll eat. I'll only be a minute." I walk back to my room after giving her a quick smile.

His phone goes straight to voicemail. His custom message plays and I'm struck by how deep his voice is. It's all timbre. When he talks to me in person, I always hear a softness in it. At the beep, I leave a message.

"Hi Reece, It's me, Lucía. I just wanted to say thank you so much for everything. For the hospital, for calling Jess, for staying to help her and spend time with me. I hope you're having a great day. I'm going to try and get some work done today, so I'll be home if you want to call me or stop by. Okay. Bye."

I hang up and go back out to the breakfast prepared by my best friend and get ready to do some reading.

I'M half way through my read through of my last session with Dan and Todd when my doorbell rings. I've been working for four hours straight and I'm glad for the distraction. Editing with one hand is frustrating and slow.

I look through the peephole. My mood picks up right away and anticipation makes me feel flushed. It's Reece. I open the door with a wide grin on my face. He smiles back, his eyes warm as he takes me in. I'm tingling all over; I'm hyper-aware of his presence.

"How are you, Luc?" He hands me a brown paper bag and the familiar, spicy aroma makes my mouth water.

"Come in," I say as I peek inside the bag. "Bahn mi?" I ask with excitement. I look at him grinning. "How'd you know?"

"Jessica told me," he says looking proud of himself. Oh, Jess. I should have known.

In the kitchen I unwrap the savory Vietnamese beef sandwich that I love. It feels like Christmas morning. And I'm celebrating it with my favorite person.

"Thank you. How's your dad?" I ask as I try to decide which side of it I'm going to bite first. I can feel him hovering behind me and my back arches a little, trying to subtly close the gap between us.

"He's good. He doesn't want to follow anyone's orders and wants me to sneak him food. He's driving my mom crazy."

We both laugh at the image that creates. He's standing closer to me now and I can smell him, his aftershave has a clean and fresh scent and I wish he would wrap his arms around me. Since that kiss, all the need and longing that's been simmering between us has reached a boiling point. I can't be near him without needing to touch him.

I want to know where things stand with Fabienne. My mind is made up about keeping him at arm's length until that's cleared up.

Reece shifts his stance and I realize I've just been staring at him. He coughs a little uncomfortably. "Listen, I'm not going to stay. I just wanted to bring you lunch and see if you felt up to the meeting tomorrow. If we need to postpone, we can. Just say the word. Everyone will understand."

I jerk my head back at that "No. I'm ready. We've prepared and worked our asses off. I'm bruised and I have stitches in my hand, but I'm not bedridden."

I wrap my sandwich up, no longer interested in eating it.

"That's what you came to ask, right? Well, I'm ready. I don't want to postpone. Was there anything else?"

I tap my foot impatiently.

Reece sighs and rolls his eyes a little.

"Did you just roll your eyes at me?" I ask.

He ignores that question. "I'm not sure why me asking if you'd like to take another day off upsets you so much. Are you taking the painkillers they prescribed? Those can give you mood swings."

I groan at him. "I'm *not* taking painkillers and I'm *not* having a mood swing." I use my good arm to hop up on the kitchen counter. I sit facing him. "This meeting is important and I want to get it over with. I nearly killed Dan and Todd and myself trying to get ready. It's the only thing that's getting me through each day right now. So, I need it to happen." I know I'm just one octave away from sounding like I'm begging, but I don't care. "If we've got to start from scratch or the studio's not thrilled with what we're doing, I'd rather know now."

He walks over to me but stops a few feet away. He's just staring at me, his eyes alight with a predatory gleam as he looks at me from head to toe. He doesn't say anything. But every single nerve ending in my body feels the demand in his gaze. My whole body starts to tingle.

"Reece," I say, my lips feel dry and I lick them.

His eyes narrow at the motion. "I should go, Luc. I can't be here when you're dressed like that. You sitting up there like that. Your T-shirt is practically see through and your nipples are making me crazy. Your shorts are hugging you like they're fucking painted on," he growls as he takes a step toward me.

I look down at myself. My shorts *are* very short. Apparently my "made up" mind has lost control of my body because just as

I think to myself that I should go and change—my legs open, wide. I let him see my denim covered crotch and he takes another step toward me. I can feel my panties getting damp as the need to be touched swamps me.

"Lucía," Reese mumbles, a low warning.

"Yes, Reece?" I trail my hands up my sides and then run my hands over my nipples. They respond to my touch and I feel them stiffen under my palm.

"What're you doing?" he asks me, quietly, his eyes glittering as they follow the path of my hands.

"I don't know," I say honestly. I am just letting my body do what it will. I want him to look at me. I need him to see me.

He steps between my open thighs.

"Lucía, I'm going leave. I have a meeting and then I need to spend tonight preparing for tomorrow." But as he says this, his hand trails down the center of my chest, and spreads out over my abdomen. His touch is like a brand, even as he lifts it from my body, I still feel it.

My breath hitches, as the tips of his fingers brush the underside of my breasts. His eyes never leave mine. He looks like he wants to eat me alive. I lick my lips and his eyes dart there and then back to my eyes.

"I want to get through that meeting tomorrow and then I want us to figure out what we're doing about . . . us."

He whispers the last word, he unbuttons my shorts and slips a hand inside. I watch his eyes narrow just as his fingers breach my underwear and he feels how wet I am. He trails the pads of his middle and index finger across the lips of my pussy and I tilt my hips forward to increase the pressure. It's an instinct because like sheets of loose leaf paper in a stiff breeze, my wits have scattered. All that remains is how this feels.

"So sweet. I want to fuck you. So badly." He brings his

mouth close to mine so that as he speaks our lips brush. "I can't think straight."

I spread my legs even farther and he slips one of his big fingers inside me. The sensation of his finger filling me is unreal. I didn't know anything could feel so good. My muscles contract gripping his finger tightly. I whimper and lean back as he starts to pump in and out of me. He drops his head and bites my nipple through my T-shirt.

My arms are around his shoulders and my ass slides on the counter with every thrust of his finger and when he presses his thumb to my clit, I scream.

He starts to rub me and sucks my nipple hard before he brings his face back up to mine and brings our lips to almost touching again.

He adds another finger and slows down his thumb's assault. I feel the spark of an orgasm starting to build somewhere inside of me.

"I can feel you, baby. Your cunt is squeezing my fingers. God, I wish it was my cock," Reece mumbles against my mouth, our gazes still locked.

I feel helpless and ravaged. His fingers' manipulation of my body takes me from breathing hard to moaning to whimpering to shuddering as my orgasm rolls over me.

Reece watches me, mumbling against my mouth, the heat of his breath mingling with mine every time I open my mouth to release a sound. It's like he's feasting on my pleasure, absorbing my need.

He pulls his fingers out of me. He trails them over his lips, and then kisses me lightly.

Reece lifts me off the counter and onto my feet. I'm disoriented and so completely aroused that it takes me a moment to register that he's leaving. I just blink up at him, trying to get my bearings.

He licks his lips. A slow smile spreading when he sees the flush of heat spread all over my body.

"I'm going to leave now. Make sure you bring your A-game tomorrow, Fifty-five." And then, he's gone.

Just as I'm settling down to read again, I pick up my phone and send Reece a text.

Stop calling me that.

24

Reece

"SO, WHAT'S THE VERDICT?" I ASK THE HEADS OF MY various departments after Lucía and her team have left. They just finished pitching their script, presenting their story and giving updates on their timeline. I think they knocked it out of the park. They're seventy percent done with the screenplay and anticipate that they'll completely finish in less than three weeks. The story arc is fantastic. They've brought the book to life but they've added to it and trimmed it to make the story one that can be told well in one hundred and twenty minutes.

I face my team and feel a rush of nerves that I haven't experienced in years. I'm asking them to green light a screenplay. To give it a budget, build a crew, and start casting. It's a big ask because of the nature of the project and the timing; it's earlier in the production process than we normally make decisions like this. I asked them to consider it now so that if there are problems, we'll have time to fix them without throwing off the project's timelines. This is the moment of truth. I know they'll be fair, but just as tough on me as I am on them. I'm not an asshole, but I am anal retentive when it comes to the decision to greenlight.

Sophie, my Head of Casting speaks first. She is the most opinionated member of our team and has been pissed with me since she found out that she'd have to give Lucía the right of refusal on casting. So, I expect her criticism to be stronger than the others.

"I honestly can't believe I'm saying this, but I already have actresses in mind to play Azalia and Julio. She's making great progress, and listening to them go over the script today makes me want to read the book."

"Is this *Invasion of the Body Snatchers*?" quips Zev. "Who are you and what've you done with Sophie?" The rest of the team, including Sophie, laugh good-naturedly.

My marketing director, Joshua says, "You've got to convince her to do some promo. We won't find an actress or actor who can sell the characters the way she does. You'd think she knew these people instead of having conjured them from her imagination."

I smile at him. "I'm going to work on her. She's reluctant to do it, but I think she might be convinced."

He nods at me and says, "Then, I don't have any qualms about giving her the go ahead now. Let's find a director and get casting going."

I look at the rest of the team and they all nod in agreement. And just like that, it's happening.

When our meeting is over and everyone is gone, I stick my head out to ask Liza to get Lucía on the phone.

"Okay, but I think they left the office. I heard them saying something about heading back to Los Feliz?" Thank goodness for my nosey eavesdropping PA. "Do you want to have them come back?" It's almost five in the afternoon. Rush hour traffic is a nightmare and Lucía looked tired towards the end of the meeting.

"No, don't worry. I'm going to go check on my dad and then head home." *Or to Lucía's*, says the devil on my shoulder.

"Tell your folks hi. And give your dad a hug for me. I've been praying for him." I promise to pass on her message. My parents are well liked across the company. My dad's hospital room was so full of flowers that it took two carts to get them out.

When I leave my office, I head to Beverly Hills to see my parents. I want to spend time with Dad, but now I can't wait to get to Los Feliz, give Lucía the good news and celebrate with her.

BY THE TIME I leave my parents, I am in desperate need of a long hard swim and a session of yoga.

My dad is being stubborn and won't stay in bed. My mother is frazzled. I've never seen her like this. She's snapping at everyone, except my dad. When she screamed at me for chewing too loudly, I knew it was time to go. My dad's going to be fine. He needs to take some medication and watch his diet, but otherwise, he's in really good shape.

It was a minor heart attack. But, my mom is acting like he had a quadruple bypass and brain surgery. You'd think she'd been told he was dying. And as crazy as she's making me, I like seeing this side of her. Generally, she's not a warm person. Although I know that she loves my dad and that she loves me, she's very pragmatic and doesn't let love get in the way of what needs to be done or what needs to be said.

There are times when I've wished she was warmer. But she's one of the most amazing women I know. She's the real star in our family. The brains behind the entire operation. Our family is well regarded, widely respected and influential. She's built that and she protects it fiercely.

My dad doesn't care about these sorts of things, but her family is even older Hollywood than his. They founded this town. She believes that marriages should be alliances. And that children should be raised to take over the family dynasty. Appearances are important and must be kept up at all costs.

Seeing her go without her precious beauty sleep, miss meals and workouts and allow herself to be seen in less than full makeup has been a revelation.

The only person not surprised by my mother's behavior is my father. He only smiled and said, "She loves me," when I mentioned her transformation.

My father is the exact opposite of my mother, but he's encouraged her to be who she is. He's reveled in her career accomplishments. Her ambition is one of the things he loves most about her. So, while everyone else sees her as a stone-cold executive with no heart, my dad sees the woman he loves daring to be as great as she's capable of.

He just loves her. She's given him everything he's ever wanted; a partner and a son. And they haven't tried to change each other. That kind of unconditional love gives you wings, and that's why they both fly so high.

The prospect of losing the person you share that kind of

love with . . . it shakes you. And my mother has come undone. I hate that my dad had this health scare, but I feel like I've really gotten to know my mother in the last few days. I see how she and I are similar. People think I'm cold, pragmatic, calculating, too. But, when I care about something, or someone, I don't hold back. And the way I feel about Lucía, is a full body experience. All of my senses are engaged and I feel completely in tune with her.

During the meeting, I watched her, so poised, so prepared, and in control. She completely mastered her presentation. I hope that as she reaches for her dreams, she'll always be the bold, fearless, unstoppable woman she was today.

I want to be the only one that gets to see her completely undone. I remember how she fucked herself on my fingers. How she screamed when she came. That's how I always want her when we're alone. Moaning, coming, begging. Fuck if the past, the unchangeable past, is going to stop me from being with her.

I pull up to her house and as soon as I step out of my car, I can hear the music playing in the backyard. It's a crooning Bob Marley, telling me not to worry about a thing. Yeah, Bob, easier said than done.

I ring the doorbell and Jessica comes to the door.

"Reece, hey!" she shouts, her blue eyes huge, her blond hair moving with the rest of her as she leans out to grab my arm and yank me inside.

"We're out on the deck, cooking and having a drink. Lucía said the meeting went really well," she says over her shoulder as she walks back down the hallway that leads to her kitchen and then out onto their deck. The music is loud. They've got the remains of a meal they obviously enjoyed scattered all over the table. Several empty bottles of wine, the sight of Todd bent in half laughing, Dan and Lucía dancing along to the music.

Lucía spins around in the middle of her dance and stops abruptly when she sees me. Her laughter dies on a gasp of delight, her eyes widening and dancing happily. Her expression settles the disquiet in my mind. Yes, we've got hurdles to clear. But, when I look at her, all I see is a walking embodiment of every single one of my dreams.

"Hey, Reece. What're you doing here?" says Todd turning the music down, but still moving to beat. Dan motions for me to have a seat, and so I do. I smile at them, glad to share some good news.

"I thought I'd come and tell you in person that you guys have been green lighted. You killed your presentation today."

They all start shouting at once. Jess runs into the house screaming, "Hold on!" over her shoulder. Lucía, Todd and Dale form a group and hug for a long time. To see them sharing this moment as comrades in arms is gratifying when I recall what a discordant start they had.

Jessica comes running back out with a bottle of very good champagne in her hand. "Let's celebrate!" The pop of the champagne cork is followed by a chorus of cheers from the triumphant trio.

Lots of screenplays are written. Very few of them are actually green lighted for production. This is a big deal. But I'm feeling like I'm interrupting. I hadn't expected her to have company and I decide I should just call it a night.

"I'm happy for you guys. I just wanted to come and tell you in person. I'll let you get back to your evening." I say as I stand and turn to leave.

"Reece, wait, stay. Please. We have more food and we're

going to be up for a while." This is from Jessica who looks like she probably drank more than she ate. She's very close to wasted. Dale and Todd are a little better off. Lucía in contrast, is completely clear eyed as she looks at me from across the room.

She approaches me from the edge of the deck where she'd been standing. The well-lit deck makes her look like she's glowing against the backdrop of the twilight's violet-hued sky. She's wearing all black—a pair of slacks and button-down blouse. She didn't offer even a glimpse of skin today. Her bandaged hand was the only indication that she'd been rushed to the ER just a few nights before. She'd come dressed to meet with executives. Now, I want to strip her and put my mouth on every inch of her body, and then make love to her.

Her smile becomes suggestive as if she has just read my thoughts. She puts her hand on mine and says in a soft voice that makes my dick wake up. "Yeah, Reece, stay. I want to talk to you anyway. Come into the house with me." And then she walks inside without looking back.

I follow her in with a wave to Jess and the guys. The three of them return the gesture, all wearing knowing grins.

I find her in the living room. The wall that separates it from the kitchen makes it so we're totally out of the view of the group outside.

"Answer my question," she says as soon as I step into the room.

"What question?" Confused.

"Do you still have feelings for Fabienne? Are you guys going to get back together?"

I remember that she was asking me these questions when she fell. I'd totally forgotten that this was actually a concern of hers.

"What would give you the impression that I'm reuniting with my ex-wife?" I'm incredulous.

"Reece, she showed up at the guesthouse like her dropping by unannounced was normal. And she looked angry when she saw us together." She crosses her arm and winces slightly and uncrosses them.

"Whoa. First, Fabi and I are very much broken up. I haven't seen her again since that morning. I only gave her a ride to the offices so that I could have someone take her back to her car and make sure she really left the estate. We've also changed the code at the gate. Does any of that sound like we're going to reconcile?" I don't know why this question exasperates me so much, but it does.

"Okay," she says. She walks toward me slowly like she's not sure whether or not it's safe to approach.

"I was just asking. I needed know," she says as she continues to approach me.

As soon as she's close enough I extend my arm and grab her waist and pull her toward me. She comes willingly. When our bodies connect she nestles into me. I'm hard and she can feel it.

"Is that all you need to know, Lucía?" I say cautiously.

"No. But that was the only one that couldn't wait." She leans her head off my chest and gazes up at me. "If you had feelings for someone else, then there would have been no hope." She closes her eyes, takes a deep breath, as if she's gathering her courage.

I can feel her wanting to ask more, I decide to pre-empt her. "We were married a long time. But, we were too young when we got together. Our life experiences were so narrow. We both thought we could build a marriage out of a hot weekend hookup." I roll my eyes as I remember how stupid we were.

"It was drama, all the time. I wasn't a great husband. I

wasn't unfaithful, but I thought about it. And I didn't love her. Our divorce was messy only because she's messy. She's only sniffing back this way because her professional football playing boyfriend was just injured and is probably going to lose his contract. She's looking for a way to keep herself in the news. Don't take anything she does or says seriously. Some fool with more money than sense will scoop her up soon and she'll go away. Really. That's over."

Her eyes fly up to mine. "Really?" Her husky voice resonant with her emotions.

"Do you trust me?" I repeat the question I asked her last night.

Her eyes fly open and she looks up at me and says, "Of course I do."

I smile down at her. "You'll never regret giving that to me."

She smiles back.

"Let's promise to be honest with each other. You can tell me anything and it won't change the way I feel about you." She makes all of this feel so effortless.

"Promise," I murmur against her temple. I run my nose down the side of her hairline, and I inhale. I feel our energy— all need and impatience—moving between us like a rope. With each pass, it binds us closer to each other.

Her hair smells like peaches and it reminds me of how her pussy tasted after I fingered her the other day. I kiss the top of her ear, and her head falls onto my chest, her stomach forms a cushion for my hard cock, her hard nipples rubbing my torso through the thin cotton of her blouse.

"You're mine," I whisper.

She lets her head lilt backward, her eyes still closed. Her full lips are devoid of lipstick, they're pink and soft and I can't stop myself from bending down and sinking my teeth into the bottom one. She hisses, but doesn't pull back. I release her lip and say, "To hurt." And then lick the sting away. "And to heal." She moans. I put my hands into her hair, and thread my fingers through the feather soft, thick mane. She looks up at me, her eyes are glazed but focused on me.

"I'm yours, Reece, and you are mine."

25

If this is a dream, I don't ever want to wake up.

"I see you, Lucía. The scarred places. And the beautiful parts." He pauses and shakes his head. He threads his fingers into my hair and my entire body erupts with gooseflesh. His eyes come to mine and I know that I'm ready for this. "You've seen me at my worst, too." He tightens his grip on my hair and he leans down so his lips brush mine. They are cool, dry and when he pulls back I gasp at the sensation of loss that overwhelms me. "This connection. This feeling. It feels like a blessing and curse. I need you so much, it frightens me."

He's right. We're each other's strength and weakness, intertwined and indistinguishable. He is my undoing, this man. The thought of being laid bare in front of him emboldens me. I've never known this kind of connection. It's visceral and charged. It's freeing.

My hands come up to his face and I brush back the lock of dark hair that's fallen over his eyes.

The wild and untamed attraction that's been running between us has only been intensified by the friendship we've formed over the last couple of months.

I've made my choice. I want to be with him.

We may drag each other to hell and back before we resolve all the shit that life has thrown between us, but I know that what's on the other side of all of that is so beautiful, it will be worth the flames. "Come with me," I whisper. He nods.

The walk up the stairs feels like it takes forever. I'm very aware of Reece's body behind me. I know what I'm taking him to my room for and yet, I can't believe this is actually going to happen.

As soon as the door is closed, Reece picks me up. My legs wrap around his waist, my arms go around his neck. "Is your arm okay?" he asks me suddenly.

"Yes, it's a little sore, but it's fine," I respond quickly.

His mouth is on mine an instant later. The kiss is slow, open-mouthed and deep. Reese's hand slips through my hair and trails to cup my neck. He takes a step so that my back is against the door. Our kiss goes from intense to all-consuming. He sucks my lips and nips my chin. He's pins me to the door and holds me there using only the strength of his legs and hips. One hand remains fisted in the hair at the nape of my neck. The other is fast at work on the buttons that line the front of my blouse. I hear several of them pop off and land on the floor. As soon he bares my chest, he dips his head and takes my nipple into his mouth through the lace of my bra. He sucks it hard, his teeth nipping me at the same time. Sparks of tension fire off between my legs.

My head falls back and hits the door as I moan. I rub myself against him. He lifts his head from my breast and steps back so that I'm no longer on the wall. He walks over to my bed and puts me onto my back. He pulls off his tie and shirt. And then undoes his pants and lets them fall. He's wearing boxer briefs and he's so erect that the tip of his cock is peaking out of the waistband.

I watch him and admire that body, so beautifully crafted by his time in the pool and the gym. My eyes feast on the hollows and swells created by the muscles of his chest. He reaches for me and pulls my pants down and off, and my panties fly off right after them. He kneels onto the mattress, right between my legs. The hunger in his eyes sets my heart galloping. His strong hands roam over my body, squeezing, caressing, rubbing me into a puddle of senseless need. His thumbs brush my nipples, as he drags his hand down my torso and in between my legs.

When his hand covers my pussy, I move my pelvis so that the heel of his palm presses on my clit. I whimper at the delicious sensation and I watch his hand as it moves in rhythm with my hips. I move them even faster.

"Yeah, baby, show me. You don't have to hide with me," he says. His eyes are hooded, yet I can see the possessiveness in them. Even in the shadows cast by the setting sun as it streams through my window, I can see the flush on his cheeks as he watches me unravel at his touch.

I bring my hands up to cup my breasts in offering. I squeeze them and moan at the sensation it creates. He leans over and licks the tip of each one, back and forth while his hand continues to create delicious friction on my pussy. I can feel his fingers growing wet from touching me and my un-bandaged hand reaches between us and slips into his boxer briefs. I circle the head with my hand, it's already slick with pre-cum and I spread it over him as I start to stroke him.

He slips out of my grip as he grabs my waist and lifts me over him. He lies back on the bed and says, "I've been dreaming of this since the first time I saw you in a skirt. Climb up here and sit that pretty pussy on my face." He doesn't wait for me to comply, but hooks his hands under my thighs and lifts me until I'm straddling his mouth. And then he leans up and takes a long lick.

"Reece." I call his name. It's a plea. I need more.

"Yeah, baby. I've got you." And then he pulls me to him. I feel his tongue, lips and teeth start to feast on me. I reach behind me with my uninjured hand and start to stroke him. His cock is hot, hard and the skin feels like velvet. His hips pump into my hand and I can feel the rush of blood as he grows even harder in my hand. I try to keep a steady rhythm, but when he pulls my clit into his mouth and starts to suck, I can't sit up anymore. I fall forward over him. He flips me onto my back without breaking the wicked motion of his mouth. He takes two fingers and starts to stroke me and fuck me with them. And, that's all it takes to send me over. I come so hard I can't control the shout of pleasure it elicits. I try to pull away, moving my overly sensitive parts from his eager mouth. His hands grip the back of my thighs and he pulls me back to him.

"Again. I haven't had enough." And he eats me, making his tongue the only thing I'm aware of. I beg him to stop after my next orgasm crashes over me. I can't take it anymore. And I want him, my body needs him, inside.

He crawls up my body, kissing his way until we are hip to hip. When he kisses my mouth, I taste myself on his lips and I don't think I've ever felt closer to another human being as I do to him right now.

He rolls us over so he's underneath me. His strong, long arms circle me, pulling me so close it feels like we're conjoined. I rest my head on his chest and the beating of his heart drowns out the ambient noises of the neighborhood that seeps in through my partially open window. He runs his fingers up and down my spine. "You should try to sleep; it's been a long day."

I lift my head up in surprise and look at him. "Wait, we're done? You didn't finish . . ." I roll my hips so that his still erect cock glides in between the lips of my pussy.

"Oh, Luc." He chuckles softly. "I'll never be finished with you. But when I fuck you for the first time, I want you in my bed. You're driving back to Malibu early, right? You've got a long day and that arm of yours has a few more days of rest due."

I groan as I remember everything that's waiting for me tomorrow. He rolls us so that we are lying side by side. He kisses me softly, and pushes the hair out of my face. He smiles roguishly. "I also need to go and stock up on condoms and lube because I'm a greedy bastard and I want to put my cock in every single part of you . . . your mouth, your pussy." His hand runs down my back. "I want to fuck your tits and your ass." He squeezes the ass he just spoke of and I shiver in anticipation. Not just from his words, but from the intensity in his eyes as they land on mine. They demand that I don't look away.

His smile disappears.

"I'm going to take everything, Lucía. I'm going to fucking wreck you. But I'm going to give you everything I've got, too. Everything."

I nod and wrap my arm around his waist. I look at him and let him see the excitement, fear, power and love that I'm feeling. "Fuck, yeah."

26

Reece

Lucía's looking at me like there's an alien standing on her doorstep. I just drove down to Malibu after spending a whole week in Los Angeles. We've been talking every day, but my dad is still recuperating. Today, I've cleared my calendar. I decided to drive down early and wake her up.

She's flushed and rumpled from her sleep. Her thick, chocolate colored hair is tousled. She's rubbing the sleep out her eyes as she squints up at me.

She's wearing a T-shirt that hits her right above her belly button. Her tiny shorts might as well be panties. She's not wearing a bra and her nipples are hard underneath the strained, worn cotton of her T-shirt. They're begging for my mouth.

"Good morning, sleeping beauty," I stop to brush a kiss on the top of her head as I walk in through the door she's holding open for me. She hugs me, but I give her a wide berth so she doesn't feel how stiff my dick is. Then we'll never get anything done.

"Uh, morning, Reece," she says as she closes the door and follows me out onto her back deck.

"Yoga lesson, right?" I say casually. She's standing there, blinking like a baby owl opening its eyes for the first time. She called me yesterday and I called her back, but kept it brief. I could tell she wanted to talk, but I was really focused on my to-do list so that I could enjoy today.

"Are you okay? Why are you blinking like that?"

Her frown turns to a smile. "Because, I'm tired, Reece," she says through a yawn. She stretches, and takes a deep breath, "But I'm so glad we're still doing this. I've missed us having this time together." She looks up at me through her lashes, and a small, but happy smile adorns her face.

"I've missed it, too. The last lesson was a swimming one, so today we can do some yoga. You can't use your arm properly, so you can show me stuff that doesn't focus on them for support." I walk over to the closet where our mats are stored and pull them out. "Go get dressed… unless you're going to do yoga in those clothes."

She flushes, and tucks a stray hair behind her ear. "Okay, I'll be right back." And then she starts to walks fast back into the house. "You need some help?" I ask her.

"No," she snaps.

I'm chuckling as I watch her walk away, enjoying the sway in her hips. I have a plan for the day, and I want today to be perfect. I want to spoil her, let her relax and have a day of being together. And then tonight, I'm going to fuck her.

"Okay, I'm ready." She walks back out and sits down on the mat I've rolled out next to mine. She's wearing tight, multicolored yoga pants and a little sports bra. And that's it. Her breasts are restrained, but just barely. The bra has these cords of fabric up the side and she's got so much skin exposed to me that I'm tempted to suggest that we scrap yoga and just go back to bed.

"While I was changing, I was thinking. . .I can teach you one of the meditations I do to clear my mind and help me focus. I actually made it up, so it's not proven on anyone other than me. You can modify it if you want, but at least you'll have the basics down and be able to get a feel for meditation principles. And it will give my arm and hand a break." She waves her bandaged arm.

"Does it hurt a lot?" I ask, restraining the urge to touch it.

She looks at it and sighs.

"Not like it did the night it happened. I've been keeping it elevated when I sleep so the swelling has gone down a lot. The stitches are dissolving." She holds up her hand I can see the line of stitching in her palm.

"Okay, looks good."

She looks straight ahead and stands up, putting her palms together in the first position of the Sun Salutations, signaling that the conversation is over.

I chuckle and follow her lead.

Once we're done, and she's still in her final pose, I ask a question I've been holding onto since she told me what we were doing for our lesson today.

"Meditation? Is that part of yoga?" Her eyes pop open as if she didn't realize I was there. She shakes her head as if to clear it before she answers. "Sorry, I was already a little lost. And yes, it's essential. At least to my practice of yoga. Meditation doesn't mean just closing your eyes and not thinking. It can also be a time where you spend reinforcing your mind with positive thoughts and things that you want to influence your mood. I've actually made up my own meditation mantras. I took the first four stanzas in Kipling's *"If."*

"I read that in high school," I scan my memory for fragments of the poem that are floating in my memory. "If you can dream—and not make dreams your master; If you can think—and not make thoughts your aim." I recite the one line I can remember and Lucía looks at me with pleasant surprise.

"You know it? That's great," she exclaims and claps her hands together.

"Wow, you're easily impressed," I joke.

She slaps me across the arm. "It's my favorite poem, Reece." She rolls her eyes toward the top of her head, but this time in a look that says, *I'm heaven* rather than in annoyance. "It's *the* perfect advice on how to be happy. Don't give up. Work hard. Stay humble, be honest. For my meditations, I've broken it up into stanzas and then use each stanza as I need it."

"Which one do we need, today?" I ask. She tilts her head to the side, and taps her finger on her lips as she thinks.

"If you can dream—and not make dreams your master; If you can think—and not make thoughts your aim; If you can meet with Triumph and Disaster and treat those two impostors just the same; If you can bear to hear the truth you've spoken twisted by knaves to make a trap for fools, or watch the things you gave your life to, broken, and stoop and build 'em up with worn-out tools; If you can make one heap of all your winnings and risk it on one turn of pitch-and-toss, and lose, and start again at your beginnings, and never breathe a word about your loss; If you can force your heart and nerve and sinew to serve your turn long after they are gone, and so hold on

when there is nothing in you except the Will which says to them: 'Hold on!'

"That's two stanzas, Vega. You said one," I say with mock disapproval.

"We need those two today, Carras," she returns, creasing her forehead to mimic my expression. "We've got a lot of negative energy to dispel," she returns with a smile. "I'll say the stanza out loud once and then I repeat it slowly, really focusing on the words. I do this for twenty minutes and allow the words to help me focus and shut out the other noise in my head."

"Okay," I mumble, letting my skepticism show.

"Look, just try it. Clear your mind, think the stanzas and just be alone with them for twenty minutes. Forget I'm here. Forget you're here," she demands before she closes her eyes and starts to say the stanza to herself.

I mimic her. And I allow myself to focus on the words.

"REECE! REECE!" I hear Lucía calling my name, but she sounds so far away. And then I feel a rough shake on my shoulder and I jolt. I look up and Lucía's kneeling in front of me. Her face scrunched in concern as she scans my face. "Are you okay? I've been calling your name for almost a full minute."

The haze starts to lift, my awareness returns. I'm on her deck. We're doing yoga. I'm confused by the minutes I appear to have lost. "Did I black out?" I ask her.

"No. You were meditating. Wow. Good job, Reece. I'm so glad you took it seriously." She smiles as she stands up.

"Yeah, Luc. I got stuck on the words 'If you can meet with Triumph and Disaster and treat those two impostors just the same;' I said those over and over again for twenty minutes."

"That's a tough one for us all. It's hard to not get caught up in success and discouraged by failure. I struggle to remind myself, that they can be as valuable as each other."

As much as I want to have this philosophical discussion, I also want to get going with my plans for the day.

I grab her waist and pull her down beside me. "Yes, I mean, just look at us. Tragedy has brought us together. It's all what you do with it." She smiles, but doesn't say anything as she stares out at the horizon.

"Listen, can we spend the day together?" I ask her.

She turns to look at me and *that* smile breaks across her face. It warms me like the sun melting away frost.

"Yes. I'd love that. I'll let Todd and Dan know I need the day off."

I'm surprised by how quickly she agrees. I don't hide my surprise, and she smiles. "That's an easy ask, Reece. I'd love to spend the day with you." She strokes my cheek with the pads of her fingers. I lean toward her involuntarily. My hand trails down the side of her face. I'd only have to lean in a little, and if she met me half way, I could have my lips on hers. I want to kiss her and then fuck her so hard that we break shit. I want to spend all day eating her pussy and sucking her nipples while I'm balls deep inside of her.

She leans back. "What are you thinking, Reece?" she asks, eyes wide with alarm.

I grin at the look on her face. "What does it look like I'm thinking about?"

"I don't know, but you look like you're about to jump me. And, in a 'not so friendly' way," she says and leans even farther away from me. "You look like you want to eat me alive."

I laugh, a long, loud burst that catches me by surprise. She is so fucking innocent.

"I am hungry," I say sliding my hands down her arms and pulling her into me. She pulls away and heads toward the house and says without turning back, "Well, if you're hungry, I've got some of those cinnamon rolls that Jess made in the freezer. Let's warm them up." I laugh and follow her into the house. I'll let her go for now.

We've got a lot of shit to talk about, but once that's done, I'm done fucking around. I'm taking her tonight. She's ready and so am I.

27

Lucia

IT'S A PERFECT DAY. THE KIND WHERE IF SOMEONE offered to grant me a wish, I'd have a hard time thinking of one that would make it any better. Reece and I are in his car, top down, speeding down the Pacific Coast Highway. I have a scarf tied around my head to keep my hair from blowing. But caught up in the exhilaration of the moment, I reach under my chin and untie it. I laugh in delight as my hair blows wildly around me.

The noon sun is shining, and it's an unusually warm day for the end of October. But there's a nice breeze and it feels great. It's dry, but there's moisture that makes it feel like a sweet caress.

After breakfast, he went home to change and told me to be ready in an hour and to wear something a little nicer than casual. He said we were going to lunch at Spago in Beverly Hills; and then he had a surprise for me. I protested when he suggested that restaurant. He just waved me off and said, "It's easy to get a table and the food is great. And it's on the way to where we're going."

It's also very public. Just the kind of place I'd avoid since my book took off. Reece is a paparazzi magnet. I'm not an expert, but I've heard Jess reading from the celebrity gossip and me hearing, *seen coming out of Spago*. I'm worried that if we go to Spago, someone will take a picture of us together. People will start asking, right away, who I am; where I came from.

When I gave voice to that concern, Reece had said, "Why should you be afraid of that? Own it, Lucía. You need to stop hiding. You have the right to be here. You have a valid work permit and you're a law-abiding person. Besides, Spago is discreet. It'll be fine."

As we turn off the 405 and onto Wilshire Boulevard, he hits a button on his dashboard that starts to put his top back up. "We're almost there, not much privacy on Wilshire, even at this end of it." He grabs my hand. His fingers twine with mine and remain that way as we make our way up this iconic stretch of road.

We're passing through the greenest strip of Wilshire when Reece's phone rings. His car's dashboard announces that "Graham" is calling. He touches a button on his steering wheel and a booming voice replaces the music we were listening to.

"Yo, R. Are you in LA?"

"Yup," Reece responds.

"And you didn't even let your bros know you were coming?

You've disappeared to that house in *fucking* Malibu. You've left O, D, and me to handle all these thirsty hoes on our own."

I can't stop the gasp that comes out of my mouth.

"Graham, you're so dramatic, man. I'm in LA, but only for today and I'm with my lady, so watch your mouth."

"Oh, shit," Graham drawls. He has a deep, very strong Southern accent. God, it's sexy. And I know who he is because *everyone* knows who Graham Davis is. He's a very sought after personal trainer. He has his own TV show where he helps people lose weight. He's got a line of workout clothes, diet supplements and his own line of sports drinks. He's also a notorious womanizer and a professional bad boy. Jess has a picture of him on the wall of her pottery studio. She calls him her muse.

"Excuse me, Reece's lady. If I'd known you were in the car, I would have tried to sound like I have some manners," he says and I look at Reece, not saying anything.

"Graham, shut up. And you could always come to Malibu if you miss me," he says.

Graham scoffs, "Yeah, right. Meet us for dinner tonight. I'll text you the details and you better be there. Don't say no. I'm hanging up." Then the line goes dead. I turn to him, excited by having been in a car where Graham fucking Davis was just talking.

"Sorry about that. We don't have to go to dinner," he says apologetically.

"Are you crazy? Of course we have to go to dinner. Can I invite Jessica?"

"You want to go to dinner? I thought you'd want to go home early."

"Why would you think that?" I ask him, perplexed. "I'm having the best day."

He smiles, but it doesn't quite reach his eyes. "Yeah, sure. We can stay in LA for dinner."

He pulls past Soul Cycle in Beverly Hills and I see all the women sweating their asses off and I remember that I promised myself to add some sort of cardio to my workouts. I've been eating all the food Jessica cooked for me. ALL of it. My half-assed yoga isn't going to cut it.

And then he's turning onto North Canon and we're at the restaurant.

The valets come and open each of our doors and only then does Reece let go of my hand. As soon as we're standing together, he grabs hold of it again. "I promise Graham is much nicer than that phone call might lead you to believe. Omar and Dave will be there, too, so yeah invite Jessica if you want." As soon as we enter the restaurant, a young man, dressed in a suit and tie says, "Welcome, Mr. Carras, Ms. Vega. Your table is ready. Please, follow me."

I turn to Reece and whisper, "You must come here a lot. They're acting like you're royalty or something." He chuckles. "Yeah, my dad loves it here. Since I was a kid, this has been our spot. When I'm in LA, my parents and I meet here for lunch almost every day. It's convenient, great food and they're more discreet than a lot of other places in town. We'll have privacy here."

We walk through the restaurant, which is tasteful and understated in its decor, but it feels *special*. It's a beautiful space full of beautiful people. I see several very famous people as we pass by and all of them stop Reece to say hello. He introduces me to everyone by saying, "This is Lucía Vega." And nothing else. And to my amazement, some of them have heard of me. Their faces brighten. One woman who is one of my all-time favorite actresses grabs my hand and says, "I cried reading your book. You told a story that everyone needs to hear. So glad to meet you." I am so star struck, I'm unable to do more than nod and mumble, "thank you."

As soon as we reach our table, before I even sit down, I ask for the lady's room and run to go and text Jessica. I have to tell her right away where I am and what's happening. And I have to invite her to dinner tonight.

I'm not crazy about celebrities, but Reece's friends are in their own galaxies when it comes to fame. Graham, Omar, and Dave are the hottest guys in their respective professions. Dave is the head violinist for the Los Angeles Philharmonic. He's made classical music cool again. He's very private and rarely appears in Jessica's magazines. Omar is the newest European soccer player acquired by the LA Galaxy. His family is from the Pacific Island of Tonga, but he was born and raised in Los Angeles. An injury cut his Premier League career short, but he's still a star. Known for fighting with paparazzi—and his wanderlust. His Instagram is full of pictures of his perfect body laid out on one exotic beach after another.

Gossip magazines dubbed them the Four Horsemen, because they all met when they were young polo players at the California Polo Club. They are all big, athletic and so very sexy.

I know that meeting these men is on Jess' celebrity bucket list. All three of them at once is crazy. I tell her I'll send her details, but that she should be ready for the night of her life.

And then I look at myself in the mirror, I see a smile on my face that I don't recognize. It's huge. We're coming to the end of a really dynamic couple of weeks. There's been so much pain, but so much to celebrate as well. I know Reece and I aren't in the clear. But it feels like we've both decided to not waste time being apart when we both want each other so much.

I'm nervous about how he'll react when I tell him I've never had sex before.

I walk back out to our table, trying not to gawk as I walk past table after table of movie stars, models and the crème de la crème of Hollywood.

Reece is scrolling through his phone, but as I approach, he drops it into the inside pocket of his jacket.

"I ordered a bottle of water for the table, but they'll be right back to get you a drink," he says as he takes a big sip of his own water.

"Thanks, this is great," I say excitedly as tears swim into my eyes.

"What's wrong?" Reece asks with concern.

"Nothing. I can't believe this is my life. Mine. Lucía Vega, née Ana Maria De La Vega Rios. I used to stock shelves in grocery stores, I used to scrub toilets for a living. Now, I'm in Beverly Hills with the most amazing man holding my hand. People I've grown up watching on my television are telling me that they've heard of me."

The concern on his face morphs into understanding.

"You've come a long way, Fifty-five. And you've done it your way. You have a lot to be proud of." The nickname is starting to grow on me, and I smile at him before I speak.

"I wish Julian was here." I say wistfully and when I see his smile falter, I reach across the table to grab his hand.

"Please. I know it's only been a week since everything's been out in the open. But, I want to talk about him. But if you're not ready, I understand," I tell him

"I'm ready. I want to learn more about him, too," he says, squeezing my hand and looking me in the eye.

"I was so young when he died, so my memories of him are things like tagging along when my mother sent him to the store. We'd always stop at a little playground near our house and he'd push me as high and fast as I wanted. That's *the* playground, you know."

His eyes widen in surprise.

I laugh at the memory and say almost to myself, "I wonder if it's still there." Just then, our waitress comes back with my water and an iced tea for Reece.

"Mr. Carras, good afternoon. Welcome back to Spago. We have your regular, unless you'd like something else?" she says pleasantly to Reece.

"Please serve my guest first," Reece says in return, his voice icy.

The girl flushes and turns to me, "I'm sorry, Ms. Vega. Have you had a chance to look at the menu or can I recommend something?" she asks politely. If she is chagrined, she doesn't show it.

"How about you recommend a salad? One with seafood," I say warmly, eyeing Reece, my expression asking, *'What was that about?'*

"We have a great Lobster salad. The lobster is flown in overnight from Maine and kept alive until you order your salad."

"That sounds wonderful," letting my excitement show.

She smiles brightly and faces Reece, "Mr. Carras. Will you have your regular?"

He nods, not smiling in return.

"I'll go put that in. Would you like anything else to drink?"

I shake my head no and she leaves without another glance at Reece.

"Reece, what in the world? You terrified her," I whisper at him.

"Good. She knows that she should serve you first. The

women at the table always get served first here. She must be new." The muscle in his jaw flexes.

"Reece, I didn't even notice. Give her a break, it's not exactly an easy, high paying job. Who knows what her day has been like? Maybe she's got a sick kid or a sick parent. Or maybe she's just an asshole," I add trying to lighten the mood.

He sighs and shakes his head. "I'm sorry. You're right. I just want today to be good for you."

I tilt my head at him. "I'm having a great day," I assure him with a smile.

"So, tell me about swimming. I watched you swim in the Olympics." I blush when his smile turns knowing. "I mean, I watched everyone, but I remember you. All your gold medals. It was so exciting to see an American on the top of that podium."

Reece looks thoughtful. "So, you think of yourself as American?" he asks, seeming to be genuinely curious.

But that question hurts, especially coming from him, one of the DREAMERs' biggest allies.

"I don't *think* of myself as an American. I *am* an American. This is my country. even if they don't want me," I say to him,

He muffles a curse and takes my hands, I glance around the restaurant immediately, wanting to make sure no one's watching us.

"This is the most private table in the entire restaurant, no one can see us clearly unless they're standing right in front of us." Reece's voice has a tinge of irritation. "And that was a stupid, insensitive question. I'm sorry."

"It's okay. Let's talk about something else. Tell me when you started swimming?"

He looks relieved by the subject change and I *know* I am. I don't want anything to put a damper on today.

"I was swimming before I could walk. My dad's Greek. He

comes from a family of sailors, and he insisted that I learn how to swim. And I love the water. There's something about being immersed in it that makes me feel invincible." He laughs at himself. "I know that sounds ridiculous. But it's true. And when they realized I was fast, they put me on a team. My parents tried to encourage my love of film and I knew that they'd expect me to join them in the business when I was old enough. I interned at Artemis every summer from the age of fifteen." He laughs ruefully.

"I started in the package delivery room. As long as I did that internship, they let me swim. The only other rule in our house was that I needed to keep myself out of the press. I had no interest in that life anyway, so that didn't feel like a sacrifice. Sophomore year of high school, I was recruited by a coach who'd come to one of my meets. My parents agreed to let me work with him as long as I kept my grade point average at school above a 3.5. So, I did. That was good enough to get into UCLA which also had a competitive and well-funded swimming program. I swam in my first Olympics my junior year, but I took a year off to train. I promised my parents I would go back and finish my degree."

His eyes drift a little. "Winning gold was so unexpected. Even though I'd been working hard that year and I knew I was competitive for a medal before I got in that pool, winning gold was surreal." The proud grin falls a little as he continues.

"Gold brought the spotlight and people all over the world started asking who I was. I went from Reece Carras the swimmer to Reece Carras the Olympic Gold Medalist and son of 'Hollywood Royalty.' And the rest is history."

"Wow, how conveniently you erased me from your life history." I look up to see who the owner of the sultry, slightly accented voice is and see Fabienne standing there, her perfectly styled eyebrows raised. I'd been so absorbed in Reece's story, I hadn't even heard her walk up.

"Hello, Reece. I was just sitting down to lunch when Martha Tierney told me you were here." She looks pointedly at our joined hands and I immediately start to pull my hand back.

He tightens his hold on it.

"Fabienne," Reece says not hiding his irritation.

"Aren't you going to introduce me? This is actually the second time we've met, after all. I always seem to catch you two when you're having a moment." Her tone is pleasant, but the expression in her eyes is anything but.

Reece sighs, gives me a reassuring smile, and then looks up at her.

"This is Lucía Vega. She's the author writing the screenplay for a project we're developing. Lucía, this is Fabienne de Olivera." His use of her maiden name must annoy her because her eyes narrow at it. "Thank you for stopping by to say hello," he says in a tone that is just civil.

She turns to face me and says, "Enjoy your moment while it lasts."

"Goodbye, Fabienne," Reece says, his tone making it clear that she was being asked to leave.

"See ya," she says with a cold smile. And then she turns and strolls away. I stare after her and think that for a woman who was blessed with so much physical beauty and natural talent, she seems pretty miserable.

"I'm sorry about that."

I don't say anything, but I'm curious about how someone as conscientious and kind as Reece was married to someone who's the exact opposite of those things.

"When did you meet her?" I ask, that curiosity overriding my good manners and discretion.

"Are you questioning my judgment?" We both laugh.

"No, I'm just wondering, you're complete opposites," I say honestly and he sobers a little.

"I was in Australia for a swim meet. I was just eighteen. And she was in Australia for a fashion thing. We met at a night club, hit it off and that was it. Honestly, Luc, I didn't put much thought into things, then. Not for years. I swam and when I wasn't swimming, I was working at Artemis. My parents discouraged the marriage and that just made me want it more. We eloped to Vegas. And she didn't really want anything more than fame and I was just a vehicle to get there. So, we grew apart pretty quickly. She started cheating on me. So, I stopped fucking her." He grimaces and says, "Sorry, I stopped sleeping with her."

"Call it whatever you want. Either way, it makes me want to vomit. You can skip this part," I say with a grimace.

His expression is sheepish as he continues. "Anyway, she was gone a lot for work so she didn't notice. When I was injured, I moved in with my parents because she was gone on jobs for months at a time and I needed help after the surgery on my shoulder. That's when I found out about . . ." He pauses and looks at me before he says, "Everything that happened with Julian."

Hearing him say Julian's name pokes at the never-healing crack in my heart and I feel myself wince.

Reece stops talking. "I'm okay, Reece. Go ahead." I prod his calf gently with the toe of my shoe. He looks unsure, but goes on.

"It scared me straight and it got me fired up to do something. And that was when things with Fabi really started going south. Before, our relationship had been kept alive by a sort of mutual indifference." He grimaces.

"Then she lost her contract with her agency and all of her work along with it. She was still beautiful, but she'd stopped taking care of herself and designers weren't booking her anymore. So she moved home. And that's when she decided that it would be fun to make both of our lives a living hell. I put up with it for a while because I'm Catholic. Divorce is frowned upon. And I didn't want to hear my parents say I told you so. So, I stuck it out. She wanted to party, travel, shop, snort coke and fuck. I was trying to get my foundation off the ground and I'd just gotten my first major promotion at Artemis. We just wanted different things from life. So she started traveling, partying and fucking . . . without me."

He says this, smiling so broadly, I wonder if I've missed something. But so captivated by his smile, that I don't want to ask and risk that he'll stop smiling. He's such a beautiful man. I want to pinch myself. I can't believe this is my life.

Our waitress approaches the table and I slip my hand out of Reece's as soon as I see her. Reece's smile disappears. I groan inwardly. We're going to have to talk about this.

She places my napkin in my lap for me; I almost slap her hand before I realize what she's doing. She walks off quietly, leaving Reece and I to eat and talk.

"Eat up, I want to get to my parents' soon. We have to meet the guys for dinner and I don't want us having to rush from place to place."

I drop my fork at that.

"Wait, we're going to your parents' house? Today? Are they there?"

Reece doesn't stop eating, and nods casually.

"I'm not ready to meet your parents, Reece! Isn't your dad recuperating?"

"We won't stay long. Don't worry, they'll love you." And then he digs back into his steak.

I can't imagine how that could be true and I have a hard time finishing my meal after that. But Reece seems so unbothered that I decide to try and relax. I tell him about the first time I met Jessica.

"She started the nickname thing right after that first class. We'd started talking while we were packing up. She said, "you're such a little treat, aren't you? You remind me of all my favorite pastries.""

When we get up to leave, we're in a good mood. As we approach the front of the restaurant, Reece stops short. He loops an arm around my waist and starts to walk back into the restaurant. His face is a mask of barely controlled anger.

"What's happening?" I whisper, looking around the restaurant in alarm.

"Someone called the paparazzi." I look over my shoulder and through the tinted front windows of the restaurant, I see a throng of people standing outside with cameras. He stops again and when I look back at him, his gaze is focused on something and when I follow it, I see that he's staring at Fabienne. She smiles maliciously and widens her eyes in feigned innocence.

He shakes his head in disgust pulls his phone out as he walks us back toward our table. "Liza, send a car to Spago. Back entrance. And please, send someone to pick up my car. I have it valeted here."

The man in the tie who'd taken us to our table walks up to us. "This way, Mr. Carras, I'm so sorry, I didn't realize they were outside. Someone must have just called them. Can I order you a car?" His nerves evident in this rapid-fire line of questioning.

Reece is calm when he responds. "I have a car on the way. We'll wait at our table until they get here." He leads us back to the table we just vacated. It's cleaned and reset and he leaves us to sit down and practically sprints away.

He sits down and pulls me into his lap. When he looks at me his eyes are full of regret. "They don't know who you are, yet. But we're going to need to get you a publicist sooner rather than later." He looks stressed and I want to alleviate that. I look around and see that we're back behind the wall that had hidden us from the rest of the restaurant.

I wrap my hand around his neck and massage it with my fingers. "Mmmm, I need that," he murmurs.

"Let me give you something else I think you need." I tilt my face up to his.

He smiles slowly as he bends to meet me. Our eyes locked on each other until the moment our lips touch and just as they do, I whisper, "Yes."

And my eyes flutter shut. If anything in my life has ever felt as right and sure as this kiss, I can't remember.

It's an exploring kiss that he starts to deepen right away. I open my mouth for him and his tongue feels hot as it sweeps the inside of my bottom lip. My awareness narrows to Reece. His hands in my hair, his mouth taking the offering of mine with avarice. I feel it right at the center of me.

A vibrating sensation against my thigh, makes me jump back, breaking our kiss.

Reece is a sight; his hair mussed, his mouth smeared with my lipstick and his eyes bright. He looks down at himself and it's a few seconds before he realizes the vibration is coming from his phone's buzzing.

He grabs it and simply says, "We're coming out." And hangs up.

"Come on, Vega. Let's get out of here." Reece hurries me through the kitchen and out a backdoor into the alley. The

SUV's rear passenger door is open and Reece climbs in and pulls me inside with him.

He puts the privacy screen up and leans back in his seat, covering his eyes and swears under his breath. I eye him expectantly and when he doesn't say anything else, I poke him in the ribs.

He opens one eye, and when he sees my worried expression, he sits up and smiles. But it doesn't quite reach his eyes. "Sorry, it's just . . . that was a close call. We really need to get you a publicist soon."

I groan. He squeezes me reassuringly. "We can talk about it later. I hoped we'd have a little more time before all of that."

"All of what?"

"We're only a few minutes from my parents. Let's just enjoy the rest of the day." I nod my agreement, but I can't shake the little kernel of unease that I'm feeling at the thought of publicists and paparazzi. But before I can worry about that, I've got to get over my most immediate challenge—meeting Reece's parents.

28

The Carras' home is nothing like Reece's place in Calabasas. Just a mile down the same street as Spago, it's Beverly Hills grandeur at its finest. Black wrought iron gates open up to a long, manicured bush-lined drive. The drive crests near the front door of a red brick mansion.

"This is where you grew up?" I ask Reece as he parks his car on one side of the massive drive.

"Yeah, my parents have lived here for almost thirty years. They moved here when I was little. It was my mother's grandmother's house before it was theirs."

"Stay there." He opens the car door for me and takes my hand to help me out.

"You're very gallant today," I joke. I have butterflies in my stomach as we approach the door, I tug his hand and come to a stop. "Reece, I'm nervous. I'm not sure I'm ready to meet your parents."

"Why not? They're just regular people." He grabs my arm and tucks it into his side.

They're the furthest thing from regular, it's laughable to hear him say that. My insides feel like jelly, but I plaster a smile on my face as I walk into the house with Reece.

It's like stepping into another world.

The floor is cream-colored stone, punctuated with black diamond-shaped tiles every five or six feet. The entryway's huge crystal chandelier hangs from a huge silver dome in the thirty-foot ceiling. The stairs look like they're carved out of ivory and the rails are wrought iron and glass. Everything is so ornate. The flower arrangement on the table in the middle of the foyer is the size of some of the small trees we have in our yard in Los Feliz. I've never seen this kind of luxury in person.

Reece heads up the stairs and beckons me to follow.

We get to the top and walk down the longest hallway I've ever seen in a home. "This place is like a palace," I mumble to Reece.

"Yeah, it is. Growing up here was fun, but it was too big for us." We walk all the way to the end and he opens two double doors.

"My parents have been spending a lot of time in the viewing room. My dad is finally taking his doctor's orders seriously and Mom takes three days a week off to keep an eye on him." His voice drops to a whisper as we enter a huge room.

"It's why I'm still in LA. I've had to work with the rest of the executive team to come up with a plan for my dad's absence."

The room has three walls that are movie screens. The screens all have their own seating area. In the one that's across from the doors, I see two heads, bent together in one of the huge reclining chairs. Playing on the screen is of all things, *Love Actually*. The scene where the office worker chick finally gets it on with the guy she has a crush on is playing. There is no sound coming from the screen.

"They've got earbuds in," Reece explains. He walks over, lays a hand on the woman's shoulder and says, "Hey, you two, I want you to meet someone."

Reece's mother pops out of the chair and turns around to face us. She pulls her earbuds out of her ears and glares at Reece.

"Are you trying to kill your father? Why would you sneak in here like that?" she yells at him.

"Diana, darling. *You're* going to kill me with that screaming." Reece's father stands up and smiles at his wife. I stare at Reece's mother. If I wasn't sure that's who she was, I wouldn't have recognized her as the woman I've seen in magazines and on TV. She looks so young and relaxed. Her dark hair is down. She always has it up or back. Her usually expertly made-up face is completely natural. She's wearing a white T-shirt and some colorful leggings. She's barefoot.

I realize I'm still staring when Reece comes to put his hand on the small of my back.

"Mom, Dad, I'd like to introduce you to Lucía Vega. She's the author of the book we're scripting for production and she's the sister of Julian Rios."

His mother gasps, but so do I. I had no idea he was going to tell them who I was.

His father's eyes narrow on me but otherwise, he doesn't react.

I step toward them, my right hand outstretched to shake her hand. She hesitates, glances at Reece and then reaches out to shake it.

I turn to his father whose eyes are still narrowed. I think he's going to leave me hanging when he reaches out and hugs me instead.

"I read your book. I think you're remarkable."

I look at him curiously.

"Reece only told me about you,"—he gives his son a stern look— "last week. I've been reading your book and I have to tell you, Ms. Vega, if you lived a tenth of what Maria has, then it's a miracle you're even standing here."

A rush of pride has me straightening my spine and look him in the eye as I say a very heartfelt, "Thank you."

I look back at Reece's mother. Her expression is not even close to warm.

"Reece, why are you and Ms. Vega here? It seems a little odd for you to be spending time with a screenwriter that you've hired."

The effect her words have on me remind me of the first time I got caught in the sprinklers at school. I was startled, chilled and embarrassed.

"Di . . ." Reece's father says, his tone chiding.

"Mom," says Reece at the same time, his tone angry.

She looks at both of them with annoyance and then sighs. She puts a hand on my shoulder.

"I'm sorry, Lucía. It's been a very stressful month, but you didn't deserve that. Please, come sit," she says as she leads me to one of the sofas in the seating area. I go only because I think it would be rude to say no.

She considers me very thoughtfully. "I have a lot of reservations about this . . ." she searches for the right word, "association. I don't think Reece should be carrying on with someone our business has a contractual relationship with. You'll be the talk of the town. I don't like negative attention." She looks over her shoulder to where her husband and Reece are still standing. She drops her voice. "But, I can see the way Reece looks at you. So, I'll just ask this of you." Her face takes on a softness that is unexpected and disarming. "Be sensible and be discreet. At least until the film is out. Anything that's said about you or that happens to you will impact it. And it's my job as the COO of Artemis to make sure that Reece's division has the operational support to make his films successful."

Her face hardens slightly. "As his mother, it's my job to make sure he's well equipped to navigate life successfully and to advise him when I think he's making a mistake."

"Mom," Reece interjects. I don't react, what she's saying doesn't surprise me. If I was his mother, I might be saying the same thing.

She sighs and says, "It's clear you make my son happy. He's been smiling for no reason. All week." She rolls her eyes and I smile at that. She's trying. I won't throw it back in her face. Now I see why she's so successful. She's domineering, but knows when that approach won't work.

She stands up suddenly and walks over to her husband. She doesn't even wait for me to respond, clearly she is used to being obeyed.

"Reece, you've interrupted our movie. Thank you for stopping by to introduce Lucía, but if you could run along so we can enjoy the rest of our afternoon, that would be lovely." His father lets out a hearty laugh before he grabs his wife and nuzzles her neck.

"Let's leave before they do something even more embarrassing," Reece says. They're totally absorbed in each other as they walk back to the chair and put their earbuds back in and start their movie again.

"Before my dad's heart attack, they hadn't set foot in this room for anything other than entertaining," he says as soon as we've closed the doors behind us. "I'm sorry about my mother. This family is her everything. So, she's very protective of us and of our image. Our studio wants our movies to be in the news, never us. She's got a good heart."

"She's your mother. She loves you. I understand." I mean it. I didn't like everything she said, but I'm glad Reece has parents who love him so much.

"Okay, now that you've met them, I want *you* to show me something. I just want to swap my car for my motorcycle, it's a nice day for a ride." He starts to lead me back downstairs, but I tug on his arm to stop him.

"Reece, where are we going? What could you want *me* to show *you*?"

"I want to see that playground. The one where that scene in your book happened."

I stop, my throat tight, not with emotion, but with anxiety. I'm not sure that I'm ready for that. When I tell him that, he turns me to face him and puts his hands on my shoulders.

"Okay, what about it scares you?" he prods gently.

"I'm not scared," I answer honestly. Unable to meet his eye. "I just don't want to go back there. I escaped that. I've built a new life. That neighborhood, that playground, it's all in the past."

He takes my hand and sits back down next to me.

"Okay, I get that. But you have to also know that the life you've built, your book, even your new name, can't be taken away from you. You've earned them. They're yours and always will be."

When he says it, I almost believe it. But it's not really my name and I still have moments when I feel like I'm living an imposter's life. But, maybe I need to prove to myself that stepping back in that neighborhood won't turn my carriage back into a pumpkin.

"Okay, if you really want to see it. I'll take you."

29

Reece

WE LEFT MY PARENTS' HOUSE ON MY MOTORCYCLE. IN LOS Angeles, most guys drive Ducatis or BMWs, but my baby's a Harley. I always love riding her; but, tonight with Lucía behind me, it's a fucking joyride. Her thighs hug my hips, I can feel the heat of her body through my jacket. My most fervent wish is that we could go straight to my house and take all our clothes off and really get acquainted.

When we get there, there won't be any going back for me. This tiny, vulnerable, woman with the courage of a lioness has become my hero. I've known her for such a short time, yet our relationship feels substantive and grounded. Watching her go after her dreams, has made me want to step up my game. I want to be as badass as she is. I made a decision this week and I'm going to tell her tonight.

We pull off the 101 at Whittier Boulevard in the part of the city that is usually known by the monolithic reference of "East Los Angeles." I'm familiar with this part of town. I volunteered at a recreation center in Salazar Park before the city shut it down. When Lucía asked me to take us there, I didn't need directions.

We pull up to the park and it's as I suspected; the playground is still there, but the equipment is rusty and in desperate need of replacement. The recreation center, once a beautifully maintained building decorated with wall-sized murals has a tarnished chain holding the front doors together.

"See, it's changed so much. It used to be so beautiful," Lucía mumbles as she walks toward the playground. She sits down on one of the swings. I'm dubious about its ability to hold her up. The rusted chains creak as she uses her legs to propel herself forward, but it's clearly sturdier than it looks.

"Push me?" she asks, shielding her eyes from the low afternoon sun. It shadows most of her face, but I can see a smile playing across her lips.

I stand behind her and give her a big shove. A little cry of excitement fills the air as she gains momentum.

"Faster!" She shouts as she swings back to me.

I push her harder and she soars, her hair flying, her laughter ringing out. If I close my eyes, I can imagine a five-year-old Lucía on these swings.

I push her until she tells me to stop and I grab the chain of the swing to slow her down. I hold onto the metal— warm from where her hands had grasped it. I slide my hands down and let them rest on her shoulders. She tips her head and leans back, turning my torso into a backrest. I start to sift my fingers through her hair, caressing her scalps. She moans her approval. A comfortable silence falls between us. We're lost in our thoughts as we stare out at the park. I see possibility and I want to do something to make this a place that serves the community again.

"You feel okay?" I ask after a few minutes. I know she'd been anxious about coming here.

"Actually, yes. I'm fine. I thought we'd get here and someone would recognize me and call me Ana. I used to think about this park and remember the day that girl hit me and my mother did nothing. Now, I'll think of it and remember today with you." She laughs and it's so light and melodic. "So, thank you."

"You're welcome, Luc."

"I'm Ana," she declares. "I'm Lucía, too. Neither one cancels out the other. Maybe they can even co-exist. Ana was actually a pretty remarkable girl. This neighborhood was my home. I'm glad to be back," she says, wonder tingeing her tone.

I almost sag with relief. "I'm glad you feel that way because I have an idea."

"Of course you do," she says wryly as she uses her foot to push herself on the swings again.

I speak to her departing back. "I want to make a difference. I want to do more than put a Band-Aid on a problem. Knowing you, seeing how you're putting yourself out there for the sake of what you believe in—it's made me want to do the same."

She uses her foot as a brake this time and stops herself mid-swing. She looks over her shoulder at me expectantly, her expression growing more worried as I speak.

"I'm going to run for City Council. Obviously, I couldn't run in this district. But the First Council District has a long-time council member who's retiring. I've decided to throw my hat in the ring."

She pales. "You're running for office. Public office?" she asks, sounding like she hopes she heard me wrong. There's silence as I try to decide how to answer her.

I was prepared for this reaction, but actually seeing it makes me nervous. If she and I are really going to be a couple, I need her support in this. I walk around to stand in front of her. I bring her hands to my lips and press a kiss to each of them. I pull her into me, she doesn't resist, but she's stiff in my arms. Her hands rest lightly at my waist, and I can feel her heart beating a flagrant staccato against my torso.

"Tell me why that upsets you," I ask her, hoping she can hear the sincerity in my voice. I won't do this if she can't get behind it. I run a hand soothingly up her back.

"Reece . . . I," she shakes her head in a short, stuttering movement. "No, it's not about me. I don't want to make it about me. You should tell me why you want to do this."

That's a question that's easy to answer. I push her back slightly so I can look at her. She closes her eyes and doesn't open them. "Look at me, please." I need to see how she's feeling while we talk about this. She does as I ask, all of her apprehension sitting at the surface of her expression. My chest tightens, this is going to be a hard sell.

"It doesn't feel like enough to just donate money or time anymore. I want to have a real stake in the future of this city and this country. Who knows, maybe one day I'll even run for Congress," I say, my excitement building as I complete the sentence.

"Okay, well, congratulations," she says, her eyes cast down. "I think that's wonderful. You'll win, of course. Who could stand a chance against you?" She's trying so hard to smile, but I can see the effort it's taking. I narrow my eyes and cross my arms.

"Now that you've gotten that out of your system, why don't you tell me how you really feel? Or was that promise to be honest you mentioned the other day only meant to apply to me?"

She flushes and pulls away. She walks back to the swing and sits down again, clutching her hands in her lap.

"I feel so selfish for even thinking this way, Reece. If you want to do this, then of course I'll support you. I'm worried what that means for us."

If she'd told me she was an alien, she couldn't have surprised me more.

"What's this got to do with us? Why would anything change?"

She steps back clearly exasperated. "If you're running for office, you can't have a girlfriend or significant other that's undocumented."

"Why the hell does anyone need to know? What's that got to do with anything? I know it's important to you, but it doesn't always have to be an issue, Luc. Part of the problem in this country is that people don't think about this issue. No one's going to look at you and wonder if you here legally or not," I say knowing that I sound agitated.

"Says the man dripping in privilege," she returns acerbically. I flinch at that.

"That's not fair, Lucía." My voice is low, and curt.

"Maybe not, but it's true," she snaps. She sighs and looks up at me. Her eyes contrite and her lips pursed. "Of course most people don't walk around thinking about immigration all the time, most people don't have to." She runs her fingers through her hair. "I wish I didn't have to. But I do. And it's frustrating to hear you say that I shouldn't worry about something just because you don't have to. I know that as soon as people hear I'm Mexican, that'll be the first thing they wonder about."

I acquiesce. I have no clue what that would feel like.

"I understand. But maybe we can just keep you out of the spotlight when I'm campaigning. If you want to just be there, but not play a public role, we could do that. How many City Council member's girlfriends can you name? They're not being drafted to be in the *Real Housewives'* shows or anything."

"Right, but I know the Governor of New York dates some Food Television Network star. I know that the Senator from New Jersey is married to some actress. If their significant others are well-known, they are in the news, too. Reece, you've just asked me to stand in an international spotlight to do promo for the film. I won't be able to step out of the spotlight once I'm in it, will I?"

She bites her lip in frustration. "I know you are on the right side of this issue, but you don't understand. I don't want people to know. It's not even about shame or pride; it's survival. I'm an American. I've lived here since I was two years old. This country is all I know and I don't want my life to be even more distilled than it is. I want to have a place where I can just be Lucía, the girl who loves yoga, tacos and writing."

She puts a hand over heart. She rubs the spot, slowly. "I have a tattoo. Over my heart. It says *Libertad.* It's Spanish for freedom. I got it when my first DACA application was approved. Suddenly, I could go to work, rent an apartment—all of that. I promised myself I'd never live like a prisoner again. If I can earn money, support myself and live quietly, then maybe I can stay here and no one will notice." She stops talking. Her shoulders heave like she's out of breath. I feel her fatigue and her hurt.

There's a new distance between us. Borne out of her recitation of all the reasons why not. "I didn't know . . . I haven't seen your tattoo. I didn't know they were the same," I say, desperate to make a connection, to soothe her . . . and myself.

"They're not the same," she says quietly. "Yours is a declaration." She points her chest. "Mine is a plea." Her shoulders square and she looks at me.

"I don't want to call attention to myself. Every decision I make has real consequences and I need to weigh them. See if they're worth the risk. If they see me as an agitator, I could be detained at any moment. And they wouldn't have any trouble finding me. Let's go to YouTube and we can watch prominent activists being detained outside of speaking engagements, even outside their offices."

I'm alarmed at the picture she paints, but confused.

"Why would they deport you? You're enrolled in DACA. You're productive, you're contributing."

She bows her head and says softly, "I applied to renew my DACA application four months ago, Reece. It's still pending. They might not approve it."

These words send a shot of real fear down my spine. "Why wouldn't they? You haven't committed a crime, you're not on any social services," I say, trying to fight my own rising fear.

"They can do whatever they want. It's not guaranteed and it's never taken this long for an approval. This is my third application in five years. I'd planned on leaving when this project was over. If I leave before they deport me, there's a good chance I can come back in a few years."

My heart skips a beat. "You planned to leave? Were you going to tell me that?"

"Of course I was. But, I haven't thought about leaving since I met you."

I walk over to her, not letting myself even think about the

possibility she would have to leave. I'd do everything in my power to make sure it doesn't come to that. I cup her cheek, tilt her face up to mine.

"We'll face that if it comes to it, and I know you're worried, but trust me, I wouldn't let you be deported. I don't throw my weight around, but I will if I need to. I'll take care of you. You don't have to do this by yourself anymore."

30

Lucia

I CLOSE MY EYES AND SAVOR THOSE WORDS. THE PROMISE in them buoys me.

"Thank you. I think if I lay low a little, it'll be fine."

Reece's thumb had been stroking my cheek and at my words, he stops. His smile falters and his eyes close.

"Are you okay?" I look over my shoulder to see if he's seen something.

He smiles again and grabs my hand, pulls me to standing. He lowers his face to mine and pulls me into a hug. He voice is gruff and his breath lifts my hair a little as he speaks.

"Yeah . . . no. I need to talk to you." I'm still in the fog of desire his little tease created, but I hear his last sentence and I start to wake up.

"What's wrong?" I ask wearily.

"Today in the restaurant, you said it made you happy to meet the people I introduced you to?"

I nod wearily. I have no clue where he's going with this.

"I had an ulterior motive for taking you there today."

I grimace and he continues.

"No, it's nothing bad. I just wanted you to see that it could be okay to be out in public. I want you to help us sell this film. Our marketing team created a strategy, or at least the sketch of one, and you being available to talk about the book and the issues it raises are part of that strategy."

My heart sinks. I feel cold suddenly and I rub my hands up and down my arms.

"Do you want me to stop talking?" Reece asks.

I whisper, "No, I'm just trying to grasp what you're saying." I understand perfectly, but I wish I didn't.

"I'm saying that you need to come to terms with being in the spotlight. A few late nights, a morning show or two and a feature in an upscale magazine. As soon as you say okay, Sol's going to get working on getting one of those lined up. You're beautiful, they're going to want to know who you are. I'll be there with you. We can control the narrative, make it about the film, the book and not so much you."

A feel a frown form on my face. "Are . . . you giving me media training?"

"No. But you're going to need some, soon. You're overdue for interviews for the book. We'll do them together and I'll talk about why we're making film," he says brusquely.

"What's soon?"

"Three weeks. We're flying to New York to do TODAY,

Good Morning America and a spot on a CNN morning show. We'll be back two days later and you'll do one of the late night shows here a week or so after that."

I'm afraid my eyes are going to pop out of my head. I don't know how we got here. "Reece, my contract. It says no press."

He nods, "Yeah, it does," he says with a challenge in his voice. "But you can decide to do it anyway. Who knows your status besides your family, me and Jessica? You'll be fine. You're about to the be next hottest thing. Sol's going to be very busy fielding offers for endorsements."

I laugh nervously. "Reece, you're getting ahead of yourself. I haven't said I'd do it."

He comes to stand in front of me and drops down to his haunches so we're eye to eye.

"Luc, you've got to make a choice. You put that clause in there because you were afraid of being the center of attention. I get it, but you can't be ruled by your fear."

I consider him for a moment. I know that he's right about my original motivation. But that fear is real and it's not baseless. I want the movie to do well but I don't want the focus to be on me.

"Okay, but we need to compromise. I have conditions. And I know you won't like them, but you're not in this alone."

He smiles triumphantly and says, "Hit me with it."

"Well, there's only a couple, really. I don't want to parade our relationship in front of the press. It will only make them curious about me and I don't want that right now."

He pulls his head back in surprise. "You want to hide?"

"We don't have to hide, Reece, I just don't want to point a neon sign at us. Don't you understand?"

He closes his eyes for a second but says grudgingly, "I do. What else?"

"I'll do the interviews, but by myself," I say.

"Hell, no," he says almost immediately. "You've never done this before and I'm not sending you out there by yourself." He puts up a hand just as I start to protest. "We can come up with talking points ahead of time if you'd like. Our agents will let the shows know that we won't talk about certain subjects. We can even ask for a list of potential questions. But you are not doing it by yourself." His finger jabs the air to punctuate every word of that last sentence. I blink back my surprise at his vehemence. I make a quick decision.

"If it's that important to you, we can do them together. We'll just have to make sure they don't turn into segments about us."

He takes my hand.

"It'll be fine. I promise. The studio will manage everything. We'll need to talk to Sol about getting you set up with PR. You need someone good and discreet, who can craft a bio that's satisfying without giving away too much. We'll pick reporters we can trust and shows we've got relationships with. They'll treat you like a princess."

I can't even comprehend the warp speed at which my life has changed. Ana Maria feels like distant memory. But I'm still tempted to look over my shoulder. I can't let myself get too comfortable. As long as I'm out of status, getting comfortable isn't a luxury I can afford.

I'm overwhelmed, but I don't want to feed the feeling by worrying about this. I can't let my fear rule me. I'll just need to spend the next few weeks busy if I'm going to stay sane.

"I've got to get some writing done with Dan and Todd. I need to work longer hours the next few weeks to get everything done. I should probably get back there tonight, so I can get an early start tomorrow."

Reece looks slightly disappointed, but I'm not sure why. I just agreed to do what he asked. Before I can ask, the look is gone and he's smiling. "That's a good idea," he says, but I hear a hesitation in his voice.

"Are you sure?" I eye him.

"Yeah, of course. I'm just thinking," he says as he starts to scan the park. I close the gap between us and take his strong, warm hands in mine. He looks down at our joined hand and then up at me.

"Are you sure you want to take on the mess of my life?" I ask him, earnestly. He doesn't hesitate when he responds.

"Your mess is my mess. My mess is yours."

"Okay." I smile, take a deep breath of relief. "Julian used to say, 'fear or faith' all the time. I'm afraid. But I won't let that stop me."

He cups my face. "I see that fear baby, and I feel it too. But, I believe in us. We're on the right side and we're together."

I nod at him, unable to look away from his mouth. I remember how soft it was when I kissed him in the restaurant. His hands flex, his fingers moving into my hair. I exhale as my scalp tingles at the touch of his fingers. He tilts my head a little and brings his mouth to my ear. "You're so beautiful, and I'm desperate to kiss you," he mutters, biting my earlobe before he sucks it into his mouth.

I groan, "Mmmm, well that's perfect, because I'm desperate for you to kiss me," I whisper back.

That's all the invitation he needs. The tip of his tongue traces my lips, and he murmurs, "This mouth." Before he brings his mouth to mine. My arms twine around his neck and I come up to the tips of my toes to try and close the distance between us. The kiss . . . it's everything. It's like a big gulp of fresh air. My lungs open. My heart expands. I'm hurtling through time, forward to my future. It's full of promise and pleasure and I try to get even closer to him as feelings I've never experienced assault my senses. His hands come to palm my ass as he fuses our hips. I can feel him against my stomach, his hard thickness pressing into me. He deepens our kiss, our tongues sliding against each other. I moan into his mouth. When he pulls back, pressing soft kisses on my cheeks and neck, I let my hands delve into his hair. And suddenly he pulls back from the kiss. He presses his forehead to mine and takes several breaths before he speaks. "You're going to be the death of me." He chuckles. "We're making out in the park like two teenagers and if we don't stop I'm going to pull your dress up and fuck you right here."

I pull back from him at that, my eyes wide. He laughs at my expression and puts an arm around me and steers us back toward his motorcycle.

"We're meeting the guys in Venice and I need to go get my car. If we're going to make it in time for dinner, we should get going."

I loop my arm around his waist and we walk back to the bike, then start to strap on our helmets. Reece sits down and just as I start to climb on behind him, he stops me. "Thank you for coming here with me. Today has been one of the best days I can remember in a long time."

I smile at him, knowing that my eyes are holding nothing back. "Ditto."

31

"REECE. YOU'RE EMBARRASSING YOURSELF, MAN."

I glance at Dave and shrug. We're at dinner at Ponte in Venice. The food and drinks are phenomenal and it's a local eatery that's casual and easy. Lucía and Jessica just got up to use the bathroom and I'm watching her walk away. Her hips have this great swing to them that gives her a bounce when she walks.

"You just wish it was you." I go back to watching Lucía as they disappear down the dimly lit corridor where the restrooms are.

"Hell yeah, I do. She's fucking hot," Dave says.

"Yeah, and she's a little young for you, old man." He ribs

me with his elbow. "How old is she, eighteen?" I slant a glance at him and grin.

"Hell yeah, she's fucking hot. Most beautiful woman I've ever seen. And she's twenty-three." And they all laugh out loud. I laugh too. I sound whipped. But that doesn't bother me. Lucía could be fifty-three and she'd still be the woman I'm crazy about. Yeah, she's young, but she's got more emotional maturity than almost anyone I've ever met.

Lucía's lit from within. She's brave, brilliant and totally out of my league.

In LA, in the business, women like her are like myths. I want to be like Jay-Z and shout, "I got the hottest chick in the game wearing my chain." Because she's mine. She has been since she moved out to Malibu. God knows I've done my share of shit talking about them and their women, so I'll take all the ribbing they want to dish, because I know I hit the fucking jackpot.

I look at Omar who is being unusually quiet. He's been nursing one beer since we got there and has barely said a word. He also hasn't taken his sunglasses off. In LA, that's not unusual, but he's wearing them to hide a black eye. He lost his mind and fucked his coach's daughter. It's been in the news, and it's made his professional life a living hell. He got sucker punched by her brother a couple of days ago and he's been laying low ever since.

"And you're turning that book into a movie? Sort of different for your studio," Dave says as he pops an olive into his mouth.

"Yes. So what?" I snap at him irritably.

"Easy, man. Just asking. Anyway, they're coming back," he says and then nods his head in the direction of the bathroom.

As they make their way through the restaurant, every single head turns to watch them.

Lucía's wearing a long black sundress. It's simple, but on her it looks like lingerie. She's got her hair up in a messy bun that is just begging for me to take down.

"We're back," Jessica sings as they get back to the table. She's a real party girl. You can tell she's always up for fun and she's been flirting outrageously with Dave all night and he's been flirting back. But I know he's not going to take it any further than that. He's got a very serious girlfriend in New York and I think he's planning on proposing to her soon.

Graham ambles back to the table, he left to take a call more than ten minutes ago.

"Sorry folks, I've got to love you and leave you. I've got a client who needs a FaceTime session to help talk her through a craving."

I look at him and raise an eyebrow. "Since when do you do those?" I ask, knowing how covetous he is of his rare free time. He usually doesn't take clients' calls any later than three in the afternoon.

"Since this client started craving my cock, but is out of the country for work. FaceTime and my hand are going to help her get out tonight."

Lucía chokes on her wine and Jessica laughs out loud.

"No one needed those details, man. You could have just said you had to go."

"I did. You asked why. I answered."

He turns to Lucía, his expression taking on a warm sincerity I rarely see from him. "It's really nice to meet you. Good luck working with this guy, he's a slave driver." He takes her hand, places a kiss on the back of it. She flutters her lashes and blushes back at him.

I roll my eyes. Graham and women.

"I'll see you at the premier if I don't see you before." He gives both her and Jessica a peck on the cheek and then strolls out."

We settle back and I look at my clock, it's getting late. I know Lucía's got an early start in the morning, but I'm driving back to Malibu with her tonight and I don't plan on leaving until it's time for work.

I'm just about to say something to that effect when Omar speaks.

His sunglasses are still on but it's clear he's looking at Lucía when he speaks. "I read your book," he says it quietly, but loud enough that we can all hear a note of displeasure in his voice.

Lucía looks at him, a little warily. "Thanks . . . what did you think?" she asks a bit hesitantly.

"Well, I think it glorifies a bunch of law breaking people who have convinced themselves they have a right to be here."

The mood at the table goes from jovial to hair trigger tense.

"Well, that's rude." This is from Jessica who has started to put a protective arm around her friend's shoulder.

I look at Lucía and she looks relaxed, so I let myself relax, too. He's entitled to his opinion. I know he has strong ones. We've argued about this issue for years.

Lucía moves slightly so she's not under Jessica's arm and says to her, "It's not rude. I know that he and a lot of people feel that way. Tell me why you think it's glorifying anything."

Omar puts his beer down on the table and takes his sunglasses off. His right eye is red, and swollen with skin that ranges from dark purple, to mottled green all around the outer edge of it.

"Because everyone in that book is made out to be some sort

of hero. All of them are criminals." This is a tone I've never heard him use before.

"Hey, man. Careful," I warn him.

Dave groans and pulls his baseball cap down even farther on his forehead and slumps in his seat. He can tell that this is going to get messy, quick.

Omar glances at me. "Careful with what? My parents are immigrants to this country, too. They waited until they could enter legally and I did things the right way. But people like the ones she writes about, they give us all a bad name. Why couldn't that family just go back to Mexico and use the skills they learned here, there?"

Lucía tips her head at him, her eyes narrowing and I see all my plans for tonight go up in ball of flames. I'm going to fucking kill Omar.

"Go back Mexico? Don't you think that people would LOVE to be able to go back to the country of their birth? You think they all want to have to leave just to feed their kids? Good for you that you had the luxury of choosing when you immigrated. My characters came here as children. What choice did they have?" she demands.

"Why is that now the entire country's burden?" Omar throws back at her.

"What burden? They work, virtually every single social service excludes them from access even though they pay taxes. They can't access health insurance; they can't get proper identification. They do work you couldn't even imagine. They fucking contribute." Her voice raises at that last sentence and people at the adjacent table turn to look at us.

She lowers her voice a little. "They're your neighbors. Not all undocumented people are criminals and drug mules. I bet your soccer team has someone on staff who is undocumented and who lives in fear of exposure every day."

"If they're so afraid, they should find a way to go back home." Omar's keeps his voice down.

"I'm undocumented."

All of us stop and turn to look at Jessica. She looks completely sober and more serious than I've ever seen her.

"I am. I came here to study. When my visa was running out, I got married. To the love of my life, but he died before he could file for me. My husband left me all his money when he died and it's made it easy for me to blend in. But, I'm basically stuck here. If I leave, I wouldn't be able to come back."

I had no idea about Jessica and apparently Lucía didn't either. She looks dumbstruck. But she just moves closer to her friend and puts an arm around her.

She looks at me. "Reece, last year there was a man whose legal fees your foundation paid. He was born in South Korea, but he'd lived here since he was three. He was married, had children, owned a restaurant. At the age of forty-two he committed a petty crime. He went to trial, was found not guilty of the crime, but because he was undocumented, they deported him anyway. He had to leave his wife and kids and go."

Her eyes blaze at Omar.

"They drop you off with a hundred and fifty dollars and tell you good luck. He didn't speak Korean; he couldn't find a job or a place to live. The South Korean government, like most nations, doesn't have any resources available for people like him. He was homeless for months before he killed himself. I know it's against the law to enter or remain in this country without paper. But, for those of us who didn't actively break that law, it's unfair to treat us as if we did." She takes a sip of her drink and continues. "It's easy to say, go back home. Or tell me that now that I'm old enough I should go to Mexico and petition to enter legally. What would happen to my work, my bills, my friends, my life if I did that? I would have to wait three years to apply for re-entry. What would I do in Mexico for three years? My Spanish is barely conversant.

"Thank God for DACA or I'd probably be gone by now. God knows I wouldn't have had time to write a book without it. When I couldn't get documented jobs, I worked in restaurants, valet stands, grocery stock rooms. I had to have three jobs to survive. When I got my work permit and could get a real job, I was able to cut down to one job and that gave me time to write this book . . ."

She trails off as she notices that all of us are staring at her. Omar in surprise, Jessica and me, in alarm.

"What?!" she exclaims. "Why are you all looking at me like that?"

Omar speaks before we can. "You're undocumented?" he asks her, looking back and forth between us.

Her face drains of color when she realizes that in her rant she's given herself away. She doesn't want it to be public knowledge. That's why she wrote under a pen name. It's why she has avoided publicity.

She lifts her chin at Omar defiantly, but even I can see that she's not feeling the bravado she's trying to put on.

"Yes, I am."

He looks at me. "Reece, you knew? And you're employing her? That's illegal," he whispers at me.

My hackles rise. I hunch my shoulders and look down at the table before I speak. I choose my words carefully. "Omar, you need to watch it. Don't cross a line we can't come back from, man." I don't look up at him.

He doesn't back down. Instead, he gives me a dismissive glance before turning back to Lucía.

"What are you even talking about? I'm stating facts. And you know how I feel about this already. I'm sure she's a great woman. But she's still illegal."

"Omar—"

"Reece, it's okay." Lucía touches my arm and shakes her head. I hadn't even realized I'd stood up. I sit back down. Trying to respect her, but what I really want to do is to make his other eye black and maybe knock out some of his teeth.

I look him dead straight in the eyes and tell him, "I'm sitting down, out of respect for my woman. But if you speak about her like that, one more time, you and I can take it outside."

His jaw drops, not because he's afraid of me kicking his ass, but because I just threatened to kick his ass. And because of a woman, at that. He knows that fighting is a last resort for me. I'm not a violent man, but when it comes to Lucía, I want to fuck up everyone who disrespects her. Everyone, not just Omar. The table is quiet while they take me in. Omar's face drops and he runs a hand over his face.

"Reece, I'm sorry man. I didn't mean any disrespect. Lucía, it was nice to meet you. I mean that. I'm sorry that we're just so far apart on this issue. But, Reece, you're my brother and you know I've got your back. I'm going to get out of here now." He stands up without saying anything else and leaves.

"Fuuuuuck, man. You guys know how to kill a buzz," Dave groans. He sits up and pulls his cap off and runs his hands through his dark red hair before he puts it back on. "I was nice and buzzed when I came in here. Now I'm stressed the fuck out."

He looks at Lucía. "Omar's an asshole. But he's our asshole.

He may talk shit, but he's loyal as fuck. He's had a rough week. Try not to hold it against him." He rubs his hand together in glee. "If you want, I'll kick his ass for you."

We all laugh at that. Dave is at least four inches shorter than Omar, he's also about fifty pounds lighter. He's a violinist and he's got the most beautiful hands I've ever seen—on a man or a woman. He sleeps with gloves on. He won't even attempt to open a jar that's tightly sealed, much less fight Omar.

"Anyway, I'm getting out of here. Going to hit up my girl and then get some practice in. I might come out to Malibu if you don't get back to LA soon, Lucía. We need to hang out."

He gives me a pat on the shoulder, throws some bills on the table and then saunters out.

"Well, I'm ready to go home," announces Jessica. She looks at me and says, "You should be careful how you choose your friends." The combination of too many cocktails and her anger makes her accent, which is normally very subtle, more pronounced.

"Hey, Jess." Lucía gives her a hug so their heads are touching. "Omar feeling that way doesn't mean he's a bad person. He was honest, said what he felt and he allowed me to do the same. Yes, I wish he didn't see things that way, but as long he doesn't try to hurt me, I have no reason to dislike him."

She's an amazing human being. "I'm so crazy about you, Lucia." I say, inserting myself into their conversation and clearly surprising them both. She and Jessica both look at me, mouths agape.

Her mouth opens and closes a couple of times. Jessica grins broadly. "Oh, Reece…" she sighs, turning the soft "c" at the end of my name into a "z."

Lucia slides in her seat so that she's pressed against my side.

She brings her hand up to cup my cheek and says, "Can you take me home? We've all had a long day."

If Omar had still been there I might have made his other eye black. There go my plans for tonight. I've been building up to it all day, but I can tell she's tired. It's been an emotional day; I should have known she'd be tired when it was over. I feel my cock start to lose interest and I say a silent apology to it before I answer Lucía.

"Of course, I'll take you back to Malibu tonight."

She looks up at me through her eyelashes. A small, shy smile plays about her mouth. She leans close to me and whispers so that only I can hear. "Can I stay with you tonight? I was thinking that since it's so late, maybe you could take me back in the morning? We'd have to leave early, but. . ." She bites her lip nervously. "What do you think?"

As if I'd say no to that. "I think it's the best idea I've heard in months."

She laughs and looks back at Jessica. She's drooped over in her seat and looks like she could fall asleep right there. I make a note to ask Lucía about her later. I think every time I've seen her, she's been totally smashed.

"Let's get her home," I echo to Lucía, and she nods. Jessica scoots out of the booth. I try to take her arm, thinking she needs the support. But she pulls her arm out of mine. "I can walk just fine," she huffs indignantly and walks out ahead of us.

I put my arm around Lucía's shoulder and pull her into me. She wraps one arm around my waist and presses herself even closer. And just like that, we've reached an agreement. I'm about to fuck her so hard she'll find sitting . . . memorable, for at least a couple of day. I've never had sex with a woman I felt this way about. I can't wait.

When my car pulls up, we all pile in. I'm glad I went home

to get my car before dinner. I don't think Jessica could have made it home on her own. I give my driver Jessica's address and we drop her off. We sit on opposite ends of the bench seat in the back of the SUV. We don't speak, we don't touch. I know the minute I do either of those two things, I'll be pushing her panties to the side and fucking her where she stands or sits. I don't want our first time to be in the back of my SUV, so I'm keeping my distance until we get home. But then, all bets are off.

She's quiet, too. She's watching the road and not speaking either.

When we get to my house, I hop down. I let my driver help her down as I rush into my house.

She walks into the house a minute after I do. "Reece, you left me outside!" she calls. I grab her, push the door shut behind her. She gasps as I stoop down to hook two hands under her thighs and lift her up, her dress rides up to the top of her thighs. I back her against the wall and grind my cock against her pussy. I can feel the heat of it through my jeans.

"Did you come here so I could fuck you?" I growl into her ear. I run my nose along the soft outer shell of her ear, nuzzling her silky hair, breathing her in, reveling in the familiar scent of her.

She nods.

I use one hand to push her hair back and I put my mouth on her neck and start to suck. When I feel her flinch, I ease up and lick the spot I've just bruised.

She's panting and winding her waist, trying to find some relief. Her fingers dig into my back.

"Reece." She pauses to catch her breath and then says, "Did you give me a hickey?" She sounds shocked.

I grin into her neck. "Yeah."

"People will see it," she protests even as she reaches down and cups my ass, pulling, telling me she needs more. I'm about to give it to her.

"That's the point," I say and then I take advantage of her mouth being open and put mine over it. I lick the inside of her mouth, stroke her tongue. I want to fucking drink her. I want to know what every single part of her tastes like.

I walk us down the hallway and kick the door of my bedroom open. I flip the lights on, put her on my bed and then lay on top of her. She feels so good beneath me, I might come just from this. I need inside her.

"You ready?" I say to her. Her eyes are dazed, she looks like she might not even know what her own name is if she were asked.

"Yes. So ready," she says. But then I look in her eyes and she looks at me warily.

She shakes her head and says the last words I want to hear. "Well, maybe not quite."

32

Lucia

REECE BLINKS DOWN AT ME LIKE I SPLASHED COLD WATER in his face. "What? Are you okay? You changed your mind?" he asks me, starting to roll off me.

I pull his arm to hold him still. "No, no… It's just that, I've never done this before and I don't want to let you down."

He blinks, slowly like he can't believe his ears. He smiles, widely. "You're a virgin?"

I cringe. "I don't like that word. It implies naïveté. I'm not naïve, I get off to Tumblr posts just like everyone else." His smile turns to a grin. I roll my eyes.

"I just haven't done *this*. You may have to give me some

guidance," I say, annoyed that he's reacting like this. "Are we going to do this or are you just going to sit there and grin at me?" I ask him.

He bursts into laughter and puts his face into my neck while he chuckles. He tangles his fingers in my hair and says, "Oh, yeah. We're going to do this. I'll go easy on you tonight. A little."

I shiver in anticipation as his hand moves down from my hair and trails down my neck. He stands up and starts to strip. He unbuttons his shirt, and yanks it off. His body. It's so . . . manly. He's got chest hair, he's big, a little rough. His muscles are honed from swimming and polo, and he's lean. My eyes feast on him and he laughs. "You're looking at me the way I'm always looking at you." He pulls his jeans down over his hips and takes off his briefs with them. He's magnificent. So hard and muscular everywhere. And his cock is standing at attention. It doesn't look like it's going to fit inside me. I look at him with wide eyes.

He reads my mind. "Don't worry, you're going to be so ready, I'll glide right in." He kneels down at the foot of his massive bed and pulls me to the edge, lifts the skirt of my dress and ducks underneath. He hooks his fingers in my panties and pulls them down.

I close my eyes and gasp at the first touch of his tongue to my pussy. He brings one hand up and grabs my hand. He laces our fingers together as he starts to lick me, softly, slowly.

"You like that?" he asks from underneath my dress. I use my free hand to reach down and pull my dress up so that I can see his head.

The sight of his dark head in between my legs while his tongue dips in and out of me is out of this world. I'm so turned on by it that I feel the beginnings of my orgasm. Reece mumbles, "Delicious," as he sucks the lips of my pussy into his mouth and kisses them like he would kiss my mouth. He sucks on my clit, sending me closer to the edge. He puts two fingers inside of me and coats them in my wetness. Those same fingers slip between the crack of my ass and he teases my pucker with one of his wet fingers. He rubs the wetness all around it and then inserts just the tip of his finger into my ass.

My orgasm crashes over me without any warning and my hips lift off the bed, his mouth doesn't lose his grip, but he slows in his intensity as he lets me come down. I feel wrung dry and am catching my breath when I feel Reece start to pull my dress up my body. He pulls it off and then stands up and walks over to his nightstand. He pulls out a pack of condoms, a bottle of lube and a little plastic thing I don't recognize.

"Move up," he orders as he comes around to the front of the bed. I do as he asks without hesitation. I'm tingling from my orgasm and feel myself starting to grow wet at the sight of him.

He reaches over and grabs a condom. He watches me as he rolls the condom down his cock and then pours lube on it.

He arranges the pillows behind me and lays me on them. He kisses me gently, as he lays down on top of me.

He props himself up with a hand that rests next to my head. The other hand goes in between us and he tickles the lips of my pussy with his fingers.

"Fuck, you're incredible." He hisses as he slides a finger inside me. "You're so ready, Luc." He grabs his cock and lines it up with my entrance. He lifts his dark gaze to mine, and watches me as he starts to move forward. I feel the first press of the wide, blunt head of his cock. It's so different from his fingers, it's heavy and stretches me as he slides in. The effort that he's putting into going slowly shows on his face. He's sweating and grimaces with each small thrust.

A drop of sweat falls from his face and lands on my chin. He dips down to lick it off and then moves down my face. "I love this mouth," he says as he sucks my lower lip. I groan as he tilts his hips and gives me another inch. I feel so full and yet it's not enough. I wrap my legs around his waist and tilt my hips and pull him almost completely inside.

We both groan. The sting from his initial thrust has morphed into something that feels like heaven. "Reece, please, I need more." He looks at me, nods, hikes my legs even higher around his waist, grips my hips and then he's filling me. The muscles in his chest and his shoulder flex and relax as he moves over me and I'm mesmerized by how beautiful his skin is. I lean forward to press a kiss to his shoulder and he captures the back of my head before I lean back down.

"You okay?" he asks with his voice gruff. His face is flushed and his eyes are burning as he watches me.

"Yes," I huff out. "So full, Reece. I want . . ." I trail off unable to articulate, but I squeeze myself around his cock and he groans. He withdraws slightly from me and looks down between us as he slides back inside of me.

"You want that? This?" He pushes himself into me, fusing our hips as he fills me completely.

I moan as the friction sends a current of pure lust through my body. I reach up and grab my breasts, my fingers pinch my nipples in concert with our hips and the world starts to chip away, one claiming thrust at a time. With a swipe of his arm, he pushes the pillows he's propped behind me to the ground. I fall flat on my back, my ass raised and resting on the top of his thighs as he kneels between my legs. "Touch yourself, baby. Let me see you," he orders.

My hand snakes down to where our bodies are connected and I rub my clit. His eyes watch my fingers as he fucks me. I wish I could see what he sees. I want to watch us. What I'm feeling couldn't look anything other than beautiful.

Our eyes meet and even though no words pass our lips, we say profound things to each other. His eyes make me promises, conveying the depth of his devotion. He leans over me, puts his mouth on mine and speaks to me through his kiss. The demanding probe of his tongue implores me to trust him. The prolonged pulls on my lower lip tells me he never wants this to end. The slow, tender play of his mouth on mine tells me that he treasures me.

I start to come, and open my eyes to find his open, too. "Let go, baby, I want to watch you." In a haze of almost unbearable pleasure and with my heart full to bursting, I let go. And as my body releases all the pressure he built up, my heart falls. I bring my head back up and take his lips in a searching, desperate kiss that begs him to catch it. I tell him I'm his and that he's mine.

He holds me while I tremble in his arms, covered in sweat. He wipes my tear stained face with his fingers and holds me. He's still hard inside of me and he rolls his hips.

Suddenly, he lifts me off him "Turn around."

I obey. Anticipating him, I get on all fours in front of him. He leans over me and pushes my head down so that my face and forearms are pressed into the mattress.

"Reece?" I ask, him suddenly unsure of what to expect. My heart races at the unknown. He must hear the uncertainty in my voice, he leans down to press a kiss to my back. He places the flat of his hand on the spot he kissed and says, "If it hurts, I'll stop." And then I feel a cool, blunt object press against the pucker of my ass.

"Mmmm. What is that?" I ask as I tense against it.

"It's a small plug. I bought it for you last week," he says as he rubs my back. "Bear down, baby. It'll feel better." I do and I feel the cool rubber push past the tight ring of muscle.

The moan that escapes me is guttural. It's a strange kind of pleasure. Deeper and more intense than anything I've ever felt. He lines himself up behind me again and I feel him pushing inside my pussy. My hips start to move. "Yes, that's my girl. Fuck yourself on my cock." Reese slips his fingers between my legs and starts to rub my clit. I rear back as he pushes forward, our bodies united in common purpose.

This pleasure is beyond what I could have imagined. The fullness of his cock and the pressure of the plug in my ass are so intense that my knees buckle. I fall forward on the mattress and Reece lays down on top of me bearing his weight on his forearms as he starts to fuck me. His lips ghost over the back of my shoulders and press kisses to my neck. He grips my hips, squeezing me so hard I know he'll leave a bruise. That bit of pain only intensifies my pleasure and I feel my climax start. His pace is fast, constant and punishing. Each one makes his headboard knock the wall behind it. I can smell the scent of us in the air. I am so aware of him as he surrounds me, fills me, makes my senses scream.

The scratchy texture of his hair as his legs brush mine gives me goosebumps. I can feel the heat of his breath as he exhales with each thrust. I reach my arm around to grab his firm ass and pull him into me. Every rock of his hips, sending a ripple through the muscles in my hand. I can feel him restraining his body's power, I know he's going easy on me because it's my first time. I can't wait for him to give me everything.

Suddenly his hips jerk and then his pace picks up. "You ready? I'm coming," he says as he pounds into me, each time more forceful than before. And my orgasm breaks, as strong and as overwhelming as a riptide, deep inside me. It spreads from the inside out and soon my entire body is riding a wave of pleasure that makes me unaware of everything but it.

I hear Reece call my name, followed by a satisfied, guttural groan as he reaches his own climax. He pulls out and falls down next to me. My eyes drift close as a haze of bliss and fatigue overwhelm me. He's panting as he sits up and gets off the bed.

I prop one eye open. "Where ya going?" I mumble sleepily.

"To the bathroom." He steps into the en suite bathroom and I hear him turn the water on. I start to doze off as the sound of the water flowing turns into white noise.

I startle awake when I feel a hot, damp towel on my back.

"Sleep, I'm just cleaning you up," Reece whispers.

Then, I feel the towel moving gently between my legs. It's soothing on my tender skin. "There's blood. I wonder if I should keep this towel as a memento of your deflowering," he mumbles through a laugh and then goes back to the bathroom.

That has me sitting straight up, sheet wrapped around myself, I call after him. "You used a towel? Please don't put it in with your laundry, I don't want whoever does your laundry to have to clean it."

He sticks his head out and rolls his eye at me. "I'm not a total asshole. I left it out and I'll wash it myself." I give him a proud smile and he rolls his eyes again before disappearing into the bathroom.

A few minutes later, he's back, turning off the lights and getting into bed next to me. He pulls me so that my back is pressed against his chest and my ass is in his lap. I reach for his hands and wrap them around me, then rest mine on top of them.

"I took your virginity," he says, his voice a mixture between disbelief and pride.

"You put a plug in my ass," I mumble.

"You liked it," he responds.

"I did." I grin. "A lot."

He kisses my cheek and says, "Let's go to sleep. Tomorrow's going to be a long day."

I yawn in response. My last thought as I drift off into a dreamless, deep sleep was that today is the best day of my life.

33

Reece

New York City in the fall is quite possibly the most perfect place in the world. I love Los Angeles; I can't imagine ever living anywhere else. But here, I feel a freedom of movement that I don't have at home. I don't need a car; I get to run in Central Park. This time, it's even more special because I've got Lucía with me. This is her first visit and we decided to stay an extra day, because she wants to go the 9/11 Memorial and the Statue of Liberty.

She and her team have been working sixteen-hour days for the last month. The screenplay's first draft is done. We're heading to New York with that under our belt. It feels great.

We took the red eye from LA and are headed straight to our first appearance this morning. We have three more after that. Only one is in-studio, the rest we'll join via video feed. Now, in the back of the limousine, I look over at Lucía. I laugh when I see that she's plastered herself to the window with her neck craned up so she can see the city as we drive by.

She doesn't take her eyes off the view, but says, "I can't believe I'm here. It's like being in a different country." Her voice is full of wonder and happiness.

She slept for almost the entire six-hour plane ride. She said, "When we land, I want to be wide awake. I'm afraid that if I'm tired, I'll miss something." She'd even packed her SLR camera in her carry on.

The last month has been just like this. Seeing everything I take for granted through Lucía's colored lenses. Her optimism, courage and curiosity make everything seem bright. They make anything seem possible.

All the staff at the Malibu estate love her. She asks about their kids, remembers birthdays and makes them feel special.

She does the same for me. Because, no matter how brightly she smiles at everyone else, the smile she reserves for me alone is the brightest.

Our publicists advised us that the best way to keep our relationship out of the news was to lay low. We've been spending a lot of time in Malibu. Lucía's swimming— basic chest stroke, but swimming. I've mastered the first three *Asana* and am feeling stronger than I have in a long time. I'm also sleeping really well.

That last part has to do with the fact that I spend most nights next to Lucía.

Our limo pulls into the garage below Rockefeller Center.

We roll to a stop and my door is opened almost immediately. A man, with a tan too orange to be anything but sprayed on and teeth so white I have to force myself not to squint when he grins at us, leans down to greet us in a very warm, but professional manner. "Mr. Carras, Ms. Vega, welcome to Thirty Rock. I'm Rick O'Banyon. I'm one of the show's producers and I'm here to escort you to your greenrooms." When I get out of the car, I start to reach in to grab Lucía's hand, but he steps around me and beats me to it.

"Ms. Vega, I'm such a huge fan of your book. We've all been dying to meet you. We're honored that you're giving our show your first live interview," he says as he helps her out. He doesn't let go of her hand immediately, but Lucía doesn't seem to mind. She's smiling warmly back at him. "Thank you Mr. O'Banyon, I'm so happy to be here. This is just amazing."

And I see it happen, the way it always does when she smiles, he falls a little in love with her. He grins at her and says, "They're going to die when they see you upstairs. You're gorgeous. Oh, you're going to be a hit." As if he suddenly remembers I'm here, too, he faces me. "Oh, both of you are. The staff is buzzing."

She blushes but squeezes his hand before she comes to stand next to me again. My arm instinctively goes around her shoulder. Rick's eyes widen with realization, just for a second, before he schools them.

"Well, I'm sorry to keep us standing out here while I blather on. Let's get inside." He turns and leads us into the building. He's practically hopping with excitement and I groan inwardly. It's going to be a long day.

"You have separate greenrooms, but we can always put you in one together if you'd like," he says casually, but I know he's fishing. He'll probably be on the phone to some entertainment reporter as soon as he leaves us. I don't even give a fuck.

Lucía asked me to wait until the screenplay was done. I've waited. I'm sick of not being able to tell the world she's mine. I've had to watch the staff flirt with her, some of the guys have asked her out. I hate all that shit. I'm not a kid. I stopped sneaking around when I was a teenager. I hate doing it now. So, this trip is going to be our coming out—whether she likes it or not. Whether she thinks she's ready or not.

"We'll share one," I tell Mr. Not Slick Rick. He actually claps before he catches himself. "That won't be a problem, we have both of your rider items completed, so we'll just take you to Ms. Vega's room and move your items over there." He pulls out his phone and starts to make a call.

"What's a rider?" Lucía whispers as we follow him down the long hallway leading to the greenrooms.

"It's everything you request when you're doing an appearance. Sol filed one for you, but I didn't see it. I thought he would have run it by you?"

"Request? What would I request?" she whispers back, sounding perplexed.

"It's not a big deal. They like to make sure their guests are comfortable, so they ask if they can get you anything special. A particular snack you like . . . you know, things like that. I'm sure Sol just told them to have something for you to eat and didn't get too specific," I explain.

We turn right from the garages tunnel into the brightly lit, chrome, marble and glass lobby of Thirty Rockefeller Plaza. Lucía grinds to a halt and just stares. Her eyes wide as she takes in her surroundings. "I've only ever seen this on TV. I can't believe I'm here." Her grip on my hand tightens as she surveys the lobby.

"After you're done, we'll make it possible for you to come back and take a private tour of the plaza. It's quite a marvel. And the view from The Top of the Rock is a must see," says Rick.

"Oh, thank you, I'd love that," Lucía, exclaims. I smile, but inwardly curse him. After we're done, I'd been planning on taking her back to our hotel and fucking her hot, tight pussy for dinner.

I just smile at him and say, "Yes, thank you, Rick." My tone is warm, but my eyes when I look at him are anything but.

He smiles nervously and says, "Well, let's get going. We've got to get you in makeup and we'll send our producers in to give you a quick prep, and then you'll be good to go."

We step onto the elevator and climb to the fifty-first floor. When we step off the elevator, the scene that greets us is what I'd call ordered chaos. A lot of people moving rapidly, but with purpose.

"This way, please," says our erstwhile guide. "We've moved your rider items into one greenroom. We're going to start makeup right away." He smiles coyly at Lucía. "Not that you two need it."

She giggles. I groan. She elbows me in reprimand just as we're shown into our greenroom.

There's a rack of dresses and suit jackets on the left. There is a sitting area that frames a huge television screen on the right. A woman is standing in front of a huge vanity with lights and a counter. She's dressed in all black with light blond hair, cut very close to her head. She smiles and walks toward us. "I'm Mila," she says, revealing an Australian accent. "I'll be doing makeup for you both today." As effusive as Rick was to Lucía, she's even more so toward me. She sidles up to me, a cool, but very suggestive smile on her face. "I'll do you first," she says, the innuendo unmistakable.

This isn't new or surprising. I'm relatively young, wealthy, famous. So, wherever I go, women try their luck with me.

In the world I live in, most women don't care about anything but what I represent. But, I'm used to them, so Mila's flirtation barely registers.

I feel Lucía tense. Mila doesn't notice though, and she puts her hand on my arm to lead me to the chair. I remove her hand politely and keep a pleasant look on my face, but my message is clear. "Actually, I need to make a call, so I'll go last."

I turn to Lucía, who is eyeing Mila, and grab her shoulder. She looks up at me then and I lean in fast and press my lips to hers. It's a quick kiss, but for the fraction of a second that our lips touch, I forget where I am and why we're here. And she does, too. I expect her to tense, but she doesn't. She deepens the kiss, putting her arms around my waist and stepping into me. She steps back and smiles at me. And then I remember Mila is standing there. She's blushing furiously and staring at her phone screen.

"I'll just go sit down and make my call, have fun in make-up," I say to them both, before I turn and head toward the seating area. I pour myself a cup of coffee and pull out my phone and get on a call I have with the Chairwoman of California's Democratic Party Committee. As I'm prospecting the idea of running, I think it can't hurt to try and start building some relationships. I want to be ready in case Lucía decides she's in.

Thirty minutes later we're done. My call was a good one, the party's interested in talking. We have a face-to-face when I get back to LA next week. Out of the corner of my eye I watch Lucía step out of the chair and walk over to another woman.

Melanie, as I'd heard her introduce herself earlier, is from wardrobe.

"Okay, Lucía, let's get you into something that's going to knock them dead."

Lucía looks down at her black, sweater dress that she's paired with a pair of black knee boots and then looks up.

"Oh, I though what I was wearing would be fine."

Melanie looks her up and down, no recrimination in her eyes, but says frankly, "We can do better. You should wear something jewel toned. It's fall, and you've got great skin and hair. I've pulled some things. We got your size from your agent, but we've got everything in alternate sizes, too. We'll get you something that works." She walks over to the rack of clothes and beckons for Lucía to follow her.

Mila beckons me with the tip of her head and I sigh. She clearly hasn't learned her lesson. Lucía doesn't handle this sort of thing with the same flippancy that I do. In the last month, I've learned that she's as possessive as I am.

When I sit down in her chair, she makes a show of walking back and forth in front of me, digging in the drawer of the vanity, ass in my face, trying to find "that damn brush," she keeps calling it.

She comes to stand in front of me and I notice that two of the buttons on her shirt are undone. I roll my eyes, not bothering to hide my boredom.

I crook my finger at her and look over my shoulder, pretending to check to see if Lucía's paying attention. She comes, bringing her ear to my mouth. "Hey, I get what you're trying to do, but I need to warn you. My girlfriend's over there." I mimic her head nod in Lucía's direction. Her eyes widen in understanding and I start to feel relieved until she speaks again.

"Hey, if you want to wait until later, that's cool. I didn't realize you were a couple. But I get it."

I shake my head. "No, there's no later. You seem like a nice girl and I want to save you from getting cursed out." She jerks back as if I spat in her face. "I'm not interested. At all. I need you to stop disrespecting my woman by coming on to me."

Her face takes on a stony expression; I can see the flush on her cheeks. Her jaw clenches and she swallows a few times before she speaks without looking at me. "I really had no clue about you two and this week has been . . . rough. I'm sorry." She cuts herself off and gathers her composure and says, "Let's get your face done so you two can meet with production."

She's done with me in ten minutes. I hate the makeup they cake on your face for television. I sit through most of it, but stop her when she tries to put gloss on my lips. Thank God I'm not wearing a tie and my collar is open, or I'm sure I'd be worried about smudging my shirt with it. My hair feels like a helmet.

I thank Mila who mumbles a barely audible, "You're welcome," and hop out of the chair. Lucía's in the bathroom changing so I go back to the seating area and pull my phone out to check email.

A couple minutes later, a pair of black leather stilettos appear in my line of sight. I let my eyes travel up her legs. They're encased in skin tight black leather pants that show of her incredible figure. Her blouse, emerald green, silk button down, fits her like it was tailored for her.

She's gotten the camera-ready makeup, and her eyes are kohl lined and look huge in contrast to the rest of her face, and she's wearing a coral-colored lip gloss, completely different from her trademark red. The only thing about her that looks like she normally does is her hair. Free, flowing down in dark chocolate waves, and pinned up on the sides.

"Well, what do you think?" she asks me. She sounds apprehensive, but I don't understand why. I stand up and lay my hands lightly on her shoulders. In her heels, her mouth is much closer to mine than it normally is when we stand face-to-face.

"You look amazing." I try to reassure her and then lean forward to kiss her. Her eyes widen in alarm and she pulls back. I stop and look around. "What's wrong? We're alone."

"You'll ruin my lipstick." She walks back to the mirror on the vanity and looks at herself and muses, "I like this color. I'm going to find one when we get home."

I walk to stand behind her and try to hold her close, she steps away. "Stop! You'll wrinkle my shirt, that poor girl just pressed it."

I groan. "Oh, my God, I've created a monster. I can't kiss you or touch you now that you're TV-ready," I quip.

She whirls on me, and even though she's clearly pissed, I just marvel over how beautiful she is. "Leave me alone. You've done this plenty of times. It's my first time. You're lucky I'm not throwing up right now. Stop making it worse. When we're done, and I haven't made a fool of myself, you can smudge, tear, wrinkle, rip…whatever, but please, I'm just trying to hold it together." And then her scowl deepens. "And that *puta* who was doing our makeup and hitting on you is really lucky that I'm not trying to get arrested." I grin at her and she sneers back. She turns back to the mirror. "It's not funny. I know you set her straight. She couldn't even look at me when they walked out of here."

"Fifty-five, it's normal to be nervous. Don't worry. You're ready. I'll be right beside you. You got this. You've been prepped and you're well rested. It's going to go by so quickly it'll feel like a blur. We've given them a list of topics that are off limit. Nothing about where you come from. We're focusing on the book, the film and the issues."

She smiles, a reluctant tilt of her lips, but I can see her posture relax.

"Can I get a fist bump at least?"

She taps my fist with hers and says, "Fuck, yeah."

34

THERE ARE MOMENTS IN MY LIFE THAT, AS THEY HAPPEN, I know will leave me changed forever. This trip is one of them. I'd never left California. I never thought I would. And I'd told myself I was content with that. Now, I know I'll never be again. I just want to see more of the world.

California is a huge state and in lots of ways, the world has come to me. LA is the ultimate melting pot, where people have carved big chunks of their culture onto the city's psyche. But I know, without a doubt, after visiting New York City, that I'm missing out. No movie, television show, book, postcard, can do this city justice. The buildings are gargantuan. You feel your insignificance when you stand next to one. They are majestic and soar into the clouds. And there are so many of them. The streets teem with people who are living their lives without caring what the person next to them thinks of what they're wearing.

I mean, this is the world's style capital, but there is not a single trend that dominates. Standing on the balcony of our suite at the Four Seasons, located in mid-town right between the world famous Park and Madison Avenues, I feel like I can see forever. And the cherry on top of this spectacular ice cream sundae of an experience is that I'm here with the most incredible man in the world. I love him so much that I'm terrified to explore it.

I glance at my watch.

It's late, after ten. I should be tired, but my mind is still on California time, so sleep will elude me for a few more hours. Reece is inside on the phone with his publicist. At ten in the evening the streets look even more crowded than they did during the day. Yellow taxis play kamikaze, bobbing and weaving through traffic as they snake up East 57th Street.

Our interviews were all amazingly fast. Not having a studio audience helped me relax and answer the questions. Having Reece by my side made me feel like I belonged there. It was awe inspiring; sitting down with reporters I've seen on television every morning for years.

I can hear his raised voice from inside and I know he and Lacy, his publicist, are going at it.

I hope she's tearing him a new one. Reece went off script today. Majorly. He answered every question about us with complete candor. By the time we'd made it to the recording for the evening show, pictures of us were everywhere. All the coverage of the movie is intermingled with stories about us. His phone has been ringing nonstop. The only people who've called me are Jess, Sol and my mother. Sol sounded very worried. Jessica sounded happy. And, my mother only said, "We'll talk more when I see you on Sunday." When I asked her what she thought.

When I'd been online earlier, I checked Facebook—my account doesn't even have a picture—to see if I saw any mention of us. That was a mistake. Our names had been combined, Reecia, they called us, and we were a trending topic. Most of the articles focused on Reece. They didn't really know much about me, yet anyway. And suddenly I was glad my Facebook page was sparsely populated. Without any information, they started making it up. They were calling me a rebound for Reece. That was fine. The less they knew about us, the better.

The last two months with him have been an experience. One that created a bond unlike any other I've ever had. He's my favorite person. My mind is unfettered, my heart joyous when we're together.

I'd never had a relationship like this. We're each other's safe place. His heart is so beautiful. His graciousness is totally unexpected. He isn't perfect, but when he sees room for improvement in himself, he's not afraid to admit it. He feels a real calling to try and use his platform for good.

When we're alone with each other, it feels like nothing can touch us. Reece has awakened my mind, my heart and my body. I am learning new things about myself every day. I have moments, long swaths of time each day, where I feel invincible because I know I'm not alone anymore.

But standing here, on this balcony that may as well be the edge of the earth, I realize how destructible I am. I feel the vulnerability in every pore of my being.

I need Reece.

I walk back inside. He's sitting on the plush brown leather couch, listening now instead of talking. I take a look around this suite. It's more like an apartment than a hotel and it's the definition of understated luxury. I walk over to him and he opens his arm and invites me to join him. I crawl onto his lap and lay my head on his chest. I hear the strong, steady beating of his heart. My whole body rises and falls with each breath he takes. And it's like being plugged into an energy source. I feel my fatigue start to lift and my nerves start to soothe.

I used to lament being so short. But it seems I was perfectly made to fit him. After listening to Lacy talk for almost five minutes, Reece finally says, "You've made yourself clear, Lacy. But, we're not going into hiding. We'll be in Malibu unless being in LA is absolutely necessary." She tries to cut him off, but he speaks over her. "It's late here, I'm tired and hungry. And we can't turn back time." He listens again and then says, "Fine. Yep. Bye." And hangs up. He immediately powers his phone off and throws it across to the couch opposite us.

He adjusts his position and my legs move to straddle his hips. "I thought she'd never let me hang up," he says as he starts to run his fingers through my hair, gathering it into a ponytail in his fist.

"You were a very naught boy today, Reece Carras; you deserved that talking to," I say to him, mock disapproval in my voice.

"I don't regret it." He leans forward and kisses the tip of my chin and then tugs softly on the handful of hair he's holding, and looks at me. "Do you?"

"No," I answer honestly. "They seem more interested in you anyway. They're just referring to me as the author Reece Carras is seeing. No one really cares *who* I am. And that's fine with me." I'm surprisingly relaxed tonight. "You know, I'd been dreading all of the publicity and attention. But, I can understand how important it was for the movie and the story. Thank you for pushing me."

"I'm proud of you. You did good today, Luc. And when we leave tomorrow night, we'll go straight to Malibu and lay low for a while. In a couple of days, someone will break up, get married or post naked selfies on Instagram and they'll forget about us." He loosens his grip on my hair and I let my head fall back on his chest.

His big hands start to roam my back. Caressing, searching for spots of tension and then rubbing them until they disappear. I doze off several times in the twenty minutes we sit there. Each of us lost in our own thoughts.

We had to forgo our tour of Rockefeller Plaza earlier because of the media circus our presence caused. But even that change didn't bring the disappointment I would have expected. I know that I'll find a way to come back to this city. I feel unshackled. Reece has expanded my entire world. My heart is lighter. I'm less afraid and I see paths of ingress and egress where I hadn't before.

Tomorrow morning we're visiting Ground Zero and going out to see the Statue of Liberty before we go to see the site for what will be Artemis' New York office. The company is buying one of the larger news networks and has started setting up shop in preparation for the move. It's an acquisition that his father has been working on for almost two years, and the announcement has been causing waves in the entertainment world. Lots of discussion about the independence of news and what will happen once it's owned by a company that is profit driven. Reece told me today that his father wants him to run the office, but he's not sold on the idea, especially if he decides to run for political office.

"You're tired?" Reece murmurs, his warm breath tickling the fine hairs on the side of my face. I reach up and caress the back of his neck, let my fingers run into his hair. He presses warm, open mouthed kisses on my neck.

"Yeah, a little, but I don't want to sleep. Let's go sit out on the balcony and watch the city . . . can we?"

"Your wish is my command, Fifty."

"This nickname is devolving, Reece. I've stopped signing with my initials because of you. I've been horrified at the idea that there're a bunch of people who I email that are calling me Fifty-five behind my back."

He laughs and lifts me off his lap as he stands up. "Your imagination is pretty out of control there, Fiddy."

I dissolve into giggles at this, and he takes my hand and pulls me up to standing. "I'll grab the Glen Fiddich, you grab the glasses. Meet you outside."

I go to the suite's little micro kitchen and grab two tumblers and walk outside. It's a cold November night, but the heat lamps on the deck make it possible for me to be comfortable in just a Henley and pajama bottoms.

Reece settles onto a chair and puts the things he's carrying on the table in front of us. Along with the bottle of whisky, he's also got a tube of lube and a dildo I've never seen before. I feel myself clench at the sight of them.

I have turned into a sexually insatiable woman. Reece and I fuck all the time. I can't get enough of his cock in my mouth, in my pussy. I hadn't had him in my ass yet. But tonight, I think I'm ready. New York City makes me feel like testing my limits.

Reece pours us each two fingers of whisky and then beckons me to come to him. I sit, my back to his chest, my legs bent at the knee, my feet perched on his thigh. We sit there silent as we take in the noises, the lights and each other.

When we're in Malibu, Reece and I usually end our evenings outside. Sitting and listening to the ocean as it plays us a symphony of cresting, crashing and receding waves. I take a sip of my drink and savor the burn as liquid travels down my throat, warming me from the inside out.

Reece pushes my hair forward and starts to feather kisses on the slope of my shoulder where it meets my neck.

"I love you." The three words that his actions have been telling me for weeks, fall out of his mouth in supplication. My heart flutters, and I feel myself grow wet as a throb comes to life between my legs. He kisses the base of my neck and my head falls backward, blanketing him with my hair.

Before I can respond he says, "This trip has been amazing. I've loved being here with you. I feel fucking invincible with you by my side. And I wanted the whole world to know that we're a team. In every way that matters. The last two months have been incredible. He continues kissing his way up. I turn my head, and lift my arm to wrap around his neck.

"And I love you, Reece."

"Fuck, yeah you do," he says against my lips before he claims them in a kiss that I feel straight down to the tips of my toes. I can feel him filling me with his kiss, healing me with it. The ache that lives in my heart disappears when Reece kisses me. The worries that plague my daily life vaporize as I completely immerse myself in the experience of sharing my love with this man.

Without breaking our kiss, he plucks my drink from my hand and I hear the clank of glass as it lands on the table.

His hands come up and cup both of my breasts. I'm braless under my shirt and he takes my nipples in between his fingers and squeezes, rolling them as he does. A moan floats out of my mouth in a sigh that's more like a hallelujah. I've ached for him all day, for his touch, the pleasure and the pain and I'm dripping wet already thinking about what's to come. I writhe in his lap, dropping my legs so I'm straddling him, sliding back and forth on his rock-hard cock.

I stand up and turn to face him, and drop to my knees.

He drops his head back in anticipation, puts his hand in my hair and caresses it absently. The sounds of the city are muted now and my mind focuses on the task of unbuckling his belt, unzipping his pants and freeing his cock. My mouth waters in anticipation. I bend down and place my mouth on the tip of his head that's already protruding from his briefs. I swirl my tongue over it and he hisses as his hips thrust up.

I use my hands to pull his briefs down, taking him deeper into my mouth as I expose him. He hits the back of my throat and I feel the sting of tears as my throat protests. I pull my mouth up, running my tongue along the underside of his length until I reach the tip. I suckle it.

"Lucía, baby. Yes," Reece whispers as his fingers wrap themselves in my hair and he starts thrusting into my mouth. I put my hand between his legs and cradle his balls, I rolls them in my fingers and Reece moans and then says, "No, stop." He lifts me to standing and yanks my pajama bottoms off and then yanks me back on his lap. His cock slips up and down in between the desire-drenched folds of my pussy and he reaches to the table for the lube and the dildo. He mumbles into my neck in between kisses, "I want to put this in your ass." My thighs clench. "You ready for that?"

"Reece, I want *you* in my ass tonight. I'm ready," I say insistently, knowing that he wouldn't need much convincing.

"You don't need to ask me twice," Reece says. He's already lubing up the pucker in my ass, pushing a finger, then another inside to lubricate and stretch me.

My hips start rolling, my pussy clenching eager to be filled. When he picks up the dildo, I startle a little "I thought you said . . ."

He kisses me to silence me, and with his tongue slicing through the last of my wits, I forget about the dildo and feast on the meal this man is feeding me. And then I feel it, the cool, plastic, dildo pushing into my pussy. I bear down on it and let go of the remnants of the day's stress. He pushes it in to the root and then leaves it there.

I contract around it enjoying the sensation it causes as it rubs against the bundle of nerves deep inside me. And then he shifts me, grabs his cock and lathers it in lube. He lifts me up and positions his cock at the entrance of my ass and says, "You're driving, let me know if you want help." I feel the broad tip of him at my pucker and I look at him as I lower myself onto him. The sensation is indescribable. It hurts, but in a way that is exquisitely delicious. I slide lower, slowly. My eyes closed, trying to focus on all of the sensations assaulting my body right now. I don't even hear the street noise. I hear only my blood rushing as my heart works to pump blood to the places that are demanding it.

I feel his cock rub against the dildo as I take more of him inside me. This is peak pleasure. I grunt as I finally sit down fully, resting my ass on his thighs. I feel impossibly full. My pleasure is tinged with a trill of fear that this might be too much. Can a body handle this much bliss?

"Lucía, my God. I . . . you've got to move."

I start to rock my hips, lifting and then coming back down to take him again. I grunt at the effort I'm making and Reece's eyes open.

"You can take it, baby." He squeezes my ass and dips his head to pull my nipple into my mouth through my shirt. The hot wet recess of his mouth sending sparks of electricity straight to my core.

"Reece, it's too much. I can't." I moan as I feel something flip inside, it's the beginning of an orgasm, but it's from a place inside of me I've never felt.

"Too much? It will never be enough, Lucía." And then he starts to thrust his hips upward. I cry out from the powerful tremors inside of me. My thighs start to shake so badly that I have trouble balancing myself. Reece's arms band around me. I reach between us and touch my clit and as soon as I do, I explode. Reece's arms tighten as I shudder my release, one that feels endless and threatens to overwhelm me. I feel like I've been shot from a catapult and am hurtling through space and time, completely untethered. Caged in the arms of the man I love, I find a new kind of freedom.

Reece's rhythm falters as he starts to make slower, more powerful thrusts inside of me and then, he's groaning into my neck, grinding up into me.

Fifteen minutes later, we're showered, and in our hotel bed. One hand is holding mine under the covers, the other is stroking my hair as we both start to drift into sleep.

Reece mumbles at the edge of sleep and wakefulness, "You make me so happy, baby. Thank you for this trip, I know what a big deal it is."

"I've had the time of my life," I whisper back.

"You ain't seen nothing yet." And then he yawns and squeezes my hand.

And just like on every other night I've spent with him, I fall in love, at a thousand miles an hour, all over again.

35

Reece

WE'RE HAVING DINNER WITH LUCÍA'S ENTIRE FAMILY tonight. Well, the ones that live in California anyway. All five of them. It's inconceivable to me, even as an only child, that she has such a small family and just a couple of friends. My extended family is huge—I have cousins, aunts, uncles. Even my parents' close friends are more like family. And I have a good group of friends. I feel a pang of pain as I remind myself that part of the reason her family is so small is because of me. I realize how alone she's been until now.

We stand for seconds that feel like minutes, on the doorstep of her uncle's house. I stare at the nondescript door that fits in with the nondescript house, in this nondescript neighborhood.

I look down at Lucía. She looks calm; chin up, eyes on the door, a sweet smile on her face. Only the death grip she has on my hand tells me that she's anything but. I give her hand a return squeeze and she glances up at me and gives me a self-deprecating smile.

"Sorry. It's just that I haven't seen them in so long." She loosens her grip on my hand. "At least we're not going back to that house," she says with a shiver. "I have such bad memories." She looks around the stoop, taking in the house. I clench my jaw to keep from asking why the hell we were even here. I don't know if I can sit politely in the same room with people who I know treated her unkindly. We were supposed to be going to her mother's, but she called this morning and asked us to come here instead.

She told Lucía that she wanted me to meet everyone. And my girl couldn't say no to her mother; and, here we are. I would have liked this first meeting to be just us, so I could say the words of apology I needed to say to her mother privately. I'll have to find a way to pull her aside when the opportunity presents itself.

Keeping my voice neutral, I say, "You'll be fine. We're here together."

She leans into me and sighs. I press a kiss to the top of her head. Letting the familiar fragrance of her soothe my nerves.

And just then, the door swings open and a woman, who looks to be in her late fifties, answers the door. Her green eyes glittering, her bright red lips parted in a grin that reveals tiny white teeth set in massive gums. She gazes at Lucía, her expression almost theatrical in its attempt to look genuinely happy to see us.

"Ana, come, come. Let me look at you," she says as she

rushes forward and gathers Lucía into her bony arms, giving her a bear hug.

Lucía looks up at me, raises her eyebrows and returns my questioning looking with an expression that says, *Fuck if I know.*

She pulls back and then looks at me, her smile even wider now. "Oh, and, Mr. Carras. What an honor it is for us to have you in our humble home." And then she curtsies.

I don't know whether to laugh or help her up to standing. Instead, I just say, "The honor's mine, thank you for having us."

She rises out of her pose and her eyes widen, and she says, "Oh, I'm sorry. Please come in. We are very glad to have you visit our home."

Lucía told me they had two children. Two girls, who she'd practically helped raise, are about ten and twelve years younger than she is.

The house is deathly quiet and smells like vanilla. It's immaculate and decorated very tastefully. It doesn't look like a house where two little girls live. A short hallway leads to a large living area, where a man and a woman are sitting. They both stand up as soon as we walk in and the woman, who I know is Lucía's mother as soon as I see her face, walks over to us.

She's taller than Lucía, and she's almost wiry in build. Her dark her is pulled back in a severe bun and it reveals a face that is softly lined and beautiful. Her eyes, dark and intensely sad move over us. "Mama, this is Reece," Lucía says as her mother reaches us. If she notices her mother's expression, she's not reacting to it.

She presses a kiss on each of her mother's cheeks, lingering on the second one. Her eyes closing for a second as she savors the touch.

Her mother turns to me and the weight from the sadness in

her eyes lands right on my chest. She smiles though, and steps up to give me a hug. I'm surprised at first, but return it. She hugs me for a long time and then with a final squeeze lets go.

The man, who I assume is Lucía's uncle steps forward. He's short, shorter than his wife, with a full head of very dark hair and a full mustache that hides his upper lip.

Lucía moves to stand behind me slightly in a move that surprises me. My eyes dart back to her uncle and I don't miss the censorious glance he gives Lucía before he turns to me and says, "Well, I see Lucía's forgotten all the manners we taught her. I'm Jaime Rios. Welcome to our home, Mr. Carras." And he puts his hand out. He said that like it was funny and that he thinks himself charming. I look at his hand and am tempted to refuse to shake it, when I feel a surprisingly strong finger poke me in the back.

"Thank you for having us," I respond, without any warmth.

Out of the corner of my eye, I see her mother walk past us, back towards the couch. She whispers something in Lucía's ear as she passes and Lucía's eyes grow large and she looks at her mother.

She follows her and says, "What do you mean you're sorry. Sorry for what?" Her mother doesn't respond, only sits back on the couch and puts her face in her hands. I look around and realize that the house is still very quiet. We were invited for dinner, but if anything is cooking I can't smell it. They look dressed for company, but something else is going on here.

An alarm goes off in my head and I forget my attempt at politeness.

"What's going on?" I turn to her uncle and ask. He and his wife are exchanging meaningful glances, but neither one of them answers me. I walk over to her mother and put an arm around her.

"Mrs. Rios, whatever you're sorry for, you can tell us in the car. We're leaving," I say and Lucía doesn't miss a beat, standing up and grabbing her mother's purse.

"No, we can't go," She says pitifully through her fingers that are still covering her face.

"She's right. You can't leave." Her uncle's echoed statement is unequivocal and I turn to look at him

"The hell we can't. What the fuck are you even talking about?" I ask him as I turn my attention back to Mrs. Rios.

"Tell them, Marisol," her aunt pipes in, sounding a lot less friendly.

"Tell us what?" Lucía asks, finding her voice finally as she squats down in front of her mother. She pries her fingers off her face.

Her eyes are red and glassy and she closes them as soon as she sees her daughter in front of her.

"I can't. Lucía, I'm sorry. I didn't know what else to do." And then she starts to cry, hysterically.

This scene is turning very bad, very fast.

I turn back to her uncle and grab him by his arm.

"Tell us what's going on, now."

He smiles what I'm sure he thinks is a calming and somewhat charming smile.

"Why don't we all sit down. This doesn't need to be contentious. Let's just talk." And as if to lead by example he and wife sit down on the love seat across from the couch.

I make a snap judgment when I see Lucía still crouched in front of her mother, trying to comfort her.

I sit and say, "Okay, talk."

His eyes flit to his niece and then back to me.

"What's going on is that Lucía's rich now. We are the ones

who took her in and raised her. We deserve to be compensated for that."

Lucía hops up and turns to them, her eyes wide and hot with rage.

"You raised me?" she hisses at them. "You made me your live-in maid. You ignored me. Made me eat alone in the kitchen." She turns to her aunt and her eyes narrow. The woman pales. "And *you.*" The "you" is filled with venom. "You stole from me." Her teeth are clenched.

Her aunt's eyes widen in mock horror. "You little liar. You owe us," she says her voice trembling, lacking the bravado of her husband.

Her mother surges out of her seat and makes a beeline for the woman. I grab her just as he reaches her, arm drawn back and ready to strike. She doesn't resist my restraint, but leans toward them to say, "You are vile people. You have so much, and yet you want more."

"Who doesn't want more? What we're asking for is nothing for someone like you. Pay us or we'll make sure that everyone knows who Ana really is. We watched your interviews. Your little story about her being a girl from LA was cute, but we know better. Three million dollars and you can rest easy that we'll leave you alone." Lucía pales and she staggers back to the couch to sit down. Her mother starts crying again and I just look at him.

He's wearing a straight face, but I can see the strain. I want to laugh at the absolute brazenness of his statement.

"Three million dollars," I repeat slowly.

"Yes. Insignificant really. I mean, you've got planes, and own buildings. I saw you two all over each other, but that Lucía doesn't really exist. It's a new day in America. All those undocumented activists who walked around like they had a right to, they're being rounded up and deported. And when they find out she's getting rich off her crimes, they'll kick her out so fast, her head will spin."

Lucía's mother is on the move again and this time I can't stop her. The room is silent as the crack of her palm on his face reverberates.

Her eyes grow wide and she covers her mouth with her hand.

He doesn't even flinch.

"You just battered a police officer, Marisol," he says with cold eyes glaring at her. She doesn't even look his way. She lifts her chin, in the same way Lucía does, grabs her purse and walks out of the room.

Lucía is still sitting on the couch, but her eyes are glued to the floor, her face expressionless.

I walk over to her and put my hand on her shoulder. "Luc, go with your mom. Get in the car, I'm coming." She nods numbly and without looking at me walks out of the room, too.

I turn to her uncle. I assess him, he's a bully and his wife is a fool. But these are the most dangerous types of people.

"Mr. Carras," he says as if we're old friends. "Let's take the emotion out of it. Now that it's just us men we can make a deal." I glance at his wife whose existence he seems to have forgotten.

I sneer at him and say, "I don't see another man in this room. Don't come near Lucía or her mother again, or I'll ruin everything you even think you care about and leave you intact to live with the devastation."

"She is my niece." His voice shows emotion for the first time, anger emanating from the last word. "We took care of her. She's basically won the lottery. She needs to take care of us, too.

That's how blood works." He's spitting at the end of his sentence.

I look at his wife. She's sitting with her head hanging down between her shoulders. I can't tell if the pose is one borne of shame or defeat, but either one makes me want to shake these people.

"She owes you shit. Exactly what you gave her. Don't call her or her mother again. Unless it's to apologize." I turn to walk out. He calls after me.

"You're making a mistake, Mr. Carras. I know you think you're powerful and can't be touched by someone like me, but Lucía's not."

I don't stop walking until I'm at my car. I can see Lucía and her mother inside. Through the windshield, I can see that they are having a furiously heated conversation. They are both in the backseat, their hands gesturing wildly as they talk.

Lucía notices me just before I open the door and as soon as I do, they stop talking.

I sigh, but don't say anything. I start the ignition and pull out of the driveway without saying a word. Neither do they and we sit like that, in a fraught silence for a long time.

We're on the 405 headed south, not quite sure what my final destination is tonight, before I decide to speak.

"Tell me what's going on. If you knew what they were going to do, why didn't you warn us?" My voice is gentle. I try not to sound accusatory, but right now, that's how I feel. I don't understand the role her mother plays in all of this.

"Reece, I'm sorry—" Lucía starts.

"No." Her mother's voice is stronger than I've ever heard it before. "No, I'm sorry. I did what I thought would keep Lucía safe."

"Safe from what? From them reporting her?"

"Yes," she says her voice losing all its confidence.

"Mama, why didn't you say anything? All this time. They're always going to want more from us. It won't ever be enough." She sounds anguished and it's like every single nerve ending in my body can feel it.

"And I'll give them more. And you should, too. You need to keep them quiet."

I feel a chill run through me at the exchange.

"Have you given them money already?" I ask her, not able to hide the disbelief from my voice.

"She's given them everything I've given her," Lucía responds for her, anguish now layered with frustration. I don't respond. I'm not sure how to.

She responds with equal emotion. "If I hadn't, your name would be in the papers by now. I've seen all those young people being arrested. DREAMERs, like you. The country has changed and it doesn't matter if you're breaking the law or not, they will send you back to Mexico. And I've already lost everyone. I wasn't going to lose you, too."

Lucía sighs wearily.

Through my rear view mirror, I see her mother reach out and smooth back her hair. "I'm sorry, Ana."

She meets my eyes in the mirror and I wonder if it's just today or if that heartbreak is part of her permanent visage. I see her shoulders square before I look back to the road and then hear her say, "If you want this to go away, if you really want to be free, you need to leave this country and go back to Mexico."

36

MY EYES IMMEDIATELY GO TO THE REAR VIEW MIRROR TO
try and catch a glimpse of Reece's face. It's too dark and all I can
see in the shadowy darkness of the car are pieces of his forehead
and part of his nose. His eyes are hidden. But I can feel his
hackles rise at her words. I'd hoped to have this conversation
with him when we were alone.

"I know," I say to my mother. All my earlier sadness is gone,
replaced with outrage.

"You could come back. But it would take time. There's a
penalty period, but maybe you could get a waiver," she says, her

voice sounding hopeful and I find myself stunned speechless for a moment.

"I know. I talked to a lawyer," I return.

Reece hasn't said a word, but he speaks up then. "You talked to a lawyer?" he asks. I nod.

"But why? Why haven't you said anything?"

I want to plead with him to understand. I feel sadder now than I have in a long time.

"It's best, Ana. You should go." This comes from my mother. I turn to look at her. Resentment wells in me.

My mother, who sent me to live with those monsters. Who distanced herself from me and as soon as I think we might be able to salvage a relationship, is talking about sending me away again. Except this time, she's not the only person I'd be leaving behind. I look at Reece again and this time when I meet his eyes, I can see that he is angry.

My mother's eyes follow mine to him and what she sees causes her eyes to widen.

"Please, just listen. Those people, they will report you if you don't pay them. And if you pay them now, they'll be back. You should leave, just drive down to the border, and walk across."

I stare at her in horror. "You want me to leave? To just go? And only *hope* I can come back?" I ask her incredulously.

"They'll let you come back. My friend did it."

"We're not paying anything. You're not leaving." Reece's voice, so deep and cold, cuts into our exchange.

My mother looks at him, her voice sharp and caustic, "You've already sent one of my children to detention. You won't do it to another."

The words are a poisoned-tipped bow hitting its target. Reece's entire body jerks. But he doesn't say anything.

"Mama!" I gasp in horror.

"I'm sorry, Reece. I'm just scared," she says quietly. She lets go of my hand and scoots away from me, pressing herself against the door of the car. She looks at me, like she's afraid of me. I'm torn between defending Reece and reassuring her that a part of me understands. Because I do.

"Lucía, I have never been able to protect my children. Every threat that came near them, touched them and ruined them. Your brother is dead. You were molested by a boy who's shit I'm still wiping up."

I look at Reece, I've only recently told him that story and he'd been so angry that I'd refused to tell him the family's name.

"I had to send you away to live with those people knowing that they would make it difficult for me to see you." Her eyes flit to Reece and I feel my stomach twist. This is a nightmare of epic proportions.

"If you love my daughter, you'll encourage her to do this. If you marry without her doing this, her status won't change. She'll have your children and just like me, she'll be living in the shadows, unable to protect them from anything. What about when you want to take your kids to see Europe for the first time? She won't be able to go. Are you going to hire a driver to get her around? Do you want to live with the fear that she'll be deported? Once the film is out, she'll only become more famous. It won't take a blackmailer. Just someone who is creative enough to connect the dots," she says to Reece, her voice beseeching.

Reece looks at me and I look at him. I let all my emotion show in my eyes, I pray he understands what I'm saying. *I'm sorry. Get me out of here. I love you.* His eyes soften slightly and he looks at my mother.

"Okay," he says on a big exhaled sigh. "It's been a long day. We all have a lot to think about. I think we should get going."

She doesn't say anything. She only looks down at her hands.

"I only love you, Ana. I'm just trying to make things right."

"I know, Mama. I love you, too. I'm just tired. I'll call you this week. We can talk some more."

NEITHER OF US has said a word since we got in the car. Reece is pensive and I can feel the angry energy radiating from him. We were supposed to spend the night at Reece's house, but when Reece passes the exit for Calabasas and gets on the I-10 instead, I know we're headed to Malibu. We need to be there.

"Reece . . . I'm sorry," I say, feeling how wholly inadequate and thin that is right now, but it's all I've got.

He only squeezes my hand in response. His eyes never leaving the road.

My shame knows no bounds. He's seen the raw underbelly of my life. The part that I've cultivated this exterior to protect. My uncle blackmailed him. My mother threw Julian's death in his face. And she painted the bleak picture of the life we're facing if I continue to live here in undocumented status. My uncle is right that since this new administration rode a wave of anti-immigrant sentiment into office, people who had been safe were no longer. And my DACA application is still under review.

I hear my mother's voice, "*It won't take a blackmailer.*" She's right. I know she is. I need to think about this and plan for a way to leave the country before I'm deported. That will make coming back much more difficult. I growl in frustration.

Reece sighs and glances at me. It's dark and I can't see his face, and part of me is glad. What would I see there? Sadness? Anger, maybe? Other things I'm too afraid to give voice to.

"Luc . . . I don't know what to say. There are a million

things running through my head, but none of them feel like they're ready to come out." Reece sounds just the way I feel—tired and defeated. "Let's try to get some sleep and see how things look in the morning."

His voice is neutral, but his knuckles are white as they grip the steering wheel. I see the flex of the muscle where his jaw hinges. Guilt mixes with my shame and that growl wants to become a scream. I'm afraid I may never sleep again. My life for the last couple of months has felt too good to be true. I'd forgotten the realities of my situation. I feel myself starting to descend that very dangerous and seemingly endless ladder of self-pity that I've avoided for most of my life.

I've always worked around the roadblocks, pursued my goals even when I had no real hope of seeing them realized. And now, I have to figure out how to plan a future when I don't even have the right to live in the same country as the man I love . . . if Reece wants that. We haven't talked seriously about where we're heading. I love him, desperately, and it's happened so quickly that my feet have barely touched the ground since that day in the pool when he told me, "I lied," and then pressed his lips to my neck.

I glance at his profile again taking him in. Tonight at my uncle's house I was worried that things would turn even uglier. Reece isn't used to anyone making demands and threatening him. My uncle and aunt are nasty, greedy people. I'm sure this is just the beginning of their blackmail. A niggle of self-doubt worms its way into my inner dialogue. Is Reece wondering if I'm worth all this trouble? My heart skips a beat at that thought. Is he going to leave me? I don't know that I would blame him. I'm not sure that I would invite this much trouble into my life voluntarily.

"Fifty-five, I can practically hear your mind working. I only suggested we sleep on it, but if you want to talk we should. I don't want you going to bed with this weighing on you."

His voice is kind, his spirit generous. I want to crawl into his lap and stay there. To bask in the cocoon of safety and security that he's provided me. I want to fuse myself to him so that I never have to be without him. I can't imagine what today would have been like if he hadn't been there. Actually, I can. My uncle and aunt were abusive when I lived with them. She hit me whenever the fancy took her and he berated me, reminding me of the debt I was accruing in their house.

And two years after I moved in with them, when I was fourteen, my can of money, the one I hid under my bed, disappeared. It contained every penny I'd saved from the odd jobs I'd taken after school. I didn't tell her that I was working, I hadn't wanted them to know. And it wasn't very much, but it was everything I had. She didn't even try to deny having taken it. She told me their utility bill had increased since I'd moved in. When I told my mother, she'd only told me to pray. I left as soon as I was able and I never looked back. He's my father's cousin and the furthest things from family I can think of.

"Reece, we can't pay them."

"Of course we're not going to pay them. I'm not even going to give them a second thought. And you shouldn't either." His voice is sharp and bruising. He doesn't say anything else and neither do I. The silence in the car is uncomfortable and I don't know how to make it better. We pull up to the gates of the Malibu estate and Reece punches in the code to open the gate.

I need to think about what I'm going to do, but I also need to find a lawyer. I need to explore my options and then decide what's going to be best. I start to say this to Reece when he says, "I'm just going to drop you off tonight, Luc. I'm headed back to

LA. I have an early meeting . . ." His voice trails off. Early meetings hadn't kept him from staying with me before.

My heart sinks. I swallow and try to keep my voice from quavering. "Is this too much? More than you signed up for?" I quietly ask one last question. "Are you thinking of breaking up with me?" I'm not prepared for him to answer that honestly. I don't look at him; I just stare straight ahead.

He doesn't answer, the gate opens and the car doesn't move. When the gate starts to close again, I finally look up at him. And my breath catches. He's staring at me, looking at me with eyes full of naked, unabashed love. And behind that is something much harder to identify, it's need, promise, helplessness and anger all blended together.

"Reece . . . " It's a question and a demand.

Without responding, he turns the car off and gets out. He closes his door with a slam that makes me jump. His stride is long and angry as I watch him round the hood of the car. In a flash, he's snatching my door open. He reaches across me to unlatch my seat belt. He grips me by the forearms and yanks me out of the car. I yelp in surprise as he turns me around, and presses me against the side of the car. He kicks my legs apart and then steps into me. I feel his rock-hard erection pressing into my lower back and I start to squirm. I rub my thighs together and my entire body clenches in anticipation.

"I fucking love you," he growls in to my ear. "I've been waiting for you my whole life." His hands tangle in the hair at the nape of my neck and he pulls my hair back to expose my throat. His mouth hovers over my ear, sending a chill through me and causing a whimper to escape me. "We were made for each other. You were looking for freedom . . . I thought I'd already found it. I had no idea." He puts his open mouth on my throat and starts to suck it. Hard and fast. My hips move of their own volition. He groans, his hand leaving my hair and moving to my side. One of them cups my breast through the thin fabric of my dress and squeezes. The other runs down my thigh and yanks the dress up around my hips exposing my bare flesh to the cool night air. His rubs my ass, squeezing and kneading it.

"You think that it could ever be too much? That what happened today would scare me off?" He bites my ear, then moves to my throat. "Lucía, I'll ruin anyone who tries to hurt you."

I feel him lean his hips away and tear the zipper of his jeans as he pulls them down. It's dark, but we're outside, just off a main road. Anyone could drive by. I feel a surge of moisture at the thought. I turn my head and look around. "You looking around because you want to make sure no one sees?" He tips my hips back while dipping his hand inside my panties. "Or are you hoping someone will drive by while I'm fucking you?" I grind myself against his fingers and a moan rips from my throat.

"Yeah. You like that." He laughs and then grunts as he puts two of his thick fingers inside of me.

"You're always so ready for me. Fuck. I need in you," he says before his fingers leave me. He pushes my panties to the side and then with one strong thrust, enters me. His cock is hard and with every thrust he sends a jolt through me that runs from the top of my head to the tips of my toes. He grabs my waist with both hands and sets a punishing pace. I groan, long and low at the sensations he's creating inside of me. "Tell me you love me," he whispers frantically in my ear as he fucks me out in the open like our entire lives depended on it.

"I love you." I manage to get out.

"Yes. You do. Don't fucking doubt us. I'm not going

anywhere." He pants in my ear. One of his hands leaves my hips and circles around to find my clit. It's pulsing and when he touches it, I feel my orgasm start to build.

"Shit, yes. Come for me, baby," Reece mumbles in my ear. He keeps talking but I don't understand a word. I'm lost to my climax and soon Reece is, too. He shudders and groans at my back as he comes. His finger digging into my hips so tightly that I know I'll be bruised there tomorrow.

He lays over me for a few minutes when he's done, breathing hard as he pulls out of me.

"Stay right there," he says as he runs over to his side and comes back with a hand full of tissues. He kneels in front of me, lifts my dress up and wipes me clean.

Still on his knees, he looks up at me. His eyes have lost the anger and helplessness, but the love and promise remain.

"I'm not going anywhere, Luc. Unless you're coming with me."

I stroke his face with my hand, caressing his cheek and looking back into the eyes that have come to be a compass for me. I look at them when I need to find my true north.

He's it. And I need to fix things so that I can be a real partner to him. Before I started this journey, I'd thought about coming out of the shadows and finding my path to citizenship or at least to legal residency. My life has been a series of dramatic events that propelled me in a direction I have little control over. I don't want this to be like that. I want to plan and do it, and give myself the best shot at being granted re-entry.

37

"I'M GOING TO CALL THAT IMMIGRATION LAWYER *tomorrow. See if I can get an appointment," Lucía says as we lay in bed, she's drifting off and I was too, but at her words, I'm suddenly wide awake.*

"Okay . . ." I respond not sure what else to say.

"I just need advice, Reece. I need to know what my options are."

"Options?" I repeat, dumbly.

"Yes, my options for trying to change my status. I can't live like this anymore."

"I understand; do you want me to help you find someone?" I ask calmly, even though my mind is screaming "no." I know

she needs to do this. I'm just afraid of what happens when we open this door.

"I'll let you know. I'll see what the lawyer I spoke to before says," she responds, through a yawn.

"If you could write the answer to your problem, what would it be. If you could have anything you wanted?" I ask after a few minutes.

"I'd be an American citizen."

I'M AT MY PARENTS' for breakfast, replaying the conversation I had with Lucía last night. My mother's voice interrupts my thoughts.

"Reece, you haven't graced our breakfast table on a weekday in over a year. To what do we owe the pleasure?" She asks as she and my father come into their dining room.

I feel a twinge of guilt. I stand up to kiss her and to give my father a hug. "I know, guys. I'm sorry. You know how life gets." They sit down on either end of the table and it feels like I'm back in high school. I look at both of them before my eyes settle on my father. "I need your help."

I drove back to LA after Lucía fell asleep. I left her a note telling her I'd call her later. On the drive here, I'd replayed the entire evening. Her aunt and uncle's fuckery. Her mother's hard truths. Me fucking her against the car yesterday. Trying to fuck away our fear, trying to say with my body what I couldn't with my words. I need her. And she needs me. I've let her down so far. I've buried my head in the sand about this issue, thinking that this love would insulate us. Or that my money and influence might be enough to protect her.

Yesterday, I watched real life puncture holes in the little bubble of avoidance I'd been living in. I'm glad my illusions have been destroyed, because they've rendered me useless when she really needed me. I wasn't prepared for any of what happened yesterday. Lucía took hits on all sides yesterday, and all I'd done was watch.

"Not every day that you ask me for that, son. Tell me what you need." My dad puts his coffee cup down and folds his hands on top of the table. He doesn't smile at me, because he knows that whatever this is, it's not something to smile at.

"It's Lucía," I say and his brow furrows.

"Things not working out?" my mother asks from her end of the table.

I glance at her, not hiding my irritation. "Sorry to disappoint you, Mom, but we're fine."

She actually looks affronted. "Reece! Is that what you think? That I'd take delight in you being unhappy? Never. Yes, I don't believe you're well-suited. I would have liked to see you with someone who understands our world. But I know you love her—"

"She's the love of my life," I interrupt her, not wanting the conversation to go off the rails.

"Then what's wrong?"

"Her uncle tried to blackmail us yesterday. He wants money or he'll reveal her status," I say quickly.

I look at my father and he and my mother are looking at each other. They're having a silent conversation. Clearly this has been something they've thought about.

"Yes, we figured things like that would start happening. This is an easy one to dismiss, but..." My father sighs. "I warned you. And it's only going to get worse."

"I know you warned me. You were right. You can say I told you so. But I need to figure out to how to make this right."

They exchange another glance.

"She needs to see a lawyer," my mother says. "But, Reece, honey, you have to be very sure that this woman is what you want. Things could get ugly before they get better."

"What could get ugly?" Coco says as he saunters into the living room.

"Nothing." I'd forgotten he was living here again. He'd been driving some of our other talent since he'd been re-assigned from Lucía, and I hadn't seen him in months.

The conversation is over. I look at my parents and say, "Thanks for the chat, guys, I have to get going."

"Oh, don't leave on my account. How's Lucía? I hear you're tapping that these days," Coco says with a shit eating grin on his face.

"Coco, don't be so crass," my mother admonishes. My father though doesn't say anything, but I can see him looking at Coco with disappointment in his eyes. He loves Coco like a son. He's his brother's only surviving child. But I can see that Coco's general state of being a fuck up is starting to weigh on him.

"You're lucky that I'm tired and that I don't really give a shit about what you think," I say as I stand up.

"Yeah, Reece, I'm really lucky," he scoffs and rolls his eyes.

My dad stands up, too. "I'll walk you out, son." And we leave the room together.

"I'm sorry about Coco interrupting us. I've been working on something, Reece, and I need you to fly to New York this afternoon to get the ball rolling. Clarissa's looking for flights as we speak."

I stop and look at him. "Today? Now? The screenplay is being handed over officially on Wednesday. I have things to deal with here."

"Reece. You are the president of the film studio, not Lucía's social worker. She doesn't need you here to help her hand over her work and she doesn't need you to take her to see a lawyer. You need to remember your priorities and your obligations. Think about your family and the legacy we've built. This thing you're doing with her could bring a very uncomfortable spotlight on Artemis. We've tolerated your activism, hell, I even support it. But not at the expense of things that are really important." I'm too shocked to respond and he puts a hand on my shoulder.

"Son, I know you're feeling things now. But you need more than love to build a successful marriage. You'll find that with someone who's better suited. Trust me. I had a beautiful, sexy girl who let me walk on the wild side for a while before I met your mother. But I did my duty to my family. I married well and your mother and I have had a very good marriage. She's been a real partner. She hasn't held me back in any way. This woman's going to hold you back. I know why you want her, but you have to decide if it's worth it."

If he'd punched me in the face, I don't think I could have been more surprised. I didn't know that he only "tolerated" my activism. I'll clearly need to work this out on my own. I can see now that neither one of them really want Lucía to be a permanent part of my life. And that is not an option for me. I don't just want her, I need her. I love her. She's changed my life.

I give him a curt nod.

I look at him, as if seeing him for the first time. The disappointment I feel, is crushing. But all I say is, "I understand. I'll go to New York." I then turn and leave to head to the office. I've got a lot to do.

38

Reece has been in New York City since Monday. He left while I was sleeping and I haven't seen him since Sunday night. This morning, he called to say he's extending his trip for one more day. He wouldn't be back until Friday. The project he went to work on needs more time. He sounded so happy when we spoke that I didn't want to tell him about my conversation with the lawyer.

She'd been able to squeeze me in on Monday afternoon. I left her office with a chasm in my heart as wide as the Grand Canyon. I'd wished that I was the kind of person who could bury my head in the sand and pretend that everything was fine.

What she told me devastated me. I don't have any good options. My DACA application is still pending. She's seeing a trend of the revocation of the status of vocal immigration activists since February of this year. She thought it likely that ICE was already aware of my status and was just waiting for the application to be denied before they pounced. My heart leapt into my throat. Fear, real and potent, chilled me.

She advised me to voluntarily depart. That it would increase my chances of being able to re-enter. I'd be barred from even trying to re-enter for three years. And there was no guarantee they would grant my request when I made it. Yet, it was my best hope. There were no other options for me to stay in the United States legally. When I was leaving she gave me her card and told me that I should call her if I got into any trouble and that she could help me with the voluntary departure process. I thanked her and left.

Three years. I'd have to find a way to live in a foreign country for three years. I wonder if my mother will come with me. I certainly have the money to support us. I could get us a house; I could still write. I don't have to be here to publish my books. The screenplay was done, I'm sure everything else that needed to be done could be done by email or over the phone. I *could* leave. But I can't leave Reece. Not for three years. What would happen to us?

Dan, Todd and I submitted our screenplay this morning, signed all the paperwork and then went out for a celebratory drink. I'm going back to Malibu to get my things. With Reece gone, staying there alone hasn't felt comfortable. And with the screenplay done, it's time for me to go back to Los Feliz. I need to tell Jessica and my mother everything that's happened and I'm dreading it.

My driver drops me off and I ask him to come back in the

morning. I need to pack and clean and I think I'll be here for hours, so I might as well spend the night. And that's how I spend my day. When Reece calls, for the first time ever, I don't answer. I can't make small talk right now and I want him to come back from New York so I can tell him this face-to-face.

My whole world is crumbling. I can't believe it's come to this. I know that I can't expect Reece to wait for me. The lawyer's words are starting to swirl in my head, and I put on my headphones and go for a run on the estate. I'll miss it here, but it was all just a temporary escape from my reality.

WHEN I GET BACK from my run, I see a car I don't recognize in my driveway. I feel a flick of alarm when the door opens as I approach. Coco steps out and I feel my stomach drop. I'm suddenly acutely aware of how alone I am here. There's not another soul within shouting distance.

He leans on the doorframe grinning at me. I haven't seen him since that day in the boutique. The smile on his face is sinister and I stop my approach and make a stand. "What are you doing here, Coco?" I say, trying to sound like I'm only annoyed. My heart is beating wildly in my chest,

"You and I need to talk," he says in a singsong voice.

"Can we do this at the office in LA? I'm expecting someone soon," I say, hoping he'll leave.

"It won't take long," he returns.

"Coco, I'm not sure what we have to talk about, but I want you to leave. We can do this at work."

Without warning he pushes off his perch on the car's door-frame and walks quickly towards me. He's even bigger than Reece and he's moving fast. His facial expression changes from sinister to downright dangerous. Before I can decide whether to run or try to face him, he's standing in front of me. He grabs my arm so tightly that I feel tears sting the backs of my eyes.

He drags me toward the car and pushes me roughly against it so I'm facing him. He steps into me, pressing me back, his body flush with mine. And I go from being alarmed to being terrified. "Coco, stop."

"Shut up. You're a fucking cock tease. You smiled at me and then dumped me when you found out Reece wanted to fuck you, too." He seethes into my face. I am trying to not let my fear show. "Well, now I know all about you. I know your secret, and if you want me to keep quiet, you're going to start being really nice to me."

I can't restrain my whimper when I feel him rub himself on me. He's hard and he has me pinned there with his full body weight. I start to struggle. I'm not going to stand here and let this happen. I land a blow on his shin and he steps back and howls in pain. I take the chance to dart past him, but he grabs my wrist and throws me back against the car. My head hits the doorframe and I feel dizzy. I feel the sting from the open palmed slap he gives me before I even see his hand move. He presses himself against me again. Pinning me in place with the full weight of his body. He licks the side of my face. "Oh, don't worry. I don't want you right now. You stink," he says putting his nose in my hair. "I'll be back for you tonight. Take a shower and cook me something. And if you even think of not being here, I'll have you turned in and deported so fast your head will spin."

He brings his hand up and cups my breast, squeezing it painfully. "I know why Reece is so addicted you. But he's just fucking you." I flinch. "Aww, what? You thought you were going to marry Reece? People like him don't settle down with people like you." He chuckles. "Don't worry, you'll see how good I'll make it for you. I promise you'll like it." He thumbs my nipple and I have to bite my lip to contain my plea for him to stop. I won't give him the satisfaction.

He yanks the strap of my sports bra down and bares my breast. A tear rolls down my cheek. "Just a little sample before I leave." And when I feel his mouth close over my nipple, I can't stop the sob that escapes. He lifts his head and eyes me with a satisfied smile. "I like that. I want you to cry. It turns me on."

He pulls my strap back up and says, "Go. I'll be back in three hours. And you'd better be here. And don't even think of calling the police. Because if they come looking for me, they'll also find you, and then you can kiss this country goodbye." He releases me and air rushes into my lungs, and I feel bruises in the places that he had me pressed down.

And like he doesn't have a care in the world, he gets into his car and drives away.

I stand there staring after him, and when his car disappears from the drive, I turn and run into the house. I grab my suitcase and throw all my clothes inside. And then, I call Reece.

He answers almost immediately. "Babe, I was just about to call you. I'm just getting back to my room—" He stops talking when he hears me crying.

"Lucía, what's wrong?"

The concern in his voice and that he's so far away, break the dam I've held on to my emotions this week. I completely break down. I tell him everything. About the lawyer and about Coco. I am a fountain of pain. It gushes from me leaving my body through my tears, my sobs, my words.

"Reece, I have to leave." Each word feels like the tug of an anchor. They pull me down to a place I thought I'd left behind. My life as I know it, is about to end. Again. "I can't live like this anymore. I can't. It won't end, Reece. It will just get worse. I have to leave."

Reece is silent. If it wasn't for the noise in the background, I might have thought he'd hung up. I know this is a shock to him. I know he feels helpless. But what just happened with Coco has spurred me into action.

I stand up and start putting my things in a bag while I continue to speak. "I need to get to Los Feliz, get Jessica squared away and let her know I'm leaving. I only need a week to find a place, pack and go. The last week has been too much. How much am I supposed to lose because of a crime I didn't commit? I didn't ask to be brought here. I didn't ask to be raised here. But I was. It's the only home I've known. I've only tried to make something of my life, but I know now that I'll never be able to do that here," I say into the phone.

Reece has been silent and when he speaks I almost don't recognize his voice; it's lost its timbre. His tone is robotic and hollow. "I'm going to make sure Coco never touches you or anyone else again. I've just ordered a car to come for you. The driver's name is John, he's one of the office drivers who drives my father. He's going to take you to my parents' house. Please wait for me, I'm heading to the airport now." His voice breaks on that last word and he clears his throat. When he speaks again he sounds more like himself. "I'm so sorry that I left you. I'm so sorry that he touched you. God, I'm just so sorry for everything." I can hear the depth of his anguish. I can't quantify my own feelings. I just know that I need to get out of here.

"Reece, I love you. When you get here, we'll figure it out," I say and curse the distance that's depriving me of the ability to touch him.

"Go and get Jessica and take her with you to my parents. I

don't know that you'll be safe in Los Feliz. Coco knows where that house is."

I start to protest; I don't want to go to his parents' house.

"Please, I know that you're not crazy about my mom, but you will be safe there. I'm calling them now; they'll be expecting you."

I sigh, too tired to argue. "I'll ask Jessica to pick up my mother. Would it be okay for her to come, too?

"Yes, of course," he replies sounding relieved.

39

Reece

It's been two weeks since I got back from New York after all hell broke loose. I'm pacing my parent's living room waiting for Lucía and her mother to come down. I'm taking them to the airport. They're leaving. The last two weeks have been full of planning and putting out fires. As I traveled back from New York, I was in denial. I was sure I would get back and be able to fix things.

I begged Lucía to let me find an option that didn't include her having to leave. I'd spoken to a lawyer and told her that she could apply for advanced parole while her case was pending. That would have meant she could stay during that time.

She refused. That conversation was, by far, the most heated

we've ever had. We'd been having breakfast at my house a couple of days after I got back. Her face was still bruised from where Coco had hit her. I wanted to kill him. Not just figuratively. She had a bruise on her breast that wouldn't fade and I swear I wanted to cut every finger off the hand that put them there. My anger is inconsolable. But so is my fear of her leaving. The panic I felt when I realized that she was determined left me shell shocked. But it was nothing compared to the unnervingly humbling knowledge that she was also right. But I didn't give up without a fight.

Her response was potent with anger and when I'd brought up the idea of Advanced Parole, she'd said, "I'm not going to be a conditional resident, Reece. I've had enough of it and you can't ask it of me." Tears trailed down her face and I hurt for her. But, I'd felt like I was fighting for my life in that moment. This woman had begun to feel like the most important part of my life. I loved her. I didn't want her living in another country where I couldn't protect her.

When I'd told her as much, her response was laced with a bitterness I'd never heard before. "You can't protect me here, Reece. If they walked into this house right now and put handcuffs on me, you couldn't stop them." She looked away from me, gazing out the window. The sun was shining, the birds were chirping . . . like it was just any other day. And not the worst day of my life.

That truth, delivered like rapidly fired arrows, hit their mark. "I fucking know, Lucía," I seethed at her. My hands gripping my coffee mug so tightly I'd heard the ceramic protest and threaten to crack. "But I am the man who loves you. I need to try."

She got up and came to sit on my lap. She looped her arms

around my neck and looked at me. Her dark eyes luminescent with a plea for me to understand.

"Try by helping me to leave. Let me go so I can come back to you. I want to be a full partner to you, Reece. I want to travel with you. I want to be able to vote. I want to drive. I want to speed down a deserted highway and know that if I get pulled over by a cop, the worst thing that will happen is that I'll get a ticket." She touched her bruised cheek. "I want to be able to call the police when I'm in danger and not worry that it will mean I'll be thrown out of the country that is the only home I've very known."

I stared at her, my heart pounding as I settled into the realization that I couldn't stop this. "Okay. Let's do it." And then I picked her up, took her back to bed and started saying goodbye.

MY PARENTS, very quickly, realized how vulnerable Lucía is. What Coco did to her—the way he violated and terrorized her —shook them. My response showed them, that no matter what they said or did, I wouldn't be giving up on the woman I love. They have thrown all their weight around as we've all worked to help Lucía get ready to leave. My father has been good friends with the Mexican Foreign Secretary since they were both young coeds at Yale. He called him and made sure Lucía wouldn't have any trouble settling in Mexico. He coordinated with various agencies to get her updated Mexican identification documents.

My mother flew to Baja to look at the house they'd chosen online, herself. She's also played hostess to Lucía's mother for the last week.

I look down at my bruised hand and smile at the pain in it as I flex my fingers. I went to Coco's arraignment this morning.

It was only going to take five minutes, but I wanted to see him, and I wanted him to see me.

He's lucky the police found him before I did. After I saw Lucía's bruised eye and arms, I saw red and I went looking for him. I drove to all the places he used to hang out and only stopped when I found out he'd already been arrested.

I watched him as he trudged into the courtroom, accompanied by the police. Apparently, he's spreading his special brand of charm to his fellow inmates. He looks like he got his ass beat. He's got black eyes, and a bloody lip. Good, I hope there's plenty more where that came from.

I didn't know this kind of rage was possible. I abhor violence. But right now I feel like I could tear Coco apart with my bare hands. He threatened Lucía. He fucking touched her.

I watched him as they led him into court. He scanned the court room as if he'd been expecting someone. His bruised eyes widened slightly when he saw me. His lips curled into a sneer. "She tastes real good, Reece," he said with a wink. I didn't care that he was handcuffed and it wasn't going to be a fair fight. I didn't give a shit about anything but making him pay. I lunged for him.

My movement caused a commotion in the courtroom, but no one managed to stop me before I reached him and I punched him twice, hard in the ribs. "If you even think about coming near her again, Coco, you'll wish you were back in jail."

I say this in his hear as they pulled me off him. He laid there groaning, covering his head. "Fuck you, Reece," he mumbled as he was helped to his feet. I didn't even respond; officers cautioned me and told me to leave.

Now, I'm standing here waiting for Lucía to come down. She's leaving tomorrow. It's her last night and I'm taking her back to Malibu for the night. We've spent the last two weeks planning, house hunting and saying goodbye. After what Coco did, my father did a one-eighty. He still thinks this is the best plan, her leaving, but he also saw the strength of Lucía's character and how undeserved she is of all the shit she has to deal with because of her status.

She meant it when she said she'd had enough. But she wasn't giving up. We talked to her lawyer and decided that she would voluntarily depart. She can apply for re-entry in three years and while that's pending, maybe she'll be granted permission to enter the country. That's three years away. But we're going to conquer that three years. And we'll conquer anything else that gets in our way. Even if that's the United States government. This love of ours is an infinite source of stamina. If they put an obstacle in our way, we'll get over it, dig a hole underneath it, outlast it. We both have the same exact end goal. To be together.

She's been stoic about this since that morning we argued. The focus has been on logistics. We've put our feelings aside so we could do what we needed to do. We hadn't really talked about what we'd do once she was gone. How often would we see each other?

We bought her a car here that we're shipping. She needs to take an official driving class, and then she's got to get her license. She also had to open a bank account and set up her life there.

She'll continue to write her book. We've agreed that she can do remote interviews around the movie's release and premier. And I'll be back and forth until we can finally live in the same place.

Three years is a long time to live separately. But if it meant that we could have a lifetime together, we'd do it.

My mother walks into the foyer as I'm waiting. Her

normally enigmatic expression is full of sympathy. Her dark hair is pulled back, her mouth smiling, but tense. "Is she ready to go?"

"I think so. We'll be back tomorrow morning for her mother," I say staring up at the stairs. Waiting for her to appear. I was hungry for every glimpse of her now. Knowing that I wouldn't be able to see her every day, or even every week is killing me.

My mother puts an arm around my waist and pulls me in for a rare hug. I hug her back. I need the comfort right now. I've never looked to my mother for that before. Lucía was the first person to ever give me any real peace. She's handled things amazingly well. She's helped me really believe that what happened to Julian wasn't my fault. That my role in it was a very cruel coincidence, but nothing more. She's shown how generous and gracious love can be.

"You'll be fine. This won't be easy, but it's the best thing, Reece." Her voice is gentle, but I can hear the steel in it, too. She knows the separation will be hard, but she's sure it's the only way forward.

I hug her back, the knot in my chest constricting as I'm reminded yet again, that the best thing for me is to send the woman I love to live in another country.

"I know. Thank you for everything," I say. And I mean it.

She sighs. "I wish I could have done more. But, you'll be fine. She's a smart woman. And she loves you. Those will be the secrets to surviving this."

I look down at her, smiling, but surprised. "I never took you for a romantic," I say to her.

"Who do you think you got it from?" And with a quick peck on my cheek, she continues down the hall.

Lucía comes down a few minutes later. She's dressed in a short red top and black shorts that are, as usual, too short.

The shirt is unsubstantial and as soon as I see her, I want to take it off. I know I'll find her completely naked underneath.

She's half way down the stairs when she sees me. She goes from walking to running and I meet her at the landing, where she launches herself into my arms. Her legs wrap around my waist and she kisses me like it's the last time we'll kiss. And I reciprocate.

I'm scared about her leaving. Terrified for her to be in a new country, having to learn how to navigate all by herself. I know she's capable of doing it, but it feels wrong that she's going to be doing this without me. I can't move to Mexico. My work is here. I head a studio that's my family's legacy. No matter how much I need her. No matter how much she needs me.

She understands. This is her home, too. Her life is here and this is just until she can come back. But it's going to kill me to be away from her. To not be able to protect her. The stories I've read this week, of what happens when undocumented people are deported or leave voluntarily. They often end up on drugs, homeless, exploited or dead.

Lucía's one of the lucky people who can actually afford to leave. She's got money and she's got me. She's also got family in Mexico. She'll be able to draw on the money in her US bank account anywhere Visa is accepted. She'll be fine.

Tonight I'm going to have a meaningful talk with my woman, and then I'm going to make love to her. And then, I'm going to let her go.

WE'RE OUTSIDE, at my house in Malibu. This has become our place. It's where we always come when we need to be alone, but together. The fire pit is roaring and we've got a thin quilt thrown over us, as we lie together in the cabana I set up outside last month. The fire's blue and orange flames, our only source of light.

"It feels like I've come full circle, Reece. That Ana Maria has won and Lucía's having to take a back seat. I can't believe I'm leaving my home. That I may never come back. That I can't live with you anymore. I've lost control of everything." She's not crying. Her voice is clear, reflective as she speaks. Almost as if she's not talking about herself.

"No, Luc. You're taking control. You're making decisions. You're not waiting for them to be made for you. This is necessary. And we know it's temporary. You'll be back. One way or another."

She nestles her head on my chest, but doesn't respond.

I'd made a mistake a week ago. I asked her to marry me. We'd been eating dinner with Jess and I remembered that she'd married someone to get her citizenship. That night while we were brushing our teeth, I'd brought it up. She only glanced at me in the mirror and finished brushing her teeth. And then said, "If that's the only reason we're getting married, then, no."

I decided to save my protests for later. I cursed my misstep, but knew that any protests to the contrary would be futile right now.

I want to ask her again tonight, but I know that even if we are married, she'd still have to leave in order to petition for permanent residency.

And I don't want her, or anyone else, to think that that was the reason I wanted to marry her. So, I've decided to wait before I ask again. But it's coming. I want her to settle into her new life first, before I disrupt her rhythm.

I lean over to kiss her and she smiles as she ducks under my arm to sit up. I raise an eyebrow at her, smiling quizzically as she then rises to her feet. Then she lifts her little red top off and reveals her bare, unbound breasts to the night air. They are covered in gooseflesh, her nipples puckered and pebbled. My mouth waters at the sight of her.

"Come here," I say to her as I reach down, unbutton my shorts, and pull my stiff cock out. I start stroking it while I watch her.

She shakes her head and then reaches down to pull her shorts off. She stands before me, the ocean as her back drop, her hair flying in the breeze. She's the embodiment of Botticelli's Birth of Venus. I promise myself that I'm going to plan a trip to Florence, so I can show her that painting.

I shrug my shorts all the way down and pull my top off. Lucía drops to her knees in front of me. Her eyes trained on my hand as it moves in long, leisurely strokes up my cock. She licks her lips and covers my hand with her own and then she takes me in her mouth. She sucks the tip of my cock while our hands work together. Her hand falls away, and mine does too, she takes me all the way to the back of her throat and I can feel it close around my head. I groan and pull myself out of her mouth.

She comes up eagerly wiping her mouth as she climbs into my lap and then lower herself onto to me. She drapes her hands over my shoulders and clasps them behind my neck. She buries her face in my neck and we start to fuck. She's moving fast, rotating her hips every time she comes down. My hand goes to her clit and I start to rub her. She whispers my name, as she loses her rhythm. And when she starts to come, I pull out of her, flip her back onto the mattress and eat her down from that orgasm and up into another.

When she's done I pick her up and carry her into the house.

"It's our last night in this house for a long time. Let's make love in our bed," I say to her as I walk us down the hall into the bedroom.

When I lay her down, I just look at her for a long time. I know I'll see her again in two weeks, but that might as well be a light year. This move is wrong. We're separating when we should be moving in together.

As if she's reading my mind she says, "I wish you could come with me."

I can't find my voice. I am lost for words. I trail my fingers across her collarbones and trace the curved silhouette of her left breast and let my fingers rest on the tattoo that's next to her heart. *Freedom*. It's what she wants and what she needs and she's leaving tomorrow to try and find it.

And suddenly I want it, too. When I met Lucía, I'd thought I had everything I could ever want, but I didn't know what I was missing. She's been like a mirror of truth for me. I've had to look at myself and confront how I live. It's humbled me to have to stand back and just *watch* as the woman I love has to break down her entire life and start over again.

"Distance is nothing," she whispers, in between the kisses she's pressing on my chest. "We'll be okay. And in three years, I'll be back. Now, stop brooding and kiss me. I'm going to have to live on what you give me tonight for the next two weeks. I don't want to waste time talking."

"Talking is a waste of time?" I say with a smile, I dot her face with kisses, nipping at her cheeks, her chin and her lips.

"Mmmm hmmm . . ." she mumbles, her eyes following the path of her fingers as she strokes my chest. "Our hearts do all the talking for us. Our bodies do the translating. Who needs words?" She pulls my head down and this time, I don't stop.

When the sun comes up, Lucía's spent. And I've made some decisions. I have to prepare myself for what's to come. So, I don't sleep. I just watch her and whisper promises. That I'll find a way to close the gap, that I won't leave her alone for long and that tomorrow is just the beginning of our story.

AT THE AIRPORT, Lucía and I stand and hug. She's holding me so tight that my breathing constricts. It still doesn't feel like she's close enough. We stand there, trying to drag out the last few minutes we have together. I let my hands roam her back, memorizing the way her ribs feel as my hands skim them. I run a hand under the fall of hair that's hanging down her back and caress the nape of her neck. She's really leaving and even though we planned for it and talked about it, I'm not ready to let go.

"Please wait for me. Please believe that I'm coming back. I love you." She says over and over as she cries into my shirt.

Her mother comes to us to remind her that they don't have much time before they have to board their flight. I can't go beyond security.

I watch my girl walk away, and my heart goes with her. So beautiful and brave. She's in the pair of ripped jeans she was wearing the first time we met, her black shirt falling off one shoulder. Her hair flowing, her lips red; I make a mental image.

She turns and gives me one last big, brave smile and blows me a kiss before she disappears into the crowd to her gate. I don't see her again.

I return to my car and get the bag I'd hidden in the backseat. And then, I head back to the terminal to catch my own flight.

40

Lucia

THREE MONTHS LATER

I WAKE up to the smell of rich coffee and hot bread . . . and to
my mother's quiet sobbing. This, and the cock crowing is what
has woken me up every morning since we got here. My father
hasn't been to see us.

When we called to say we were moving, he'd said he wanted
to try and rekindle his relationship with us. But, that's not
going to happen. Last week he called to tell us that he has
another family. A woman he lives with and has had two more
children with.

I look at the clock by my bed and see that it's only six in the
morning. I was up until one a.m. writing, and I feel like I could
sleep for another two hours. I see Reece's picture; one I took the
last time we went to the beach in Malibu. He's looking straight
at the camera, and laughing. His beautiful mouth slightly open

in the frame I snapped and it's exactly how I like to think of him. I feel a pang of longing as I remember our conversation on the way to the airport. God I miss him. And I'm worried.

The first month we were here, he came down twice. It was glorious, we spent the weekend at one of the resorts, catching up, fucking, eating and just being together. The second month he came once and this month, he hasn't been at all. We talk every night, most nights, FaceTiming. th as we get ourselves off. But he's postponed his trip three times now. Something's going on and I'm scared that he's wavering. Maybe the distance is too much.

Our house is all wood and stone and everything echoes. I hear the front door open and close and assume my mom's gone outside to pick up our grocery delivery.

I'm going to brush my teeth and change before I head downstairs. Sometimes, she comes right back inside. But, a few days a week, I find her sitting outside, staring out at the horizon, and I have to sit with her until she feels ready to come in.

It's been exhausting.

I turn on the bathroom light. The buzz and hiss of bulbs as they brighten is something I'm still not used to. I peer at myself in the mirror and I can see the fatigue showing on my face.

"You look beautiful."

Reece's voice floats into the room, and like a mist, it washes over me. I close my eyes in relief and turn around.

"Baby..." Amazement tinging my whisper as I drink him in. He looks so beautiful. He's tanner, his hair is longer and he's beaming at me as he leans against the doorframe of the bathroom.

"Hey, Fifty-five," he says softly as I leap into his arms. I wrap my legs around his waist. He straightens and absorbs the impact and wraps his arms around me. He pulls me into a fierce hug and then in an instant, he's kissing me. It's a fierce, hungry kiss. This month has been hell for him, too. He tastes like mouthwash and Reece and I let myself relish it all. I wrap my arms even tighter around his neck and he deepens the kiss, his tongue brushing past mine and making me whimper. God, I've missed him. My heart is like a parched desert getting the first kiss of rain it's had in months. Our tongues duel and dance. Greet and welcome. I can feel him hard and eager against my stomach. He places my ass on the sink and unbuttons his jeans.

"I need you. So badly. Can I have you?" he asks in between kisses.

"Always," I whisper as I spread my thighs to make room for his hips. My night shirt rides up and I'm naked underneath.

We both groan at the first touch of his fingers.

His eyes stay on mine as he strokes me, his fingers trailing through my wet, swollen lips. "Always," he says before I feel the broad tip of his cock enter me. I am so ready for him.

He takes his time, and fills me one slow increment at a time. The glide of his flesh into mine is a divine homecoming. The pleasure of it teeters on the edge of unbearable.

"God, I've missed you," Reece rumbles into my ear as he thrusts into me. It's claiming and hard. I love it. I want more.

"I've missed you, too. Please. Fuck me harder," I beg, I grab his ass and hitch my legs higher against his waist. He tilts my hips, so that I'm almost sitting in the sink and he gives me what I asked for.

He doesn't hold back and in a minute, I'm putting my fingers between my legs and rubbing my clit so that we can come together. "I love you." He grits his teeth, nips at my lips and thrusts. I hiss at the bite, and he licks the sting. I can feel the flex of his muscled flank under my thighs as he fucks me.

"God, I need you, Luc." He pours out as he comes. My climax chases his.

"I'm going to come, Reece." I pant, almost in warning. My perch on the sink suddenly feeling precarious. My arms flex as I bow my back as the first crest of my orgasm breaks.

He whispers in my ear, "Come. I've got you." He presses a kiss to my cheek. His arms tighten around me and I fall into a blistering, blissful haze. Cheek to cheek, we stay as we are; me sitting on the sink, legs wrapped around him, his arms encircling me.

"Hi, honey," I mumble into his neck. I stroke his sweat damped back, relishing the feel of his skin under my fingers. I let my hands move over the ridges and valleys that his muscles create. I inhale the fresh scent of him and press a kiss to his cheek.

"Hey," he says as he catches his breath. "I hadn't planned on attacking you like that. I saw you, looking so fucking beautiful, and just lost my mind for a minute." He chuckles. His breath fans the hair that clings to my neck and I tighten my arms around his neck.

"That was just what I needed." I pull my face back so I can look at him.

"I hadn't expected you."

"Yes, I know," he says tenderly, his eyes not leaving mine. "I'm sorry that I haven't been here."

I look down, not sure what to say, and just relieved that he's here now. I'll need to learn to adjust. It's not reasonable to expect Reece to fly down twice a month or even once every month.

He pulls out of me and holds my waist while I hop down. I start to clean myself and he straightens his clothes.

"It's been hard. But, I understand," I say, and I do. But I hate it. The next three years are going to be miserable.

As soon as his jeans are buttoned he sits on the edge of the free-standing bathtub and watches me while I wipe myself clean with a hot wash cloth.

I take my time, holding my night shirt up, so he can see my naked body.

He groans. "I'm going to make you pay for teasing me," he drawls at me.

"I can't wait," I say, my voice low and sultry even to my own ears.

He stands up. "Listen, I have a surprise for you. We're already late. I'm going to need to you to stop tempting me." He kisses the tip of my nose, takes the wash cloth from my hands and tosses it into the clothes hamper in the corner.

"Let's go for a drive?" he says cheerfully, his grin broad and bright.

I smile back, "Of course. Let me get changed. I'll meet you in the kitchen."

We walk back to my room. I head for my closet and Reece leaves. As I get dressed my mind and heart race.

For the last two weeks, I'd been worried. I'd thought maybe the distance was wearing on him. That maybe now that I'd left, he'd see that it wasn't worth the trouble.

I throw on my clothes and do a quick brush of my teeth. A sudden, irrational fear that he'll be gone when I get to the kitchen adding an urgency to my steps.

I release a breath I'd been holding.

He and my mother are sitting at the kitchen table. They both have full breakfast plates in front of them. My mother looks calm, her eyes red from crying, but she's putting on a brave face in front of Reece. They talked before we left. She tried to apologize for what she'd said in the car. He wouldn't allow her to. They'd sat in his parents' living room, her crying on his shoulder as they comforted each other.

"Mama, are you okay?" I ask her softly.

"Yes, of course. Did you sleep well?" she asks casually. I look at her closely trying to see if she's really fine. She takes a sip of her coffee and raises her eyebrows when I don't answer right away.

"I did, thanks," I say slowly.

I look back at Reece. He's watching me, his kiss-stung lips tipped up in a lazy smile. His dark hair is tousled and his eyes are hooded. The memory of our bathroom "hello" makes my toes tingle. I smile back and walk over to give my mom a hug.

"You have a nice morning," she says absently as she butters her toast.

I give her a quick kiss on the cheek, grab Reece's hand and head for the door.

"Where are we going?" I ask when we're outside. He swings our joined hands between us as we walk to the car.

He waits until I've climbed up into the jeep's bucket seat before he answers.

"To see our house."

My head jerks back.

"Close your mouth. A fly's going to hop in," he says jovially right before he closes my door.

"Our house?" I repeat incredulously when he gets into the car. He looks at my face and laughs. "You look like I just told you I bought you a pile of plastic." He pats my knee and turns the car. He starts out of my driveway.

"Yes. I bought us a house." He sighs. "I'm sorry I've been so secretive, but I wanted everything to go through before I told you. We had to get approval from the feds—"

I cut him off. I feel like I'm in the *Twilight Zone* and he's not making any sense.

"Reece, what are you talking about? You bought us a house? Why? I don't want to live here alone. I couldn't sleep in a house here by myself. You'd only be here a few days a month." His eyes on the road, his profile shows all the emotions that pass over his face. None of them are appropriate responses to my outburst. He only smiles and then grins.

"Reece."

He just glances at me and breaks into a wide grin. "Patience, Fifty." His enjoyment obvious.

Ugh, I *really* hate that nickname.

"Okay. Fine. I'm just going to sit back and relax," I say, glancing out of the window to watch the desert go by. I marvel, as always, that the land so close to the ocean is so dry.

He pats my leg again. "It'll be worth the wait. And we'll be there in less than a minute."

He turns left into a gated community and stops at the guard post. He shows his ID to the guard and the gates open.

When we drive in, I expect to see big houses, manicured lawns. The manicured lawns were there, and the houses are beautiful, but modest. And there are scores of them. The street we're on is lined with houses as far as the eye can see.

"It's a three-mile-long road. The entire subdivision is enclosed in the gate."

"What is this place?"

"It's our new neighborhood," he says gleefully as hops out of the car.

41

Reece

Loreto Bay is said to be the greenest and most lush city in all of Baja. I walk over to open the door for Lucía after we pull into the house that I designated as ours when I bought this development. I've been keeping a lot from her, but I wanted this to be right before I told her. The deal was signed this morning and I got on a plane and came straight here.

"I bought this community from a developer who finished construction, but was caught up in a lawsuit that meant he couldn't afford to carry the cost of the development while he was waiting for people to come in and buy. It was supposed to be a retirement community for Europeans and Americans who were looking to spend part of the year here," I say as I help her out of the car.

"It was *meant* to be?" she asks as she lets me lead her up the stone tile walkway. The landscaping is perfect. Everything is.

"Now, it's going to be staff housing for the studio we're building here. Staff that's going to be made up of voluntarily departed and deported people."

She stops in her tracks and tugs my arm to make me stop.

"Hold on, stop and explain. Now. It's obviously something great, because you're grinning like you're high. So, just tell me."

"You're ruining my fun." I scowl. She scowls back . . . and it just makes me want to kiss her.

"Fine." I relent. "Let's go in and get out of the heat, I'll tell you." I open the door and lead her inside and watch her face as she takes in the coral colored stucco walls, the Travertine tiled floor, the beamed ceiling lined with sky lights. The hand crafted local furniture and artwork are things I picked out. "We can redecorate later, if you don't like it."

She spins to face me. "You're building a studio?" I laugh at her doggedness.

"In partnership with the largest media company in South America. Yes. We signed the deal this morning. It's been a nightmare because we've had to negotiate with the Mexican government to purchase the property. I had to get my parents on board. They're not thrilled that I'm moving to Mexico, but they understand and they agree that Artemis is ready for this kind of expansion."

I grab her and pull her into me. "I talked so much about my family and my duty to it. But you're my family, too. We may not have a piece of paper or blood that says so. But we've got something much stronger than either of those. We love each other. We chose each other. And so, I had to find a way to be here while you were."

She steps back and just stares at me. Her eyes bright, her smile, that smile, even brighter.

"You're moving here?"

I nod and laugh as her dark eyebrows rise nearly to hairline. Her eyes narrow.

"Reece, what about the City Council?" she asks, reaching to cup my face. She holds my eyes as if she needs to look into them to see the truth. I let her see. The truth of my heart. The truth of my life.

"Three years of us living apart is not an option. City Council isn't going anywhere. We're going to keep fighting, but we'll do it as private citizens."

She kisses me, but frowns as she says, "I'm not a citizen, Reece. And what if they don't let me come back? Or what if I decide I want to live here?

This surprises me, but my answer is the same. My motivation unequivocal. "We can stay. We can live here. My visa is one that gives me permanent residency because I bought a business here."

"So you would stay here? For me?"

"We'll be together wherever we need to be. And if you decide you want to go back in three years, we'll apply for you to enter, but as the spouse of a US Citizen."

Her grin explodes, she shrieks and jumps up, throwing her arms around my neck and climbing up my body, before I'm even done with my sentence.

I put my hands on her hips and haul her up.

"Reece, yes! Yes. You asked again and I'm saying yes."

"Well, I was going to get down on one knee and ask you

properly. I have a ring in my pocket," I say into her hair as she tightens her grip around my neck.

She stills and then scrambles down. "Oh, I want that. I SO want that. I've been waiting for this," she says, beaming.

She runs her fingers through her hair. And smooths the fabric of the dress she's wearing.

"Okay, I'm ready." She smiles happily up at me.

I drop to my knee and pull out a ring that my grandmother left me. It holds value that's more sentimental than monetary, but when I saw it, I knew it was right for her. It's a filigree of a bird in flight, set with tiny diamonds.

I slip it on her finger and tell her, "You're my freedom. You're my family. I want to be with you until I take my last breath. You've shown me what real courage looks like and I want to live with you where you can really live free. So here I am; at your feet, and I always will be." I kiss her hands, the hands that wrote the story that brought us together. "I love you in a way that I'll never be able to understand or contain. Will you be my wife?"

She smiles a new smile. I'll come to recognize that smile. It's the one she wears when she's so happy her heart's song can't be contained. It's so bright that it casts everything around into the shade.

I'll see it again next year when she says, "I do." In a few years, I'll see it when she holds our daughter, Julianna, for the first time. But today, it's new. And it's the most beautiful smile I've ever seen. I slip my ring on her finger and she joins me, dropping to her knees in front of me and says, "Fuck, yeah."

The End

EPILOGUE

FIVE YEARS LATER

"MOMMY! WAVE AT ME," Juliana screams across the room at Lucía. Lucía glances at us, and waves at our daughter and then looks at me and crosses her fingers. I lift my hand, showing my own crossed fingers too.

We're in the South Hall of the Los Angeles Convention Center, watching Lucía and nearly five thousand other newly naturalized citizens get ready to take their oath of citizenship. We've been here for a couple of hours and we had to separate while she went through most of the process herself. My parents are here with Juliana and I and my dad's recording everything on his phone.

"Daddy, I'm hungry," Juliana whines as she wiggles on my lap. She's three and growing like a weed and always hungry. My mother reaches into her purse and pulls out a bag of grapes. "Come sit with your Mimi, baby and I'll feed you."

Juliana's big brown eyes widen as she scrambles off my lap and walks over to her grandmother. My mother retired a year ago and she and Juliana spend a lot of time together when we're in LA.

We spend six months a year here and the other six months in Loreto. When we got married four years ago we decided to split our time. It's been great for Juliana because she gets to spend plenty of time with both sets of her grandparents. The studio we built in Loreto has thrived. Our little community of returners has been a success and we still live there. Some of our employees have stayed, others have used the jobs we gave them as a stepping stone to rebuild their lives in Mexico.

A few months after Lucía left, the new president ended DACA, the program that had given DREAMERs the right to work and to remain the country without fear of deportation. We lobbied congress, raised money, ran campaigns and were relentless in our pursuit of our goal. When the bill was intro-duced to give DREAMERs permanent residency and a path to citizenship, Lucia and I both cried as we watched the legislative proceedings.

A year later, *Throw Away the Key* hit box offices. The film exceeded all my expectations and when the screenplay won Artemis Films it's very first Oscar, Lucía accepted the award in person. The film, it's success and Lucia's own journey gave the DREAMER's movement real momentum.

Since then, she's published two more books and the film she wrote a screenplay for just won the Palme d'Or at Cannes. My girl is on a roll.

As the crowd of people begin to recite their oath of office, all of them with their right hand up, swearing to be loyal to the United States, I gaze at my wife.

She's solemn, looking straight ahead. Her left-hand rests on her gently rounded stomach, where our son is growing. She's my inspiration. My dream come true. And as she says the last sentence of the oath she's spent the last week memorizing, she turns to look at me. Our gazes hold and she smiles as she says, "*I take this obligation freely, without any mental reservation or purpose of evasion; so help me God.*"

And then her eyes close, and she puts her right hand over her heart and caresses that tattoo. She opens her eyes again, her smile bright enough to rival the sun as she mouths "I'm free."

THE END

AFTERWORD

Thank you so much for reading Thicker Than Water. Writing it has been a labor of love. Lucía and Reece's story ends happily, but for many people in Lucía's position, things are far from ideal or easy.

If you'd like to know more about this subject, I've included some links that you can explore.

Newspaper Article.

Article on Undocumented existence

Movie

Movie of Protected DACA enrollee deported

A Great Book on the subject

Great Article

ACKNOWLEDGMENTS

I want to thank the brave men and women who shared their stories with me. I won't name them, to protect their privacy. But please know that you are my heroes.

To my beta readers, Autumn, Cézanne, Chelé, Layla, Lisa, Margie, Nana, Rachael, Sara, and Sophie,— you guys are the reason this story is any good at all. Thank you all SO much for putting up with my indecision and self-doubt. I love you guys and am lucky to call you my friends.

Patricia and Lylian, thank you for reading it early and giving me the confidence to show it to the rest of the world.

To my editor Anja, thank you for believing in me and pushing me to do better.

To Marla, my amazing proofreader, thank you for making this pretty enough for the world to read.

To Mary Ruth for the incredible cover you created . . . your talent is awe inspiring and your spirit is just as beautiful. I'm grateful to know you.

To the great team at Foreword PR- Linda and Alissa your support and encouragement means the world.

To Crystal thanks for stepping in and saving me.

To Jeananna and Kylie at Give Me Books, you guys are the best, I love working with you. Thank you!

To my amazing author friends and mentors who read this story, encouraged me to write it and helped along this journey – you're my comrades in arms, thank you.

To Mila – Thank you for everything. I owe you more than I'll ever be able to pay, but know that for as long as you'll have me, I'm yours.

To Chelé – What would this journey be without you? I don't want to even imagine. I love you!

To my Layla – Your honesty, you constancy and your friendship are a cornerstone of my life. Love you.

To my friend Claudia – you're wonderful. Thank you for just being you and for helping along every single part of this journey.

Mara, you're a goddess. That is all.

To my friend Nana, everybody needs a friend like you. You're wonderful and love having you has part of my Ghana Massive.

To Becca, you're definition of kindness and grace. Love you, girl.

To my dearest Kennedy—no words could ever express how much I appreciate your presence in my life. And I know for sure that this books wouldn't be what it is without your input and guidance. Thank you for putting up with me. I've learned so much from you and you carried me across the finish line on this project. Thank you for everything. I love you.

To my author friends who support me in so many ways every day, I can't

To my parents for being brave enough to leave their home country and seek out the American Dream for the sake of their children, I hope we've made you proud.

To my husband and children — you are my reason. I love you so much.

To all the amazing bloggers who have shouted about my book, thank you, I couldn't do this without you.

To my Darlings you ladies are my own personal army. Thank you for your support and willingness to roll up your sleeves for me. I can't say thank you enough.

To my Day Dreamers — You're my favorite corner of the internet. You guys make my day, every single day!

And to every single reader who has given my work a chance, thank you for making my dreams come true.

All my love, Dylan

Made in the USA
Columbia, SC
12 April 2018